MEMORIES OF BLOOD AND SHADOW

Aaron S. Jones

CHAPTER ONE: JUST AN OLD MAN

Darkness cloaked the land of Alfara as a chill
swept through the fields of wheat. Tavar felt
energy shimmer in the air. The threat of cha
Of violence. An age had passed since he had felt suc
force around him. The earlier downpour had worser
muddy path. Wet and slippery. A hazard for most.
trodden along it so often that there was no need for
light other than that being offered by the moon and
above. He ambled to the stables, running his finge
through the wheat to his left.

    A strong, familiar smell of manure blaste
nostrils as he eased open the rusting iron bolt and
the creaking, wooden door open. The lone stallic
whinnied long and loud, stamping his hooves ag
stone ground, ears rolled back. The three other s
stood empty, as they had been for over a year no
just the two of them. Tavar and Marek.

    The animals always seemed to sense it,
than humans: the tension, the promise of blood
a gentle hand against the agitated horse's neck
him, resting his own head against the beast's v
closing his eyes; a silent promise that all woul
The horse kicked against the straw at his feet,
missing a huge pile of manure. Tavar pulled a
of his worn, tattered bag and offered it to his
Marek calmed instantly, distracted by his fav
If only all of life's problems could be solved

energy unleashed by nature. The rain would be good for the crops at least. Not gonna bother him while he's inside.

He dragged a chair closer to the fire crackling in the blackened stone hearth. The warmth of the blaze felt good. It hit his palms as he placed them close to the flames, instantly reaping its rewards. Not many things felt better than sitting by the fire after a long, hard day's work in the cold.

He licked his dry, cracked lips and peered up above the hearth at an old friend perched on top of two iron hooks sticking out of the wall. The emerald green handle of the thin blade glinted mischievously in the dancing candlelight as Tavar held its gaze. It would still be sharp. Fatally so, if necessary. Its maker had ensured him of that. Receiving a weapon from the greatest smith in the world came with some guarantees after all. He contemplated grabbing it, wrapping his fingers around its hilt and sliding it slowly out of its ornately decorated bone-white sheath. The beat of his heart picked up its pace at the suggestion. His body willed him to do it, urging him forward. Fingers twitched as old memories flooded his mind.

> The blood.
>
> The carnage.
>
> The screams.
>
> The bodies.
>
> The tears.

No. Not now. He wasn't that person. A blade like this didn't forget. Once drawn it must be bloodied. It wouldn't be sheathed again once released without tasting the sweet red it longed for. Tavar breathed in slowly. He closed his eyes and forced his heart to return to its regular rhythm. Standing from his seat, he opened his eyes

This is a work of fiction. Names, characters, places, and incidents either are the product of the author's imagination or are used fictitiously. Any resemblance to actual persons, living or dead, events, or locales is entirely coincidental.

Copyright © 2022 by Aaron S. Jones

All rights reserved. No part of this book may be reproduced or used in any manner without written permission of the copyright owner except for the use of quotations in a book review.

First edition 2022

Book cover by MiblArt

ISBN: 9798713353100

Imprint: Independently published

If you enjoyed this book, please leave a review on Amazon and Goodreads.

Visit **www.aaronsjones.com** for more information. You can sign up to the mailing list to be the first to find out about author events, interviews, and will always be the first to hear of new books from the author.

Also by Aaron S. Jones

<u>The Broken Gods</u>
Flames of Rebellion

Paths of Chaos

End of Days

A Long Way from Home - A collection of short stories from the world of The Broken Gods (available as an audiobook read by Mark Rice-Oxley) way.

He patted the animal's neck in farewell, marvelling at its shiny coat, as black as a starless night sky. Slinging the bag over his shoulder, he released a long, deep breath; preparing himself for what was ahead. The wooden door closed behind him. He slammed the bolt back into place and listened closely for any sounds inside. No more whinnying. Tavar turned to face the night, staring over his land into the distance. Less stars were visible and the light of the moon failed to offer much relief as dark clouds blocked its path. On the horizon, he thought he could see a small light travelling slowly.

To his left, faint candlelight flickered through the window. Without a backwards glance, he strolled along the beaten path and headed home. The wooden structure wasn't a beauty by any means, but when he looked up at the wooden beams, paint cracking and in need of a touch up or noticed the head of a nail – his fingers ached reflexively: a reminder of the labour involved in its creation and the pride he had felt upon completion. Not many things felt better than finishing a task with your own two hands. For twenty years it had stood here. Good ground. A decent amount of land. And most importantly, the nearest neighbours were over a day's ride away.

As he walked up the three wooden steps, his knees cracked: a reminder of his age. He'd seen too many winters. Too many dark nights like this one. He pushed the door open and lowered his hood, running a hand through his long, damp hair. As he placed his cloak on to the back of the oak chair, the first stream of rain hit the ground. A moment later, lightning flashed in his peripheral vision followed closely by the boom of thunder. The house itself rocked with the incredible

MEMORIES OF BLOOD AND SHADOW

AARON S. JONES

whilst releasing a long, slow breath out from his nostrils. The blade remained sheathed above the hearth where it belonged.

He scratched at the itchy stubble on his chin and gazed out of the window. Another flash of lightning with the bang of thunder. Closer this time. The rain sounded like an army of rocks dropping from the heavens. Not a night for weary travellers on the road; that was for sure.

Deciding to grab some water, he strolled into the back room, relieved that he had convinced himself to grab the water from the well earlier in the day. The buckets were where he had left them in the corner of the room, filled to the brim. An old, worn cup that had seen almost as many winters as him lay on the table to his left. He picked it up and gave it a sniff. Seemed clean enough. Before he reached down towards the water, the lightning flashed again, thunder followed but this time his ears pricked at another sound. Old habits were tougher to break than an iron wall.

Two knocks at the door.

He paused, listening intently for the sound, eager for it to have been his old mind playing tricks on him. Knock. Knock. No such luck. He rolled his shoulders back and sighed as he felt the bones crack in response.

He felt no need to rush to the door. They weren't going anywhere. Too far to travel to the next shelter. In this weather, at this time of night, it would be too risky. He placed his cup back onto the table and pulled his white, woollen shirt down over his belt, hiding the dagger sheathed at his hip. With any luck, it would stay sheathed. He doubted it. Luck had never been the most reliable of companions. A man must make his own luck. That's what he'd always been told. Tavar could make a lot of things but luck didn't seem to be one of them.

Knock. Knock.

Best not to keep them out there too long. His footsteps echoed through the house as the heels of his boots clipped against the floorboards. He pulled the door open and found two young, soaked travellers, dark hoods pulled up cast shadows over their faces. The one closest to Tavar offered a warm, weary smile, displaying a crooked row of white teeth. His smooth charcoal black skin betrayed his heritage and chestnut brown eyes fixed upon Tavar.

"Awfully sorry to bother you, sir. Dreadful weather this night has forced my companion and I to seek shelter." The dark-skinned man waved a hand carelessly to the grim man at his shoulder. His companion had light skin with suspicious blue eyes peering out from beneath his hood. A failed attempt at growing a beard had left the man to deal with patches of ginger stubble around his neck and chin. Neither of them could have been past twenty years. That was being generous. "Might be wrong but this appears to be the only place for miles. Somewhere to rest and hide out from the storm would be wonderful…"

Tavar stayed silent, eyeing up the travellers. The more vocal of the two spoke well: he was no fool. Fools were dangerous but predictable. Clever folk needed an eye upon them as they could wear a mask of joy to hide their darker motives. Give him a fool any day over men gifted with a silver tongue. Nine times out of ten that silver tongue would turn out to be forked.

Both men dressed in a similar fashion; black cloaks, olive green trousers and brown boots that made it difficult to see where the mud ended and boot began. He peered over their shoulders and spotted a couple of nervous mares; their heads flicked up and down and they kicked their legs as the thunder crashed around them once more. Turning away travellers never bothered him, but animals didn't deserve this.

"Stables to the right over there," he pointed. "Got some apples inside if they need calming."

"Very kind of you. Should be able to manage though. William, be a good chap and take them both into the stable."

For a moment, Tavar thought the light-skinned traveller would argue, his face contorting, pronouncing his grimace further. The moment passed with a grunt as he turned away and strode off towards the horses.

"Doesn't seem so happy," Tavar muttered.

"Never does. Believe it or not, he's in a good mood tonight." The traveller pulled his hood down and shook his shaved head.

"Hate to meet him on a bad day." Tavar stepped back, allowing the traveller to walk through. No point in keeping him waiting.

"Decent place you have here," the traveller said, eyes surveying the building and nodding to himself. "Name's Jassim by the way." He held a dark, scarred hand out. Tavar left it hanging, attracted by the heat of the fire.

Tavar grabbed a chair, scraping it across the floor next to the fire and sat down, eyes staring at the traveller. He watched carefully as Jassim followed suit, dragging a second chair before spinning it around and sitting down, legs spread wide and arms resting on the top of the chair. Brown eyes silently pierced him, lips curling softly in the corner. His own eyes flashed to a sheathed sword hanging low from the man's hip.

"Don't usually allow folk to come in armed."

"This little thing," Jassim said, unbuckling the clasp and pulling the weapon up onto the top of the chair. "The roads can be dangerous for two weary travellers in these parts. Bandits and cutthroats think twice if you have a bit of steel on you."

No argument there. Only a fool would travel the lands empty handed. "Won't find bandits and cutthroats in this house."

"No, perhaps not." He placed the sword carefully onto the table beside him.

Tavar kept his eyes on him, watching every movement and noting that the weapon was still within reach. "Had to use it much?"

Jassim shrugged, "No more than any other man on the road." His eyes flicked to the weapon perched above the hearth. "Had to use that beauty much?"

Tavar silently cursed himself. Old fool. Should've taken it down before he invited them in. "Only for decoration. I'm just an old man, weapons are for the young."

"Maybe you are right, but you aren't that old by the look of you. The young can only make it to such an age with a weapon at their side, I fear. These are dark times."

"All times are dark. Everyone feels that they live in the worst point in history. Believe me: it's always been this shit," Tavar spat.

The front door slammed shut as William strolled into the room. Rainwater dripped onto the wooden floor as his eyes sparked with envy at the flames to Tavar's side. Not gonna happen. William silently walked around the table, pulling the final wooden chair slowly across the floor and placing it next to Jassim's.

"I trust there were no difficulties?" Jassim grinned at his companion. William shook his head. "Excellent! Our warm host here and I were just chatting about the dangers of life on the road and the general misery of life. I'm sure you'd like to add your thoughts on such a debate."

"Things are shit," William muttered, not a man of many words.

"Insightful. Concise. This is why we work so well together," Jassim laughed. Tavar didn't find it too funny. He had met many men in his life who loved the sound of their own voice. Jassim was just one in a long line of men who didn't value the art of silence. Only in silence could a man think, arrange his thoughts and act upon them.

"Where are two men such as yourselves travelling to? Not many places out here. Haven't had any visitors in a long time," Tavar said, spotting William sliding a hand beneath his cloak. Probably grasping for a weapon. He let it slide. There was enough distance between them for now. Hasty actions often caused the biggest mess and Tavar wasn't ready for the clean up.

"Alfara doesn't have the opportunities it once did for two young men with ambition. Merchants passing through the city spoke of better chances on the other side of the river. Yorkland and the Green Isles may be smaller kingdoms but there's room for progression. They are kingdoms on the way up. Alfara is falling, and falling fast," Jassim said with a shake of his head.

"These roads won't take you to either of those kingdoms. Should have turned west when you reached

Amir's farm. Huge farm. Can't miss it."

"Must have got mixed up somewhere. We made it to Amir's. Veered too far south, I guess. Easy mistake when you're in a rush with weather like this," Jassim answered.

It wasn't an easy mistake and he knew it. Tavar had lived long enough to spot a liar. Jassim wasn't even trying hard to deceive him. He wondered how long the game would go on for; a veil of manners waiting to be pulled away so that all the audience could see the grim reality. He could play along for a while longer. What else was there to do?

"As soon as it clears up. I'll show you the way. Added about half a day to your journey."

"Thanks. Appreciate it," Jassim said. "You been into Alfara recently? Bit of a journey for you I bet but it must get lonely out here."

"Been a while. I have everything I need right here. Every other month I ride to see Amir and grab some extras. Not so good in large crowds. Too old for that now. Makes me… uncomfortable."

"What about when you were younger?" The glint in Jassim's eye unnerved Tavar. He was pressing for something.

"What I did when I was younger is my own business," Tavar growled back, body tensing like the string on a bow. His eyes shifted to a shuffle under William's cloak, readying himself for trouble.

"Easy, easy," Jassim said, leaning back and throwing his open palms into the air. "I meant no disrespect. Just curious is all. An older guy, all alone out here. Beautiful sword hanging above his hearth. You must have an interesting tale or two to tell and this weather was made for such tales. That is certain."

"My memory isn't as good as it was. Never been one for telling tales anyway. My life has been lived. That's it. Those who played their part in it know what happened and those that didn't don't need to know any more." The fire started to burn his right arm; he'd sat there too long. Almost time to move.

"I get that. It's a man's right to keep himself to himself. Not a problem with that at all. I have to say though," Jassim breathed in through his teeth and cocked his head to the side, "Seems almost like you're hiding out here. No family, away from any other signs of life apart from your horse. I'm just curious. What are you hiding from?"

"I'm not hiding from anything, boy. This is my home. I've given *you* shelter from the storm. Sounds like it's stopped now. Maybe it's best for you to be on your way." No more thunder. No more lightning. No more rain. A deep silence smothered the room, sucking all the air away from the three men. A suffocating silence. Tavar reminded himself to breathe slowly through his nostrils as he stood, eyes never leaving Jassim. In return, all he received was a wicked grin and the man's tongue licking the edges of his lips.

"Now, now. There is no need for hostility. Is it a crime to be curious?" Jassim asked, eyes flashing in the light of the flames. "I can tell you what actions are classed as crimes in Alfara now. I think you'll be shocked. It is a crime to mock the king. Three men were flayed on the wall last week for performing a play that poked fun at the king's large, crooked nose. It is a crime for one born in Alfara to marry an outsider. Even worse if they were to have a baby. Two babies were thrown from a balcony one moon past. I can still hear the cries of the parents. It is a crime to even mention the name of the of the infamous warrior who won the kingdom for the nation…"

"Choose your next words very carefully…" Tavar said through gritted teeth. His fingers flexed in anticipation. Excited energy pumped through his body, slowing time as all men stood as one; aware that the time for action was almost upon them.

"I choose all my words carefully, Tavar. Growing up in Alfara, the grandson of refugees from the bloodiest battle in history, I've learnt the importance of using words. My grandparents used to tell me tales about you. I'd be wide-eyed and silent as I devoured them all. You were my hero. A legend. Then, when I was old enough, my parents told me their tales about you. Still wide-eyed, but now in horror. Still silent, but in disgust."

"I'm not the person you think I am," Tavar warned, ears pricking at the sound of a blade slowly scraping free. "You are making a grave mistake."

"Perhaps, but I made a promise. It is one I must keep, no matter the dangers. William, make it quick."

Tavar stomped a boot down hard against his opponent's knee. It locked instantly, knocking William backwards into his chair once more with a grunt, sword half sheathed and gleaming in the light. Out of the corner of his eye, Jassim swung his still sheathed sword at him. Tavar let it land against his right shoulder and used the momentum to race forward. His knee crunched hard against William's jaw, slamming him onto the floor, sword sliding off into the open doorway.

He dropped low and rolled against the wall, feeling the air whip above him, narrowly escaping the arc of Jassim's unsheathed blade.

"You move well for an old man," Jassim admitted. "Will, get up. Grab the sword."

"I wouldn't do that if I were you..." Tavar said, breathing heavily as he clutched at his dagger. He grabbed it tightly and faced William. As soon as the emerald blade was drawn, there would be blood. It was inevitable.

William stood groggily. He held his jaw and cautiously stepped around Tavar, dagger following him all the way. Tavar kept his mouth closed now, eyes following every move; there's only so often you can warn a man before you have to let him make his own mistakes. Sometimes the harshest of lessons were the ones best learnt alone.

"I admit it. I wasn't sure it was really you at first. The years haven't been kind," Jassim said, running his mouth as Tavar had come to expect from the short time he had been in the room. "Then, I saw that blade. The emerald handle, the bone scabbard. Just the thought of the people that sword has torn through makes me get all... funny inside. A true *kyushira*. Don't see many of them around." He wriggled like a worm in the mud as though shaking off the thought.

William reached up for the blade and pulled it down from its perch above the hearth, the first time it had been taken down since Tavar had put it up there. It had waited patiently, biding its time. To be awakened after such a long slumber meant only one thing. Chaos.

"Feels heavy," William muttered. He stared at it like a long-lost lover, fingers running up and down the bone, caressing it with a smile.

"Unsheathe it," Jassim commanded, all joy fading from his voice as he stared longingly at the unique blade.

"It's speaking to me. It's asking me to draw the blade. No. *Demanding* that I unleash it," William said with his voice shaking, eyes unblinking.

"A real Al-Taabi. One of only ten made. Well, eleven if you believe the stories," Jassim answered, voice dripping with excitement.

Tavar knew the importance of timing. Surviving for this long meant knowing your limitations and taking advantages of your enemies' weaknesses. With his opponents distracted by the glory of the blade, he took his chance.

The dagger danced through the air, straight past the shoulder of William and towards Jassim. At the last second, Jassim forced his own sword up high, deflecting what would have been a fatal hit. The sound of metal clanging against metal woke them both from their trance but Tavar had not stood still to admire his throw.

He raised a knee, forcing it into William's stomach and driving all the air out of the man. In one swift movement, he grabbed the bone scabbard and snapped it upwards, straight into the throat. William fell onto the floor, clutching at his throat and struggling for breath.

Tavar placed a boot on William's chest, holding the sword at his side, eyes staring into Jassim's, waiting for the next move.

"I know exactly what you want to do, Tavar. Hell, *I* want you to do it…"

Tavar glanced down at the blade, feeling the old strength flowing through his body as he tightened his grip around the emerald hilt. Beneath him, William lay coughing, still struggling for breath. Right hand on the hilt, left gripping the scabbard, Tavar stared coldly into Jassim's eyes, wanting him to understand that he hadn't wanted this. He'd been forced into it.

His right hand flashed down and across, left hand snapping in the opposite direction. Blood sprayed up into the air, splashing up his shirt as warm droplets landed on his face. He kept watching Jassim, noticing the flicker of eyes and twitch of lips as young man watched his ally die.

Silence caught the room by the throat once more and held tight. William's body twitched on the floor for a moment and then stopped. Blood flowed from the single exit wound across the neck.

"Bravo, Tavar. Bravo." Jassim clapped, a smile breaking out on his dark face, placing his own sword onto the table. He stepped forward, defenceless, grinning from ear to ear. "Beautiful. Age hasn't dimmed your skill with a blade."

Tavar narrowed his eyes, unwilling to relax even as his enemy stepped forward with no weapon in sight. He glanced at the blood dripping from the edge of the beautiful blade and felt the warmth of satisfaction. Rather than sating his bloodthirst, he had a taste for it, as though drinking water after years of wandering in the desert. More was needed. He couldn't hear what Jassim was saying now, only saw the grin on his face and the open, empty hands.

Dropping to one knee, he slashed the weapon across his enemy's leg. The shocked scream of agony followed by a thud informed him that he had been precise. He looked down on his fallen foe and slashed across the chest. Not a killing blow but that wasn't the aim. He needed answers. He would demand answers.

"Who are you and why are you here?"

Jassim held a hand on his chest, attempting to staunch the flow of blood. His shirt was ripped along with the skin beneath it. Not deep enough to end his life but deep enough to hurt like hell. "I am who I said I am." He forced out through quick, sharp breaths, wincing with the pain. "The grandson of refugees. Born in Alfara. Raised in Alfara. The city of Kessarine to be exact. I'm a watcher and all I've seen is suffering in my lifetime."

Tavar sheathed the blade but kicked a well-placed boot against Jassim's ribs. "Why are you here?" he asked again. No unwelcome visitors for a decade and then two travellers turn up uninvited and wanting blood.

"For you."

"What would two young travellers want with an old man living alone out here. I'm nothing to you."

"Well, you're not just an old man are you, Tavar Farwan? If you were, I doubt anyone would give two shits about you. William is a hired thug, I needed someone to poke the bear; to help me decide if it really was you."

"He's dead because of you. You knew he'd die yet you didn't care."

"Care? Why should I care? He's killed innocents before. No one will cry over this loss; I can guarantee that."

Tavar allowed him to shuffle up against the wall, his breathing ragged. His hand dripped with dark red blood. He wasn't a danger for the moment. Let him get comfortable. Tavar would have his answers.

"You still haven't answered my second question."

"I have. What I said about Alfara earlier wasn't a

lie. The streets are chaos. The king is ruling through fear and soon his bastard of a son is going to take over and things will be ten times worse, as unimaginable as that is right now."

"What does that have to do with me?" Tavar asked, unable to meet his eyes.

"Don't play dumb with me. Not now I'm lying here in a pool of my own blood. I know who you are. You know who you are. It has everything to do with you. Without you, he wouldn't be king. You fought with the bastard and now we are the ones reaping from that cursed harvest. You were a legend in Alfara – the man who killed the puppet masters. Then the legend turned to disgust as the people realised what had happened. I came to see if you were ready to clean up the fucking mess you left!"

Tavar paused, taking a moment to digest the words spat out at him. Some words cut deeper than the sharpest of blades. That's what he had been told when he was younger. Admittedly, he'd rather be in his own situation than Jassim's right now. It's easy to argue a point when you're full of health but watching a man bleed out on the floor changes one's perspective.

"I've made many mistakes in my life, but there is one I regret more than any other. I should have left Kessarine well alone when I had the chance." He allowed the comment to hang in the air, giving it room to breathe and grow. He'd never admitted it out loud before, scared that the words would take on a life of their own to come back and destroy him. Often, he'd heard that the fear of something happening was so much worse than the pain of reality. Had to agree with that in this instance.

"Thousands of people are suffering, dying because of what you did. How does that make you feel?

Proud? Happy?"

"Thousands of people would be dead without me," Tavar snapped through gritted teeth, sick of being judged by this baby-faced fool. What did he know about what he'd been through? The pain. The suffering. The horrors. He knew shit. That was all. The world was full of men who excelled in judging others; moaning about what they had or hadn't done. Few men, if any, could claim to know what he had been through. "You think you know what happened? You know shit, kid. I was fighting in battles before you were born. And you dare to come here and threaten me, to take revenge for something that happened so long ago that only the dead could recall everything."

"Not only the dead. You know. You know it all," Jassim said, coughing as he struggled to force out each word. "If none of this is your fault then prove it. Tell me what happened. For once, give your version of events; speak your truth."

A pang of guilt flashed through Tavar at Jassim's words. He had to take some of the blame; no matter how he felt, he was a part of it, all of it. Without him, things would be different in Alfara. Would things be better? Who knew? Maybe the Oracles of Mareen knew but they sure as hell weren't letting anyone else know.

"For decades I've lived here, away from the backstabbing, the pain, the death. For decades I've not had to look in the eyes of those judging me. Until now. You want to know the truth, all of it?"

Jassim struggled to sit up, wincing at the pain tearing through is body with each movement. He tentatively pressed against the wound in his side before looking back up at Tavar. "I want all of it. I want to know how the son of travelling merchants ended up becoming the catalyst for a revolution. The greatest warrior in history. The last man to have a sword made by the greatest smith of our time." Jassim's eyes hardened, lips tightening. "I want to hear about the rise of a hero who promised so much and yet gave so little. I want to hear of the fall of Tavar Farwan and understand how someone who was so revered allowed the lands he loved to become blackened with greed, corruption and death. I want to know everything. Anyway, it's not every day you get to meet a man who killed a god..."

Tavar sighed, defeated. "That was no god. He was a man, just like any other, no matter what he tried to claim. Just a man, like any other. And I was no hero. Just a young fool wanting to save his friends. If you want to know it all, I'll tell you. But I'm starting from the beginning. To understand who I am and why I did what I did, you need to know what happened when I was growing up. It is a tale in three parts: like all the great tragedies of old. I'll tell you everything. The blood. The shadows. The flames. The hunger. The cries. It all started with a young boy; a naïve, young boy and a family who loved him."

PART ONE: THE EYES OF THE YOUNG BOY

"The eyes of the young boy shine with hope; glow with adventure; and glisten with transient pain. The past is a shadow; the present is fleeting; and the future is open and endless."

-Malike ir Terrasil – author of "Life in the Shadow of the Godking".

CHAPTER TWO: THE STORM

The wind howled through the fields, leading the branches of the bare trees in their autumn dance. It slammed against the merchants and entertainers packing up their belongings for the day. Weary men and women forced shut the wooden doors to their mobile stalls, fighting against the uncaring gale.

"Hate to close early but no one else is going to turn up, not with *that*!" Tavar's father gazed up at the clouds heading their way, as black as ink and threatening the worst storm they had seen that year. "Run along and find your mother; she'll be with the horses. And if you see your brother, tell him to head back to the caravan as soon as possible. I don't want to waste time looking for the rascal!"

Tavar nodded, accepting a short ruffle of his dark, wavy hair and spun away, eager to reach the woods before the storm hit.

He ran past the busy travellers and their wagons as they rushed around, grabbing at anything valuable and throwing it into the relative safety of the cart. All the men and women in this caravan had lost something of value in a storm and they weren't going to make the same mistake twice. A few of them perked up as Tavar raced past, long, wavy hair flowing in the growing wind; they waved and called out a greeting and he always made sure to wave back. Both of his parents had raised him to understand the importance of simple manners; acknowledging the people around, people who kept him safe on their long journeys travelling the Bone Road.

"Tavar!" his friend, Samira – a curious girl of his own age – picked her head up from where she sat against a tree reading a book and smiled at him. "Where you off to in such a hurry?"

He smiled back but carried on his journey. "Horses!"

Samira shook her head, smile still upon her face as she returned to her book.

As he reached the rows of trees, Tavar slowed down, panting with the effort of the run. He pressed a hand against the stitch in his side and screwed his face up.

"Out of breath already?" his mum snorted. Tavar nodded wordlessly, patting the body of the mare next to him before falling into his mother's arms, welcoming her embrace and revelling in her familiar earthy smell. "You must have been running very fast!" She planted a soft kiss on his head, her smile reaching her unusual sky-blue eyes. "Your father need me?"

"He's packing up. The storm." Tavar pointing up at the darkening clouds.

"Of course." His mother frowned up at the sky and held him close. "Go and fetch your brother so that we can get the horses into the caves; he's further into the woods with the twins."

He released his grip around her and strode off through the wood. It wasn't long before he found the three of them, each grasping long, thin branches and taking short, slow, steady footsteps whilst staring at each other. They took any opportunity they could to play hero; testing each other's footwork and reactions by slapping the oversized twigs against knuckles. Tavar could already see swollen red knuckles sticking out from his brother's fist as his hand trembled. Adam's hand looked no better but his twin sister, Alice, was once again unhurt.

"Come on boys, stop holding back," she mocked them with a smirk. "I can take it."

Whether it was her fast reactions or the boys lack of will to hurt her, she always won.

The twins had soft, gentle features. Each had the light, blonde hair of the north; Alice's long and wild whilst Adam's was short and military. Their eyes though, were identical: icy blue and full of sparkling life. They were three years older than Tavar, barely half a year younger than his brother and they were two of Tavar's favourite people to be around. Charismatic and full of life, always eager to head off on an adventure and never making Tavar feel like a younger, unwanted, unnecessary part of the group.

"We may need to stop there, sister. It seems we have a visitor," Adam spotted Tavar and dropped from his fighting stance, grinning at him before bowing low. "Master Tavar, an honour, as always."

Tavar couldn't keep a grin from his own face, bowing in response with a flourish. "Master Adam." He responded in his own mocking elegant voice before reverting to his natural tone. "The storm's picking up. Everyone's getting inside. Might be a big one."

"They always say that." Vandir sighed, throwing his wooden blade into the mud, shoulders slumping in disappointment. "It'll be like the last one: we'll hide out in the wagons and things will shake a bit. Then it'll stop and all the adults will talk about what a near miss it was. Never changes." He put an arm around Tavar and pulled him in close, squeezing him so that Tavar felt the air escape his body. Vandir released him and winked, trudging away from the clearing.

"I'm not too sure," Alice muttered as the twins followed. "Do you remember the one we got caught up in near the Old Kings' Pass? Lost three people that day. Almost tore down the statues and Samira's father said they'd been standing for over a thousand years."

"Samira's father says a lot," Adam replied as Tavar fell into line, listening to them. "Remember when he said that he'd held a real Al-Taabi in his hands?" Adam snorted. "Can't believe everything he says."

"What's an Al-Taabi?" Tavar asked, struggling to keep up with their long strides but unwilling to ask them to slow down for him.

"Tamir Al-Taabi is the greatest swordsmith in the world. Whenever Dad speaks about him, it's always in a hushed tone, as though he's not worthy to even speak about him in a normal voice. Man's a legend: his swords are perfectly weighted for each individual and he only makes one for you if he likes you. Rumour has it that the King of Hondai requested a sword be made for him: Al-Taabi turned him down, even after the king threatened to burn his city down and kill all of the people."

Tavar's jaw dropped. "What happened?"

Adam shrugged. "Nothing. Though, the King passed away in his sleep six months later. Some people think it was Al-Taabi himself who did it…"

"Gossip and rumour," Vandir called back to them. "The king was old. It was his time to go."

"And how do you know that?" Alice asked, squinted at Vandir who could only shrug in response.

"Dad said so. Our caravan passed through Hondai before that one was born," Vandir pointed back to Tavar, "and Dad said that the king was on his last legs even then. The surprise was that he even lasted that long! Al-Taabi moved to Okada after that. Stopped making blades according that merchant from the Arrow Islands who sheltered with us last winter."

By the time they reached the edge of the wood, only three of the horses were tied to the trees, whinnying and stamping at the muddy floor, aware of the storm to come.

"Took your time!" Tavar's mother scolded, the shadow of a smile showing that she wasn't really angry with them. She calmed the nearest animal down, stroking its neck gently and whispering in a soothing voice. "Most of them are in the cave already thanks to Arlo and Ben. Help me get the rest of them over there and then we need to head back to the wagons, won't be long until it starts. Alice, Adam. You father said he wants you back as soon as possible. Also said you can stay in our wagon if you'd like but he wants to see you first and make sure you're okay."

"No problem ma'am, we'll head back now. See you all later!" Alice said as the twins jogged away.

Tavar reached into his pocket and found half on an apple from earlier. He held it up to his favourite horse, a beautiful palomino he'd named Pan. The mare gratefully accepted the gift, a favourite of hers and allowed him to rest his head against her side, listening to her steady heartbeat. The two of them had grown up together and he considered her one of the family. He took her reins and pulled, guiding her away from the wood and towards the distant caves carved into the side of the mountain range. The fields between were clear as most members of the caravan had packed up and were now safely sheltered in their wagons or one of the numerous caves nearby.

"Reckon it'll be a bad storm?" Vandir asked as he led one of the horses across the field, staring up at the angry clouds.

"Looks it," their mum answered. "We'll be fine though. Been through enough haven't we?"

The horses fought against their handlers, nerves clear and obvious. A few tempting pieces of apple and a gentle stroke convinced them to make their way to the caves without bolting as had happened in previous storms. Tavar's mother was right: they had been through enough. Experience was a great teacher. That's what she always loved to say.

The many caves lining the mountains were a welcome shelter for any passing along the mountain pass. Unpredictable weather had too often been the cause of injury and even death amongst travellers and having a sanctuary available with such ease meant that the route was active and busy. Some travellers even attempted to improve the surroundings for any passing by after them, as was the case with the cave chosen by Tavar's mother.

The cave was dry and warm – exactly what they needed. Towards the back, there was a collection of wooden beams that had been dug deep into the ground by whomever had occupied the shelter last. They led the horses to the beams and, after being checked with a good push and pull by Tavar's mother, the horses were tied to the beams and given the last few treats to keep them calm.

"This is why we travel on the well-worn routes. More likely to find places such as this, prepared by those who have come before us," his mother said, smiling warmly at her two sons. "Leave the world a better place than when you entered it: that's the job of any person alive. Small things like this help you with that goal." She slapped a hand against one of the wooden beams and winked at them. "Come on, they'll be fine. Time to get back to your father before he sends out the search party!"

The first drops of rain began their descent, falling steadily from the dark sky. Tavar looked up and two drops fell directly onto his face, catching him by surprise and making him jump. By the time they reached the wagons, a deluge of rain had fallen from the sky like a demonic bucket emptying its contents out across the mountain pass.

"It's about time!" Tavar's father called out just in time for the first flash of lightning and boom of thunder to echo through the pass. He had his forest-green hood pulled up tight around his head, already soaked through as he bounced on the spot, urging them to jump into the back of the wagon. "Almost came to get you myself."

He helped his wife into the wagon carefully before turning back to pick Tavar up. Tavar grinned as he was lifted into the warmth of the cosy cart, blankets draped all around it like a secret hideout from one of the adventure stories he loved to listen to. His father winked at him, understanding his excitement before turning as his eyes fell upon Vandir's swollen knuckles. "Been playing that silly game again?" he frowned as Vandir attempted to pull his sleeve down to hide the evidence.

"Just a few hits. Nothing I can't handle…"

"I've warned you about that game," his father muttered darkly. "You either quit, or you get better! Can't have you breaking your hand when we need your help on the road. I'll have to swap you for Alice if you get any worse…" The smile returned, lightening the mood once more as he followed Vandir into the wagon. He tightened the cords around the waving flaps at the back and rubbed his hands together for warmth.

"Fingers crossed it will pass just as fast as it arrived," Tavar's mother said, leaning back into her corner and closing her eyes. They knew the routine.

"Aye. We've done what we can anyway, no use fretting over things you can't change," his father replied, checking through the deerskin bag full of food and pulling out some fruit. "Best to get our heads down and start again in the morning. Should be in sight of the city walls in a few days. We've made enough to afford a decent inn and a real bed!" That brought genuine smiles to all their faces. It had been too long since they had stayed inside city walls. Tavar loved their life on the road but the luxuries of a city were something he craved for after a long, hard journey on the Bone Road.

He sank into the comfort of the blankets, arching his back and shuffling against a feather pillow Vandir had picked out earlier that year in the Morodira Market. Best purchase they'd made in Tavar's opinion. The wind picked up, its howl growing and hitting out at the thin cloth protecting them from the elements.

His eyes grew heavy with the rhythmic song of the wind mixed with the warmth under the covers. Sleep was due to welcome him into its comfortable embrace when suddenly, a shout woke him from his slumber.

"Almost blew me into the mountains!" Adam cried, squeezing himself into the wagon and laughing at the cries of discomfort and disgust as he shook the copious amounts of rainwater from his jacket. "Bit of a storm out there! Hey everyone."

"Hey Adam, Alice." Tavar's father replied, wiping the water from his face and blinking rapidly.

"Hey guys," Alice responded, gracefully pulling herself in after her brother and squeezing between Tavar and Vandir. "Thanks for having us."

"Anytime!" Tavar's mother said joyfully. "Your parents safely shut in?"

"Mum's already asleep, typical," Alice laughed. "Dad's reading his book on the history of warfare."

The impact of the rain against the covers intensified following another boom of thunder. Tavar shuffled until he felt snug, enjoying the sounds of the storm. Though many people shook with fear at nature's wrath, Tavar found the whole thing oddly soothing. The rhythm of the storm and the patter of rain against the roof always led to heavy eyes and a quick trip to dreamland. Once the animals were settled and safe, there was nothing to worry about. The whole thing became an excuse for friends to get together and share stories. Nothing to worry about at all.

"You already thinking of sleep?" Alice asked as Tavar opened his mouth in a great yawn. "Thought you'd want to hear all of the cool stories!"

"Heard them all before," Tavar said, licking his lips and pulling his cover tight up to his neck.

"Doesn't usually stop you."

"Been a long day."

"What have you done?" Vandir snorted.

"Not much," Tavar grinned, closing his eyes and welcoming the gentle embrace of sleep.

Tavar woke to shouts and angry voices.

A stream of rain slapped against the covers on the wagon; no roll of thunder sounding in the distance. There were only raised voices fighting to assert control over one another. One of the voices sounded familiar to him.

"Stay still. Do not make a sound," Vandir whispered, holding a finger to his lips and glaring at Tavar to make his warning clear.

He felt panic rise inside as struggled to wake up, rubbing his eyes and fighting off the sleep nullifying his senses. "What's going on?" he whispered, eyes darting from Vandir who was peeking through a gap in the cover and the wagon, to Alice who was resting against Adam's shoulder with her eyes tightly shut as he muttered a silent prayer.

"Soldiers. Alfaran soldiers." Vandir shuffled back from the edge and carefully pulled the corners of his covers up. He lifted up the hidden bow and placed it on top of the sheet before heading back under, rummaging for something else. A moment later, he grimaced and raised his hand back up, fingers clutched around five arrows. He dropped them to his side and picked up the wooden yew bow again, testing the hemp string. The string fought back against his effort, taught and ready, unbroken.

"Don't even think about it," Adam warned, easing his sister from his shoulder and crawling towards Vandir. "These are trained soldiers of Alfara. Heading out there with a weapon will only make things worse. You'll get everyone killed!" Adam motioned to grab the bow but Vandir yanked it away, his face stern and determined.

"My parents are out there! You expect me to just sit here and do nothing?"

"Yes. That's exactly what I expect you to do,"

Adam bit back, "because that's what your parents asked you to do. You're not the only one with family out there, you know."

The comment calmed Vandir as he realised he wasn't the only one suffering. The tension left his face, replaced by a look of frustration and fear. His eyes softened as they fell on Tavar, his little brother looking up at him with tears glistening in his eyes.

"Stay here, brother, please." Tavar swallowed the lump in his throat, pleading with Vandir as the voices outside grew louder. Vandir nodded silently and crawled over to Tavar, allowing him to rest his head against his chest.

"The deserters were found in the same caves as your horses," a commanding voice yelled outside of the wagon. "For three days we have been tracking the scum and then we find them being sheltered by a passing caravan. Such a crime is dealt with severely in Alfara."

"There were no men or women in the caves we used last night. We led the horses in for shelter and tied them up before returning to our shelter. If any deserters were using the caves then it must have been after we left when they arrived." Tavar held his breath as he recognised his mother's voice, strong and unwavering in the face of danger.

"A story fabricated to cover for your crimes, no doubt. Luckily for you, I am in a good mood this morning, now that the storm has passed." The commanding voice had a hint of mischief about it, as though playing up before the punch line.

Tavar tensed as he held his breath, waiting for it to hit. He could feel the steady rise and fall of Vandir's chest as his breathing increased in speed. "We will take your horses and your merchandise as payment for this slight against our kingdom. Also, you and your people are banned from entering Alfara for the next two years. That, I feel, should be enough of a deterrent…" A crowd of laughter roared out at the punishment, other soldiers, eager to boost their leader's already inflated ego, no doubt.

"You can't do that!" a voice screamed through the laughter. Bergir, the butcher. A good man. He'd often given Tavar some of his best strips of bacon as he passed by, always offering a pleasant smile and a warm tale. "There's not another city within four weeks of Kessarine. You can't ban us from Alfara. With nothing to sell and nowhere to go, it'll be the end of some of us! Have mercy, please!"

Tavar jumped at the loud thud and the screams of horror that followed. He prayed that the sound wasn't what he thought it was. Vandir bolted up, grabbing the bow before Adam tackled him to the ground as Alice balled her fists, her face turning a dark shade of red.

"No, Vandir. Don't!" Adam said through gritted teeth.

"Mercy? You beg for mercy when you have been sheltering traitors of Alfara! You are lucky to be walking away with your lives!" the commander bellowed. "Lieutenant Marcus, tell your men to search the wagons. Drag anyone out who is hiding and take anything valuable that you find. This caravan displeases me."

Tavar hunched into the corner of the wagon, making himself as small as possible as more shouting and cries echoed through the mountain pass outside. Alice moved to be beside him, throwing an arm around his shoulders.

"It will be okay, Tavar," she said through a hushed breath. "You'll see. Everything will be okay." He nodded in response, not trusting his voice to speak without breaking.

The sound of covers being flung into the air mixed with screams and yells of the innocent merchants and their families being forced from their places of hiding. Heavy footsteps drew closer and a shadow passed by the wagon. Tavar felt the sweat dripping down his forehead as all four of them kept as still and silent as possible. Out of the corner of his eye, he spotted a slight movement from his brother. Vandir pulled the string back, arrow tight against the hemp string as Adam and Alice were distracted by the shadow walking towards the entrance.

The cover was thrown back in an instant, casting the harsh sunlight into the wagon, compelling Tavar to throw a hand up to cover his face. Through the light he saw a soldier, angry dark eyes peering out from a silver helmet; a navy blue and white leather top covering his torso and metal gauntlets running from the tips of his fingers up the length of his forearms. The dark eyes widened as they fell on Vandir, bow ready and taught in hand.

The twang of the bow reached Tavar's ears as his eyes watched the arrow land directly on its target, forcing the soldier back with a yell as the arrow dug deep into his shoulder.

"You little shit!" the soldier roared, clutching at the wound and wincing as he shifted the arrow nestled inside him. "Little bastard shot me!" he yelled to a nearby group.

More men raced over to the wagon, weapons in hand, spears and swords glistening with the promise of death.

"What have you done?" Adam muttered, his shoulders dropping as he looked despairingly at Vandir. Vandir shrugged back, jaw set and eyes locked on the rushing men. There was no way he could take them all down. He dropped the bow, regret soaking through his every movement.

Rough hands grabbed at Tavar, pulling him from the wagon with a scream as others grabbed at his brother and friends. Tears burned his eyes as he watched Vandir hit the wet ground, face first. The soldier he had shot strolled forward, an evil smirk clearly displaying his intentions. A boot to the stomach pushed the wind from Vandir as he coughed and rolled on the ground, struggling to catch his breath. Adam and Alice had their hands tied with rope held by two of the soldiers, unable to move.

"No! Leave him alone. That's my son!" Tavar's stomach turned as he saw his father pushing past a row of soldiers watching the huddled crowd of merchants. His mother followed, distress lining her worried face.

A broad-shouldered man stepped in between Vandir and his parents, standing out from the crowd of soldiers with his black sleeves adorned with a golden snake on either side. "Take one step closer and your son will be dead before you can do anything about it." He had the commanding voice that Tavar had heard from the wagon. The leader.

His parents stood still, rooted to the spot as their eyes locked on their fallen son, still struggling on the ground, his attacker looming over him.

One of the soldiers pulled Tavar's hands behind his back and tied them together with a length of rope. He wasn't gentle. The rope burned against Tavar's skin but he didn't complain. There was no point. He looked to his right and heaved. The body of Bergir, the butcher, lay motionless on the ground, blood still pouring from his head and pooling in the grass he had fallen on. There was the evidence that fighting back was futile. Comply or end up like the butcher: the message was clear.

"Please," Tavar's father called to the commander, "He's just a boy. He was frightened and wanted to defend himself; defend his family."

"Attacking a member of the Alfaran army, a defenceless soldier who was only trying to get him out of hiding, is a worse offence than harbouring deserters…" The commander licked his lips, looking down at the struggling boy beneath him. "Saeed here will need medical supplies and some rest to recover properly. That costs money: costs time as well, time that we don't have." He lifted Vandir's chin with his muddied boot, inspecting him with a sneer. "Dark skin like an Alfaran. Like one of us. But you don't understand our ways, that much is obvious."

"We have some coin; fast and powerful horses; and a few bits and pieces that can be sold. Just please, leave my son," Tavar's father pleaded, pain shaking his voice. He dropped to his knees, staring at his fallen son before glancing at Tavar, eyes wide.

"We will take everything, there is no doubt about that. It is all deserved. But we need more. A thousand of your horses are not worth one of my soldiers, the greatest in the world. Alfara puts a high price on its men and I fear it is a price that you peasants cannot afford." The commander stepped forward, lecherous eyes falling on Tavar's mother. He raised a gloved hand and batted away a strand of her dark hair. "However, we may be able to come to some kind of arrangement." His voice dropped low, almost to a purr.

Tavar's father jumped to his feet and stood in front of his wife, shielding her from the commander. The whole atmosphere shifted, soldiers reaching for their weapons at the lack of respect.

"You will not touch a hair on her head," he threatened, eyebrows lowered in fury.

The commander nodded in appreciation, still smirking. "You've got a bit of fight in you, I respect that." He launched a fist straight across the jaw of Tavar's father, knocking him onto a single knee. "Usually, that takes people off their feet. You're made of stern stuff." Tavar's father rubbed at his jaw, resting his other hand on his wife's shoulder as she stared at him through her tears. The other merchants could only look on in silence, caught in the trap of wanting to help their friends and not wanting to risk their own lives.

"You can carry on with your lives, peasants. You have earned my respect." The commander cried out to his anxious audience. He clapped his hands together and the soldiers moved, many clutching at ropes attached to the children around the enclosure. Tavar spotted Samira struggling in the distance as she was hauled to her feet, fear in her eyes. "We're taking the children. Alfara has need of slaves and servants. They will pay for your insolence."

The crowd yelled out, anger boiling up inside them as they watched their children being dragged away from them. A row of soldiers slammed together, blocking their path and aiming long spears towards them.

"You can't do this!"

"He's my only child! Have mercy!"

"Alfaran bastards!"

Tavar sobbed as he watched Vandir struggle to his feet, only to meet another blow to the stomach from his attacker. "I'm gonna have fun with you, kid. That's the last time you'll fire an arrow at one of us…"

Vandir leaned back and launched a lump of saliva from the back of his throat. The soldier wiped it from his face, furious with the complete lack of respect. He drew his sword, point aimed at Vandir's heart.

Tavar didn't even think about what he was doing. He raced forward, slipping from his own soldier's grasp and slammed his foot into the back of the soldier's knee, dropping him to the ground with a scream. Vandir took the opportunity to thump his knee straight into the man's face. The crunch informed those close enough to hear that something had broken. Blood poured from the soldier's nose as he struggled to open his eyes. A stream of curses Tavar had never heard before spewed from the soldier's mouth.

The crowd roared and pressed forward, led by Tavar's parents. His father pushed the closest soldier aside, surprising him and opening a gap. He wrapped Tavar in his arms and held him close, his breath tickling Tavar's ear. "Stay alive. Do whatever you can, my son. Just stay alive. We love you."

Hot blood splattered onto Tavar's face, making him jump back in horror, eyes wide open. The point of a blade stuck out the front of his father's throat, opening a wound that could never be closed. A scream broke his heart as he saw his mother rush towards them, drawing a hidden dagger from her girdle. She pulled back, ready to stab it straight into the heart of her husband's killer. Tavar willed the blade forward but the will of a young boy meant nothing against the training of a soldier.

The commander caught Tavar's mother by the wrist, smiling at her. "Your family has earned my respect, truly. Your boys will be looked after in Alfara. It is the least I can do." He thrust his sword up through her chest and straight into her heart.

Tavar cried out, unable to tear his eyes away from his mother. Her eyes lost the light he had so loved and she fell to the ground with a thump. Tavar finally closed his eyes, rocking back and forth with the lifeless body of his father in his arms. "I'm sorry. I'm sorry. I'm sorry," he muttered, as though it was a chant that could turn back time and bring them to life once more.

More sobs broke out in the crowd, the sobs of the hopeless and defeated.

Tavar looked at his brother who could only stare back in horror, purposely looking away from his lifeless parents.

Adam and Alice gazed out into the crowd. Tavar spotted their parents, holding each other close and looking straight back at their beloved children.

"I've had enough," the commander growled to the soldiers around him. He wiped his blade with a ragged piece of cloth thrown to him. Without looking up, he issued his command. "Take the kids. Kill the rest of them."

Tavar closed his eyes shut but he couldn't escape the sounds of death around him. A cacophony of cries stabbed through his heart with more force than any steel could ever manage.

He opened his eyes to see his brother on his knees staring up at him, bloodshot eyes burning with rage. "I'll kill them. I promise, little brother, I'll kill them all."

CHAPTER THREE: HOME

The next few days passed in a blur.

Tavar stayed silent as though he had forgotten how to speak. Sleep evaded him, replaced with a waking nightmare. As horrible as it was when he was awake, trudging along with his arms tied up, it was better than having to rest and be lost with his own thoughts, his own memories; the true nightmare of what had befallen him and his people.

Both his legs and feet burned with exhaustion as the soldiers pushed them relentlessly forward, only stopping for two meals a day and to sleep two hours after the sun fell from the sky. A couple of grim-faced soldiers flanked the line of children stumbling through the mountain pass and then along the muddied pathways through Greenway Forest. The trees hunched together, blocking out most of the light from the sun and confusing Tavar for the first day as he struggled to decipher whether night had replaced day. It was only when he could no longer see the feet of Adam tripping up on the twigs and fallen branches in front of him that he realised that night-time had truly descended upon the marching troops.

Another two days of journeying through the forest allowed Tavar a chance to sharpen his senses.

Some of the soldiers spread out along the narrow line of men, carrying torches to light the way. Light fell on curious eyes just out of reach of the thick trees as the flames flickered. Even the usual small talk of soldiers abated as the men glanced nervously around, their pace quickening, intending to reach the end of this cursed forest as soon as they could.

Birds that were so black that they even stood out amongst the shadows sat perched upon crooked branches above them gazing down with intrigued looks and a cocked head, beaks facing the intruders of their home.

Tavar stared up at them as they chattered with an unusual clicking sound. The closest bird spread its wings and a black feather dropped to the ground, swaying in the air before Adam's boot stepped on top of it unnoticed. The bird's black beady eyes looked down at Tavar and he met the gaze unflinching. He had heard tales of animals helping those in need but as much as he prayed for intervention, deep down, he knew there was nothing that could be done: his parents had entered the void and he was only days away from life as a slave, working for those who had taken his parents from him.

He lay on the filthy ground, a ripped sheet pulled tight over him, and stared up into the blackness of the forest, fighting off sleep. Soft snoring filled the air as the nightmare returned, unable to escape it even whilst awake. He clung to his older brother's words, repeating them gently to himself. "I'll kill them. I promise, little brother, I'll kill them all." The words swam around his head, taking on a life of their own and giving Tavar an energy that forced him to keep going.

Quiet sobbing muffled against a cover caught his ear and he sat up, looking around for the disturbance. His eyes were useless so he listened carefully to gentle words spoken next to him.

"Don't cry. We can't show weakness. These are soldiers; you saw what they did back there. We can't give up and let them win. We have to keep going. I won't let them get away with what they've done. We need to think of our parents. They can't have died for nothing!"

Alice's voice was low enough to prevent any of the soldiers from hearing but Tavar still held his breath as a torchlight in the distance made its steady way in their direction. Only when the soldier holding it had strolled past with a long, drawn out yawn did he feel comfortable enough to breathe again.

The sobs died down and there were no more hushed conversations in the darkness. Tavar wondered how his brother was coping, sore and aching from the beating no doubt. He sighed and closed his eyes, preparing himself for a sleep that would hold no rest.

The relief in the air took on an almost physical presence as the group marched through the last row of trees, boots stomping quicker as they spotted the increased sunlight streaking through the branches, welcoming them with open arms.

Tavar breathed in long and slow through his nose, allowing his chest to rise as he embraced the fresh air before letting it out through his mouth. In the distance, down the row of tied up children, he spotted Vandir looking back. They caught each other's eyes and shared a relieved smile, happy that they were alive. Even from this distance, Tavar thought he could sense the grief and pain in his brother's tired eyes.

"Keep moving, boy," a gruff voice muttered next to Tavar. "You don't want to be caught slacking. These men want to be home, been too long already and they don't need an excuse to inflict pain."

Tavar recognised the soldier: pale grey eyes,

cropped black hair and a thin white scar on his stubbled jawline. Lieutenant Marcus was respected by the others but there was a side to him that the man kept hidden from his comrades. This wasn't the first time the man had offered Tavar advice. He'd even managed to pass a water bottle to him in the forest when Tavar's body had threatened to give up in him, eyelids falling and dehydration promising a swift meeting with the muddy ground.

"Keep going. We're less than a day away," the soldier muttered, twisting around and walking backwards, keeping his eyes on the last stragglers breaking through the forest cover.

"Thank you," Tavar whispered. The soldier offered the briefest of nods before spinning and marching forward and away.

The whole company suddenly had a spring in their step. Perhaps it was the fresh air and sunlight after walking through the stuffy, enclosed forest for so long, or maybe it was just that the soldiers could sense that they were so close to home but their mood had brightened. None of this sudden joy was shared by the line of children they dragged along, unsurprisingly.

By midday, Tavar saw scattered thatched rooves on houses that formed a village in the boundary of Alfara. The soldiers grinned and slapped each other's backs, ignoring the pained and nervous glances that their prisoners shared along the line. The green of the forest gave way to the rock and sand of Alfara. A cool breeze whipped across the sand and cooled the group as they marched forward in the growing heat.

One of the children, Tavar had forgotten his name but remembered that Samira had spent time teaching him to read of late, even though he was a year older, fell to his knees and began to sob, overcome with the horror of his situation. The nearest soldier cursed and slammed a shield against the boy, knocking him to the ground.

"Hey!" Lieutenant Marcus raced forward and pushed the soldier away, chest puffing out, eyes wide and brow raised. "How are we going to get them back into the city if we keep striking them? They're on their last legs as it is. Pick them up and drag them on. No striking!"

The soldier spat on the grass, his saliva barely missing his superior's muddied boot. "Too soft on 'em, Marcus. That's your problem." The soldier shrugged and turned away. Marcus kept his gaze on the man's back, shaking his head before offering a hand to the fallen boy.

"Come on. Not much further to go."

The excitement the soldiers had displayed when stepping foot on Alfaran soil was nothing in comparison to the moment the heart of Alfara rose into view on the horizon.

On top of a great, rocky hill, the city of Kessarine had a wonderful vantage point looking down on the world from all angles. Protective stone walls circled the city with towering fortifications warning any would-be besieger that an invasion would be futile. Rising higher than the walls and sat in the centre of the city was a golden dome shining in the light of the setting sun. Numerous spires stabbed at the sky around the domed centre, less welcoming than any city Tavar had entered in his short life.

In light of his situation: parched mouth, dry throat, aching limbs, sore eyes, sand everywhere, heart almost at breaking point – it was astonishing that Tavar had the energy to raise his head and marvel at the wondrous city, as threatening as it may be. It had been over a year since he had stepped foot into a large city and Sira must have been less than half the size of the grand city towering over him.

"A beauty, isn't she?" Lieutenant Marcus muttered; eyes fixed on his homeland. "For centuries, this has been the heart of Alfara – the very spot from where the great kingdom grew after Queen Tamira defeated the Pretender." The lieutenant held out his camel skin bottle.

"Were you born here?" Tavar asked, eagerly nodding for the water. He tilted his head back and Marcus pushed the bottle forward, tilting it carefully to ensure the water didn't choke him.

"I was born close enough; the city of Kessarine has been my home for much of my life. You can see the citadel from here: the golden dome is a beacon for all to see – a sign of how far we have come as a nation."

Marcus's eyes sparkled with pride; his chest pushed out towards his home. Tavar bit back his reply. The rope chaffing at his wrists reminded him of his situation. Now wasn't the time for backchat. A silent nod was the best he could do.

The soldiers broke into song as they neared the city, chanting together and stamping their feet in joy. More of them offered water and fruit to the struggling prisoners; hostility paused or hidden by their relief and making it back home.

As the sun dipped below the horizon, thousands of lights lit up the city from above. Tavar was close enough now to see figures walking along the walls, torches in hand lit to guide their path. With the light of the torches came a horror Tavar had not noticed when staring at the grand structure earlier.

Either side of a black, iron gate were lines of what Tavar had assumed were gruesome displays of art. Choking back the bile building up inside, he spotted a flicker of movement from one of the statues. He struggled to calm his breathing as he realised the statues were in fact bodies: human bodies nailed to the wall through their hands and feet. Both men and women were displayed in this sickening way, their heads dropped onto a shoulder or their chest. Most were dead, free from the agony. But some were still alive, their bodies refusing to give up. Tavar closed his eyes, muttering a silent prayer for their passing to be swift. Never before had he seen such dehumanising torture. And this was only the entrance…

The commander swept along the line of prisoners, staring down at them with that sickening smirk of his from horseback. "Feast your eyes on the greatest city in the world, the heart of Alfara – Kessarine," he cried. "In this great city, you will live out the remainder of your wretched lives. The Outer City houses the workers of Alfara: blacksmiths, leatherworkers, woodworkers, tradesmen, and merchants. It is here that you will find your new home. You will make life easier for the lucky bastard willing to pay for you. Some of you may even find your way into our glorious army – we always have a need for shields." Scattered laughter rang out through the lines of soldiers listening. "From this day forward, you are citizens of Alfara – bound to our laws, culture, and way of life. If you still harbour feelings of hatred and resentment, I suggest you look upon those who have acted upon those feelings of late. We are always on the lookout for men and women to adorn the strong walls that have shielded us from our enemies. Make the right choices. You are home."

Tavar didn't have the energy to feel anything except a wave of nausea. The commander rode off ahead of the line of weary prisoners and buoyant soldiers, raising a hand in a salute mirrored by the soldiers seated by the gate. A moment later, the great doors opened out to them and Tavar caught the first glimpses inside his new home.

Escaping the acrid odour of the decaying bodies on the wall, Tavar finally trusted that breathing in wouldn't cause him to pass out. His nose itched, shocked by the onset of a wave of tantalising smells. Rich and powerful aromas wafted his way as the group turned right, entering a grand market, greeted by rows and rows of stalls with merchants selling spices of every colour. Tavar winced at the orchestra of sound blasting his ears. After so long on the road, the shouts and conversations of thousands of people packed into a city unnerved him. It didn't seem natural.

His stomach growled as the smell of fried fish attacked him: a reminder of his constant hunger. He licked his lips, eager for something to eat, anything.

"Fresh fish! Caught earlier today in the River Wylde. True Alfaran fish, none better anywhere in the world! I guarantee it!" a merchant sang out to the baying crowds. A few people eagerly handed over small, circular bronze coins in exchange for the large fish.

"Fruit; fresh fruit!" another called out. "Alfaran apples are sweeter than any. A delight for your taste buds!"

"Nuts and berries picked from within the great land of Alfara! The best around, guaranteed!"

"Pork, chicken, lamb! All prepared for you in our great land!"

The merchants battled each other, shouting louder and louder, eager to have their voices heard. In Tavar's eyes, they all had the same message: buy from us because Alfara is the best. In all the cities his family had traded in, Tavar hadn't noticed such determination to sell from one's own land. The beauty he had found in travelling had been the diversity and variety in food, materials, language, and people. The very idea of trade was based upon sharing with others. Not here, it seemed.

He noticed that all the men wore brightly coloured robes that matched the elaborate headgear that sparkled with silver on the brim. The women opted for black. All of the women also had their heads covered with a scarf that fell low and wrapped around their shoulders. Some of the women had gold and silver patterns stitched into the robe and scarf that caught the light from the sun. He caught a group of women giggling to one another and pointing as one of the soldiers passed them with a wink.

The paved street led on past the market until the group reached a large, beige clay building with a flat roof. Standing on the balcony, looking down at the line of soldiers and prisoners was a woman with short, cropped hair and dark skin. Her eyes narrowed as they caught Tavar's. She puffed on a long wooden pipe before blowing out a large cloud of smoke and heading into the building.

The commander called for attention. Soldiers stamped their heels together as one, backs straight and chests puffed out like pompous birds looking for a mate. The prisoners paused, relieved at the sudden break in their journey. Tavar frowned as he noticed Adam's legs shake with the exhaustion of standing up for so long.

"Welcome to Kessarine, the heart of Alfara." The commander grinned at them. "This is your first time here and we can't have any of you walking around in the light of day tomorrow looking like the filthy scum you are. You will be paired up and escorted by a soldier into Lilian's barracks. This is the South House, where most of you will be staying. Shoes will be taken off before you enter any building in Kessarine. You will bathe and ensure you look your best before you are fed. Following a night's rest, you will be woken up at first light with the call to prayer and called to the main hall. It is here that you will find your life. My advice is that you forget the old one, unless you want to head up to the wall."

"Commander Grey." Tavar's eyes shifted to the cropped haired woman who was now walking towards the commander, pipe in hand and a wicked smile on her face. Dark brown eyes gazed along the line, studying the boys and girls tied to each other. "Your welcoming speeches never fail to make my heart soar and chest burst with pride. Fifteen years have passed since I walked with you into this city and I do believe I could recall every word you said that day, though you were just a member of the infantry back then..."

The commander sniffed and stood up straight, his eye twitching slightly. "Lilian. You are an example to these vagabonds of what can be achieved with hard work and the right attitude." He turned to face the prisoners and pointed a finger at their host. "She was once where you are. Listen to her." Grey slipped a dagger from his leather belt and marched to the front of the line, obscured from Tavar's view.

Lilian curtsied and licked at her painted lips. "Commander, as always, it is a pleasure." The commander walked back into view, pulling on a rope. Tavar's heart stopped as Vandir stumbled along at the end of the robe, hands still tied. His shoulders were slumped and his eyes were heavy. Swelling around his lower lip and jaw was proof of the beating he had received. Grey gave a stiff nod and spun on his heels, striding off further down the paved path followed by a collection of soldiers. Vandir staggered along, forced to follow his captor.

For a fleeting second, Tavar contemplated calling out. He knew how that would end. Bravery was a fine thing in all the stories but in real life it usually ended up with a body six feet under. Or nailed to a wall…

He could only watch, biting his lip and feeling the heat rise behind his eyes as he stared out after his older brother, wondering if he would ever see him again.

The other soldiers remained to escort the prisoners, including, to Tavar's relief, Lieutenant Marcus.

"Soldiers of Alfara, you know the process," Marcus called out. Instantly, the soldiers grabbed for their daggers and cut the ropes along the line, taking the nearest prisoners and dragging them forward into the building.

"Lieutenant Marcus, it is good to see you again," Lilian said. "I hope your travels went as expected."

Tavar shifted to the side, turning his head to listen to the conversation as Marcus stepped towards the woman. "We have a whole new intake of orphans to look after. How do you think it went?" Marcus's voice was stiff, angry even. Tavar risked a look at Lilian just in time to see her face soften.

"Grey?" she whispered. Marcus titled his head forward in the slightest of nods. "Shit."

Marcus sighed and turned away. Tavar busied himself with staring a hole into the ground as the soldier walked over, dagger now in hand.

"Don't think about running away. You'll get hot water, food, and shelter. The commander was right: it's that or the wall." Marcus cut the rope behind Tavar and walked ahead of him, doing the same to the rope in front of Adam so that it was just the two of them connected now. "Follow me."

The building was cramped. Wooden floorboards creaked beneath his feet and doors opened either side of a narrow corridor. Marcus led them straight down the corridor, ignoring the thin staircase leading to the upper floors.

"Here we are," Marcus said, stepping into a room on the left and turning to face them.

Adam stumbled through first and Tavar followed. Marcus stepped to the side and allowed them a good view of the small room. There were two small beds, simple but better than lying in shit on the road.

"The toilet is out back. You'll be called by one of the servants when it is time to wash and prepare for the meal. Same with the morning routine. Clothes will be delivered within the hour." Marcus cut the ropes from Adam's hand. The exhausted prisoner stumbled over to the bed and collapsed on it without uttering a word. Marcus strode over to Tavar and cut his ropes.

Tavar groaned and stretched his wrists and fingers, rubbing at the red marks etched in his skin. "What is this place?" he asked.

"The South House. A halfway house," Marcus answered, sitting down on the other bed. "Orphans in Alfara can come here for food and a safe place to stay before they are… relocated."

"Enslaved."

"Look, the life ahead of you will be hard but

exactly how hard depends on you. Keep your head down and make the right choices. Whatever you do, don't push to be trained in the army, no matter what the commander does or says."

"Why not?" Tavar asked, the dormant defiant streak in him awakening once again.

"Trust me. You're not from Alfara. Surrounding yourself with Alfaran soldiers will only lead to issues you don't want to deal."

Tavar looked around the room, taking in his new home. Though it was larger than the wagon he had travelled in with his whole family, this room felt more suffocating, as though the walls were ready to close in around him. He took a deep breath and sat down on the bed. "Why are you offering advice to us?" he asked the lieutenant, genuinely bemused. "Your soldiers butchered my family and friends for no reason and you watched. They were good people."

Marcus shot up from the bed, fists clenched. "Watch your words. Remember your place, boy."

The stress, fear, exhaustion, and grief tore through Tavar, blinding him to the reality of his situation. "You're all just murderers; scumbags who—"

He fell back onto the bed, hands clutching at his burning jaw. His eyes watered with the pain but it felt good, an escape from the emotional whirlwind that had been building up inside.

"I have been too soft on you." Marcus's voice trembled with rage, threatening to break. "This city chews up the weak and spits them out. I helped you because I felt guilty. We shouldn't have killed all those people. But it's done now. You're in Alfara; this is your life now. Get used to it." He strode out of the room without another look back.

Tavar sat back, rubbing at his jaw.

"You shouldn't push him." Adam's muffled voice called over from the other bed. "We could use all the help we can get right now."

"They killed them all, Adam."

"They didn't kill us."

No, they didn't.

Daybreak found Tavar awake and restless.

He'd managed to get little rest, waking up twice to screams of terror from his sleeping, lone roommate. He'd jump up, breathing heavily before coming to his senses enough to realise that the cries were a part of Adam's nightmares. Tavar had lain in bed, struggling to calm himself whilst attempting to ignore the sobs from the other side of the room.

After splashing cold water on his face in a futile effort to fight back against the exhaustion threatening to consume him, he dressed into the new clothes that had been left by his door and took a good look at Adam for the first time since they had been taken.

His friend looked even worse than Tavar felt.

Bloodshot eyes sat on dark heavy bags. His lips were dry and cracked and every move he made looked as though Adam was doing it with the weight of a wagon being carried on his shoulders.

"How you feeling?" Tavar asked. It hurt to see his friend, usually so composed and full of life, look like this – a shadow of his former self.

"Fan-fucking-tastic, Tavar. Couldn't be better," he muttered dryly, red eyes rolling as he changed into his fresh clothes.

"Look, Adam—" Tavar began.

"No, Tavar," Adam snapped. "I don't want to talk about it; about any of it. I just want to get through this hell, one day at a time. Maybe at some point I'll be able to wake up from this nightmare…"

"Okay. I won't talk about it," Tavar agreed. If that was his way of dealing with things then it would have to do. "We'll get through it. One day at a time."

The servants Tavar had seen throughout the building so far all had the pale snow-like skin and blonde hair that was almost white. He had seen similar people before on his travels, even spoken to a few. Most came from the Crown Isles or Naviqand in the far north of the continent. The harsh conditions on the continent bred a stoic and brave culture. Wars with the Northern kingdoms across the Marrish Channel had almost destroyed their way of life. Many moved to other continents and worked as cutthroats, mercenaries or, apparently, servants.

One such servant knocked on the door. Tavar opened it with a weak smile.

"Breakfast is ready. Please, follow me," the servant said, turning away.

The kitchens and dining rooms were in a building next door. It was of a similar size but far more open with only the three, large rooms. The dining room had a high ceiling and rows of wooden benches leading down to the open window at the back of the room attached to the kitchens where cooks were busying themselves with the morning food.

The smell of cooked meat and sight of fresh fruit on the plates lined out on the wooden tables seduced every one of the boys and girls who had entered the building with caution and fear.

As most of the boys and girls took their seats, a blur of movement caught Tavar's attention. A smile grew across his face as he recognised the twins hugging each other, sobbing in each other's arms. A few of the soldiers around the edge of the room peered over but none of them seemed too bothered with the display of emotion. Tavar allowed the siblings a moment together, scanning the room futilely for his own brother before striding over.

"Tavar! I'm glad you're safe," Alice said, pulling him in for a hug. "We still have each other. That is important."

"It's good to see you." Tavar beamed.

"Where is your brother?" she asked. "Where is Vandir?"

Tavar shared a glance with Adam who finally had a bit of colour to his face once more.

"You didn't see?" Adam asked. "The commander took him away yesterday. Haven't seen him since."

The smile faded from Alice's face. "The commander? What for?" she whispered, eyes darting around the room at the soldiers who continued to stare over.

Tavar shrugged his shoulders. "I'm trying not to think about it. He will be fine. Vandir is made of strong stuff." The others nodded but he could tell that they were placating him. All three of them knew that the odds of seeing Vandir again were slim to none. He just didn't want to say it out loud; to make it real. Keeping up with any kind of hope was necessary if he was going to survive. He'd suffered enough.

The meal passed without incident. Conversation was dull and uninteresting: purposely keeping away from what had happened. The pain was too raw. Tavar knew they would have to speak about it at some point but now wasn't the time.

Following the servants' collection of the now empty plates, the quiet chattering throughout the room faded to a waiting silence as Lilian stormed into the room, on her face a look of thunder. Soldiers stood to attention and all eyes turned her way.

"Boys and girls!" she cried, her voice echoing around the cavernous room before she breathed out through her flared nostrils. "Due to the continued blasphemy of the heathens in the nation of Hartovan, the Godking, his majesty King Uhlad, is sending troops west." Confused glances filled the room at the words. What did this have to do with them?

"As a result, King Uhlad has asked that all prisoners brought into this great city are used in the best interests of Alfara." Lilian scratched at the short dark hair on her head and sighed. "As of today, each and every one of you are to be trained as part of the Alfaran army. Welcome to Kessarine, kids. Don't get fucking killed." She spun away, scarlet cloak trailing in the air behind her, leaving a room of scared and confused boys and girls in her wake.

Adam balled his fists on the table and allowed a smirk to form at the corner of his mouth. "They'll train us to fight; give us weapons…"

"What are you thinking?" Alice questioned him; voice low as nervous conversations broke out amongst the benches. Tavar thought he knew what Adam was thinking, though he wasn't sure he liked it…

"Revenge. We'll have our damned revenge."

CHAPTER FOUR: MAKING FRIENDS

His breath flew out from his lungs with the strike. Another bruise for the morning. The wooden practice blades were blunt with the chance of death extremely low, barring a fatal splinter, but each missed block hurt like the hells. Tavar gingerly twisted his torso, taking care to cover his pain through gritted teeth. Hurting was bad enough but showing weakness to Carver was ten times worse. Somehow the sly bitch was related to sharks, she could smell blood from a distance like no other.

"Barely a tap that time," the smirking daughter of an ambassador muttered. "I must be off my game today..." The usual crowd of sycophants and idiots chuckled and guffawed, looking across at her smug face like puppies with their mother. Even Qassim ir Alisson, a recruit two years their senior, gazed adoringly in her direction. After two years of training, it still gnawed at Tavar: the way they would fawn over those born into the noble families. The accident of birth took precedence over hard work and intelligence, it seemed. Unfortunately, Carver had the talent to back things up, even if it meant not having to work as hard as the others.

"Or I'm getting faster," Tavar said, voice low and threatening. A waste of time: his cheering section was always understandably muted in current company. A snap of the head from Adam and a clenched fist from Alice was all that was offered in support.

"Doubtful. If anything, you've been getting

slower over time. Still, at least there will always be a need for horse handlers in the army," Carver retorted, casually flipping her blade in the air and catching it with her weaker hand. "A place for everyone."

A place for everyone. The Alfaran phrase Tavar had grown to hate over all others. Sure, there's a place for everyone: the only downside was that your place may be bleeding and suffocating to death on the wall that bordered their great and just city.

He took his place in the fighting square and shook his head, shaking away any distractions and gripping his blade tight in both hands. Left foot forward, knee slightly bent and eyes focused intently on his opponent who was still playing off her adoring crowd of peers.

"Miss Carver," the familiar drone of Master Oden called out. "Position, please. I, like so many others in the room, wish to go to lunch on time today. I beseech you to not hold us up once again."

"Of course, Master Oden." Carver bowed low and readied herself, her lithe body slack and loose. She blew her blood red hair from out of her eyes and all joy left her. She would laugh and joke but Tavar knew that in the square, she meant business.

Carver whipped towards him so impossibly fast, Tavar had to jump to the side to avoid yet another hit. The sore skin stretched around ribs but he ignored it, every part of him focused upon his opponent. On the back foot already, he danced and twisted away from the continued onslaught, blocking out the smirk at the corner of Carver's lips as she played with him. At least there was one thing he was blocking properly.

Tavar had once heard a wise man suggest that

attack is the best form of defence. The wise man had been seven jugs deep at the time but the advice had stuck with Tavar. At any rate, if he was to do any damage then he would need to quit dodging and thrust once in a while. Overwhelm the opponent. Give them no time to think about attack and force them to focus on their own survival. It was a plan that always seemed to work for Carver; why couldn't it work for him?

It was a good plan. The problem with plans is that they require good execution. Tavar lunged forward, thrusting the blade in the direction of Carver's heart, victory filling his thoughts. Effortlessly, the blade was swiped away, forcing Tavar's arm out wide and offering his unshielded torso to the eager girl in front of him.

She was merciless.

The diagonal blow struck him hard across the chest. He fell to the ground with tears in his eyes. At first there was no pain, just a mighty roar from the sycophants circled around the pair of fighters. Then the heat of the wound hit him harder than the initial impact, a pain that made him draw a breath in through his teeth and close his eyes. When he was able to trust that he could hold back the tears, he opened them again to witness the first specks of blood seeping through his shirt.

He blinked a few times, pressing his hands into the dirt of the fighting square's ground. Old customs dictated that all fighters learn fighting on the soil of Alfara. One of many dumb customs. He coughed and gently pressed a hand against his wounded chest. There'd be a nasty welt soon enough. He was nearly an expert in the aches and pains of a fighter. Pain and suffering were excellent teachers.

Carver strode towards him, triumph lining each movement though the smug look had faded, replaced by one that was much harder to decipher. She held out a hand in his direction. He jerked away at first, blindsided by the unusual shift in her bearing.

"Take it," Carver muttered so only he could hear. "They'll just see you as a sore loser if you don't."

Tavar couldn't argue against that. He'd been beaten. No changing that fact. Now was the time to get back onto his feet, brush himself off and improve. He marvelled at the newfound maturity of his opponent as she dragged him to his feet. Where was the girl who had spent the last year taking any chance to belittle and abuse him?

"You don't belong here, Tavar. Just like your parents, you'll only ever be peasant scum unworthy of even scraping the dirt from our boots…" Ah, there she was.

He had no memory of picking up the wooden blade from beneath him but there it was, in his throbbing hand as he paced towards the person he had learnt to hate over all others. The world slowed down, cheers and calls from the audience faded from his hearing. He didn't even notice Master Oden rushing from his chair, a feat hitherto unheard of in all Tavar's time in the fighting chambers. All he knew was that he wanted to hurt Carver ir Edemer.

She fell to the floor instantly, clutching at the back of her head and groaning. Tavar just watched her roll over, staring her dead in the eye to let her know that this is what happened when he was pushed too far. Suddenly, the air flew back into the room, the volume rose and a strong pair of hands pulled him away from the maddening crowds who bellowed and shook their fists. Adam and Alice stood alone, mouths gaping open and eyes unblinking.

"That was a foolish thing to do, boy!" Master Oden. "To the stables with you. One moon of shovelling shit will be a lesson for you. Striking an unarmed adversary in the back of the head is despicable and cowardly!" Oden threw him to the ground, his face a red mask of anger.

Behind the incandescent master, Carver had finally sat up, ignoring the support from the herd of fools checking on her. Her brown eyes never left Tavar as the shadow of a smile grew on her face.

As his senses returned, Tavar realised what a fool he had been. This is exactly what she had wanted. He'd taken the bait like some idiotic animal being snared by the more intelligent hunter. His face was hot now but with embarrassment. Tavar inclined his head towards her, laughing incredulously at his error. He'd made a mistake, but he wasn't going to make the same one again.

He wasn't ready to defeat her physically, but he swore to himself he would beat her mentally. Carver ir Edemer. Tavar whispered the name to himself, boring it into his skull, never to be forgotten.

"Ever think that maybe there are better things to do with your time than shovel shit in these stables?" It wasn't the first time that Tavar had been asked the question. He was fairly certain it wouldn't be the last.

"There aren't many places in Alfara that can improve on the company…" he replied, dropping the stinking excrement into the designated corner. He dropped the shovel and wiped his brow which was covered in sweat from the evening's work. Most would only begrudgingly work in the stables but truthfully,

Tavar welcomed the opportunities he had to keep away from the others. Here, he had his newest friend, as well as his oldest one.

"I assume you're talking about Pan and not me," Hashem grumbled, washing his hands in a nearby bucket. The podgy stable boy knew these horses better than anyone else in Alfara. His father was the stablemaster and one day, Hashem would follow in his footsteps and care for these animals on behalf of the soldiers of Alfara. "Beautiful horse though, I must admit."

"She is," Tavar agreed, patting the mare against the neck and accepting a soft, playful nudge in response.

"You do know that you can visit during free time, right?" Hashem raised his eyebrows as his eyes flickered from the palomino to Tavar. "Smacking people across the head ain't the best way to come here. Piss off the right people and there'll be trouble on your doorstep. Father always tells me that." He ran a hand through his bouncy caramel curls and turned away, humming to himself. "Pissing off Master Oden. Pissing off Carver ir Edemer. That is precisely what I'm talking about. There's a system in Alfara. Got to know your place."

"And where is my place, Hashem?" Tavar sighed, feeling the weight of his poor position upon his shoulders.

Hashem paused as he reached a brown Okadan horse – his favourite. "You're an orphaned rookie in the Alfaran army. We both know that you're not exactly close to the higher rungs on the ladder in this kingdom. I wish it wasn't the way, but it is. Nothin' we can do about it."

Tavar kicked at the hay, causing Pan to snort in surprise. He rubbed at her perfect coat in apology, calming her down in an instant.

"Look, the bottom of the ladder is that damn wall around the city. Be thankful you're not there," Hashem insisted, gazing lovingly at his prized mare. "Those who don't accept their place only fall."

"What about my brother?" Tavar asked, a glint in his eye. He smirked as he watched Hashem stumble and struggle to answer.

"Well... erm... that's different..."

"Why is it?" Tavar pulled at the string he had caught and kept pulling. "Why is that a mere exception?"

"Your brother lucked out; plain and simple," Hashem chuckled, walking back over to Tavar. "Got in with the right people. Played the right games. Somehow he has the right people looking out for him. The recently promoted General Grey has taken him in under his wing and I've never seen that before. It's a strange one but that's all I can say about that."

Tavar blew his cheeks out and winced: the effects of his earlier battle. It was strange. For six months he had mourned his brother. For six months he had stifled his cries and wondered what had happened to the missing Vandir. Grief had hardened him. He'd convinced himself that Vandir would have wanted him to continue fighting; to work hard and seek revenge on those who had destroyed their family.

Then, one morning in the mess hall, he had just, reappeared.

Tavar had raced over to him, embracing him tightly and peering deeply into those familiar brown eyes that seemed heavier than before. He had grown taller in their time apart, and leaner. His tight shirt fought against his toned, muscular arms and he held his frame straight and upwards, military-like.

"Brother," Vandir had said quietly. "How have they been treating you?"

"I thought you were dead..."

"Then consider me reborn. I have been training, like you."

That was all he could get out of his older brother that first day. In the months that had followed, their meetings had been rare and fleeting. Tavar welcomed any opportunity to spend time with his brother but their training bases were on opposite sides of the city. As Hashem had reminded him, Vandir had been taken under the general's wing, though, only the gods knew how. The older brother would always change the topic whenever Tavar had raised it in conversation.

"I wish I knew what was going on with him..."

"You should be proud of him." Hashem placed an arm around his shoulder and led him to the stable exit. The end of a very long day. "He's doing something hardly anyone in this kingdom does: he's climbing the ladder one rung at a time, and from his starting position, that's admirable. Even my father knows his name. And you're able to see Pan. That's a huge slice of luck. Most of the other horses didn't make it."

The stable door exploded open and slammed against the walls either side. The silhouettes of four figures walked in from the darkened streets. Tavar turned to see a decidedly unwelcome face and realised the night might not be over after all.

"Well, well, what do we have here then, boys?" Deep chuckles chased the laconic drawl spattered by the slow steps of boots clipping the ground. "A bit of cuddle time in the stables for our dearest friend Tavar and his fat pet pig. We should have brought candles and arranged for one of the canal boat singers to join us. I almost regret interrupting this beautiful meeting." Carver grinned as Hashem slid his arm away from Tavar.

Tavar could hear his friend's teeth chattering beside him as he shook with fear. This was Carver's favourite game, messing with those who can't fight back. Make sure the odds were in her favour at all times. Her three lackeys crunched their knuckles together, attempting to look as menacing as they could. They'd been well trained by their master. Had enough practice too.

"What do you want, Carver?" he demanded, though he thought he knew. Still had to go through the motions.

"There is a list longer than the Manvel River of the things that I want." Carver bent her fingers in towards her face, checking over her nails for specks of dust as though the conversation was boring her. "For now, I want to offer you an apology."

He cocked his head to the side, thrown off guard. Time in Alfara had taught him that things that seemed too good to be true often were. A beautiful illusion veiled over the shit reality that was life.

"Yes, an apology. You see, I underestimated you. I thought you were just a lowly bug waiting to be stepped on. I never would have thought you had the balls to do what you did today. I turned my back on you believing myself safe from any attack. I was wrong. For that, I offer you an apology." She bowed low, her eyes never wavering from him this time. "My father always warned me never to turn away from men you fear or respect. Following the events of today, you have gained a sprinkle of respect and a vow that I will never turn my back on you."

Tavar listened to the words but his mind was racing, evaluating his environment and searching desperately for any weapon he would be able to get his hands on. His eyes fell on the shaking stable boy and he let out a curse under his breath. He didn't deserve this. "Hashem, leave."

The stable boy was his friend but he was no hero. There was no point acting otherwise. He stalled for a moment, his fearful face glancing to Tavar and back to the menacing group opposite. He mouthed an apology of his own before racing past them and into the bustling evening streets. Before he had even left the stable, Tavar had forgiven him. They were friends. That didn't mean getting beaten up for him. The doors closed shut behind him. No escape.

"A good decision," Carver nodded, "we would never hurt the boy: his father is well regarded across this city. Very different to having a dead peasant for a father."

Tavar looked away, letting the insult roll off him this time. He knew what was coming. There was no need to let her words affect him in the way she wanted. Not again.

"Yep, a dead peasant.," he agreed. "Yet, I'm still in the same group as you. And my brother is a favourite of General Grey. That must hurt for someone like yourself: someone from a *noble* family. Probably hurts more than that whack to the head you took earlier..."

He knew it was immature but the way her face twitched and the sound of fingers clicking as the group prepared to make him pay was worth it. He'd got to them. Got to her. They could beat the crap out of him but he'd won this time.

"I bet you think you're really funny, don't you?

We all know what your brother has been doing to get into the general's good books… I wouldn't drop that low to get anything. Everything I get, I have earned myself, don't you forget it, scum."

Weapon or no weapon, he'd heard enough.

It was the comment about his brother that triggered him. Always, it was family with him.

His fist flew past Carver as she leant back, dodging the blow by barely a whisker. A big boot to the ribs sent him flying back but he stayed on his feet, ready for the next attack. One on one, he still wouldn't have fancied his chances. Four on one and he stood no chance.

He accepted the next blow, twisting his shoulder back to ride the impact of Kelson's fist. The big brute's attack felt surprisingly soft from what he had expected and his form was sloppy, dropping his body low into the attack and opening himself up for a counter. Tavar breathed in and exploded forward, slamming his elbow hard against Kelson's cheekbone with his outward breath, dropping him to the floor.

The rare success knocked his focus as he stood staring at the unconscious body at his feet. A rookie error. The next blow landed, catching his jaw clean and forcing him back. A barrage of kicks and punches followed, knocking him onto the floor beside Pan. He coughed, spraying blood from his mouth as lights flashed each time he closed his eyes with another attack. The three aggressors continued their relentless assault, not allowing him a chance to even get to his knees.

"Not so funny now, are you?" Carver knelt, clutching Tavar's hair and forcing him to look up at her. "Scum like you and that disgusting brother of yours dilute this great kingdom. I was being honest earlier when I said you earned my respect. Earned a bit more with that attack on Kelson. Wouldn't have come here tonight if I thought you weren't worth the effort. Still scum though, don't forget it." She dropped his head against the ground and raised a boot, knee almost touching her stomach.

The impact of her boot against his jaw was the last thing Tavar felt that night. Darkness wrapped its cloak around him and all the aches and pains disappeared.

"Can't exactly pass that off as a fall."

"No one will ask too many questions; you know what it's like here." Tavar groaned as Adam held the jacket open. He slowly slid his arm in through the sleeve and turned, wincing. He stretched out his legs and bent over, testing his body. The response didn't surprise him. Pain coursed through most of his body and he swayed, dizzy with the effort. His arms naturally spread out as he stumbled. Adam snapped forward and caught him, ushering him to the bed.

"You need rest today. The fighting chambers can wait. Master Oden will understand." Wise words but Tavar was in no mood to listen.

"Rest can wait," he moaned. "I need to show them that they haven't won. That I'm not scared of them."

"I'm scared of them enough for the both of us. They're thugs, Tavar. Even worse, they're thugs from noble families. And what are we?"

"We're peasant scum. Peasant scum with nothing to lose."

"You seriously believe that?" Adam scoffed.

"Life in Alfara is shit but we both know it can be so much worse. I know you were hit in the head but I'm fairly certain that enough time hasn't passed for you to have forgotten those bodies hanging from the walls. Fight against these people and you will have to stand alone. I have my sister to think about."

Tavar nodded, face stern and unmoving. "Then I guess that I'm alone."

He let Adam click his tongue in frustration and storm out of the room without a word. A ghost of an apology danced on his tongue but his they stayed shut. He didn't want any of his friends getting hurt, even if that meant standing alone.

"Just a fall." Tavar brushed off Master Oden's question with a shrug. "Clumsy. Won't happen again."

The old master raised his eyebrows, clutching at Tavar's jaw and shifting it to the side to get a better look at the bruising. He frowned as light hit the fresh wound. "Stables are, in my humble opinion, much safer places than fighting chambers. Perhaps it would have been best if you had taken the day to recover from your *fall*." He released Tavar's jaw but not his gaze.

"I'm fine. I'd rather be here keeping busy than resting. The pain will pass soon enough."

"Hopefully the lessons learnt from your *fall* are not so fleeting. Just watch for today. We don't want your injuries worsening." He offered Tavar a knowing look before waving him away.

Tavar shuffled to the side, ready to watch the training. Oden raised three fingers and the boys and girls scattered across the room, finding their group of three. Adam and Alice strode over, wooden blades in hand.

"Adam told me what happened," Alice screeched, nervous eyes darting around the room to ensure no one was listening. "You're poking the bear and that's a dumb thing to do at the best of times. Doing it here, in this city, it's madness!"

Adam purposefully looked away, unable to forget their earlier conversation and Tavar's dismissive tone.

"Don't worry. Just a few cuts and bruises. Calm down." Tavar shuffled his feet and chewed at his lip. "I can handle it."

"It certainly looks like you're doing a good job!" Alice spat, eyes furiously wide.

"We'll speak later. Master Oden will be annoyed if he catches us jawing here instead of going through the exercises. That's the last thing we need right now." He glanced over at the master who was strolling around the square, offering glimmers of advice and reprimands to the young recruits.

The twins fell into their fighting stances, going through the motions they had learnt over the past year, working on familiar combinations. Both had picked the techniques with ease. Tavar enjoyed watching the siblings spar, the clap of wood-on-wood echoing through the chambers as they quickened their strikes. He watched intently as Alice took control, forcing her brother back with a flurry of strikes that were blocked in the nick of time. Adams's face reddened with the effort, his tongue lolling out the side of mouth with concentration. His impatience always got the best of him.

Annoyed that he was once again on the defensive, he lunged forward, striking low and fast, aiming to catch his sister off guard. The hint of a smile appeared on her face as she raised a leg to dodge the attack and countered with a strike against his shoulder. The first point was hers.

Tavar clapped and smiled. Adam threw his blade on the floor in frustration, unable to look at the victorious grin on his sister's face.

"Every time…" he muttered.

"Take your time. The last strike is the most important. The finishing blow is the one you must aim to deliver." Tavar spun, ignoring his aching body and smiling wide at his brother. Vandir stood there, hands behind his back, shoulders wide and chin raised. "Don't rush. Rush and you will make mistakes."

Adam sighed and picked his blade back up. "Can't even beat my own damn sister…"

"Your own amazingly talented sister…" Alice corrected him after waving at Vandir.

"Come, little brother," Vandir said. "I would have a word with you." He turned away, expecting Tavar to follow as he headed over to the raised wooden benches, stepping effortlessly between the soldiers in training. Tavar spotted a glance from Carver and her crew as they noticed the newcomer.

With everyone in training, the wooden benches were empty, perfect for a private conversation. He took a seat next to his older brother and looked down at the sparring below. Vandir waved at Master Oden who inclined his head in response.

"He allowed me to take you from your training for this word of caution."

"Word of caution?" Tavar repeated. Vandir

ignored him for a moment, staring out at the fighting below.

Vandir breathed out and pressed his arms back to rest against the rear of the bench. "Those marks are not from a fall."

"Of course not."

"Last night I received word that you had hit someone after the fight was over; striking them across the head." Vandir's voice was low and even, eyes still focused on the fighting. "I want to know why you did it. It's not like you."

"And how would you know?" Tavar bit back. "You're never here anyway!"

Vandir exploded in an instant, clutching Tavar's wrist staring into his eyes with a cold fury. "Everything I am doing is for you, little brother. Do not mistake my absence for a lack of care." He relaxed, releasing his grip.

Tavar rubbed at his sore wrist and frowned. "And what exactly are you doing?"

"I can't tell you, yet. Don't roll your eyes, I'll tell you at the right time," Vandir insisted. "Now, why did you do it?"

"Carver ir Edemer," Tavar said the name like it was a curse. "She looks down on everyone and most people just fawn all over her. She mentioned our parents. I saw red and snapped. I know I shouldn't have done it, but I couldn't control myself."

Vandir breathed in, nodding silently. "Edemer. Not the best family to cross. Look, brother, you need to control yourself. This city will grind you down and destroy you if you give it a chance. We need to be smarter. How do you think Mum and Dad would have felt if they knew you had struck a defenceless training opponent?"

"How would they feel knowing you are working with the person who killed our friends and family?" he said it without thinking, instantly regretting it.

"They taught us that there are times when we must swallow our pride and think of the future. That is what I am doing. Nothing has changed, Tav. I hate this city. I hate these people. I just want to go back on the road and forget any of this happened but I can't. *We* can't."

Vandir bit his fingernails, gazing down at his feet. For the first time in a year, he looked like the older brother who had read to him at night, who had brought him food and water when he was ill.

"I'm sorry. I just miss them so much. I miss you. I hate this damn place." Tavar kicked at the bench in front of him but all it did was cause his toe to throb with more pain.

Vandir sighed and stood, brushing down his jacket and motioning for Tavar to stand. He rested a reassuring hand on his shoulder and looked down into his eyes. "We are brothers, Tav. I'm always going to look out for you, no matter the danger. Just be a bit more cautious, cuter with your actions. There's more than one way to skin a rabbit."

"Can't I just hit the rabbit until it goes away?"

"Doesn't work like that, unfortunately." Vandir turned and narrowed his eyes, the cogs in his mind twisting and turning. Tavar knew that look. "Leave Carver to me."

"She's from a noble family. Gotta be careful."

"I don't think you're the best person to give advice regarding caution in this matter, little brother." Vandir smirked. "She may be from a noble house but I've friends in high places too. Give me time and I'll see what I can do."

He slapped a hand against Tavar's back and walked away, raising a hand in farewell.

Tavar rolled his shoulders and blew out a long, deep breath, wincing at the aches and pains left from the attack. He stayed in amongst the benches for a moment longer, eyes drifting towards his foe.

Carver ir Edemer had stopped training. She stood still as a statue, staring up at Tavar with what he thought was a worried look.

Tavar grinned back.

CHAPTER FIVE: THE BANISHMENT

"Reckon you can stand?" Tavar walked over to Jassim. The wound had stopped bleeding. A good sign. The recovery would be long and hard. He'd delivered enough such wounds to have a better understanding than most in the world. Jassim was no threat now.

"I can give it a go," Jassim responded, reaching out with a bloodied hand.

"Try anything funny and the next one goes straight through your heart," Tavar warned, stepping forward and grasping the man's wrist. There was a silent nod in response followed by a groan as Tavar pulled the wounded man to his feet, offering him a chair by the fire. "Drink?"

"Got anything strong?"

"Okadan Whiskey."

"Perfect."

Tavar shuffled out of the room and into the back room. Rummaging through the cupboards on bended knees, he found what he was looking for. Okadan Whiskey. His favourite. He could still remember the first time the liquid had burned his throat. The thrill of breaking the rules. The nerves of excitement and fear that they would be caught. It was all so long ago. That was also the night when…

He swallowed and stood back up, clutching the bottle in hand. He blew the dust away and grabbed two nearby cups, strolling back into the main room. Jassim's focus was elsewhere. He had procured a bandage from somewhere and was now tying the ends together so that it tightly pressed against his wound. His breathing was shallow but he would live. Wasn't going anywhere soon though.

Tavar stepped over the corpse and placed the cups on the table before pouring the drinks. The smell alone took him back to the days of his youth: pine and almonds mixed with fresh bread.

"Gonna have to do something about him." Jassim nodded at the body on the ground. "Start to smell soon enough."

Tavar grunted, leaving the cups on the side as he lifted the motionless body and slung it over his shoulder with the ease of a man half his age. Heading out back, he dumped the body on the wet earth. He could burn it in the morning. There was no rush.

Returning to the main room, he found Jassim swilling the whiskey around the cup, eyes looking but not seeing. It was the look of a man lost in his thoughts. Or a man contemplating his death. Tavar had seen it far too many times.

"Good whiskey. Much have cost you a fortune."

"A gift from an old friend. Had it for quite some time. Haven't had an occasion worth drinking it."

"And sharing a drink with someone who tried to kill you moments ago is an occasion worth raising a cup?" Jassim asked incredulously.

Tavar only shrugged in response. "Seems as good a time as any."

They sipped their drinks, the cracking of the

flames filling the silence.

"Did you have your revenge?" Jassim asked out of nowhere. "On those who attacked you in the stables?"

Tavar scratched at his beard and breathed out, watching the liquid swirl in his half empty cup. "We were young, all of us. We were stupid. We all had our petty little arguments that seemed so important back then. It was only with hindsight that we realised how foolish we all were. To answer your question, a year had passed since the incident in the stables. I had my revenge, though it was bittersweet, like so much in life…"

The Godsquare bustled with excitement and activity. People from all over Alfara packed into the square like fish trapped in a barrel, pushing against one another to reach the front of the mayhem where the address would emanate from. Only once before had Tavar been allowed access into the Godsquare and just like then, he marvelled at the grand palace surrounding it on all sides and the golden dome looming overhead behind the balcony from where the Godking's speech would begin.

"How often is The Banishment celebrated?" Tavar asked, staring around at the silver and sapphire statues and ornaments that lined almost every inch of the palace.

"Every four years," Marek answered, the son of a merchant in the city. He'd befriended Tavar half a year earlier after joining up with Master Oden's class. He was one of the few people who didn't seem to care about bloodlines and nobility. Tavar had instantly liked him. "It was our current ruler's grandfather who started it. Banished the dwarves from Alfara and drove them from this continent. He resented them for the way they would enter city and take over the smith businesses and push out the local workers. The Banishment changed Alfara forever. We celebrate it every four years as it only took four days for him to banish them all from this kingdom. A great victory."

Tavar held his tongue. Though he liked Marek, the friendly boy had been born and raised in the city, never tasting the delights of travel and wonder. "Is he worshipped as a god, too. Like his grandson?"

"The whole line is, going back to Avaron the First. The story goes that he descended from the heavens and defeated the demonic army of Scarth before founding this city."

He made certain that Marek wouldn't see his rolled eyes. Alice caught the action.

"Tavar loves the tales of Alfara. You should tell him more," she said, nudging Tavar in the ribs.

"*After* the address," Tavar said, glaring at Alice and Adam as they sniggered. "I need to focus. It will be another four years before we are given the chance to witness such a monumental event."

Marek frowned, finally realising that perhaps his friends weren't being completely honest with him. Adam spotted the look and cut it off expertly.

"Ah, there's Hashem! I'm glad he could make it."

The stable boy pushed through an annoyed clutch of people standing on the tips of their toes, all frustrated with the chubby boy making his way past them. He wore a look of distress on his face, embarrassed to be causing such a problem. Finally, he squeezed through and wiped the sweat from his brow.

"Even busier than usual!" he cried, smiling and glancing around the square. "When's he due out?" He craned his neck and peered over those in front, looking out for any sign of the ruler.

"Any moment now," Marek answered, inclining his head to the balconies either side. "Look." Tavar followed his gaze and spotted a steady stream of Lords and Ladies making their way onto the balconies. The best views in the Godsquare. No pressing up against strangers for them.

Most of the men wore frilled white shirts covered with a navy-blue tailcoat that fell close to the floor. Some wore tall hats that seemed to Tavar as though they would fall with the slightest breeze and a couple of the older gentlemen were wearing rounded eyeglasses to aid their vision. The Ladies were a sight to behold. Silver dresses flowed down to the ground in a range of extravagant styles. His eyebrows shot up as he spotted Master Oden chatting to a beautiful, young woman who had a pained smile etched upon her face.

"How come he gets to go up there?" Tavar wondered out loud.

"A lot of the soldiers are still out dealing with the rebellion. With them gone, there are spaces that need to be filled. As the head trainer of recruits, Oden is able to fill one of those." At times, Tavar would have liked a shrug from Marek. He seemed to have an answer for everything.

"That woman doesn't look too keen on what he's saying," Alice laughed. "Reckon he's blabbing on about the heroic days of yore like he does with us?"

"If that's the case, I expect her to jump within the hour!" Tavar snorted.

"Within a minute would be my guess!" Adam added with a laugh of his own.

As Tavar turned to smile at his friends, his eyes landed upon the balcony on the opposite side to them. Dressed in military gear were three familiar faces: Commander Grey, Lieutenant Marcus, and Vandir. Two unfamiliar men stood next to them, draped in gold. Even their spears and shields were shining gold in the sun. Tavar had never seen anything like them before.

He slapped against Alice's arm with the back of his hand, eyes not leaving the balcony. "You see what I'm seeing?"

Her eyes widened, the smile leaving her face. "Shit…"

The others followed, staring across to the balcony.

"How the…" Adam muttered with a shake of his head.

"Whatever your brother is doing, you need to find out so I can copy him. A foreign peasant standing on the palace balcony during The Banishment address… The guy's a hero…" Marek said in a hushed tone, as though he respected Vandir more than anyone else.

"Who are the ones in gold?" Tavar asked, looking at the two men stood like statues.

"Immortals," Marek answered. "Ten of them are allowed in the army at any time. No more. No less. They are the Godking's elite warriors. They are the greatest warriors in the world. Completely silent; they do their talking on the battlefield. Some people say that they have their tongue ripped out during initiation so that they can't spill any secrets. The first immortals were the ten men and women who survived the Alfaran civil war. King

Dominic the Merciful squashed the rebellion but these final ten soldiers remained undefeated, using the shadows and their knowledge of the city to stay alive and strike when needed. Dominic was amazed by their prowess in battle and made them an offer: join his army as Immortals and he would spare their lives."

Before Tavar could reply, trumpets blared throughout the square, signalling the arrival of the Godking. Tavar's gaze lingered on his brother and the Immortals whilst all others turned to face forward. Muttered conversations died down into silence as all present stared up at the open balcony, awaiting their ruler. Finally, Tavar tore his gaze away from Vandir and joined the herd, looking out for the Godking.

"People of Alfara." A voice called out from the balcony, addressing the hushed crowd before him. "On this, most holy of days. It is my great honour as Herald of Alfara, to announce the arrival of the Godking, the Saintly One, He Who Will Save Us All – King Uhlad the Second."

The entire crowd roared as one. Tavar winced with the cacophony of sound blasting around him. Grown men and women openly wept with joy, some fainting with excitement, forcing the soldiers dotted around square to push their way through and drag the overwhelmed individuals away. The fanatics clapped and screamed out for their ruler, as though he would be able to hear each and every one of them. It was madness.

The twins shared a confused look which turned into a smirk as they turned to Tavar. Never before had they seen such adulation, such an outpouring of emotion. He looked to his side and was surprised to see both Hashem and Marek joining in with the cries, arms waving wildly in the hope of the Godking spotting them. The

Lords and Ladies were slightly more reserved: waving handkerchiefs in the air or fanning themselves to cool down in the heat of the passionate moment. Vandir, like all other military personnel on the balcony, stood straight to salute, chin raised and hand across his chest. Tavar prayed it was an act, hoping that his brother wanted to blend in and wasn't really being dragged into this wretched display of love for the ruler.

Tearing his gaze from his brother, Tavar looked up and for the first time in his life, he saw the Godking of Alfara. King Uhlad the Second.

It wasn't what he expected. But then, he had no idea what he had expected. There was no reference for him, he realised. In all the towns and cities he had visited with his family on the road, he had never laid eyes on a member of royalty. Only in books had he seen crude drawings of men and women dressed in lavish, impractical robes with too many gems and crowns on their head that seemed as though they would be a hindrance more than anything else.

King Uhlad the Second was nothing like that.

He had a thick build, broad shoulders ready to carry the weight of a kingdom. Unlike some of the pictures Tavar had seen of kingly men, this one had managed to escape the adverse effects of gluttony and hedonism. His outfit was unique but not lavish as had been expected. A crimson shirt and cape were lined with strips of black that matched his dark trousers. Impossibly sharp cheekbones near pierced his smooth, tanned skin as his dark, painted eyes gazed lovingly out over his people.

"Where is his crown?" Tavar queried, only seeing raven-black waves of hair cascading down onto the man's shoulders.

"He is no mere *king*," Marek laughed. "He is the Godking: a man above all other kings. He doesn't need a crown."

Uhlad walked to the edge of the balcony and raised a hand. Silence covered the square in response.

"Alfara. My people," the Godking began with a melodic voice that sang out to all corners of the square. Two more Immortals stood in his shadow, keeping watch. "This day is a day for all the sons and daughters of Alfara to join as one. We celebrate our past, enjoy the present, and look to our future. My grandfather, Uhlad the First, banished the scheming dwarves from this land and a brighter path was paved for the future of Alfara." Cheers rang out as men and women screamed their approval whilst some uttered curses and spat at the mention of the hated dwarves.

"Vandir had always loved to hear tales of the dwarves. Great craftsmen, my father used to say…" Tavar whispered almost to himself. His brother stood unmoved as the crowd beneath him calmed and the noise faded once more.

"Today is a time for celebration, but…" the Godking continued, his pause followed by a collective held breath in the crowd. "Today will also be a warning. Since Avaron the First turned back the horde of scum threatening to turn our land to darkness, Alfara has been a beacon of light shining on this dark continent. Our mission has always been to better ourselves and those who are unable to better themselves. A place for everyone. That is our goal. To achieve such an ambitious goal, we have taken our way of life and introduced it to other nations. Many have embraced us with open arms, aware of what must be done. Others have only embraced ignorance and hatred. Like the dwarves before them, they think only of themselves. Alfara is currently fighting a war, holding back a wave of petty-minded fools who believe they would be better without our gentle guiding touch. Unfortunately, there have been whispers of betrayal amongst our own ranks…"

Hushed conversations broke out in the crowd, fearful looks shared between friends and loved ones.

"Who would betray Alfara?" Marek asked, his face a mask of horror at the thought.

"There is a plague spreading within this kingdom but I am strong enough to withstand it. This plague will be burned out before it can spread any further. Anyone daring to go against myself or this great kingdom will be punished in such a way that none will even dare to think of betraying me ever again!" Even the birds had halted their flying over the crowd as the Godking raised his voice. He didn't shout but there was a spike in the melody of his song that shook Tavar and he felt suddenly cold.

"I have a bad feeling about this," Adam said, holding his sister's hand and squeezing it.

Uhlad's lips curled into a smile and he clapped his hands together, easing the tension and allowing all to breathe again. "Now, this is a celebration! Remember The Banishment; be thankful and praise Alfara; a place for everyone." His cape jumped in the wind as he spun around, closely followed by two soldiers marching with spears glistening in the sunlight.

"Well, that was…" Tavar scratched his head, thinking for the right word.

"Interesting," Alice suggested with a forced smile.

"Come on," Hashem said, throwing a sweaty arm around the twins. "It's not often we all have time off together. Let's enjoy the city!"

Kessarine morphed into something else entirely during The Banishment festivities. Dwarven effigies were hung from posts and balconies all around the city and children were encouraged to keep a stick to hand to smash against the bearded avatars with demonic red eyes and angry faces. As the sun fell beneath the horizon, men staggered through the bustling streets, slamming into doorways, bending over in alleyways to vacate whatever they had eaten for the day and some even grabbed torches and lit the hanging effigies to wild cries of encouragement from all around.

"This is crazy," Tavar said, passing one such event.

"This is The Banishment," Marek shrugged. "People release some steam, some tension. No matter what is going on in life, it allows us a chance to forget for one night and remember what makes our city so great."

Tavar noticed an elbow dig sharply into Adam's rib at the same moment he had opened his mouth to respond. Alice raised an eyebrow and pursed her lips at her brother.

The rookies in training for the army, like most workers in the city, had the evening off. Lilian had warned them to be back by midnight or face dire consequences but that still allowed for another four hours of freedom. Rare freedom to explore. The group strode through the crowds, wondering at the waving Alfara flags reaching out from the windows and listening to the old songs being sang all the way from Dwarves' Ruin to the Merchants' Square. Small triangles painted in the blue

Memories of Blood and Shadow

and white of Alfara were joined by string and ran across the city, hovering above wherever Tavar and his friends travelled.

"What a lovely surprise!" Tavar tensed at the sound and muttered a curse. It had all been going so well. "Look, friends, more of our fellow recruits, and some of my favourites I must admit…"

Carver was dressed immaculately. She had forsaken the traditional white and blue of her house for a tight, midnight purple outfit flourished with a black cape that hung from a golden clasp near her breast on one side. Her red hair fell softly, brushing against her right shoulder as she walked their way.

"Carver…" Tavar said through gritted teeth.

She mockingly opened her mouth wide and cocked her head to the side in feigned shock. "I know what you are about to say. Cut those words from your mind and listen," she said, her usual horde of followers staring at her in confusion. "We've had our differences. Both of us can agree that. Tonight is a celebration of The Banishment, in honour of this great festival of my people, let us banish our differences and past transgressions and start afresh. What do you say?"

Tavar looked down at the gloved hand offered out in friendship. He could feel the heat of his friends staring at him but asking for their opinion would seem stupid. It was time to prove he was the better man. He took the hand and shook it briefly.

"To a new start," he agreed.

"Excellent!" Carver flicked the hair out from her face and flashed a stunning smile, white teeth on show for everyone. "We are just returning from an establishment owned by a cousin of my father's. The Carved Boar. The food isn't great, truth be told, but the drinks are some of the best in the kingdom. There's even a dash of Okadan Whiskey available," she leaned forward as though sharing a huge secret with them. "Just tell them you're friends of Carver ir Edemer. They'll know what that means. Enjoy The Banishment."

Tavar moved aside as the posse followed their leader silently. After they had passed, a confused silence smothered them all.

"Anyone able to explain what just happened?" Adam asked, eyes still following Carver and her crew even though they had since blended into the bustling crowds of people still celebrating.

"Must have fallen asleep and dreamt with my eyes open…" Alice said.

Incredulous laughing broke out from them all until Tavar saw a sparkle in Adam's eyes. "What are you thinking?"

"Okadan Whiskey," Adam said to groans all around. "Wait, wait, hear me out. It's meant to be the best drink in the world. It's mad that anywhere this far from the empire would have it. If there's a chance and it's being offered to us…"

"We're not of age. Maybe in another year," Marek argued, scratching at his increasingly red neck.

"Where's your sense of adventure? How often are we free to do this?" Adam argued.

"I would love to," Hashem said, stifling a yawn "but it is time for me to leave. Gotta be up early in the morning."

They said their goodbyes and waved as the stable boy trudged through the crowds, squeezing through the mass of celebrations.

"I'm gonna head home too," Marek said, stretching his arms wide before rubbing his eyes. "Tired."

"Marek…" Tavar motioned to follow, to make sure he was okay.

"No!" Adam cried, stepping in the way. "He's Alfara. The three of us aren't." He placed his hands on Tavar's shoulders and leaned his head forward so that their eyes were almost level. "I don't know about you, Tavar, but I still hear the screams when I close my eyes. I still remember the laughter of the soldiers as they killed a whole group of innocents like animals being slaughtered for food. I still remember them killing my parents and forcing us into this shit city."

Tavar backed away, slapping Adam's hands aside. In the corner of his eye, he saw Alice cautiously step towards them. "I still remember, Adam. Don't ever ask me if I still remember." His voice shook, fingernails digging into his palms as the memories flooded back.

"Then let's have a night where we can act like three friends without a care in the world," Adam argued, face alight with an energy Tavar hadn't witnessed in some time. "Let's have a couple of drinks and share stupid stories. Let's watch the world pass us by and for one night, let's forget the horrors of Alfara."

Tavar sighed and glanced at Alice, always the more reasonable of the two. She shrugged. "Can't argue with that. If anyone deserves a drink and a moment to forget the past, it's the three of us."

Defeated, Tavar turned his back on them both. "So, which way is the Carved Boar?"

The Carved Boar, similar to almost every other establishment during the festival, heaved with hot sweating bodies squeezed up against one another like sheep in a pen. And like sheep, the smell crinkled Tavar's nose as he entered the tavern. He followed the twins to the bar, Adam leading, and apologised to the mass of people he guided from his path with unease. Most patrons ignored the youngsters and continued their loud conversations, barely glancing at the trio as they moved out of the way. A few glared and clicked their tongues against the roof of their mouths, eyes rolling before they turned back to their discussions.

"This was a great decision. I can feel it!" Adam grinned at the two of them as they reached the long, wooden bar, squeezing into a small gap next to the many other people waiting for their drinks. "Finally a chance to relax in Alfara and have some fun, just the three of us!"

"Yeah," Tavar agreed. "Shame that Hashem and Marek couldn't make it."

Adam shrugged. "I guess. There'll be other times."

"I have to admit," Alice interjected. "It is good just spending time with the two of you without Master Oden or Lilian breathing down our necks. I only wish your brother was here, Tav. Then it would be just perfect."

"Vandir probably has more important things to do, like always." Tavar's tone was sharp and bitter, much more so than he intended.

"He's doing what he needs to do, Tav," Alice said, resting a hand on his shoulder and smiling softly. "After all we've been through, it would be foolish to berate him for his actions."

Uneasy with the conversation's direction, Tavar focused on the numerous bottles and barrels in sight behind the bar, squinting to read the labels on each one.

"No point in looking at any of that, my dear friend," Adam said, licking his lips and rubbing his hands together. "Okadan whiskey. There's no other choice. Plain and simple. It's got to be done, Tav."

As if on cue, one of the barmen strolled over, cloth in one hand and a murky glass in another. He frowned as he made his way over, as though weighing the trio up. "You know the rules." His voice was tired and strained. "Come back in another year or two. The Banishment doesn't mean I can serve folk your age."

Adam cleared his throat and straightened his back, his voice suddenly deep and authoritative. "My good sir, we are perplexed as to your thoughts behind such a decision. My friends and I are celebrating on this grand day whilst adhering to the laws of the greatest kingdom in the world." The barman raised an eyebrow, threatening to lose it amongst his dark, shaggy hair. Adam leaned over the bar and beckoned the barman over. "We were sent here by Carver ir Edemer. She's a friend of ours..." he whispered, adding a wink to punctuate his statement.

Tavar made to turn away, certain they had been tricked by Carver, a practical joke at their expense. It wouldn't have been surprising, really. In fact, it made more sense than anything else.

"Friends of Carver..." the barman smacked his lips and absently wiped the glass. He peered at them under his bushy brows, nodding faintly. "Carver did mention something about friends coming earlier. She's set a booth aside for you upstairs. I'll get a drink for you while we prepare the booth. What would you like?"

"Three Okadan whiskeys please, my good sir!" Adam stammered, surprised that his audacity had actually paid off.

The barman nodded, turning away to fetch the drinks.

Tavar slapped Adam's back and laughed; amazed that it had worked out.

"I never thought I'd say this but, maybe Carver isn't that bad..." Alice said.

"Always thought she was one of the good ones," Adam added to groans. "What? I did..."

Waiting for the drinks to arrive, Tavar took in the atmosphere, listening to the snippets of jovial conversation near him whilst Alice and Adam discussed their excitement of having their first drops of alcohol. The twins were speaking about their parents and how they had often carried bottles of Tramero Red. Tavar remembered his own parents sharing a few cups of the wine but their favourite drink had been ale; especially Bayford ale. He would never forget the way his father would smack his lips and rub his hands in expectation when a passing traveller was willing the trade the golden liquid. Vandir had been old enough to sneakily enjoy a sip behind their mother's back when their father had been in a pleasant mood but Tavar had been too young.

"The Marauders have crossed the Eastern Sea, I heard," a man well into his cups was saying to his friends, many who themselves had crimson faces and swayed where they stood. "Trouble's brewing. We need to put down this stinkin' rebellion soon so that we can turn our eyes elsewhere. For too long has Alfara stood still on this continent. Them blood warriors need putting down before they feel too big for their boots."

"Blood warriors? Those sand savages won't be a problem," another argued, slamming his drink onto the bench next to him, not noticing the splash of ale jumping from his cup and landing on Tavar. "Marauders won't be an issue either. Tire themselves out before they can do much. The fact they crossed the sea is a feat in itself but they won't last long over here. Not built for it."

"Tales of what those blood warriors have done give me the shivers," another said, shaking his head and brushing himself down as though the thought itself crawled upon his body. "They cut the scalps off those they caught. Ain't right. Some say they paint themselves in the blood of those they kill…"

"Bah! Rumours and tales that grow with each telling!" the second man jumped in. "We have the Godking and the greatest army in the world. Let them come, I say. The only blood they'll be covered in will be their own!" The rest of the group praised this comment. Cheering and raising their glasses and jugs. The fearful man took a moment, steadying himself before joining the rest.

"Here's your glasses. Three Okadan whiskeys, as requested." The barman placed the three glasses on the counter.

Tavar licked his lips, eyeing the brown liquid. There wasn't much in the glass but from what he'd heard on the road, it would have a kick.

"How much do we owe you?" Adam asked, reaching into his pocket for the meagre allowance they had been handed for this moon.

The barman waved a hand. "On the house.

Friends of Carver have no need to pay here. Not for their first taste of this special drink…"

"We'll have to come here more often!" Alice chuckled, grabbing two of the glasses and passing one back to Tavar.

"It's almost enough to forgive her for beating the shit out of me," he said, ensuring his voice was low enough to only be heard by the twins.

"In her defence," Adam began, pausing when he saw the dark looks on his friends faces. "You did smack her on the back of the head with your blade…" his voice had lowered until it was barely audible.

"She deserved more than a smack on the head. Still, if she's willing to move on, then I guess I am too," Tavar said, swilling the liquid around in the glass. He wasn't sure why he did this but he'd seen others do it and thought it made him seem older, more mature. "So, what are drinking to?"

"I dunno," Adam said, pinching his lips and turning to his sister. "What do you reckon?"

Alice held her glass, eyes dropping to the floor in the way they always did when she was deep in thought. "This whiskey is special, that's what you said, Adam. So it needs to be a special toast that we raise together. We'll never have this moment again; it needs to be worth it." Tavar shared a nod with Adam, both agreeing with the comment. It was important, a splash of ink on the page that would be remembered forever and never erased.

"What do you think, Alice?" Tavar urged her on.

"To family and friends lost. To new friends found. To friends yet to come." She raised her glass and smiled, flicking her hair back and breathing deeply. "And to the three of us. May this bond never be forgotten." She threw the drink back in one go, slamming the glass back down and exhaling long and hard. "Shit..."

Tavar followed in time with Adam, each copying Alice's action. The liquid burned his throat, warming his entire body in one go. There was something primal about the experience, the way it seemed to energise his whole body, burning away the old him and starting something fresh, like a phoenix born again from the ashes.

He laughed as Adam continually stuck his tongue out, licking at the air around him and wincing. "You okay, Adam?"

"Yeah, just tastes... weird."

"I liked it." Alice grinned.

"Me too," Tavar agreed, still smacking his lips as the taste lingered. "I think."

"The booth is now ready," the barman interjected. "Please, follow me."

Candles lit the long, narrow room on the floor above the bar. Velvet and leather seating adorned either side of the room along with circular tables. In contrast to the bar area, the room was near empty with only a small gathering placed at the end of the room, their low conversation and laughter barely reaching Tavar and his friends.

"Another three Okadan whiskeys," Adam informed the barman, taking his seat and stretching his arms wide across the furnishing. He received a nod in response before the barman turned and strode back down the stairs, closing the door on his way. "Not bad for our first celebration in this city."

Tavar had to admit, the night had gone better than he had hoped. Celebrating the history of the nation that had taken so much from him would have made even the finest drink taste like ash in his mouth; celebrating their past and their continued friendship was something else altogether, something that would never cease to put a smile on his face.

"Even a stroll through Hell can have its advantages in the right company," Tavar said, remembering a line from one of the books his mother used to love reading when he was young.

"Speaking of Hell…" Alice flicked her eyes to the back of the room where one of the patrons had stood up and began to walk their way.

"Finally! The entertainment for the evening has arrived!" Tavar swore an oath under his breath as Qassim ir Alisson stumbled his way, a wicked grin on full display, his usually immaculate dark hair a tangled mess covering half of his face. "Carver said that more of her *friends* would be joining us. We've been expecting you."

"Qassim, I've no idea what you're on about but we just want to have a good, relaxed evening here. You can carry on with your friends and we'll keep out of your business," Tavar said, attempting to diffuse any trouble before it flared. Qassim was close to Carver and Tavar hadn't forgotten the look on the young man's face after the incident in the fighting square.

The floppy haired noble dropped into the booth, placing an arm around Alice and leaned in close. Too close for her comfort and everyone else's in the booth. Adam's eye twitched with the action, his face reddening in response.

"I thought it was odd when Carver mentioned

you'd be joining us here. The Banishment is an Alfaran celebration. Alfara is the reason you are all orphans. Odd of you to join in, really. Foreign peasants have no place in joining in the festivities. My father thinks it would be better if we banished the lot of you as well, just like we did with the dwarves." Qassim's voice slurred with his swaying, his eyes struggling to focus on Alice. "I agree, mostly. Though," he moved his hand, brushing his knuckles against Alice's red cheek, "I'm sure you have your uses…"

Tavar erupted, launching himself across the table, clutching at Qassim's collar and pulling a fist back. Strong hands pulled at his arms and shoulders, dragging him from the booth and throwing him to the ground before he could strike.

He ignored the first couple of hits, struggling to stand and defend himself. He swung an elbow and heard a satisfying groan from one of Qassim's cronies. Tavar lifted his hands, using his forearms to shield his face from the blows raining down on him from the three bastards still standing. Through the gap in his arms, he glimpsed Adam throwing wild punches at Qassim, who could only cower in the booth, covering his face and screaming at his friends for help.

"Get him off me, you fools!"

Alice had leapt to her feet and was now dragging one of them away, her arm expertly pulled tight around her opponent's throat, cutting off his air, a look of fury on her face.

Tavar swung a fist at the nearest attacker. It landed cleanly on the cheek but there wasn't enough power. The bastard smiled and encouraged another strike. Tavar shrugged and struck again. This time, his opponent was ready for it. He ducked the blow and speared into

Tavar's stomach, taking him to the ground and aiming further punches at his face. Tavar curled up, doing his best to block the powerful hits from his face.

"Get off him, Qassim!" Tavar heard Alice scream, her voice high and distressed. "Adam!" Her cry was cut off and punctuated with a thump as something hit the floor.

Tavar roared, grasping at all of the energy he had left and snapped his head forward, smashing it into the brute's face. A flash of blood splattered before him but he didn't stop. He snapped forward again, this time managing to knock the bastard off him. Tavar stood, dazed from the attack and staggered forward. Qassim was wrestling with Adam, his size and age giving him a clear advantage.

It was Alice who Tavar helped first though. She was clutching at her chest, struggling for air after landing heavily on her back. Qassim's sister, Nahra, stood over her, heeled shoe pressing against Alice's bare hand. The bitch was smirking, enjoying the torture. Ignoring words of wisdom his parents had given him about attacking women, Tavar pushed forward, lowering his shoulder and slamming her away and into one of the empty booths. Alice rolled onto her side and stood up, her hand shaking with the damage it had taken.

Alice didn't pause. She raced to help her brother, her boot connecting with Qassim's lower back, forcing him off the fallen Adam.

Alice's eyes widened as Adam lay motionless, blood pooling next to his face. She shook him, calling out his name. He responded with a soft groan but nothing more.

Tavar's fists tightened before he knew it, poised

to make Qassim pay for what he had done. Before he could reach him, the room swam, his eyes unable to focus and his legs no longer felt solid. He dropped to the ground at the same time Qassim stood up. He could only watch as the bastard threw Alice to the floor and shouted for his sister to resume her violent ways.

Perplexed, he tried to lift his hands but he couldn't move. A throbbing pain emanated from the back of his head as the candlelight danced above him, broken up by a wide-shouldered, shadowy figure – another of Qassim's cronies.

Five against three. Yet again, the odds were against them. That was always the way, he thought, another boot slamming into his side. More aches and pains to add to the ever-growing collection.

The taste of the Okadan whiskey had long since left him, now it was replaced with the copper like taste of his own blood. A taste becoming too familiar for his liking. He had no energy to fight back; he was just a toy for them to play with until they grew tired and bored and moved on.

Qassim stood over him, a hand rubbing at his red neck where Tavar was pleased to see a few scratches, reminders that he hadn't had it all his way.

"Carver said there would be five of you," Qassim said through ragged breaths. "She only wanted to hurt you, to remind you of your place. She said it didn't matter about the others. Didn't want them missing out on all the fun though. We're nice like that." Nahra laughed, a cackle that didn't suit her beauty. "You upset her again, and I promise this will all seem like a fun game in hindsight. There's no one to care for you, no one to worry about you should you go *missing*. Or your friends. Think about it."

Tavar coughed, spit flying from his mouth. Pain shot and twisted through his body and his vision blurred.

A hand slapped him across the cheek, followed by more laughter.

CHAPTER SIX: THE LADDER OF ALFARA

The medics released both Tavar and Alice after a thorough check. The beds were mainly full of fools who had let the festivities get the best of them: too much alcohol; too much excitement; too many petty arguments leading to fights. Black eyes, bloodied noses, broken bones. At the worst end of the scale, a few had stab wounds: fights that had gotten out of hand. Some were lucky to be alive. Some were not as lucky.

"Who did this to you?" One of the medics had asked once Adam had been taken away to rest; a woman with pale skin and freckles that dotted her face like the stars.

"We've never seen them before," Tavar jumped in before Alice could say anything. Naming names wasn't going to get them anywhere but a second trip to this festering pit of misery and gloom. "All they said was that we didn't belong here."

"Hmm..." The medic didn't seem too convinced by the answer but seemed used to the response. "Best to stay inside and out of the way this time of year. Folk can get mighty rowdy. Get some rest and stay out of trouble. We'll look after him," she said, smiling and glancing over to Adam to reassure them.

They reached the South House with the city still cloaked in darkness. The sounds of the festival rang out in the distance, loud enough to hurt Tavar's already sore head.

"Training will be fun tomorrow," he said as he pushed the door open, peering behind it to make sure he didn't wake any of the others.

"You should be used to this by now," Alice whispered, purposefully stepping on the tips of her toes as they walked through the dark corridor. "Don't know how you do it." Her right hand was swollen and red. The medic suggested it may be broken and that she would need to take care for the next moon or so.

Tavar stared into her glistening eyes and swallowed, finding it difficult to look at the effects of the night. A swollen cheek. Bruising on her jawline. Numerous scratches and cuts. "I'm sorry you both got caught up in my shit. If I could have changed it so—"

"Shut up," Alice said, stopping him from finishing. "You know Adam and I wouldn't have it any other way. We just need to be stronger, faster. That won't be the last fight we get into; not with the way you and my brother behave…"

Tavar chuckled for a moment before realising the action hurt. "True. Anyway, just wanted to say thanks. I'll see you tomorrow."

He stood there for a moment, watching her climbing the stairs, one at a time.

Shuffling in his pained state, he made his way down the corridor.

"Did you see him? Is he well?" A worried whispered voice rode through the empty corridors, reaching Tavar through the small gap left by a door that should have been closed. Soft light from a candle escaped the room, casting a ray of light at his feet where he stopped and listened, ear cupped to the wooden door.

"Yes. He's moved again. Almost got caught this

time but he's safe now. No one saw him," another voice replied. Lieutenant Marcus. "He wants to head to Hartovan and help out. He's getting sloppy. Reckless."

"He was always like that," the first voice said. Listening carefully, Tavar recognised it this time. Lilian. "It's why I fell for him…" Her voice dripped with a sadness he had not previously heard from the hard woman.

"Yeah but this isn't a game. This is life and death. You know what will happen if he gets caught. Years of running and causing trouble. The end of a spiked noose is where he'll finish if he isn't more careful. All of our time and efforts wasted."

"It's difficult for him. You know that. The sacrifices he's made."

"We've *all* made sacrifices…" Marcus bit back, his voice rising with his temper.

"You know what I mean," Lilian said, soothing him.

"I do. I'm sorry, just tired. I best be going. I'll see you in a week's time." A chair scraped across the floor, alerting Tavar of the danger of his position. He slipped away from the door, moving as fast as he dared in the silence towards his room.

He nudged the door open, creeping into the gap and closing it behind him. He ran his hands through his hair as he looked at Adam's empty bed. Sliding out of his clothes with difficulty, he dropped onto his bed, resting his head against the pillow and closing his eyes. In the dark silence of the room, there were no distractions from his injuries. He forced his mind to think of the hushed conversation he had stumbled upon but he didn't have the energy to focus.

Marcus and Lilian. What had they been talking about?

He drifted in and out of sleep, waking with each slight roll of his legs or twist of his arms. His dreams were filled with conversations spoken in a language he couldn't decipher. He tried to explain this wasn't his fault but was met with violence.

The morning found him tired and sore.

Tavar hobbled to his seated trainer, holding his breath to alleviate the likelihood of him wincing in pain.

"Fall over again, Tavar?" Master Oden mocked, looking him up and down. "Seems like your friend had a stumble too. Isn't that right, Miss Alice?"

"Nothing to worry about, Master. I'll beat the floor next time," Tavar said, forcing a grin onto his sore face.

"Every scar is a story," Alice said, trying to see the good side.

"As long as the story isn't that the soldiers I am training can't even stand up properly without hurting themselves," Oden snapped. "That is a narrative I would wish to quash as soon as possible."

"Not to worry, sir." Tavar's eyes darted over to Carver and Qassim, watching as they shared a joke, picking out their shield and sword for the day. "It won't happen again."

"Make sure that it does not. Your brother doesn't appear to be here today, Alice. I received a message that he was involved in an unfortunate incident with excited revellers during the night. More than a simple fall for him. I expect to see him at the end of the week."

The two of them backed away and headed to the wall of weapons and shields lining the back of the room. Tavar caught Marek's distressed glance but shook his head. Now was not the time for that conversation.

The majority of the soldiers had already paired up and were practising their drills.

"Defence is as important as attack. Use the shield to block the first strike. Use your opponent's momentum to knock them off guard and then strike when there is an opening." Oden was demanding over the clatter of wood on wood. "Feel the rhythm of your opponent's strike and play off it. Turn their attack to your advantage!"

It was unsettling just standing there with the shield and sword in his hand as he waited for Alice to pick her weapons. Unsettling as stared at Carver and Qassim go through the motions with ease. Strike. Block. Strike. Strike. Block. Strike. It was a dance, a mummer's farce with no hint of danger. He balked at the obvious disparity between the play before him and the visceral violence of the night before and the attack in the stables. The image of Adam lying on the floor in a pool of his blood flashed across his mind and he took a sharp intake of breath.

"You okay?" Alice asked, concerned lines creasing her forehead as she strapped her arm against the shield and grabbed the nearest sword. She swung it through the air a few times, testing its balance. "Good enough," she said, more to herself than anyone else.

"Just pissed off," Tavar answered, twisting the blade in his hand and examining the grip. "Twice they've beaten the crap out of me and twice they've got away with it. Adam's lying in a medic bed and they're laughing and joking like nothing happened. It isn't fair."

"Fair?" Alice scoffed. "We've been through enough to know that the notion of things being fair doesn't apply to us."

Curious glances followed them as they walked into the square, finding an open area wide enough for their session. Their cuts and bruises from the previous night were clear and obvious to any giving them even the slightest attention. Alice rubbed at the bruise on her jaw, hiding it from the onlookers.

"Ignore them. Just focus on this." Tavar tapped his sword against the shield and dropped into the defensive stance. "Come on, you attack first."

Alice nodded with grim determination. She placed her left foot forward and bent her knee slightly, twisting her body in preparation.

The ferocity of her attack almost caught him off guard. He dropped back at the last moment, raising his shield and pushing the blow to his left, opening up her body for the attack. He regained his composure, steadily throwing a diagonal strike that would have caught her collar bone had he gone that far.

"Easy!" he cried, cracking his neck and walking back into position. "I don't need any more injuries."

"Sorry. It's just, those two fight better than us. They don't hold back," Alice said, voice soaked with frustration. "We shouldn't either. The next time they do this shit, we need to be ready!"

"Yeah," Tavar gripped the hilt of the blade tighter and raised his shield again, staring at Alice as the previous night's actions played once more in his head. "You ready?"

"Don't ask. Just hit me."

He exploded forward, thrusting with the sword and aiming for her heart. She whipped the shield up just in time to knock his blade to the side, jumping into his guard in an instant and launching her blade in the direction of his neck. Instinctively, he lifted his own shield, slapping her weapon away before dropping to a knee and slamming the shield across the back of her knee. Before he could even blink, she was on the floor, breath pushing out of her body as she landed on her back. Tavar dropped both the sword and shield and leaned over to check on his friend, surprised by the sudden fury of his own attack.

"Alice!" he cried, a gentle hand resting on her shoulder.

"That," she said, "was a hell of a lot better!" Regaining her breath, she broke into contagious laughter. Tavar offered her a hand and dragged her to her feet. She brushed herself off and grinned.

Tavar licked his lips, feeling energy coursing through his body, ignoring the pain of his injuries and touching on the spark he had felt in the attack.

"My turn," Alice muttered, a mischievous glint in her eye.

He was ready for the attack this time. His shield knocked the first attack aside and the sword in his right hand flashed forward. Alice's sword connected with his blade this time, forcing him to improvise. He stepped to the side, striking low. Alice caught the strike with her shield and in a flash, she thrust her sword over the top of her shield and straight at Tavar. He spotted the attack at the last moment. Twisting his hips, he turned his back on his opponent, slapping the strike away with the shield and using the momentum to spin through her defence, whipping his right arm around and stopping his blade an inch away from her open throat.

They both paused, breathing heavily, sweat dripping down their faces.

"Not bad," Alice said, genuine joy in her smile.

"Thanks, you weren't so bad yourself."

"Not bad? That was dreadful!" Master Oden screeched, striding through the square, pushing aside any in his way as though they were mere furniture waiting to be moved. He stopped in front of Tavar, breathing through his nose like a bull.

Tavar thought the man was moments away from emanating steam from his hairy ears.

"You turned your back on your opponent. How many times have I told you not to turn your back on your opponent?" he spat. "A more competent fighter would have had your head like that." He snapped his fingers together, offering Alice a withering look. The joy from seconds ago faded to be replaced with shame and embarrassment.

"We're sorry, Master," Alice said, head bowed. "We just thought—"

"Well don't!" he cried, arms waving in the air furiously. "That must be the problem. Thinking. Do as I say. Do as I command. I am the one with the years of experience. You are two fools playing pretend. At some point, everyone in this room will be involved in a battle of life and death. *Thinking* at the wrong time will not just lead to your own death, but to the death of the people either side of you who are relying on you to do your damn job." The enraged master grabbed at Tavar's sword and shield and pushed them up for him. "Follow the pattern. Strike. Block. Strike. Three movements in a sequence between the two of you. If that is too difficult for you, then I suggest another evening in the stables is due."

Tavar glared daggers at the master but kept his mouth shut. They both knew how that turned out last time. Oden spun on his heels, navy cape flying behind him. Soldiers parted to the left and right, opening a path for the furious trainer as he returned to his seat, still mumbling in anger.

"Been a rough couple of days for the two of you," Carver said, just loud enough for them to hear. Qassim stood opposite her, grinning like a fool. "And that poor brother of yours. Perhaps some time in the stables with that fat friend of yours would be good for you."

Tavar's reply was cut off before it could begin. The doors to the fighting chambers opened with a bang, alerting all inside. His face lit up as he spotted Vandir. His joy drained away when he saw the look of thunder on his brother's face. Behind him, Commander Grey closed the doors before facing Master Oden whilst Vandir stood there, eyes flashing around the room.

"Master Oden, a moment of you and your students' time." Commander Grey's words were good enough but they were laced with something that unnerved Tavar. He felt like the horses did before a storm would hit. They were unaware of exactly what was about to come but knew it meant danger.

"Of course, Commander Grey. Is there a problem?" Oden answered, standing from his seat with a look of confusion.

"Not one that we can't deal with," Grey answered dismissively, following Vandir onto the fighting square.

"I have heard good things about the young men and women training here and have been waiting for an excuse to visit for some time. It appears that the day has finally arrived!"

Tavar heard the words but his focus was on Vandir. Never before had he seen such a venomous look from his brother, a cold fury threatening to boil over any moment.

"A demonstration would be useful, if that is fine with your good self? Vandir here has been trained by some of the finest fighters in Alfara over the past year or so. I would like to see how he fares against one of your fighters."

Oden nodded, a look of resignation on his weary face. "As you wish."

"Qassim ir Alisson!" Grey called out to the silent room of onlookers. Qassim stepped forward, sword and shield still in hand. "Ah yes! I know your father, a good man."

Qassim bowed, acknowledging the praise with an untrusting gaze. "He lives and breathes for Alfara, Commander."

"That is good to hear," the commander smiled, warmth not reaching his cold, grey eyes. "We must all do the same. A united Alfara is a strong Alfara. A place for everyone, as we say. Pick your weapons, Vandir."

Tavar's brother silently marched over to the array of weapons in grim determination. The crowd of rookies spread out, struggling to get out of his way. Tavar glanced at Qassim who stood silently, ignoring the worried gaze from Carver. He spotted the shaking hands with a perverse pleasure, thinking back, once again, to Adam's motionless body.

"Two daggers!" Grey said, impressed by Vandir's choice. "Bold! This should be interesting."

Vandir stalked the square like a trapped lion. He spun the twin blades effortlessly in his hands, eyes fixed on the shaking Qassim ir Alisson. The noble's son was a good fighter, he had proven that in front of Tavar time and time again. The unease he displayed now was purely due to the almost visual fury pouring from Vandir's being.

"Shall we say, the best of five?" Oden suggested hopefully.

"Let's just see how it plays out," Grey growled back, arms folded.

Nervous looks shot across the square. Tavar caught Carver's eye for the barest moment and the worry for her friend was obvious.

It had been a long time since Tavar had seen his brother playing with sticks in the woods. Vandir's stony composure was a thousand miles from that playful child. An air of arrogance swept around him as he stood opposite his unnerved opponent.

"Let the battle commence," Grey said, licking his lips as though salivating over a piece of meat for his evening meal.

Vandir held the daggers loose at his side, tips pointed at the ground. He stood still, baiting his opponent.

Qassim glanced to his friends, looking for any sign of support or encouragement. There was none. Master Oden looked at the scene with arms folded across his chest, his face unreadable. Still, Vandir stood statue-like, eyes never wavering from the nervous young man dancing in front of him.

Qassim flashed his left foot forward, feigning a strike with his shield and pulling away at the last moment, gauging Vandir's reaction. There was none. Encouraged, he snapped forward and slapped the side of the blade across Vandir's face.

The smack of wood against his brother's jaw made Tavar wince and look away. The room erupted with noise as the shocked audience burst into conversation following the first strike. Qassim looked at his cheering friends, holding shield and sword to the side as one corner of his lips curled up into a smug smile. The smile faded as he turned back and saw the icy glare on Vandir's face.

"First strike to Qassim ir Alisson. Wonderful," Grey said, stepping forward to get a closer look at the display. "Resume your positions." Sweat dripped down Qassim's forehead as they returned to their places. "Let the battle commence."

Vandir moved like lightning. His blades were a blur of motion, impossible for Tavar's mortal eyes to track as they slapped aside Qassim's shield and cracked against the knuckles on his other hand, forcing the blade to drop to the ground. Vandir raised his knee straight into the stomach of his opponent and brought his elbow down with all his weight against the back of his neck. Qassim dropped like an anchor to the ground, coughing violently.

Shocked murmurs broke out in the audience as Vandir turned his back and resumed his position.

"Someone's been training." Alice nudged Tavar, watching her old friend with a newfound respect.

"Seen the look on Carver's face? Not so smug now, is she?"

The next round was the most impressive. To the bafflement of all in attendance, Vandir threw the blades behind him and stood tall, ready and waiting. Qassim stood and gazed at Master Oden, arms wide open in confusion.

"What should I do?" he called out to the master.

"I'd suggest hitting him!" Oden barked back, visibly distressed with the unusual tactics.

Qassim rushed forward, eager to end the fight.

This time he led with the blade. Tavar thought the plan had worked but at the last moment, Vandir ducked and rolled past Qassim, catching his opponent's leg with a passing hand and pulling hard, taking Qassim completely off his feet. Vandir ripped the shield from his grasp and threw it away. He backed off, allowing Qassim time to stand. Furious with the disrespect, Qassim raced forward again, swinging the blade wildly, slashing at the air as Vandir dodged each strike.

Tavar watched in awe as his brother caught Qassim's wrist and twisted it to the side. With a scream, Qassim dropped the weapon. Vandir snapped his elbow forward and cut the scream off with one strike to the jaw. Not content with immobilising his opponent, he followed up with four quick blows with his fist, blood splattering Qassim's face with the impact.

Master Oden stood from his seat but a raised hand from Commander Grey kept his mouth shut, his fury boiling inside with no chance of release.

"Tavar..." Alice muttered as Qassim fell to the ground, clutching his face and sobbing.

Vandir stood over Qassim and grabbed at his hair as he himself dropped to one knee, their faces inches apart. One immaculate and pristine. The other a bloody, unrecognisable mess.

111

"I don't want to have to train with you again," Vandir said, so all could hear. "I'm guessing the feeling is mutual. If you ever want a fight again, you step into the square and do it like a soldier of Alfara. Do you understand me?"

Qassim's gurgled reply seemed good enough for him. He dropped him back to the ground and stood, brushing the dirt from his fighting gear.

"An excellent display," Commander Grey sang out. "A valiant effort from Qassim ir Alisson here; I shall ensure that word reaches your father of this display. As Vandir said, we must behave as soldiers of Alfara. There is a time and a place for fighting…" He waved to Master Oden who still stood, frozen with repressed rage. "Master Oden, I thank you for your time. Carry on."

Tavar attempted to catch his brother as he followed Grey out of the square and towards the exit.

"Not now," Vandir snapped, his face informing Tavar that now was not the time for arguments.

Oden clapped his hands and tried to restore order to his shocked group of boys and girls. "Back to training. All of you!" he screeched as he bumbled across the square, pushing away the crowd of people standing over the fallen mess that was Qassim ir Alisson. "Miss Carver. Take two others and escort Qassim here to the medics. He will need cleaning up."

Tavar couldn't help but smile as Carver pulled Qassim to his feet and dragged him through the chamber. She purposefully averted her gaze, letting him know that things had changed. Her closest ally had fallen a rung or two down the ladder of Alfara.

CHAPTER SEVEN: JUSTICE

"That's three in a row," Tavar said, impressed. "I think you've got this." The arrows stuck out from the red circle painted on the wood at the end of the range. They were huddled together, the feathered shafts almost touching. "I've not seen Master Oden fire three so close in such quick succession."

Alice curtsied in jest, happy with her work. The wooden bow was an extension of her body, reacting with each movement. She pulled on the tightened animal gut used the propel the arrow and smiled at the familiar twang. "Don't you remember my dad taking me out hunting? Adam could handle the skinning and the carving but I was always the one he allowed to practise with the bow and arrows. Hit a squirrel once," she boasted, wandering off to collect her arrows. "A moving squirrel!"

"That was an accident!" Adam called after her. "You admitted it yourself!"

"Well, maybe it wasn't!" she called back with a grin, enjoying playing her brother up.

Adam clicked his tongue against the roof of his mouth and threw his own bow into the dirt. He stared at his sister walking away. There were two arrows in his own wooden board. A third lay to the side of the board on the ground, mocking him.

"It'll take some time," Tavar said. "You did better than me and you're not back to full health. You'll get there." He looked at his own arrows. The three had landed on the board but were scattered and apart from each other. One had managed to brush the edge of the red circle in the centre but he couldn't take much heart from that. It was sheer luck.

Only four days had passed since Adam had been released by the medics. Even then, they had warned him that he needed rest and time to recuperate. The bruises on his body and face were yellowing now and the swelling had died down. The cut opened beneath his bottom lip still drew the gaze of onlookers and he had been told that it would scar; a reminder of the beating he had received.

"I should have been the one to teach Qassim a lesson," Adam said, his body shaking. "Vandir should have stayed out of it. It was none of his business. Ever since we've been here, he's lived his own life, away from us all. Why did he choose now to interfere?" The bitterness in his voice unnerved Tavar. He understood the anger and frustration Adam had but didn't understand why this was Vandir's fault.

"He was only trying the help. You should've seen how angry he was when he entered the training square," Tavar reasoned, flashing his eyes to warn Alice as she returned with the arrows.

"*Help?*" Adam scoffed. "Where has his *help* been over the years since we arrived in this cursed place? Where was his *help* when they beat you in the stables?"

Silence. Tavar didn't know how to respond to that. He knew his brother. No matter how much he may have changed, he was still that same kid that would read him stories in the storm.

"He's been doing his own thing," Alice shrugged, catching onto the theme of the conversation. "Vandir heard that his friends and brother were attacked. I'd hope that you would have behaved in the same way if it was me."

"It did happen to you!" Adam exploded, spit flying through his gritted teeth as he paced about like an animal, trapped. "I feel so useless. I saw those bastards attacking you and there wasn't anything I could do about it. It's eating away at me." He picked his bow up and stormed off. "I'm heading back to the South House. I'll see you later."

"We can come with you?" Alice suggested, though she knew the answer.

"No. I need to rest."

Tavar chewed his lip and watched his friend walk off into the distance.

Alice sighed, bow and arrows still clutched in her tight grip.

"He'll be okay," Tavar said, needing to fill the silence. "Just need to give him time."

"Needs another bang on the head more like," Alice said, shaking her head. "Fancy a little competition?" She stuck the arrows into the ground next to her and waved her trusty bow. "If you have the guts…."

Tavar laughed and tested the string on his own weapon, feeling the tension. "We both know how this is going to end. Maybe you should do it with a blindfold."

"Maybe you should try harder!"

"Best of three?" he asked her.

"Best of three."

Tavar collected an arrow and pulled back the string, eyes focused on the red circle at the far end of the range. He breathed in slowly and held it for a moment.

Then he released the arrow.

The South House bustled with activity as Tavar took his seat beside Alice. Lilian stood at the front of the common room speaking to Master Oden as more boys and girls poured into the room. The midday sun shone through the window to Tavar's left. Horses pulled along carts of merchandise as they travelled up the road; the city of Kessarine carried on as normal.

"How many times do you think we've all been in here since we arrived?" Adam asked. "Three times? Four?" His frustration had eased in the months following the attack. He was almost back to the Adam that Tavar had known before the beating: friendly and quick to jump in with cheeky comment that would always make those around him laugh. "Must be important. Reckon old man Oden is retiring at long last. Can't have much longer left in him…"

"Gotta be bigger than that," Tavar argued. "Gathering all the recruits at such short notice... It's odd."

The last few latecomers drifted in, uttering their apologies and looking flustered and red-faced as they look their seats at the back of the large room. Tavar could see why it was rare to call a meeting for this number of people. They were packed in tighter than Alice's arrows on a target. The heat shot up with the number of bodies all shuffling and nudging against each other. Hopefully, it wouldn't be a long meeting.

As if on cue, Lilian turned to face her audience and cleared her throat. She looked out at the room before her as he lips moved, silently assessing the numbers.

"I think that will have to do," she said to Master

Oden next to her. "Recruits!" Her voice shut up all in attendance. The woman had been the one constant in their lives since they had arrived in the South House. For some she was a mother figure. Others saw her as an overbearing teacher. All of them would admit they wouldn't have survived without her guidance.

"Master Oden and I have gathered you here today for two announcements. Over the past few years we have watched you grow into young men and women; into true citizens of Alfara. The path of a soldier is a difficult one and it was chosen for you. You have all displayed resilience and a determination to succeed. Those are qualities necessary for a soldier of Alfara; and those are qualities that you will be needing more than ever in half a year's time."

Intrigued conversations broke out in the audience at the pause.

"What the hell do you think that means?" Adam asked, leaning forward and looking across at his sister and Tavar.

Tavar shrugged, none the wiser.

Master Oden raised his palms out and rolled his eyes whilst asking for calm. "Settle down, settle down," he said, waiting for absolute silence before he began. "You were selected to be trained as Alfaran soldiers due to our need in the fight against a growing number of fools who believe they can test the might of this great nation." Oden scratched at the grey stubble on his chin, looking almost bored. "In half a year's time, you will all be taking your final test." Uneasy mutterings spattered throughout the crowd now, shocked faces turning to the friends around them.

"Final tests?" Alice repeated. "Pass and we're in

the army..."

"The test is broken into three parts: Hand to hand combat; archery; and military history. How well you do in each section will help us to place you correctly when you join up with the lieutenants in the North House and you are assigned your barracks. Some of you may fail. In such circumstances, we will extend your training by one more year." He glared around the room, threatening any who dared to fail him. "Six moons. That is all you have until you take the test."

A further outbreak of chatter erupted as Oden turned to Lilian. She had covered her mouth, not wanting the others to see or hear what was being said.

"Half a year. That's all we have to prepare," Tavar said to his friends.

Two rows in front of him, Marek turned back and waved to draw his attention. Tavar mouthed six in shock as Marek waved the same number of fingers in the air, his eyebrows so high that they became lost with his hair. This is what Marek had wanted all his life. A chance to be a part of the Alfaran Army; a soldier to make his family proud.

"We'll be in the barracks north of the city if we pass," Alice said. "Isn't that where Vandir lives?"

Tavar nodded. The northern barracks were on the outskirts of the city, a one-hour ride from the South House on a good day. He allowed himself the chance to hope that this could be the moment that he grows closer to his brother once again.

"That's if he doesn't get sent away before then. Must be trouble if they are recruiting us this early..." Tavar said darkly, understanding the implications of the announcement.

"We could be fighting for Alfara," Adam spat. "Never thought I'd say that."

"What other choice do we have?" Tavar asked, equally displeased.

"We'll have more opportunities once we're in the army. Could have a chance to escape," Alice said, her face brightening at the thought.

"And do what?" Tavar responded, bursting her bubble of joy. "We all know what happens to deserters."

"Some ray of sunshine you are…" Adam chuckled. "We'll figure something out. Just need to stick together."

Lilian cleared her throat again, patiently waiting for her audience to quit their conversations and face her.

"The next piece of news is bittersweet," she said, pausing to alter the look on her face to one of regret. "The rebel uprising has almost been destroyed. Faced with the might of our great army, the rebels are scattering, fleeing for their lives. Whilst this is good news, it comes with a dose of sadness. Our spies have unearthed a small group of Alfaran soldiers who had been supplying the rebels with food, supplies and information. This is treason. The punishment for such heinous crimes will be decided by the council later today. There will be a gathering in the Godsquare tomorrow at midday – I expect all of you to attend. You will all bear witness to what happens when Alfara is betrayed." If anyone could have thrown flames from their eyes in that moment then it would have been Lilian. Her fiery glare shot over all the recruits who say in fearful silence. "Master Oden, is there anything else that you would like to add?"

"Be there early," he said, raising an eyebrow and drawing a quick breath. "It will be busy and believe me, you won't want to miss this." The old trainer clapped his hands and smiled. "You are free for the rest of the day. Enjoy the good weather and don't get into any trouble..." His eyes lingered on Tavar for a moment longer than was necessary. "And Carver ir Edemer, a quick word if I may?"

Wooden chairs scraped throughout the room as the majority piled out, eager to make good use of the unexpected spare time available. Questions were being asked and a plethora of answers drifted over to Tavar, bringing a smile to his face.

"Who do you think the traitors are?" one asked his friend as they left the rolled.

"Your mum and dad are the most likely ones..."

"Ah, shut up! I'm being serious!"

"Imagine if it was Commander Grey..."

"Shush! Don't want anyone hearing you say that!"

"It could be! You saw what he let that guy do to Qassim. Not exactly patriotic, is he?"

"Lieutenant Marcus has looked particularly strained recently. Looked like dog shit the last time we saw him..."

"Half a year! Half a year to prepare for the most important day of my life." Tavar knew that voice.

"Don't worry, Marek. It's plenty of time, you'll be fine," he responded to his worried friend.

Marek bristled at the assumption, sweat already dripping down his anxious face. "Tactically, sure. As an archer, my grandmother could shoot better and she's been dead for ten years."

"Ask her for some advice then." Adam butted in

with a laugh.

"Very funny," Marek said, ignoring the laughter around him. "Seriously. This is a big deal."

"We know," Tavar said. He stepped out into the bright sunshine and shielded his eyes, noticing the worried look on his friend's face. "Half a year is a long time. Tell you what, why don't we head to the archery range while we have some time off?"

Marek shook his head. "No. No, it's okay. You're right, half a year is a long time. We'll be fine. We'll all be fine," he said, not sounding entirely convinced by Tavar's argument. Nothing unexpected there: Marek would have panicked if he had been given six years, let alone six moons. "I'm gonna head to the market. Need to let my dad know. Fancy tagging along?"

"Sure," Tavar said, looking to the others. Adam nodded and Alice agreed: both eager to enjoy the glorious weather.

"Summer is definitely my favourite time of year. Any chance to spend it outside is good with me."

"Then it's decided: let's go steal some fruit from Marek's father's stall!" Tavar mocked, walking down the dusty road that would lead them to the market.

"Again, not funny," Marek grumbled. "He wasn't too happy last time, as much as he likes you all."

"It was one apple," Adam cried, offended.

"Two apples," Tavar said, thinking back to the previous moon. "And some potatoes."

"Think I grabbed some berries…" Alice added to the Adam's amusement.

"Exactly. Not enough to cry about."

"Well, let's just agree to not steal from my dad,"

Marek suggested, rubbing his temple with a finger and thumb. "Don't think I can handle much more right now. I might explode."

Wide though Market Street was, herds of customers bumped and knocked into one another due to their sheer number. The heat and light from the sun attracted the citizens of Alfara to the market like ember flies to a torch. The harsh winters imprisoned them behind the walls and beside fiery hearths but as soon as there was a glimmer of light and heat, they all came crawling out of the woodwork and the market thrived for it.

Tavar had to admit, he enjoyed people watching in the market: the back and forth between increasingly agitated customers and merchants as they argued over appropriate prices for a silk robe; parents attempting to buy fruit whilst their children ran around them, bumping into the ankles of onlookers who were barely calmed with quick, insincere apologies. Most of all, he loved the life of the market. Whereas most of Kessarine felt like a cold vacuous city to him with its gated estates and areas intended only for nobles; the marketplace welcomed each and every citizen from noble to peasant. Of course, those who could afford it would often send people to purchase what they needed but Tavar loved it, nonetheless. Every now and again he would witness an act of kindness or hear genuine laughter from those around him and it would wake him from a slumber that he had shrunk into – a slumber brought on by thinking back to his past life, life on the road.

He bit into the apple in his hand and groaned, savouring the sweet taste as it exploded in his mouth. "Seriously Marek, your dad sells the best apples."

"I know. Tastes even better when you pay for it, don't you think?" Marek asked, eyebrows raised.

"Hmm... I suppose so."

"Out the way, guys," Alice said, tapping Tavar on the back and pointing at the open, tattered wagon decorated with an array of vegetables. It rumbled down the road led by two horses that looked as though they might fall at any second. Tavar grimaced. He could see where the horses' skin wrapped tight against their ribs. Under-fed and over-worked, no doubt.

He watched the wagon pull up to an enclosure behind the stalls. The owner, a tired looking woman with a dirty face, jumped off and tied the horses to the nearest post. She whistled loudly and waved a few waiting men over to her and gave her instructions. The men began unloading the wagon and placing boxes behind the desired stall. The woman plucked one of the carrots from a nearby box and took a bite. She watched as Tavar paced over to her.

"Can I help you?" Her voice was deeper than he expected and the accent was proof that she wasn't from around here.

"Just wondered if I could see the horses," Tavar answered, patting one gently on the side and holding his half-eaten apple in front of its mouth. The horse greedily chomped away as the woman raised her eyebrow at the interaction.

"You got knocked on ya little head lately?" she snorted.

He had. No point telling her that though. "I grew up with horses nearby. They remind me of life on the road."

The woman frowned, peering down at him with

questioning eyes. "You're not from Alfara."

He shook his head. "Parents were merchants."

"Past tense," the woman replied. Her face softened for a moment before shifting back to a tense glare. "Not gonna cry you a damned river. We've all lost folk. That's the way of things."

"You'll lose the horses if they don't get fed. These two are on their last legs," Tavar argued, pointing at the mares.

"That's why they got four of 'em."

"Cost you more to buy new horses than it would to feed these two what they need."

The woman snapped forward and thrust a bony finger into his chest. "Quite the fount of wisdom, aren't ya? Listen to me, kid. Maybe it's best to keep your nose out of my business. You don't know what I can afford. Keep pestering strangers and you'll end up like those dead parents of yours." She prodded him into the chest once more.

Tavar backed off and flashed a smile, ignoring the jibe. He could handle it. "I understand," he said, nodding. "Believe me, I do. There's a stable half an hour from here. Arun's Stables. You can't miss the sign carved at the top. It's on the way to the Godsquare but not as far. The stable boy there, Hashem; he'll be able to feed these two if you're staying here for a few days. There's more than enough room and food for them at the moment and it'll be cheap."

The woman's face relaxed but she had her arms folded, not wanting to relent straight away. "Arun's Stables…" she muttered to herself. "Hashem? That his name?" she asked, relaxing further.

Tavar nodded. "Hashem."

"What's your name, kid?"

"Tavar."

"Well, Tavar. I'm Lara." She spat on her hand and held it out to him. "Pleased to meet you." Tavar mimicked her and took her hand, shaking it with a grin.

"Pleased to meet you, Lara."

She wiped her hands on her dirty, brown overalls and smiled back. "I just might take you up on that little offer. Be good to get these two a real meal for once. You ever find yourself back on the road again, you say hello."

"I'll do that, Lara."

"Have a good day, Tavar," Lara said. She inclined her head and walked off after the men carrying her wares, barking orders along the way.

"Making friends?" Alice mocked Tavar as he returned to the group.

"Always," he replied, taking the jibe with good humour.

"Playing hero to the horses more like," Adam said with a nudge. "Sometimes I think you prefer their company to us!"

"That's not true!" Tavar cried. He frowned and held back a laugh as he saw the smiles fade from his friends' faces. "It's not sometimes I feel that way. It's all the time!"

He laughed and fought Adam off as his friend grabbed him into a headlock and dragged him along the street.

"Ha ha! Funny guy!" Adam said, releasing him with a grin.

"Hey guys," Marek said, pausing and looking back to his father's stall behind them. "I might stay here and help Dad for a while. It's not often I get the chance. I'll see you all tomorrow in the Godsquare?"

"No problem. Tell your dad we said thanks again," Tavar said as they waved.

He watched Marek blend into the mass crowd of customers and sellers before turning and bumping into another person. "I'm so sorry, I wasn't watching where I—" He stopped and stared for a moment at the person he had knocked into, his mouth wide open, searching for words.

Carver ir Edemer picked up the fruit she had dropped and glared at Tavar.

Her eyes were tired and redder than her hair. She had pulled her robe tight against her and her hood hid most of the red locks from view. A flash of horror crossed her face when she realised who had bumped into her. She sniffed as her eyes glistened with brewing tears. Before Tavar could say anything else, she pushed past Adam and Alice, knocking into them and rushing away without looking back.

"What the—" Adam glared off into the distance.

"She looks like she's been crying," Tavar muttered, unable to get those bloodshot eyes out of his head. He'd never seen her look anything but controlled and dignified. She prided herself on looking better than anyone else.

"Doubt it," Adam said. "That bitch doesn't have the heart for that kind of emotion. It's more likely that she walked past someone peeling onions."

Alice punched her brother in the arm. "Don't be mean."

"Mean? After what she's done?" Adam bristled. "If someone has made her cry then I'd like to meet them and shake their hand. An enemy of an enemy is a friend. Ain't that right, Tavar?"

He could only grunt in response; lost in thought about Carver.

The following day brought grey clouds and enough rainwater to risk the banks of River Wylde overflowing. The recruits were woken early and tasked with aiding those living near the river by constructing blocks around any properties in danger of being destroyed. Lieutenant Marcus stood nearby, scowling as he watched the recruits carry what they could from the village to the river and barking out orders over the howling wind.

Once complete, Tavar could barely utter a reply as the villagers thanked them for their help and offered small token gestures.

"Please, there's no need," he said to one elder woman who looked as though she had seen too many harsh winters. He waved away the offer of fruit and vegetables. "Keep it for yourself and your family. There is more than enough in the city." The toothless smile in return was enough thanks for him as he watched her return to her waiting family.

Even wrapped up in thick layers with their hoods up, Tavar marvelled at how underfed the villagers seemed. Like the horses from the previous day, he bet that under those layers he would see the definition of bones sticking out through thin, stretched skin.

"Why do they all look so under-fed? They grow their own food, farm a large group of animals: they should be in better condition than this. Our help shouldn't have been needed."

Alice trudged up the muddy hill next to him, her eyes focused on the boots digging into the ground in the hope that she would not slip. "Food tax," she said through her own ragged breaths. "Three quarters of what they grow and make they give to Kessarine."

"Three quarters?" Tavar cried in shock. "They break their backs to only keep one quarter of what they make?"

"Marek told me some time ago. In return, the city handles any disputes between farmers and the army and new recruits help out with stuff like this."

"It doesn't seem fair," Tavar said.

"There you go with that word again," Alice laughed darkly. "Best to let that word get washed away with the river today. No point saving it."

"Tavar, you using the F word again?" Adam joined in, taking great leaps up the hill to catch them up and followed by a weary looking Marek. "What did we say about that?" He clapped Tavar on the back, nearly sending him flying into the mud.

"Guess I just hope for something better."

"Ah, *hope*," Adam said looking up and squinting at the clouds as the rain fell onto his face. "I hoped for good weather today for the Godsquare. It is summer after all. This is what we got in reply." He held his hands out, allowing the rain to drop against him.

Tavar admitted defeat and pulled his cloak tighter. He looked around at the crowd of recruits all heading back to the city. Uniformed soldiers mixed into the crowd, keeping order and encouraging speed amongst the younger men and women. He scanned the crowd, searching for a familiar face that he hadn't seen so far that day.

"You're looking for her, aren't you?" Alice said, leaning close so that the others wouldn't hear.

"What?" Tavar feigned ignorance but his face gave him away.

"Carver. Still wondering why she was in tears yesterday. She's not here. Must be something serious," Alice suggested. "Qassim's here though. That prick has been silent since Vandir…"

"Give it time," Tavar replied. "They'll be back to their annoying selves before long and we'll be wishing we'd have appreciated these moments more!"

"I dunno." Alice pushed a strand of hair behind her ear. "Maybe they've learnt their lesson."

Tavar chuckled, unable to hold back his amusement.

"What's so funny?" Alice asked, frowning.

"Now you're the one with too much hope," he answered. "They'd learn their lesson if life was fair. But guess what…" Tavar mimicked Adam and looked up at the dark sky in the middle of summer.

"Yeah I know," Alice sighed, rolling her eyes. "Stabbing me with my own sword there. Let's hurry up, don't want to be late."

The dismal weather failed to prevent the mass of people gathering in the Godsquare. Tavar joined the shuffling crowd of citizens under the grand archway decorated with the shield and twin scimitars of Alfara. Past the archway, the square became choked with the swarm of the eager audience. Word had been passed around by the Heralds of the Godking as they rode throughout the city and to the nearby villages, informing them that a demonstration would be taking place today. Excited whispers had sped the announcement along its way into even the darkest shadows of the land and so thousands of people stood together in the pouring rain, awaiting their ruler.

"Could have picked a better day," Adam muttered to Tavar as a drenched merchant squeezed past the two of them. "I much prefer this place in the sun."

"I dunno, smells less," Tavar countered with a grin.

"Smells like Hashem's family dog when he jumped in the river last month. I nearly puked. I swear some of these people don't wash properly." He turned his nose up at one particularly foul-smelling man making his way through the crowd. His wild black beard still had crumbs from his day's meal hung between strands of the messy hair. "Disgusting."

From where he stood, Tavar could see the wooden gallows that had been readied the previous day. Its base was raised high to allow all in attendance to witness the justice of Alfara. A long wooden beam ran above the structure, close to the balcony from where the Godking had stood during The Banishment. All that was needed was the rope and the gallows were complete. It seemed that the decision had been made. No trial. It was almost enough to make Tavar whip out the F word again.

"They've already decided the punishment," he said, inclining his head to the structure of death.

"When treason is involved," Marek butted in, "a group of five men and women are chosen to decide guilt and then the punishment is decided by the people. No decision has been made in that regard. The Godking listens to his people, Tavar." Marek's voice took on a scolding tone so Tavar felt it best to keep quiet, not wanting to offend his friend.

Fortunately for him, the usual silence draped over the crowd as the Godking was announced on his balcony.

This time, he was dressed all in black. His face had been painted white with black markings dripping beneath both eyes, imitating tears. Even his pursed lips had been painted black. Once the announcement was complete, King Uhlad the Second shut his eyes and held a hand across his chest, a wealth of rings covering his long, slender fingers.

"It pains me, Alfara," he said, opening his eyes and gazing out at his people. "It pains me that we are not as united as I had thought." Many in the crowd sunk their heads in shame, unable to look upon their ruler and witness his disappointment. Tavar felt a nudge in his back and turned to see Adam grinning and cocking his head towards a tearful Marek. He bit back his own laughter and looked up at the Godking as he continued.

"Rebels in Hartovan continue to fight against us, unaware of their *need* for us, their *need* for structure and routine. For guidance and rule. *Ignorance*, I understand. *Ignorance*, I can forgive. They are like children still learning to walk. They will make mistakes; they will fall and we will be here to pick them up. What I cannot forgive, is my own people of Kessarine, those who have stood in my presence and listened to my words, turning against me and aiding those poor, misguided children to their doom. We gather here today to decide the fate of four men and women who have betrayed me, who have betrayed Alfara, who have betrayed *you*!" He balled his gloved hand into a fist and raised it, shaking above the square.

A smattering of angry cries erupted from the crowd, all eager to punish those who had betrayed their dear leader.

"Bring in the guilty," Uhlad said with a wave of his hand.

An outbreak of venomous curses and disgust flew from the crowd as a door opened from the side of the square.

Led by two uniformed soldiers were two men and two women. All had their hands chained together and were linked together by a rope. Memories of his own capture flooded back as Tavar's head throbbed with pain. He felt Alice's hand squeeze his own and he squeezed back, letting her know he was okay.

The prisoners were all naked. Every part of their body had been shaved and it was clear to see the effects of the beatings that they must have endured since their imprisonment. Bruises of all colours painted their naked bodies and Tavar even spotted a few open wounds. The prisoners ducked and cowered at the onslaught of rotten fruit pelted their way by the furious citizens in the crowd. They stayed silent, trying to ignore the curses and anger flying their way. A few overexcited men managed to push past the guards lining their path and land a few punches before being dragged away. One of the male prisoners began to sob, his chest rising and falling as tears mixed in with the falling rain.

Tavar looked away as the bile rose inside him. He hunched over and coughed as he felt the burning in his throat and saliva filled his mouth. He spat down on the ground, thankfully ignored by the bloodthirsty crowd.

Alice's hand rubbed against his as his breathing became ragged and uneven.

"I know it's difficult," Marek said, noticing his discomfort but completely misjudging the reason. "I feel sick at the thought of their betrayal." Blood had left his face, leaving him pale and sickly.

The soldiers guided the prisoners up onto the gallows. The sobbing man had his head bowed, unwilling to look out at the crowd. The women stared out with black eyes, unblinking. Tavar knew that look. It was the look of those who had given up hope.

The last prisoner was a tall man. His large, muscled frame reminded Tavar of the statues in the Summer Garden east of the palace. He had the body of god and even stripped naked and beaten, he still held a slither of dignity. It wasn't his frame that caught Tavar's eye though. It was his eyes. Familiar, piercing eyes that had not lost their sparkle like the others standing beside him.

"Caleem Umarsan. Tanee Rivers. Haleema Ushmae. The three of you, experienced soldiers, have been found guilty of aiding rebels against your country, against your Godking," Uhlad cried out so that all could hear him. "What punishment do you deserve?"

Caleem Umarsan's sobs grew whilst the women bowed their heads, accepting their fate.

"Hang 'em!"

"The rope! Give 'em the rope!"

The shadow of a smile flickered across the white paint on Uhlad's face as the cries from the crowd continued. He raised a hand for silence and stepped forward, peering down at the prisoners.

"Captain Marissa. Prepare the rope for our three traitors."

The soldier standing beside the prisoners offered a curt nod to her leader and pointed at three of her men waiting for instructions. They each grabbed ropes at the side of the gallows and threw them over the bar where assistants on the balcony tested the knots to ensure there would be no relief for the three prisoners.

The prisoners were cut from each other, hands still bound in an iron clasp. The final prisoner was pushed to the side to await his fate.

"Why is he separate from the others?" Adam asked, thoughts following Tavar's.

"He is a noble. His punishment will be different..." Marek answered darkly.

"How do you know?" Tavar asked, curious.

"You'll see."

The three stood on wooden blocks as the noose was readied. Tavar grimaced as he saw the edged iron and thorns sticking through the round noose given to each of them. As it tightened around their necks, drops of blood dripped down their naked bodies as they each cried out in agony.

Their cries only further enraged the audience. Stones and rocks now flew through the air. Most missed but a few landed on their target with a thump and a stifled cry.

The captain nodded at her soldiers as they pulled their ropes tight. A moment later, they kicked away the wooden blocks to a huge cheer.

The bodies wriggled and struggled like worms in the mud. Their feet fought valiantly to reach the ground but there was no escape. Every movement only forced the iron and thorns further into their skin and more blood dripped to the amusement of the animals in the crowd.

"I can't watch." Alice turned from the scene with a curse and wiped at the tears streaming silently down her face. "We can't stay here."

Tavar squeezed her hand gently. "I know. We won't."

The hanging prisoners continued to struggle as the Godking raised his hand a final time. "Justice. That is what we want today. This, *this* is justice. Paying for sins that have been committed. There is one final person who must pay."

All eyes turned to the final prisoner. He stood as dignified as he could, shoulders back and head held high as the three soldiers wriggled to their death. Tavar felt a rush of pity and respect for the man.

"A noble. An ambassador working on behalf of the greatest nation in the world," Uhlad spat. "You had the world at your feet and yet you chose to conspire and corrupt the people in your power to aid rebels against this kingdom. There is only one punishment fit for you…"

"The wall!"

"The wall!"

"Flay him on the wall!"

All the crowd agreed. The Godking had but one choice. The air grew thick and the rain paused for a moment, though the grey clouds still blocked out all light in the sky.

Tavar held his breath, though he knew what was to come. This man's fate had already been decided.

"Khaled ir Edemer. You will face justice on the

wall."

Tavar felt the breath leave him at the name.

"It can't be…" Alice said shaking her head.

"This is why she was crying," Marek said, putting two and two together as he gazed up at the solemn man awaiting death.

The crowd roared their approval as the naked noble was dragged through them and towards his final destination.

Tavar couldn't believe it.

Carver ir Edemer's father was a traitor to Alfara.

Carver ir Edemer's father died that day, for all to see, in the worst possible way.

CHAPTER EIGHT: ONE OF US

The following day started in complete contrast to the previous one: the sun returned and brought along a stifling heat that encouraged many of the men to wander through the streets shirtless and smug, smiling and winking at the ladies they passed. The sweat on their bodies only further illuminated the copious patches of dark hair on display from chest to trouser line. Tavar even spotted that a few had large patches growing out on their back and shoulders. The range of reactions was wide and varied. From blushing giggles to open disgust. Regardless of the reaction, the men seemed to be enjoying themselves, proud of what they had on display.

Training for the day was to be held in the afternoon so Tavar had the morning free. A simple note on ripped parchment had been delivered to him after breakfast from Hashem, asking for Tavar to join him in the stables. He had left his friends in the South House Gardens enjoying the sunshine and began a leisurely stroll through the city.

The sudden sunshine added to the illusion that the previous day had been an anomaly, an outlying nightmare dreamt up in a fever haze. He had struggled to sleep, eyes staring up at the ceiling as he thought about Carver and her family. From what he knew about them, they were a proud, dignified family whose line did not diverge too far from royalty. The fact that Ambassador ir Edemer was a traitor who had helped the rebels of Hartovan was incomprehensible.

The crowd had spat their venomous fury, whistling and cheering as soldiers lowered Edemer onto the wall from the battlements at the front of the city. Tavar had swayed, dizzy with disgust as the man was cut open with a spear in his side. Through it all, the ambassador didn't cry out or protest. He winced and closed his eyes, his chest racing up and down as he struggled to breathe; to stay alive. More rocks were thrown at him but most missed: the crowd was too far from the high wall and more likely to injure their own people than the unmoving figure stretched out above them.

Eventually, they had grown bored and disinterested in the display. Small pockets of the crowd heard the boom of thunder and used that as their cue to leave and head back home, bloodthirst sated for the day. Others followed like sheep until only the dead kept ir Edemer from being alone.

Tavar shook the memory from his head and focused on the present. Hashem sat swinging in his chair outside the stables, slurping a brown meat stew with relish.

"Bit early for that, don't you think?" Tavar said as he approached his friend.

Hashem looked up with a grin. "Never too early for mum's beef stew. I could eat it all day."

"I think you have," Tavar said, poking his friend's large belly.

"Pure muscle." Hashem placed the bowl on the ground and stood, flexing his arms as though to display imaginary muscles.

"I believe you. Why did you send the note?"

"Got a surprise." Hashem's eyes twinkled with

the secret. "A good one."

"Lead the way."

Tavar followed his friend to the stable door.

"Wait here," Hashem said, opening the door barely enough for him to squeeze through before shutting it again.

Tavar waited, curious. He took a moment to look up at the shining, golden dome that dominated the city's skyline. Marek had told him the story of how centuries ago, the dome had been built by King Haasim the First. The king had longed for a structure to act as a sign of the legacy he would leave on the land. The best workers in the land had been tasked with designing the grand dome which sat on top of the palace and still housed royalty and those closest to the king. The dome itself had taken a century to build. The gold had been carried from the continent across the Sapphire Sea near a land of fiery mountains. Haasim had died before its completion but his grandson, Haasim the Second had lived to witness the opening of the dome.

Marek's eyes had shone with pride when discussing the magnificent structure.

Tavar saw it as a waste of resources and the physical embodiment of one man's hubris. Of course, Marek hadn't liked that analysis. He had pointed at the dedication and effort of the workers: surely, this was recognition for all that they had done?

Tavar's thoughts were broken by the sound of the stable doors opening with a kick.

"Seeing as it is such a lovely day," Hashem said, his smile as wide as the Sapphire Sea, "I thought we could take these two horses for a ride in the fields east of the city. Father has given me permission. What do you think?"

The stable boy walked between two horses, each hand holding a reign. His favourite was in his right hand, a black Alfaran Kingshorse he had named Nightswift. It was the horse in his other hand that caused Tavar to take a step back, his mouth becoming dry.

"Pan," Tavar muttered, not wanting to blink in case it would break the illusion before him. The palomino lurched forward, recognising her old friend. Her ears flicked forwards as she whinnied a greeting. "You're letting me ride Pan…"

"We're not just looking after her now. Heard father talking about a good-tempered palomino one of the nobles had bought a while ago. The noble got into a bit of an issue due to his gambling in the faze dens in the eastern quarter. Father managed to get her for an incredible price. She's ours. That means you get to ride her again." Hashem's face lit up with the joy of helping his friend.

Tavar scratched at the mare's neck and held his head against hers, lost in the moment. Never in his wildest dreams had he thought of being able to ride her again. The noble who had bought her kept her in the stable but lowborn sons of dead merchants would be killed if they tried to ride a noble's horse.

"Hashem, I have no way of thanking you," he said, bringing the stable boy in for a hug.

"You're my friend," Hashem said, patting him on the back and laughing. "It's what friends do. You don't need to pay me back. Anyway," he backed away and scratched nervously behind his ear, staring at the ground. "I left you when Carver and the others attacked. If anything, I still owe you."

"Well, how about we say it's even," Tavar replied, "and let's take these for a ride!" The smile returned to Hashem's face and they marched the horses away from the stables.

The wind whipped across his face as the palomino raced forward, enjoying the freedom of the fields. For the first time since his life in Alfara started, Tavar felt free, unrestrained. The glimmers of light from his life on the road now shone fully, almost blinding him in delight. He clicked his heels against Pan and urged her forward, willing her to catch up with Hashem and Nightswift who had led most of the way.

Hashem peered back and urged his mare forward, outstripping Tavar and his friend with ease.

He had to admit it: there was no catching Nightswift.

Finally, Hashem slowed down and raised a hand to signal Tavar to do the same. They had been unable to shield themselves from the blaring sun as they rode but the apple trees in the field would give them protection. Tavar slid from the saddle, wincing at the soreness in his thighs. It had been too long since he had ridden. It would take a while to get used to it again.

He tied Pan to the tree and grabbed one of the red apples that had fallen. Pan greedily accepted the offering and a hug before pacing into the cooler shade of the tree.

"I heard about what happened yesterday," Hashem said, sitting down and leaning against a tree. "Can't believe the ambassador..."

Tavar took a seat of his own and picked at the

grass. "Three hanged. One on the wall. Be thankful you weren't there."

I've seen it before. Don't want to see it again. I don't care what the crime is, no one deserves *that*."

"Did your father attend?" Tavar asked, aware of the man's position within Alfara.

"Yeah, had to. Hated it though. Of course, if he said that to anyone then he would lose his place. Best to keep your mouth shut in Alfara."

For a while, they sat in silence. Tavar dropped onto his back and gazed at the white, puffy clouds lazily floating by.

"You ever wanted to leave Alfara?" he asked. He heard shuffling as Hashem moved closer to him, lying in the grass and frowning.

"You know what? I've never thought about it. I was born here. My father was born here. We've never left. Well, father's been to Hartovan a few times on business and once even rode to Yorkland to purchase a couple of horses but that's it. It's comfortable here."

"I can't stay here, Hashem," Tavar blurted out as he stared into the shimmering blue sky. "This isn't my home."

"But you can't leave. They'll kill you," Hashem said, sitting back up and staring at Tavar with concern.

Tavar sighed and pushed himself back up, stretching his arms and rolling the stiffness from his shoulders. "They want me to live in Alfara. They want me to fight for Alfara. But I can't get it out of my head that Alfara is the reason I don't have a family. Alfara is the reason I'm trapped."

"Fifteen years. Fifteen years of service and you

can go. That's the deal in the army."

Tavar knew the deal. Fifteen years serving in the Alfara army and soldiers were essentially given their freedom; a chance to leave the nation with a hearty handshake and a *thank you very much for your service.*

Lilian had informed the foreign recruits early in their enslavement. The way she had said it made them think it was an incredible offer and that the recruits should be bowing down in gratitude to their kind, benevolent leader. The truth of it was, most of the recruits wouldn't make it through the fifteen years. Any dangerous assignments were given to units consisting of mostly foreign recruits; there was no point risking pure Alfaran blood when there were others to shield them from harm. The offer was there to keep the recruits in line, dangle the fruit high above their heads to watch them jump. The aim was for the jump to lead to a fall to their deaths and nothing more.

"I can't wait that long!" It felt like someone had placed a boulder on his chest and he was unable to move it. "Seeing Pan reminds me of what my life could have been. What it should have been. I need to be out on the road, and not in fifteen years. I need to do it soon, Hashem. Once I've passed the test I'll be called into service. I'll be out of Alfara and able to escape."

"You know what they do to deserters." Tavar didn't need reminding about deserters. Screams echoed in his head mixed with the sounds of many bowstrings being released at once.

"I know what they do to innocent travellers minding their own business." His voice grew louder than he wanted. Hashem turned away, unable to look him in the face. "I'm sorry Hashem. I just can't stay here."

"I know," Hashem dropped back on the grass with a thump that scared the horses. "I've always known. You're my best friend, if there's anything I can do to help you that doesn't involve me getting killed, then I'll do it."

"Thanks," Tavar said as the tension eased. He stood and walked over to Pan, patting her against her ribs. "You'll look after her, won't you?"

"I look after them all. She'll have extra apples, if that's what you mean." Hashem stood and wiped the grass from his shirt and trousers. "Guess we only have a year or so together then. Better make good use of it."

"How about we grab some food in the city? We can race back, I'll let you win again!"

"You had me at food…"

"The most foolish thing a soldier can believe is that one man can win a war. Often young, reckless soldiers high on their own hubris will storm into battle with the intention of winning it single-handedly. In this room, we have studied the history of war; we have studied tactics that we can learn from. We do this in the hope that we can learn from past mistakes that others have made and ensure that we do not repeat them."

Tavar yawned and fought back the urge to shut his eyes. Each week he had dragged himself to the scholar's room in the Alfaran library adjacent to Hashem's stables. Each week he would listen to Lady Alara drone on and on about the failings of the past and what they needed to do moving forward. The old woman was revered by the people of Alfara: the first female to be accepted into their army. Her tactical genius allowed her to leap over the barriers that had been placed before her until Alfara had to accept that victory in battle was much more likely if one half of their population did not have to sit at home twiddling their thumbs and weeping over husbands, fathers, and brothers.

He respected what she had accomplished but being an engaging teacher and orator were not requirements of a tactical genius and Tavar would rather spend a day on the wall than have to listen to her old war stories for too long.

"In battle, you cease being an individual and become a team, a family. The only way you will make it through the day is if you can trust the soldiers either side of you."

Tavar glanced at the young woman to his right. Carver had moved into the South House a day earlier. Rumours ran rampant between the recruits: some claimed that her mother had also been killed for withholding information; others said that she was a spy who had already fled to Hartovan to continue her husband's work; others spoke of the mother throwing Carver out and suggesting that she had too much of her father in her and that it would only lead to destruction if she stayed in her family home. Tavar didn't know what to believe and knew better than to listen to the casual gossip in the mess hall. What he did know was that Carver ir Edemer looked broken. She was a poor imitation of the girl who had laughed carelessly and beat the crap out of him in the stables.

To his great surprise, he found he pitied her more than anyone else in the room.

"One weak link in the chain can lead to downfall. I remind you of the tale of Bale the Dragon. He thought himself invincible. One loose scale was all his enemies needed to drop him from the sky. A myth of course, but one with a valuable lesson for you all. Your test is less than half a year away; earlier than I wanted but there is nothing I can do about it. Tears would be a waste of salt so we press on. Read up on the principles of King Dominic the Wise and the history of Kaamir al-Masoud. Read. Read. Read." The woman tapped her walking stick against the stone floor with each word and peered over her seeing lenses. Even withered and hunched over, she could give an intimidating stare to rival some of the relatively younger trainers.

"Now, Master Oden informed me that you have sword drills. It would be best to work in pairs. Those in the last row," Alara motioned at Carver's row with a wrinkled hand. "Look to the person to your left, they will be your partner for today. Dismissed."

Chairs scraped across the floor and the recruits began to file out.

"Out of everyone here…" Adam said, shaking his head but not trying hard enough to hide his amusement.

"Who have you got?" Tavar asked, picking up his notes.

"Cassie. She's pretty cool. Not bad to look at either. Trained with her once before and we managed to make it out without any cuts or bruises."

"Isn't that the opposite of what we're aiming for?" Tavar smirked.

Adam shrugged. "Strike. Block. Strike. Strike. Block." He mimicked Oden whilst shadow striking Tavar. "That's all I remember. Anyway, good luck." He patted Tavar on the arm and left, catching up with Cassie who offered him a wink and a smile.

No distractions left, Tavar slung the strap of his bag over a shoulder and took a deep breath.

"So, we're training together today."

"No shit. Surprised you noticed: I thought you'd fallen asleep." Carver dragged her own bag across the floor and walked towards the exit with barely a look at him. "You coming, or not?"

For the second time in a minute, Tavar found himself face down in the dirt of the fighting square. He blew out some of the soil from his lips and rolled over, breathing heavily as Carver casually turned and readied herself for the next dance.

"What am I doing wrong?" he asked her, frustrated with his failure. Any thought of Carver being unfocused had been dispelled in short time.

"You think too much. I can see every move painted on your face before you do it. You might as well write me a script beforehand to save each of us the effort." Carver's voice was monotone, lifeless. She'd barely uttered a word on the walk over, more comfortable with the silence between them.

"I'm doing exactly what Master Oden told us to do." Tavar found his feet and slowed his breathing. He picked the twin blades from the floor and faced his opponent.

"That's even worse," Carver barked back, annoyance flashing across her face. The first sign of emotion she'd shown all day. "You're following *his* script. Fuck what he told you. It's a fight to the death; think for yourself. This isn't a dance. If you act like it is, you'll end up dead!"

The room fell silent. Swords hung loosely at their

owner's sides and all eyes turned to face Carver following her outburst. Tavar spotted Adam pause from a conversation with Cassie and glance nervously his way.

Carver flung her own blades on the ground and exhaled sharply through her nose.

"I'm not going to learn anything fighting a peasant like you." She stormed away, only to be blocked by an old friend.

"You're not a noble anymore, Carver. Not now your traitor daddy is dead." Qassim ir Alisson towered over her, arms folded across his chest.

"Let her go, Qassim." Before he knew it, Tavar stood next to Carver, looking up at the noble. "Training's over."

"I don't need you to fight my battles for me," Carver whispered through gritted teeth.

"You need all the friends you can get," Qassim mocked. "You heard the old hag. No individuals. You're a weak link. Probably for the best if you leave: we don't want you costing us in battle or betraying us. Tainted blood."

This time, it was Carver's actions painted on her face.

Tavar caught her wrist before the punch could be thrown. A rush of recruits ran across the room, led by Adam, Cassie, and Alice. They stood between Qassim as he laughed at Carver struggling against him.

Carver's eyes burned with loss and hatred. The pain of the previous day tore through her as she wrestled against Tavar.

"I told you not to fight my battles," she said, breathing fast.

"I'm not fighting your battles," Tavar informed her. "I'm making sure you choose the right ones." Carver's eyes softened for a moment. "He's not worth it. Every person in this room knows you could take him. He just wants you to make a mistake so you get kicked out. Don't help him." He felt her body ease in his arms as he released her. "You want to hit anyone, hit me. At least I won't go running to Oden about it."

"I might hold you to that." She pushed past him, glaring at Qassim as she left the fighting chamber.

"You think she was difficult before?" Adam said, wandering over to Tavar and blowing out his cheeks. "I don't think we've seen the worst of it."

Tavar's gaze lingered on the door a while longer after Carver had passed through. "Maybe…"

"So… you two reckon I'll pass the archery test?"

Tavar craned his head up from his slouched position on the bench and peered past Alice at the multitude of arrows on the target. Only one had missed the small red circle in the centre. "If you don't pass then I'll drink my own piss."

"Might be worth failing just to witness that," Adam said, sitting up on his bench and stretching his arms up high.

"I need to make sure that my arrows fly true. Cassie said that if a recruit shows an exceptional talent in one area, then failures in the other two tests can be overlooked. Becoming an expert archer might mean I don't need to perfect swordplay and military history," Alice informed them.

"Still, wouldn't hurt to brush up across all areas," Tavar warned. "We need to get through this together and we've not seen how well the others are doing with archery." The lack of resources meant recruits only trained in small groups, unlike the other disciplines.

"You spoke to Cassie? When?" Adam was fully awake now: alert like a wolf catching a scent. "She say anything about me?"

"Hmm…" Alice skipped over to her brother, lips pulled to one corner as she rubbed at her chin with a finger and thumb. "Let me think. Oh yeah, she did actually!"

Adam's eyes lit up, his teeth gently biting into his upper lip. "What did she say?"

Alice tapped her brother on the head and laughed as he jerked away. "She said it was such a shame that your sister had to take all the brains *and* looks in the family."

Tavar burst into laughter as Adam tried to swat his twin away. She was too fast.

"You can be a right bitch sometimes, you know?" he said to her, sitting back down as lines creasing his forehead.

"It's one of my many talents," Alice said with a bow. She jumped up onto the bench next to her brother, ignoring his dark mutterings. "She didn't say anything about you. We don't just giggle and talk about boys. There are far more interesting things to talk about than that."

"Like what?"

"None of your business!"

Tavar stifled another laugh as Adam gave up

arguing with a roll of his eyes.

With the sun shining high in the sky, the archery range was the perfect setting to sit back and relax after training. Loosing arrows felt effortless. They could take their time without Oden shouting after each shot and most of the recruits preferred improving their swordplay, so the range was often free. It had become their escape. A world away from the orders and demands of Alfara. Sometimes Marek would join them but a moon had passed since Tavar had seen him outside of training. The nervous recruit looked more drawn and pale each day as the weight of the momentous task ahead of him grew closer. In his mind, Marek didn't have time to socialise. Nothing was more important than passing the tests.

"If we do pass the tests, when do you think they will send us to fight in Hartovan?" Tavar wondered out loud as he watched a small robin flittering across the range, looking for food.

"Doubt they'll wait too long," Adam guessed. "They want the rebellion squashed as soon as possible so they won't want us waiting on the side-lines."

Tavar thought about what that meant. He would be instructed to kill people; people he didn't know. They could be innocent for all he knew, undeserving of death. The dead knew he would do almost anything to escape Alfara but did that include killing people who didn't deserve it? A cold chill swept over him as he realised that he couldn't answer that question.

"It's terrifying, isn't it?" Alice said, her eyes glassy and unfocused as they stared at the target in the distance. "This time next year our lives will have changed so much. We'll start to see the world outside of Alfara again. That's if we survive long enough…"

"Don't say that," Adam snapped. "We've got to survive. We owe our parents that. There's no chance I'm letting their deaths be for nothing. Anyway, you've both got to come to mine and Cassie's hand fastening ceremony."

All three of them erupted into laughter then,

Tavar wiped a tear from his eye as the laughter died down. "Does *she* know about this?"

"Not yet, she will though, soon enough."

"Hmm..." Alice smirked. "Not so sure about that, lover boy. Might be best if you cast a wider net instead of targeting just the one fish."

"Might be best if you don't refer to your future sister-in-law as a fish."

It was then that Tavar heard footsteps round the bend. The three of them stood and brushed themselves down, ensuring they looked presentable in case a soldier was there to check up on anyone using the range. They had been warned once before that the range was for training only and that the South House would be the preferable setting for laziness. The tone of the reprimand led them to believe that there wouldn't be a second warning.

Carver stepped around the bend. Her eyes flashed in recognition before they rolled with frustration. They lingered on Tavar but the usual disgust was missing. "It feels like you are my shadow of late."

"Don't worry. We're leaving anyway," Adam said, jumping to his feet and pulling at Alice's hand. "You have the range all to yourself!" He strode away, pausing only when he realised that Tavar hadn't moved. "You coming?"

Tavar looked between Carver and Adam. He'd hated Carver since the first day she'd sneered at him in the fighting square but the pity he felt for the lone woman dealing with the fresh wound of her father dying in such a horrible fashion easily outweighed that hatred. He'd been there. He understood.

"What are you staring at?" Carver muttered, dropping the ornate bone bow from her shoulder and eyeing the arrows stabbed into the earth.

Tavar ignored Adam silently mouthing for him to walk away; instead, he watched Carver pick out her first arrow with slumped shoulders and said the first thing that popped into his head. "I could give you some pointers, if you'd like? Training as a pair is better than training alone."

He was unable to decipher the look Carver offered him as she lowered the bow and arrow and stared at him.

"Most of the time, I'd say that's correct. Now, you couldn't be more wrong. Leave with your friends, Tavar. I'm not one of you." She turned to the target and pressed the bow against her cheek. Tavar went to turn away but Carver stopped and lowered the weapon, turning to face him again. "Though, we do need to finish our training in the fighting square. You're still not good enough and I need to keep up training with a partner."

Tavar felt the glow of victory rising in him. "Sure. When?"

"This time tomorrow," Carver sighed, readying her bow. "And Tavar." She let loose the arrow and it *thumped* against the red circle. A perfect shot. "There's no need to defend me. I can handle myself."

"Your technique is sound, but you don't have the natural speed to fight with two swords. Ever tried a longer blade on its own?" Carver mulled over the wooden weapons leaning on the shelf at the back of the fighting chamber. "It'll help you with your reach and stop your opponents from getting inside your defence easily."

Tavar wiped the sweat from his brow and replaced his twin blades before catching the longer sword Carver threw at him.

"Master Oden said—"

"Fuck what Oden said. He's training us to be silent, walking copies of himself. That's not going to help you when the blood is flowing in Hartovan. You need to think for yourself, see what works for you. Forcing it will only get people killed. Try the sword and see how you feel. Stop thinking about what he told you; go with your gut, right in the pit of your stomach."

He flexed his wrist, testing the weight of the blade. It felt foreign after using the smaller, dagger-like blades for most of his training.

"Use both hands. Don't think too much. You have greater reach and more power. Use that to your advantage," Carver advised.

She'd barely broken a sweat. Her breathing was even and unrushed. She might as well have been lying out in the fields basking in the sunlight.

"How are you able to do this with such ease?" Tavar ran an arm across his own sweaty face but it was pointless. Seconds later, it would be drenched again. His eyes stung as the droplets managed to fall into them, affecting his vision.

"This isn't the only time I train," was the only answer he received. She raised her shield, eager for Tavar to begin.

This time, he took it slow.

Oden always insisted that the first strike was crucial in any battle: land it properly and it may well be the last strike. Now, with the longer, heavier weapon; Tavar felt it better to take his time and wait for his moment.

He waited, watching for any flicker of movement from his opponent. He took a careful step to the side, crossing left foot over right and studying every mirrored move Carver took.

She was proving to be just as patient.

The energy burning through him urged him forward, to attack, just like he had been trained. Sense won out. He'd been told to use his gut, to ignore his training and do what he felt was best. Right now, his gut was telling him to wait, allow her to make the first move.

And so she did.

The wooden blade managed to get halfway past Tavar's longsword before he knocked it away with a backward step. Carver stepped back, easing into her guard and waiting for the next opportunity. For a second, he thought there was a hint of a smile on her face.

The next attack was just as fast. There was no humour to it.

He blocked the strike again but this time, it was followed with a shield slamming into his shoulder. He rolled back with the blow and decided that now was the time for his own attack. Both hands pulled the sword to his right and cut a downward arc that smashed against the shield. Carver fell back with the strength of the blow and took a dizzy step back before regaining her composure.

"Better. Much better," she said, her breath not as easy now. "However, you allowed me time to recover. Don't. Take any advantage you can. I won't go easy on you; I demand the same back."

The next half hour brought with it more bruises for the collection. Even though his body screamed in pain, Tavar felt a slither of satisfaction as he placed the sword back against the shelf.

"Two strikes," he reminded Carver as she put her tools away. Like him, she was dripping in sweat, clumps of her dark red hair stuck to one side of her face.

"Two against twenty," she said in return, rolling her shoulder and wincing at the reminder of the strikes. As always, she had been too fast and too accurate. Tavar had managed his small victories using his power and breaking through her defence, twice landing hits against her left shoulder after knocking her shield out of the way.

"An improvement," he said, unable to keep a victorious smile from his face.

"From your starting point, the only way was up."

He rolled with the verbal attack and shrugged. "Still happy with it."

"You would be."

They strolled together out of the fighting chamber and onto the busy street.

"I know you probably won't want to but, you don't have to sit alone in the mess hall. You can sit with us. You don't even have to say anything. Or you can curse us and call us all peasants and fools like you've always done. We're thick-skinned. We can handle it." He didn't know why he was offering her the chance to sit with them. She'd made his life hell and never apologised for it. Tavar and his friends still bore literal scars from her actions, actions that couldn't be brushed over and forgotten.

Carver looked into his eyes; her brow furrowed with confusion. "Why would you want to help me? We hate each other and I'm fairly sure your friends would rather see me dead."

"You're probably right. Still, no one should sit on their own. We're used to nobles treating us like shit; you're not. Might be good for you if you can see how we do it." He held a sweaty hand out and gave an uncertain smile. "What d'ya say?"

"Put your hand away." Carver scoffed and began her walk home. "I'm fine on my own."

Tavar's shoulders slumped in defeat. There was one last play he could make but he was uncertain how it would land. He hesitated, struggling with the dilemma of whether he should open his mouth.

"I'm sorry about your father." The words stopped her in her tracks. She didn't turn around, but Tavar saw the tension shooting through her body, paralysing her. "I watched my parents die and could do nothing about it. Peasant or noble, I doubt it feels any different."

He allowed the silence to take over as he watched her, unmoving. Eventually, she turned her head to the side, voice strained with the effort of speaking.

"After watching that, how do you get up every day?"

"That was my lowest point. It's like you said earlier, the only way was up." He watched as the tension left her body and relaxed. "You were right before. You're not one of us. But would you rather be one of them?"

Two weeks passed by. Tavar sat in the mess hall, goat's milk squirting from his nostrils as he laughed at one of Adam's popular impressions of Master Oden. The scrape of a chair next to him shook him from his laughter as he turned to see an unexpected face.

"Offer still open?" Carver asked, glaring at the table, daring any of them to question why she was there. The rest of the room had fallen silent, all curious as to why Carver would be speaking to them. Some, Tavar thought, were expecting a fight to break out. Fortunately, they would be disappointed.

"Take a seat," he said.

CHAPTER NINE: THE TESTS

Complete darkness. Yet, Tavar still struggled to get to sleep. The usual booming snores shook the room: Adam clearly had no pre-test nerves to deal with. Extra training with Carver had helped Tavar improve his prowess with the blade but he still felt a wave of anxiety hit him in the chest, suffocating him. He tried to calm himself; deep breaths, closed eyes, and focusing on what he was in control of.

He breathed in through his nose and blew slowly from his mouth, opening his eyes back up and allowing time for his eyes to adjust to the lack of light. He tried to convince himself that tomorrow would be just another day, like any other. It wasn't. Passing the test would be the beginning of his journey away from Alfara. Back on the road, like his family had always wanted. He remembered the way his father would struggle after a few days inside a city. The man would develop nervous ticks: rubbing his bicep furiously or snapping whenever he was asked a question. He hadn't been built for city life and it was obvious.

Accepting defeat, Tavar rolled out of his bed and threw on the trousers and shirt he had thrown lazily on the floor earlier that night. If sleep would elude him, he might as well use the time wisely. The library in the South House was small and most of the books appeared to have been written by men and women striving to outdo one another in an attempt to see who could bore their audience to death. Still, just holding a book put him at ease, the smell of the paper. The touch of the paper in his hands. The thought that someone years ago had shared thoughts and ideas that affected so many helped him feel less lonely, somehow. Even dead, they were having an impact. The Grand Library in the eastern quarter had a much wider range of books from around the world but it would take too long to get there.

He thought of his mother and how she used to love writing on sunny days. She'd make notes on different cultures, languages, food, drink, plants; anything she'd come across. Often she would quiz Tavar, testing him on what she had written as he had always been a willing accomplice, unlike his father and brother. It felt like a lifetime ago.

Reaching the library, he was shocked to find candlelight already flickering in the room.

"Miss Lilian," Tavar stuttered.

She looked up with those warm, brown eyes of hers and sat up, pulling her robe tighter around her slim frame. She closed the book in her hand and smiled at him.

"Tavar. Of course not. This library is yours as much a mine. However, I thought you would be asleep. Aren't the tests tomorrow? It's an early start."

She patted her hand on the leather seat next to her.

Taking the offer, he sat down, stiff and nervous. "Yeah, can't sleep. Nerves."

"Nothing unusual about that. It's a big day. Especially for everyone in this house. A chance to make something of yourself. To rise up in Alfara. Not many people get that chance, that opportunity," she said. She grabbed the glass sitting on the circular table to her side and took a swig of the dark red liquid. It had a fruity smell. Wine, most likely.

"Is that what you did? After you arrived in Alfara?" he asked. Her face tightened, lips pursed and jaw set. He regretted the question instantly, realising he may have stepped too far.

"Yes, Tavar." Her face softened as she took another sip and stared into the flame of the candle. "That's exactly what I did."

"I'm sorry if the question offended you," Tavar said, hoping to ease the slight tension in the room. He hadn't wanted to upset her in any way. Through his whole time in Alfara, Lilian had been a kind and gentle presence, keen to offer suggestions and comfort when needed to any of the recruits no matter where they were from or who they were.

"There was no offence taken." She stared into the light for a while longer, lips closed. Tavar shifted in his seat, uncomfortable with the silence. "I was born away from here. My mother left me with my father when I was a baby. Father couldn't cope. I was sold to Bone Road merchants. Could have ended up somewhere much worse than Alfara." She pulled at her collar to reveal a raised cross on her skin. The sign of a slave. "An ambassador took pity on me. I grew up in this very house. I was fed and looked after. Given an education in the army and taught how to fight. I have no regrets."

"Did you ever think about going home?"

"In the beginning, yes." She exhaled quickly through her nostrils and gave him a smile that didn't reach her eyes. "I missed the white sand. I missed the food. I missed my people."

"What changed?"

"I changed. I made friends. I got used to the food.

We even have some fruit and vegetables from my homeland that make their way over here from time to time," she added with a laugh. "More importantly, I fell in love." She sighed and stood from her seat, downing the last of the wine.

"Are you glad you stayed here?" Tavar couldn't think of any reason for staying in Alfara. He'd miss Hashem and Marek, certainly, but life in Alfara choked him. He wanted to breathe freely.

"I've felt pain. I've suffered. But Alfara has given me happiness that I wouldn't trade for all the gold in the world." She playfully ruffled his hair and walked towards the exit. "I know times are hard for you. What happened to your family will never go away. Nothing will change that. Alfara is right, there is a place for everyone here. Up to you what place that is."

"I'll remember that, miss."

"Do you know why foreigners are given the name Farwan, when they enter here?"

"It means nothing. We are nothing to the Alfara nation," Tavar replied. His family name didn't matter. It hadn't mattered since his parents had been slaughtered.

"Not nothing. That's a misconception. It means blank," Lilian answered. "If you want that to mean nothing, that's your choice. For me, I chose it to mean a new start: a blank slate. This is your chance to paint on a clean canvas and become whatever you want to be. Don't be nothing Tavar. No one deserves to be nothing."

The archery trial passed in a haze. The sun beat down above Tavar but that wasn't the only reason for his excessive sweating. The moisture affected his usually tight grip on the bow, forcing a slip in his first attempt. The arrow still landed on the target but further from the red circle that was his intention.

The next effort caught the curve of the red whilst his final shot, to his surprise and joy, was even more of a success.

"Good efforts, Tavar. Shame about the first one," Master Oden said, impressed with the display.

"Slipped with the first one. Hot day," Tavar explained, placing his bow back into its groove on the wall.

"Not an excuse I'll accept. You'll have more difficulties than the heat and perspiration to deal with when we head to Hartovan. Next!"

Tavar felt he could breathe for the first time that day. Cassie offered him a high five and a beaming smile as she passed him. He slapped his hand against hers and felt a wave of relief come over him as he took a seat next to Qassim ir Alisson.

"Good luck, Cassie," he called out as she picked her first arrow.

Qassim just sat slouched in his seat, a bored look on his face. He had done well: two bullseyes and one that had barely missed. Through the whole test he had barely said a word, ignored his peers and only spoke when Oden had asked a question.

Cassie did well enough. No arrows hit the red circle but all of them hit the target – consistent. She bounced back towards the two of them as Master Oden made his way over wearily. She smiled at Tavar as she pulled a leaf from out of one of the two ebony buns of hair that sat on her head.

"A good effort from all of you. The military history test will begin after your evening meal. Make your way back to the South House and wait for the others. Results are announced once all three tests have been taken," Master Oden told them as he beckoned the next three students over to him: Marek, Carver, and short, nervous, skinny boy named Sitar.

Qassim bounded ahead of them, eager to get away. Tavar wished the three newcomers good luck as he made his way from the range with Cassie. Marek nodded, unable to look him in the eyes. He'd turned an unfortunate shade of green and Tavar worried that he would be too weak to even draw back the string of the bow. Carver gave her usual eye roll and blew the red hair from her face, her focus unbroken. Sitar returned a hopeful smile, warmed by the simple words of encouragement.

When they were out of earshot, Cassie looked back over her shoulder with a concerned glance. "Marek doesn't look too well, does he?"

"This means everything to him. It's just nerves," Tavar explained.

"Poor thing. I hope he does well."

"Me too. He deserves it. Works his butt off!" he laughed. "So, which of the tests do you think will be your weakest?" he asked, eager to move the topic away from his worried friend. The thought of Marek failing was one he didn't wish to contemplate.

"Hmm..." Cassie clicked her tongue against the roof of her mouth a few times as she thought about her answer. "I'm probably weakest with the sword. Military history isn't too bad. It just involves a lot of reading and I'm fine with that. Archery was my weakest, but Alice has been giving me some tips. What about you?"

"Same, I guess," he coughed as a horse and cart rode past, throwing dust up into their faces. "Carver's been helping me with a few things but I barely land a hit on her. She's so fast!"

Tavar just caught the curl in the corner of Cassie's mouth before she spoke. "Alice mentioned you were training with her. Bit of a surprise, I've got to admit, after all that happened with you two. Still, she's not as much of a bitch these days. As long as you're happy, that's all that matters."

It took Tavar a moment to realise what she was getting at.

He snorted, hands waving in protest as his cheeks burned with embarrassment. "It's not like that! Not at all! I haven't forgotten what happened and I'm well aware she's only helping out as she has no other friends. It's a relationship of convenience."

The arch of her eyebrow told him straight away that he had misspoken. "A relationship?"

Tavar snorted. "Not that kind of relationship! She needs someone to train with and I need to improve. It's beneficial to us both."

Though Cassie's dark lips shook with the effort to contain it, they both broke out in a fit of laughter.

"Could you imagine the two of you together? I always thought her and Qassim would get together. Marek said their families were close," Cassie said, wiping a tear from the corner of her eye. "Have to say, she might be a bit of a bitch, but she is a beauty."

"She's not bad," Tavar admitted begrudgingly. Hard to dispute the way she looked, even if her personality needed some work. "For someone who beats the crap out of me time and time again."

Walking down any road in Kessarine, it was impossible to ignore the incredible number of Alfara flags blowing in the wind. They hung from the backs of carts bounding down the road, out of windows of people's homes, shops, and every other building. Scribbled messages were painted in the shadowed alleys of the city showing support for the king and his army. Other messages were written about the rebelling nation, in contrast, they were foul and crude messages denouncing the people and their way of life. Merely twenty paces from the South House, Tavar and Cassie passed a burning flag of the Hartovan. A group of men stood around the fire, singing and dancing with bottles in their hands.

One of the men wore a long, braided beard full of silver tokens. His headdress was blood red and skewed slightly to the left. There was an air of malice about him as he called over to them, wild-eyed and leering. "Girl! Think you should go back to where you came from! We don't need your rebel scum in our city!"

Cassie pulled her hood up to hide her hair, lowering her head and quickening her steps. Aghast with the idiocy of the man burning the flag, Tavar stopped and faced him.

"She was born in Alfara, just like you," he snapped.

"You know what I mean. Don't get hair like that in this city. Skin's too dark as well. She's one of them!" The wild man roared back to laughs of approval.

Tavar stormed up to him, furious at the complete lack of respect for his friend. He could smell the alcohol on the man's breath, enough to kill wildlife. The man peered down at him, chewing his cheek and opening his arms wide.

"Tavar," Cassie muttered as a crowd began to gather. "Leave it. It's not worth it. *He's* not worth it."

"Brave of a boy to stand up to a man. Especially to protect some rebel bitch."

Before Tavar could respond, arms were wrapped around his, dragging him away.

"That's it, take him away. For his own health," the man roared after him. He threw back the last dregs from his bottle before launching it into the fire.

Tavar fought against the restraints but it was useless.

"Lose, lose situation there, kid." Marcus. He was the one dragging Tavar away from the fire and the idiot still roaring obscenities. "That man is Lieutenant Farrokh. An idiot, certainly, but he has a lot of powerful friends. You could win the fight but still lose the war with him. He's on leave, lost two of his men last week. Now isn't the time."

Marcus released Tavar from his grip outside the South House. Tavar smoothed out his shirt and pulled himself together. He gave Cassie a sheepish apology that she waved off.

"No apology needed. I'm used to it," she shrugged. "Not everyone is going to like you. Nothing I can do about it."

The casual way she shrugged the comments off hurt almost as much as the initial taunts. That someone serving in the army could have such disdain for a recruit hurt even more.

"Head inside, take your mind off it. Military

history test later this evening. You need to be ready. Forget this nonsense," Marcus suggested. "I'll speak to Farrokh once he's had a chance to sleep the drink off."

The military history test went as expected. Questions of old military strategies and conquests filled the paper. Tavar knew most of the answers after pouring through the right materials over the last half a year though, around a third of the questions he had blindly guessed at. Inspiration behind the cavalry manoeuvre in the battle of the Undying Sands was something he could not recall ever reading about. The same went for the use of the Immortals and the archery units in the second war of Okada. His mind drew a blank. Still, he felt reasonably confident with his efforts.

"Why do Alfaran infantry wear red instead of the historical white and blue? Did we even cover that question in class?" Adam asked as they walked through the market.

"Gurav the Bold came up with the idea after the bloody battle of Sufwa Hill. He fought valiantly until every enemy was dead. When he looked around, he saw that all his surviving men were dressed red, covered in the blood of enemies, as well as themselves. In honour of their victory, he made a request to Queen Almaha to change the uniform. She granted it with pleasure," Marek answered in his book-like response. "Of course, it wouldn't have been denied. They were married with six children."

"Sometimes it sounds like you've swallowed all of your notes and then are able to vomit them on command," Adam said, shaking his head. "That was tougher than the archery. One more test to go!"

"Don't remind me," Marek whimpered. "One more chance to fail."

Tavar couldn't help but smile. Marek would never change. Most likely, he'd just scored a perfect test and yet, here he was, moaning that he might fail the next one.

"One more test and then that's it, Marek: you'll be an Alfaran soldier, just like you've always wanted." He saw the twitch of a smile and continued. "Think about how proud your father will be!"

"He said he's inviting you all over to celebrate after the welcoming ceremony. I'm not certain but, he keeps hinting that he has bought some Okadan whiskey for us. He never buys Okadan whiskey!"

"There you go!" Adam thumped Marek on the back and leaned closer to his shorter friend. "A celebration! Satisfaction and some alcohol. All we need are some girls and it would be perfect!"

"You sound like an expert," Tavar scoffed.

"Well, Cassie always seems happy to see me. Where is she anyway?" Adam asked, easing past a camel and carefully dodging the pile of mess it had left behind.

"She's with your sister. They wanted to take the horses for a ride after the test so Hashem readied a couple for them," Tavar answered. He'd suggested taking Pan out for a run and Alice had nearly snapped his hand off, eager to ride the beautiful Palomino.

"What about Carver?"

Tavar lifted his shoulders and looked away. "No idea."

Adam offered a wry smile. "Sure. Looks like it's

just us lads then! Market food and a night-time stroll? I'm dying for a wrapped kebab with those herbs your father suggested Marek. I've been dreaming about it for the past week!"

"Lead the way."

"This is the final test. Upon its conclusion, I will sit down and discuss the results with a select committee and then decide who will be making the cut. Those who have failed will have a chance to take the tests again after one more year," Oden told the nervous recruits gathered in front of him. "It is of the utmost importance that we ensure you are all at a suitable standard when entering the life of a soldier, now more than ever. The hostilities with Hartovan must come to an end and that means blood. The less of our blood that is spilled, the better. Focus, remember what I have taught you, and good luck. May the ancestors guide you."

"Is it just me, or is the room spinning?" Adam asked, his heel rising and falling furiously against the floor as they sat in the raised seats in the stand.

"Just you," Tavar said with a grin. "Take it easy. You've got this. We've been in enough fights," he added calmly.

He didn't feel calm. The outcome of the one-on-one sword fight depended on who was chosen as an opponent. For moons now, he had trained with Carver. To be given another partner would bring with it a whole host of new challenges. Challenges he now wasn't sure he was ready for.

"I'd feel significantly better about that if we hadn't lost every fight we'd been involved in," Adam said with a dark chuckle. "Just one win would have been nice."

"I will call out two names at a time and you may choose your weapons and take up whichever stance you believe will give you an advantage," Oden informed them. "It will be the best of three. Losing does not mean you have failed. Your form, attitude, and skill will all be assessed and taken into consideration when evaluating your final score. Zarayesh guide you."

The first three matches weren't spectacular. Nervous recruits chose the sword and shield or twin blades favoured by Oden and followed the patterns they had been taught. Carver had been right. Tavar could see it now. Each of them moved as though Oden himself was pulling strings, guiding them on a path they weren't able or willing to break from. There was no freedom in their movement. No elegance. Only the stiff repetition of what had come before.

The recruits sweat through their uniforms. They screamed and shouted. They breathed heavily as their eyes darted from their opponent to the watching master, wondering what their fate would be. Through it all, Oden watched impassively, his elbow resting against the arm of his chair and his jaw squashed on his fist. He had seen it all before.

"Qassim ir Alisson," Oden barked, ready for the next test. "And Nahra ir Alisson."

The recruits took a collective breath in and whispers swept through the fighting chamber. Brother and sister.

The siblings chose their weapons, a sword and

shield each, just like the others. Qassim made the sign of the One on his forehead and crossed an arm across his chest in respect. His sister mirrored the actions before settling into her fighting stance, low and ready for attack.

Tavar assumed the siblings would hold back and create an edgy battle, each unwilling to hurt the other.

How wrong he was.

The strikes were vicious and powerful. Qassim had improved since falling in devastating fashion to Vandir. His strikes were like the wind, deftly whipping forward towards his sister. She managed to block most with her shield and parry a few before launching her own offensive strikes. Qassim dodged them, moving like water in a stream. Four points were scored altogether. Three to Qassim and one to his sister. Breathing heavily, they crossed an arm once more across their chests.

"An honour, sister."

"And you, brother."

They shelved their weapons and left the square.

Qassim smirked as he caught Tavar's eye. He knocked his shoulder into Tavar's, knocking him a step back.

"Good luck, peasant. Your brother won't always be around to bail you out."

"Just ignore him," Alice whispered, a look of disgust on her face as she stared after the departing Qassim and his smug sister. "Just wants you off your game for the test."

"I know." Tavar rubbed at the ache in his shoulder and stretched his arm out, trying to focus on what was before him.

"Marek Iravani." Marek stumbled his way onto

the fighting square, swallowing the lump in his throat and muttering to himself. Sweat dripped down his dark face, droplets catching in the patchy buds of a beard he had begun to grow. "And Tavar Farwan."

Shit.

Tavar tasted ash in his mouth as he stepped forward and pushed through the crowd of intrigued onlookers. He blocked the whispers out as he strolled over to his weapon of choice, the longsword. Gripping the leather handle with both hands, he caught the look on Oden's face, lips slightly parted. It was nothing compared to the despair exuding from every pore of Marek's body.

"Master Oden," he said, wide eyes not leaving the longsword in Tavar's hands. "I've not trained against such a weapon."

Oden brushed away the concerns with a lazy wave of his jewelled hand. "Informing me of your shortcomings before a test, Master Iravani would not be the wisest of strategies."

Tavar's stomach twisted at the look of dismay his friend gave him at those words. Marek's eyes pleaded with Tavar for help, for support. The blade and shield in his hands shook as he stepped into the starting position, a despaired look of resignation on display for all to see.

Anyone else. Tavar would have taken anyone else over Marek. He knew how much this meant to him and how much he would hurt if he failed this final test.

In the crowd, he spotted Carver. Her face tightened as she caught his gaze. She raised her hand and squeezed her fingers into a fist for him to see. The message was loud and clear: there was no time for mercy. He had to pass this test.

Tavar looked across at his opponent, his friend,

and crossed an arm over his shoulder in respect, as was expected in these honourable tests. Marek just stood there, sword and shield pressed forward in defiance, grimly staring back at Tavar. He would do whatever it took to pass, to make his father proud.

The first point was won with an ease that unnerved Tavar.

Marek rushed forward but he seemed sluggish, unsure of his own movements. Tavar sidestepped a lunge and followed with a swing across the back that dropped his friend to his knees. He casually placed the wooden blade against Marek's neck as Oden called the point for him.

Tavar returned to his starting position with an impressed nod from Carver. Adam and Alice stood to his right. The twins watched with identical postures, hands in their mouths and worry lining their pale faces. He blocked them out of his mind and focused on what was before him.

Marek's pained face spoke of betrayal as he raised his shield for a second time, tears swimming in his dark eyes.

The second point was over almost as fast as the first.

Tavar took the lead this time. He feigned straight but shifted onto his right, swinging the weapon up with both hands towards his opponent's chest.

Marek saw the strike at the last second and aimed to parry the blow with his sword. His eyes widened with the power of the attack and his sword flew across the square and stabbed into the soil a good five paces away.

Tavar eagerly pressed on, slapping Marek's shield to the side and thrusting his sword at his heart. The tip of the blade pushed against the Marek's chest which quickened as he realised he had lost the second point. Marek's head dropped and shoulders slumped. He threw his shield onto the ground and stared daggers at Tavar.

"Two points to zero. Final point if Tavar scores again," Oden said, leaning forward in his seat, amused. "Pick up your sword and shield, Marek. Do not let me see you drop them again."

Tavar mouthed an apology at his friend but received only a scowl as he stormed away to collect his fallen instruments of battle.

Compared to Carver's speed, swift footwork and measured strikes, Marek had all the grace of a drunk, rampaging bull. His attacks did not lack ferocity but Tavar saw them as though time had slowed. He raised his weapon when needed to parry the strikes and stepped around his opponent with ease, leading the dance even when defending.

Marek's strikes grew desperate, his breathing heavy. He roared, slicing high and aiming for Tavar's chin. For the briefest of moments, Tavar wondered if he should allow his friend this one point, a token strike to regain some honour and a sign of their friendship. Before he could make the decision, he felt his wrists twist and snap the strike away before deftly turning the blade and smashing it against Marek's shoulder, knocking him into the soil.

The collective intake of breath from the audience told him all he needed to know.

"Three points to zero," Oden droned, sitting back in his chair, eyes focused on Tavar. "Weapons away. You may leave."

Tavar crossed his arm again across his chest as

Marek threw his sword and shield against the shelf. Marek passed him, glaring daggers. His fists were balled at his side as he stomped across the fighting square.

"I will never forgive you for this. You were supposed to be my friend," he spat on his way.

The accusation cut through Tavar worse than the sharpest of blades. "Marek…" He was only doing what he was supposed to. It was a fight. A test. What should he have done? Allowed Marek to beat him and put his own position on the line?

"Leave it," Adam warned, gripping his arm tightly. "Let him cool off. You know what this means to him."

The rest of the recruits stared at him, their eyes accusing him just like Marek's. Tavar shrugged Adam off and walked away, confused. How was he suddenly the bad guy?

Footsteps behind stopped him. He threw his hands on his hips, not turning. "What should I have done, Adam?"

"Exactly as you did." Not Adam. Carver. The tension tightening his body eased slightly at the sound of the unexpected voice. "You did what you have trained to do. There's nothing to feel guilty about. Your friend will get over it. If not, then he was never your friend. Look after yourself, Tavar. No one else will."

"You knew this meant everything to your friend, yet you destroyed him completely." Jassim laughed but the joy turned to pain as the action reminded him of the wound in his side. "That's cold."

Tavar continued to stare into the fire, watching the dancing flames and listening to the sounds of burning wood. "I'd got used to fighting Carver. I didn't realise how much my body had taken on board during her training. My muscles reacted without thought. To defend and strike was natural to me now, like breathing. Each movement snapped like the string of a bow. I couldn't hold back if I had tried. I didn't know how."

Frowning at the memory, Tavar stood with a sigh. "It is getting late. Stay here the night and we will continue the tale at first light. You need rest." He pointed at the wound. There was no chance the man was going anywhere soon.

Jassim nodded in resignation. "It is more than rest that I need."

"Well, I'm afraid that's all you'll get. I'll heat some water up for you so that you can clean yourself up. May have some clothes that fit that I can leave out for you in the morning. You can get out of those bloody things."

Jassim stood with effort, exhaling through pursed lips as he got to his feet. "Before you go. Tell me. Did you pass the tests?"

"Yeah. Most of us did. They needed bodies for the war."

"And Marek?"

The pause was pregnant with dreadful expectation as they each stood there, knowing the answer. Tavar scratched at an old scar on his right hand and fought back the dark memories.

"He was held back for one year." His voice cracked slightly at the memory. "He swore that he would never forgive me for what had happened. Said that I was the reason he didn't make it."

"But he'd have another chance to make it, a year later," Jassim insisted. "That's what you said. What happened then?"

"He made it, that time. But, things were different. Painful. I'll get that water ready for you. Lie down. You must rest. Tomorrow, I will tell you about what it was like to live as a soldier of Alfara. And it is not for the faint hearted…"

PART TWO: THE EYES OF THE SOLDIER

"The eyes of the soldier focus on the present. They see each thrust of the sword, each parried blow. They see their superiors through the rose-tinted lenses they are commanded to wear and with such instruments they do not see the blood they spill."

-Malike ir Terrasil – author of "Life in the Shadow of the Godking".

CHAPTER TEN: THE POISON OF ALFARA

"**D**id you sleep well?" Tavar asked Jassim. The Alfara native struggled with the buttons of his clean shirt, still favouring his right side. The wound didn't appear to be infected, which was good news for him.

"Well enough."

Tavar placed the cup of water at his side and took a seat on the table and waited for Jassim to do the same. When Jassim finally sat opposite him, Tavar tapped his fingers against the table and licked at his dry lips.

"You wanted to know everything. My life isn't an easy tale. It is full of grief and misfortune, as is anyone's. I had to make tough decisions without a guide, without anyone to help me. There were offers of support but trusting anyone in Alfara at that time irked me. In my eyes, they were still the people who tore me away from my family.

"Still, I had a reason to be happy at this point. Passing the tests meant I was in the army. And that meant I had my brother back, Vandir. But of course, like in all the old tragedies, the sweet taste of joy soon turned bitter in my mouth…"

"The theatre? Seriously?" Adam scoffed. "You remember what it was like last time, don't you? Two people dancing about on stage in masks reciting ancient Alfaran poetry of which neither of us understood a word of. The only ounce of fun I had was laughing at Marek mouthing along to every word and I presume he's not coming."

"He's not," Tavar said bluntly. Marek had dodged all his attempts at reconciliation since the final test. Three moons had passed. "Come on, this one is a modern play. Violence, romance, and in a language we can actually follow. And the best bit: it's free! Vandir got us tickets."

"If it's awful, then I'm never letting you decide on our plans ever again."

Tavar laughed and jumped on Adam's back with glee. "Deal. Meet you out the front of the barracks at sunset. I'll tell the others."

Tavar sat patiently on the bench out the front of the barracks he had called home for three moons. The evening sky was brushed with a pink that warmed him as he watched the sun drop below the horizon.

"You have such a dopey smile on your face right now." Tavar's grin grew as Carver took a seat next to him. "Haven't been on the whiskey again, have you?"

"Nope. Just feeling good for a change."

"For some reason, that terrifies me," Carver said, wrapping her black shawl around her shoulders and gazing out into the pink sky. "The others meeting us here?"

"Yeah, any moment now. In fact, here's Alice and Cassie." The two girls were giggling, both dressed in bright dresses with golden belts tied at their waist. Their silver embroidered niqabs draw the gaze to their dark eyes as their shawls swayed behind them in the light wind.

"Where's Adam?" Tavar asked, looking around for the final member of their group. "Thought he knew we were meeting at sunset."

"He's taking ages," Alice groaned. "Think he needs some help with his egal and ghutra. I've never known someone take so long to get ready!" The girls giggled again and even Carver smirked.

"Here he is," Cassie said, nudging Alice and looking over her shoulder. "Looks slightly wonky…"

"Don't say anything," Adam warned, breathing harshly through his nose and scowling at them all in turn. "Bastard thing doesn't sit right on my head." He cursed and pulled at the black egal holding the grey ghutra on his head.

"What brought this on?" Tavar asked, shocked with the traditional Alfaran dress on his pale friend.

Adam leaned in close so only Tavar could hear his response. "Heard the girls talking earlier. Cassie mentioned how much she likes traditional Alfaran dress. Thought I'd give it a go. Worth a shot."

Tavar ran his eyes over his friend, from the ghutra all the way down to the sandals on his feet. "Not too bad," he laughed. "It's a good look for you." He winked and clapped his friend on the back. "Come, it's time to go."

With the sun down, the walk to the theatre was much cooler. As they drew closer to the theatre, they blended into steady streams of people all dressed up and heading in the same direction. The crowd was a dazzling mix of bright colours highlighting the fashion of Alfara.

Some of the wealthier citizens wore silver and gold chains linked to their robes and even some from their ears and faces. One woman smiled at Tavar as he spotted a gold chain hanging from nostril to ear.

Still, there were some who made their way in carriages pulled by powerful horses, their windows blocked with deep red curtains to prevent the passengers from having to look out at those they deemed beneath them. Truly, the theatre was for all the people of Alfara.

"What's the show called?" Adam asked, his eyes peering up at the skewed egal once more.

"*Love Across Lines.* It's a famous play from Albion, apparently," Tavar replied.

"It's a good play. My father took me to see it to celebrate his promotion to ambassador." All eyes turned on Carver at these words. The reminder of her father's fate choked the air as they all struggled to respond. Adam looked away from Tavar, careful to miss his gaze.

"Well, I'm looking forward to it. If something can get through your stone heart then it will be interesting to see what happens to the blubber twins over here?" Tavar eventually said, pointing over at the twins.

"Hey, that was one time!" Alice shouted, hitting him on the shoulder.

"Yeah, and that was a sad tale. Nothing wrong with a few tears," Adam said, finally dropping his hands to his side and leaving his headwear, resigned to defeat. "Marek just has that sad voice that works perfectly with a tragedy."

The theatre, like most buildings in this part of the city, was a gaudy display of overindulgence and flamboyance. The round building was draped with golden banners that displayed the titles of historic plays held in the building. The banners hung on either side of the elaborate doors that were opened to the excited audience making their way in.

"I cannot believe this is the only way in," a thin, wiry man said to a beautiful, young woman on his arm. "There's no separation. We just head in with the riffraff. Most displeasing." Tavar inclined his head in greeted as the man passed, looking down his nose before quickening his strides.

The woman gave a shrill laugh as though the man had uttered the funniest joke she had ever heard. Such false laughter. Tavar marvelled at the fake display. It seemed that the higher up on the ladder you climbed, the more intricate the mask you had to wear.

"I don't know how you managed it," he said to Carver as she ambled along next to him, head raised high as though she belonged here. "I feel more nervous around these people than I do in the fighting square." He flattened his robe down and felt the moisture of sweat that had begun to pool. It was a cool evening: no chance he could blame it on the heat.

"There's a lot of shit involved, I'll give you that," Carver responded, glaring at an old man stroking his long, grey beard while eyeing her in a knowing way. A ghost from the past perhaps. "Thing about shit though, it falls. Better to be at the top than at the bottom. Otherwise you just end up covered in the stuff."

The steady stream heading into the theatre slowed as they reached the open doors. Six men and women stood in a semi-circle blocking their path, checking the paper tickets to ensure the right people were being allowed in.

"No pushing, my friends!" one of them bellowed.

He had braided his bright blue beard and decorated the ends with two silver bells that rang every time he moved his chin. "There is enough time for you all to enter before the greatest play of all time begins! One at a time please. That is a glorious headdress my dear. Fabulous beard, sir! Alfara truly has the greatest of people in all the known world!"

"And the acting begins…" Carver spat.

"I thought you liked the theatre?" Tavar said, pulling the tickets out from his pocket.

"I do. I like the stories. Doesn't mean I like the people."

The bell beard enthusiast continued to pander and entice the crowd. He pulled one woman in for an impromptu dance to the beat of the claps from the laughing audience. He called out compliments and tributes to many who passed him into the building and all with a wide toothy smile on his face. As Tavar drew closer, he could see the light of torches catch a golden tooth embedded next to the sparkling white.

"Ashkan ir Hamson." Tavar snapped his head to see who Carver was speaking to. An older man: grey beard and an elegant, fluted hat with silver trim. At the sound of Carver's voice, the man's eyes darted to her and then all around him, as though looking for anyone listening.

"Carver. Seeing you here is… unexpected," he said, rubbing at his neck that started to redden. The woman at his side peered out from her niqab with intelligent eyes.

"*Most* unexpected," the woman agreed with a voice that cut sharper than any sword.

Carver flinched and lowered her head. "My

father's blood has not dripped through the wall to stain me in such a manner that I cannot attend the theatre. I am a soldier in the Alfaran army. I fight to regain my honour."

"His blood runs through you, girl," the woman replied, her eyes unblinking. "And the people of Alfara do not forget the names of people on the wall." The man took out a golden cloth and dabbed at the sweat pooling on his brow.

"You often welcomed me into your home. I dined with you and your whole family, your daughters and sons," Carver said, voice shaking in a way Tavar had rarely heard before. "It saddens me that people I once called friends now look on me in the same way that they look at shit they have stepped into on the street."

Ashkan braved a look at Carver and then turned away again, as though merely looking at her may earn him a place on the wall. "We treated your whole family with the honour and respect the merciful one asks us to. For that, we were given only the actions of a traitor. The pain you feel is dealt by your father, girl. Do not reflect the blame onto us. Come, dear." He led his wife away through the crowd, begging forgiveness as he pushed his way through.

Carver stood still as the crowd started to pass her, not letting the tears forming in her eyes to drop.

"We don't have to go in," Tavar said softly. "Not if you don't feel up to it."

She sniffed and used her sleeve to wipe away the tears. When she lowered her arm, the hard mask had returned. She was the stoic, determined fighter he knew. She wasn't going to let anyone see how much she hurt. Carver was too proud for that. She may have fallen down that ladder but she wasn't going to let anyone see just how much shit she was in because of it.

"It's a good play. Father liked it. We will watch it and forget those bastards."

"Tickets! Hand in your tickets and you may pass through! Anyone without a ticket will not be allowed entry!"

They finally reached the front of the line. The bell beard man showed off his golden tooth with a wide smile and greeted Tavar and Carver like family as the twins and Cassie were squashed up behind them. "Good evening my brother and sister. Welcome to the Circle Theatre, world-renowned home to the greatest plays in the known world. Tickets, please."

He held out an expectant hand with fingers adorned by the most garish rings Tavar had seen in his life. Even some of the less respectable merchants he had grew up alongside on the road wouldn't have attempted to sell the monstrosities on this man's hand.

Tavar held back a chuckle and handed the five tickets over. The smile on the man's face faded as he counted the tickets and peered past Tavar at the uncomfortable trio behind him.

"Are these three with you?" he asked, looking askance at them.

"Yes. We're soldiers of the Alfaran army," Carver said, her voice menacingly lowered as she studied the change in the man's demeanour.

"Then you must know the rules. This play is only for the people of Alfara. There are no exceptions. No matter what you are wearing." His voice grew stern and heavy, laced with threat that warned Tavar there would be no arguing. However, Tavar had never really been a fan of letting things be.

"People of Alfara? We fight for Alfara. That's your exception right there." He felt the heat rising as the blood rushed to his face. "How can you—"

A sharp stamp on his foot broke him off and he turned to see Alice peering at him. "It's no problem at all. You two go in. Enjoy the show. We'll see you after."

Tavar wanted to fight back, to battle this injustice. Before he could say another barbed word, Alice and Cassie left, dragging away a confused and angry looking Adam with them. The crowd parted with curses uttered under breaths at the three foreigners pushing against them.

"Leave it. We're going in," Carver whispered to Tavar. She grabbed his wrist and gave a smile that even the most socially inept individual would not have been able to claim passed for warmth. Bells rang as the man looked away from them, satisfied that the matter had been dealt with.

She let go when they passed the staircase leading to the upper circle and found their seats on the floor in front of the raised circle where the performance would be held.

Tavar sat down on the crimson carpet, still flushed with frustration and annoyed at Carver for letting it go so easily. He thought she would have been up for any sort of fight at the moment.

"You realise he didn't bother to stop you gaining entry," Carver said matter-of-factly. "You look like one of us, especially next to those three."

"But I'm not," Tavar argued. Even as he said it, there was a shadow of doubt growing in his mind.

"Then where are you from? And your parents, what about them?" Carver pressed him.

Tavar shrugged, unable to give her a clear answer. "My parents were born on the road. When we spoke of heritage, we only spoke of the life of a traveller. They never mentioned any city, or nation for that matter." Saying it out loud, he realised how strange it was, to not belong anywhere. To have no knowledge of his roots.

"Rihla," Carver said under her breath, as though speaking to herself.

"What?"

"Rihla. They were a race of people with no home. They lived life between cities, always travelling. Some of the books in the Library of Wisdom speak of them. They once resided in a place near here before the founding of Alfara. That would explain your complexion and why that idiot couldn't see that you're not from here."

Tavar scratched at the buds of a beard growing on his cheek. He'd never given much thought to how he looked. Growing up in such a community gave him a blindness to some of the differences that some people in the city would see. He had known no different.

"You're still a stinking peasant in my book," Carver added, "but it's interesting, nonetheless."

"You're still a noble bitch with a stick up her arse. We all have our issues."

As the last of the audience members strolled into the theatre, candles were lit in their sconces in the centre of the circle, informing the waiting crowd that the show was about to begin.

The smell of tobacco caught Tavar's nostrils as a few members of the audience lit their pipes and sat back, ready to enjoy the evening's entertainment. The smoke rose to the upper circle where there was much more room for the elegant nobles to sit and enjoy the proceedings in more comfort, away from 'the riffraff'.

The flames circling the outside of the room blew out as the doors closed, darkening the room and focusing everyone's attention on the circle in the centre. The hairs on the back of Tavar's neck stood with anticipation as drums boomed throughout the room, slowly building to a crescendo as two figures walked onto the stage, one dressed in black with a white mask covering their face, the other in a white robe and black mask. They jumped and danced as more instruments began their instructions, guiding their movements.

Tavar risked a glance to his side and saw Carver's face illuminated in the firelight, entranced by the beautiful display, lips slightly parted. He felt his heart quicken and turned back to the two figures as they drew close before pushing one another away with the crash of a gong.

It felt as though he hardly drew in breath over the next two hours. He had never witnessed anything like it. The drama. The horror. The romance. The music. The movements. The tragedy. They all came together like pieces of a puzzle slotting together to make one final, dazzling display to capture the heart of anyone paying attention. The crowd beat their chest in appreciation as the players bowed and cheers rang out the theatre, from upper and lower circle each. In this case, Alfara was undivided, brought together by a wondrous display of beauty and heartache.

"Did you enjoy it?" Carver asked as Tavar followed the crowd out in a state of calm euphoria. It felt as though his every pore and nerve were alive with energy, tingling with the energy of the play.

"It was..." he struggled to find the right words for how he felt.

"Yeah, I know," Carver said before he could finish his sentence. "That's how I felt the first time."

"We have to see it again!" Tavar cried, steadying his breathing as they stepped out into the night. The full moon cast her serene glow over the city, surrounded by sparkling stars in the black canvas of the night sky.

A chilly breeze drifted through the crowd but Tavar hardly noticed, so energised was he from the performance. He found himself wondering what other magnificent pieces of entertainment he had missed whilst training in the square or lounging around the stables. This opened a whole new world for him. The smile drained from his face as he remembered the three friends who had missed out. The three friends who had been turned away because they didn't look like him.

"I take it that you enjoyed the show?" Vandir moved from the whitewashed wall he had been leaning against and stepped in front of Tavar.

In the last moon since Tavar had seen him, Vandir's beard had grown, black as oil and neatly shaped into a point at his chin: a reminder that he was a grown man now, no longer the child who had entered the city in chains.

"Amazing," Tavar admitted, still breathless. "Have you seen it?"

"Twice." Vandir peered out his hood at the two of them, his narrow right eye twitched at some disturbance in his thoughts. "I need to speak with you. Alone."

"I'll see you tomorrow," Carver said, giving a weak smile and heading off down the street in the moonlight. She was lost in amongst the crowd still leaving the theatre before Tavar could say goodbye.

"What in the four hells are you doing?" Vandir snapped, grabbing Tavar's shoulder and pulling him into an alleyway between two closed shops.

"What am *I* doing?" he bit back, wrestling away from his brother and patting down his robe.

"Carver ir Edemer," Vandir glowered back. "After how she treated you. The things she said about our parents. You're cosying up to her at a theatre. I thought you'd be with the others."

"I'm not cosying up to her. And the others weren't allowed in. No *outsiders*. Alfara only."

Vandir cursed and slapped his thigh, turning away into the shadows. "Shit. Should have known. Thought they'd let soldiers in. We look close enough to pass but I suppose Adam and Alice were stopped. No hiding what they are. Thought they'd be let in now they're in the army."

"Well they weren't. That's why it was just me and Carver."

"You shouldn't be friends with her. It won't end well," Vandir warned.

Tavar's face scrunched up as he laughed mockingly. "It won't end well. You do realise who *you* are friends with? She watched her father die on the wall yet she's still fighting for Alfara. Her closest friends deserted her as soon as she was seen as expendable and the only person who offered her the slightest bit of friendship was the person she'd hated for the last few years. It might not end well. But it can't get much worse for her."

Vandir groaned and rubbed at the new beard. He sighed and raised his hands in defeat. "It's your choice. Just don't come crying to me once it all blows up in your face. I warned you."

"Duly noted. You do pick your moments to act like a big brother, you know." The tone of Tavar's retort wasn't intended to be so bitter but the frustration of being away from the one surviving member of his family hurt. Vandir never explained what really happened when he was pulled away from the other recruits that first day. Tavar may as well have spoken to Pan about it for all the good it got him.

Vandir's face softened at the barb, a little bit of the fire in his eyes dimmed. "I'm just looking out for you. Even if it doesn't always seem that way."

"I know," Tavar said, already feeling ashamed for his remark. It wasn't Vandir's fault that things were like this. He was playing with the hand he'd been dealt, just like Tavar. "So why did you want to speak alone? Apart from giving me advice on who I can hang out with."

"Walk with me. I'll explain on the way." Vandir led Tavar through the shadows. Tavar didn't know the eastern quarter of Kessarine well. The area housed many of the labourers tasked with building the houses and buildings all across the city. Architects would be paid well for the beauty they added to the city but the actual workers carrying out the grand designs were given just enough to survive. Only a few of the men were walking the streets at this time, the others would be inside, resting ready for an early rise. The rows of mud-brick flats lined the empty street, a slum the city ignored that welcomed some of the desperate in Alfaran society: prostitutes, drug addicts, gamblers, and thieves. If you wanted a place to hide in the shadows, this was it.

"I'm heading out of the city tomorrow." The shock left Tavar speechless for a moment. He halted in the street, baffled.

"Where?" It was all he could manage, almost choking on the words.

"Hartovan. First wave of attacks with the Commander leading. His majesty wants this rebellion put down with haste. He's had enough."

Tavar's eyes rolled to his dirty boots. "That's... not good."

Vandir chuckled darkly. "Nope. Not unexpected though, if I'm honest. I've trained with the soldiers for long enough. What do you know of the four Judges?"

Tavar didn't know much if he thought about it. Their role in Alfara was to support the king with his decisions and ensure matters beneath him were dealt with swiftly and in the appropriate manner. That's what Marek had told him, at least. They were secretive figures, not often seen in the city outside of the major festivals.

"They help with the running of the country. That's about it."

"Thought so. That's all most people know. The problem is, they're the most important figures in all of Alfara. Think the Godking rules Alfara? Think again. And these four are true bastards. They focus on anything that will give them more power and influence. They don't care about the people of Alfara or anywhere else. If a million people had to die on the wall to make their life one step easier, then they would do it without flinching."

"Are you being serious?" Tavar asked, baffled. Surely such a thing would not go unnoticed in the busy city. The people worshipped their king as a god; to think that he was a puppet on strings by a shadowy cabal of four Judges would cause a riot that would destroy the city from the inside.

"I wish I wasn't." Tavar followed his brother as Vandir continued the journey, eyes looking out for any who may be lurking in the shadows. "The king is a front. He ensures the compliance of the commoners who worship him and do his bidding. The Judges roll him out hen needed as a reminder of what everyone is working towards. But that's it. Behind the veil of Godhood, they whisper and conspire to push the lives of people in this continent to however they see fit. It has to end."

"What does that have to do with us?" Tavar asked. The plan was to leave Alfara when they could. Not fight for it.

"Everything!" Vandir bellowed with a manic gleam in his eyes foreign to his brother. "It's not just about leaving Alfara. It's about making them pay for what they did to us. Making sure that no one else has to go through what we went through, what we're still going through! They hang people from the walls, Tavar! If there's even the slightest chance we can stop that, don't you think we should try?"

Tavar spread his palms in agreement, calming his brother. "I understand what you're saying, but what can we do?"

"Not what I can do. What *you* can do."

He scratched under his sleeve nervously and felt the skin on his arms burn. "Why me?"

"Because I trust you. You're family. And what we need to do is something that can't be given to a stranger." Vandir stopped outside of a plain building at the end of the street. A stray dog perked up at their coming, raising his head from a sleep and staring at them. Vandir stepped forwards and knocked on the wooden door three times before walking over to the dog. He gave it a scratch on the head that relaxed the animal as it returned to its rest.

"Who are we meeting?" Tavar asked, backing off, uneasy with the whole situation.

Before Vandir could answer, the door swung open, revealing a familiar face.

"Lieutenant Marcus…" Tavar muttered to himself, recognising the smiling man.

"Captain, now, actually," Marcus corrected him. "Would you like to come in?"

Vandir walked straight through as Marcus stood to the side to allow them entry. Tavar hung back, feeling itchy all over his body and not knowing what was awaiting him inside.

"Perhaps you would like to know why your brother invited you here, Tavar?" Marcus asked him, noticing his reluctance to enter. Tavar nodded and swallowed.

"It would be welcome."

"Has he not told you already?" Marcus laughed. "Look, Tavar, you have two choices. Walk away and head back to the barracks and forget any of this happened. Or you can come inside and discuss a plan we have made."

"What plan?" Tavar asked though he wasn't entirely sure if he wanted to know.

"A plan to kill a god." Blunt and straight to it. "It's time to breathe new life into Alfara, and we want you to be a part of it."

Tavar stepped inside and Marcus closed the door behind him, cutting him off from the empty streets.

CHAPTER ELEVEN: THE PUPPET KING

He could be trusted. They'd known each other for long enough now; they'd shared secrets and spent time together in the same way siblings would.

Tavar smiled and waved, watching Hashem approach with the horse. The stable boy grinned and waved back, upping his pace as he spotted Tavar, pulling the lazy horse along with him. Behind Hashem, Tavar could see busy streets of people leaving the temples following afternoon prayer, all rushing about, lost in their own drama. His own thoughts were lost in a storm of uncertainty.

Tavar stifled a yawn. He'd struggled for sleep upon returning to the barracks. The meeting with Marcus and Vandir felt like some kind of hazy dream, one which he was keen to forget. They had discussed the plan. Marcus had grown tired of the controlling nature of Alfara and the iron grip with which the four Judges used to rule to nation from the shadows. To bring them into the light, Marcus and a select group of like-minded individuals felt that killing the king would bring the four into the light, exposing them and leading to an uprising that could change the face of Alfara for the better. There would be casualties and chaos in the short term but the long term goal was freedom for the people of Alfara.

Tavar had already been pushed to breaking point here. Marcus then told him the part he expected Tavar to play. He was to be the cup bearer during the king's meeting with the four Judges and the city's council.

Marcus would ensure that a poison he had procured from the apothecary would find its way into the king's cup. Then, it was up to Tavar to ensure that the king drank its contents.

He shuddered at his recollection of the meeting. Even in the light of day it gave him the shivers. He shook his body again as though expelling a possessive djinn and forced the smile back onto his face as Hashem welcomed him into the stables.

"Wasn't expecting to see you today. No training?" Hashem asked.

"Not until later. I wanted to speak to you about something," Tavar said, nervously picking at the navy thread lining his cuffs.

"Oh?" Hashem raised an eyebrow and led the horse past its gate and pulled out a carrot from the net hanging from the wall beside him. "What's that?"

Struggling on how to form his question, Tavar made a series of gurgled noises. "Er... erm..."

"Spit it out!" Hashem snorted, laughing at his struggle.

Tavar breathed in and rubbed the bridge of his nose. "I've been in Alfara a while now. But there's not much that I truly know about it. I want to learn more. Starting with the king – King Uhlad."

Hashem scratched at the stubble forming on his chins and widened his eyes at this. "Bit of a shock. Suddenly you have interest in our history. Thought you just wanted out."

Tavar raised his shoulders and lowered his gaze. "Wouldn't hurt to know a bit more about where I live; even if I don't plan on staying."

"True," Hashem admitted, grabbing the bag of vegetables and fruit and closing the gate behind him. "Although, I must say, Marek would have been the best person to talk to…"

Tavar gave him a scathing look, knowing exactly what Hashem was attempting. "Not happening. He's made his views clear. Stubborn bastard is as immovable as an Imari Rhino. I'm not the one who overreacted and threw a tantrum." He felt the heat rise to his cheeks as he folded his arms, not wanting to budge from his decided stance.

"That's your decision," Hashem opened his palms and continued to feed the horses, stepping past Tavar and breathing sharply through his teeth. "Shame though, that's all I'm saying."

"So, do you think you can help me out?" Tavar asked, eager to steer the conversation away from his lost friend.

"Yeah, of course. Those of us who attend daily prayer know all there is to know about the king. Wouldn't do you any harm in showing your face once or twice, you know!"

"Don't start." They had already exhausted the argument of Tavar's faith and he had no intention of bringing it up again and pushing another of his friends away.

"Okay, okay. Take a seat, you might as well get comfortable if I'm going to teach you. Though, those scholars in the army need to take a good hard look at themselves. Teaching you history, reading, writing, and war games is all well and good but your life in the capital of Alfara – the least they could do is help you brush up on the history of our royal family."

Tavar found a haystack and pushed it against the wall near a grateful Pan who hung her head over ready for a scratch.

"As you know, Alora Mazta, all hail them, is the god we have worshipped since the beginning of time. Alora created the world in four days. They created the seas and rivers first, then the sands and land for people to live upon. They created the sun and stars for light and warmth and the moon to watch over us at night. At first, all was good. Life thrived and world was used as intended. Then, war crept in. Brothers and sisters, mothers and fathers, sons and daughters. All were caught up in the bloodshed. The Great One, Alora Mazta, ever wise, made a plan. She sent the Izads. Divine beings who would set an example to their followers and lead the world to a bountiful future of plenty."

"And Uhlad," Tavar said, remembering the reliefs carved into the library walls, "he is one, isn't he? An Izad."

Hashem nodded. "The royal line of Alfara is divine. Our first monarch, Queen Tamira is said to be the great granddaughter of the First of the Izads, Ahmed the Learned. The whole of the western region recognises this as truth. It's why we have not warred with the nations on this side of the continent in generations."

"What about the eastern side?"

Hashem paused for a moment and dropped the vegetables on the ground, frowning as he turned to Tavar. "We're not really meant to talk about it…"

"Hashem, please. We're friends."

"After a long, deep breath out, Hashem began, voice shaking. "Merely speaking of it could be seen as blasphemy. During the time of Queen Tamira, a rogue female warrior, whose name I will not speak, travelled the land spreading lies. She claimed that the Izads are false – that they were merely djinn trapped in human form and that they needed to be defeated if humans were to have any kind of freedom. Queen Tamira sent her army after her and the two sides met in battle. Eventually, the Queen's First killed the blasphemer and the nation of Alfara grew from the ashes of the battleground. Kessarine sits on the hill where the blood was spilled."

"And you truly believe that Uhlad is divine, an Izad sent from Alora Mazta?" Tavar had to asked, eager to know what his friend truly believed.

"I do. He is a good king, a wise ruler. Kessarine and Alfara has thrived in his reign, young though he is. I disagree with the wall and the torture but I'm a stable boy, Tavar. Who am I to question the methods of the divine?"

Tavar picked at the dirt under his fingernails and stopped for a moment, pausing to carefully measure his next words, not wanting to offend his friend. "What would happen if he was to die? There is no heir. What would happen to Alfara?"

Hashem bristled at the mere suggestion, clearly taken aback by the abruptness of the question. "Die? He can't. He is divine. His time ends when the Holy One decides and that will not happen until there is an heir. The bloodline cannot end. Such an event doesn't bear thinking about." He shook off his own ghosts of worry and sat down, steadying himself.

"Don't you think it strange, though? My family travelled across the continent. Each place we went to had their own gods to worship, their own customs and culture. Each one believes that their way is the correct one, the righteous one and that all others are wrong. How do you know that your one is correct?"

"Faith," Hashem simply replied, face stern with confidence and determination in his answer. "Asking for proof would be sinful of me. I have faith in my god and the Izads and they show me my path, though it may be unclear at times. Other people may have their own beliefs, their own paths. It is not my place to question them. I must do what I can to end up at the correct destination for me. Anything else would be cursed. I will end up where I am meant to, God willing."

"Don't you sometimes think Uhlad is just a man? I've seen him torture people on the wall. There's nothing divine about that."

"Our faith is tested in strange ways: that is one such way. I may not see the divine at all times but I believe that he is making Alfara a strong and better place. The second I stop believing that, my world descends into a pit of despair. It is how it is," Hashem finished with a shrug.

"I guess so." Tavar stood and cracked his aching back. He nudged his head against Pan's and slapped a hand against the mare's neck, offering a loving farewell. He'd got what he came here for but was still wracked with indecision of how he would proceed that night. The task he had been given would have devastating consequences whether he succeeded or not. There was no middle ground to be had here. If the Godking survived the night or not, there would be deaths. Uhlad's death would lead to an uprising to seize the throne from the Judges. If he lived, more people in Hartovan and Alfara would suffer.

His thoughts lingered on his older brother, currently travelling across the sands to Hartovan to fight in a war he never wanted, a war he had no part in. With just a small vial of poison, Tavar could ensure that Vandir came back from Hartovan sooner than expected. They could run away together using the chaos as a distraction.

They could be free.

He bid Hamesh thanks and farewell and left the stables, contemplating what was to be done.

"I was worried." Marcus exited the shadows of the summer palace and pulled Tavar in close. "Didn't think you were going to turn up."

"Neither did I," Tavar admitted, feeling a sudden chill that had nothing to do with the evening heat.

"Think about all of the people you will be setting free with this one action. Think about your brother. Uhlad has tortured hundreds on the wall over the past few years alone, going along with whatever those Judges command. Take him out and the ladder falls."

The palace boundary was littered with statues of the great stories – legends of Alfara. The apparent ancestors of Uhlad were portrayed defeating monsters and outwitting enemies in marble form. The statues stood between great columns that rose a hundred feet high, holding up the pyramid like roof of the building that Tavar remembered Marek informing him was a relic of the friendship between Alfara and the ancient nation of Pacia.

Silent guards holding deadly spears stood watch, unmoving like the statues beside them as Tavar struggled to keep pace. Marcus turned inside between two of the guards who saluted as he passed and entered past an open side door to the palace. The corridor was narrow and lined with ensconced torches that lit up a path full of reliefs of great battles over history that Tavar, to his surprise, was able to remember from his classes.

"Remember," Marcus said, keeping his voice low as he searched the dancing shadows of the corridor. "Do not look directly at the Judges or the king when they speak to you. Head bowed at all times. Never instigate a conversation and hang back until you are called to serve. Being allowed in this room during a meeting of the four is an honour not bestowed upon anyone. Your brother worked hard for this opportunity and now he has passed it onto you. Don't mess this up," he warned, voice sharp and threatening.

Tavar nodded as a wave of nausea hit him. Each step on the crimson rug beneath him was a step closer to death.

"There will be two other servants in the room. They are also soldiers, only those who are trained to fight may be in the presence of the four and the king during these meetings, in case of attack. Two Immortals will be waiting outside. They will only enter if the king calls." Marcus halted and motioned for Tavar to do likewise. "Take this." He passed a small glass vial of red liquid into Tavar's trembling hand, eyes darting either side of the corridor to lookout for any witnesses. Happy that there were none, he continued. "Make sure it goes into the king's goblet. Silver and blue. You'll know it. The Judges drink only from their golden cups." He placed a hand on Tavar's shoulder and Tavar suddenly realised how much he had grown. No longer did he have to look up to stare into the man's eyes.

"What will happen if I'm caught?" he asked, stomach turning as Marcus flinched at the question.

"Don't get caught…" Easy for him to say. He

205

wasn't the one taking the risk.

"Why are you doing this, Marcus?" Tavar asked, his skin tingled as though a thousand pins were stabbing into him. "Honestly."

A dark shadow crossed the man's face and he paused.

In that moment, Tavar felt he saw a hint of sadness and regret in the soldier's face.

"Let's just say I have a lot to make up for. And this is the first step. Go on," he waved Tavar down the corridor clutched at his neck nervously. "Climb the stairs. It's the door at the top. You'll know which one. Two golden guards either side of it." Immortals. "Good luck."

Tavar's heart hammered as he passed the silent Immortals. Their dark eyes stayed on him from when he reached the top of the stairs to when he was welcomed through to the kitchens by the head servant, a thin, energetic, balding man with a moustache that curled at the corners above his thin lips.

"You must be the new soldier. Sent by the major," the man said, snapping his fingers and beckoning Tavar into the kitchens. "Come, come! Haste is paramount this evening, his majesty and his most welcome guests do not suffer lethargy and laziness."

A team of men and women were busying themselves with a variety of ingredients. The smell of spices and herbs wafted throughout the room and forced a rumble from Tavar's stomach.

"I hope you have already eaten. There won't be time for such activities until after your tasks are over and that may not be until dawn depending on the judgement of the masters." Tavar had eaten but he'd brought up the kebab and bits of bread he'd managed to force down his throat.

"Their fast will be broken with date, as is custom. Following that, each dish will be ordered on this table when they are due to be delivered to his majesty. Do not let me catch you taking the wrong dish at the wrong time." The servant pinched the bridge of his nose and leant against the table he had pointed out to Tavar, as though struggling through a painful ulcer. "It's happened before. You don't want to know how it was dealt with. These Judges are powerful people. You do not want to upset them. That is all I am willing to say. If you follow instructions and keep your mouth shut then you will make your way out of this without a scratch, God willing." The servant stood tall, his eyes measuring every inch of Tavar. "In my haste I have forgotten my manners. How coarse of me! My name is Ahmed ir Akahn. I am the head servant in the palace in charge of the fastidious running of all items relating to the king and this palace. What shall I call you?"

"Tavar," his voice croaked from its lack of use since biding Marcus farewell. "Tavar Farwan."

"Farwan…" Ahmed repeated, tilting his head and rubbing twisting the corner of his moustache. "Not often are we sent Farwans to assist in serving in such important meetings. I wouldn't have noticed if you didn't say anything. I can see it now though, slightly lighter skin." The head servant snapped out of his thought with a slap on the table and sprang away, motioning for Tavar to keep up.

"These three young gentlemen will be joining you in your task. You've each been assigned a guest,

Tavar, yours is the king, as requested by Marcus. God knows why in his infinite wisdom so I shall not ask. Now, get dressed into your robes," Tavar attempted to hide a ripped sleeve from the servant's scan but by the look on his face, he had failed, "and then we shall begin. Haste, remember boy, haste!"

Tavar changed as fast as he could, welcoming the pockets sewed into the hips of the robe that allowed him to keep the vial hidden with ease. The robe was tighter than he expected. With pride he marvelled at the way it accentuated the muscles in his body that had grown with the tougher training he had endured since passing as a soldier.

He pulled the navy skull cap onto his head and pressed against the creases on his top, ensuring that he looked as good as possible. Pausing, he checked his beating heart, slowing his breathing in an attempt to stay calm. It felt impossible, like swinging a sword to stop a sandstorm. The futility of it weighed on him like a physical entity. He felt suddenly envious of Hashem. In times like this, the stable boy could pray to a god he felt would assist him in such matters. But Tavar didn't have the faith for such a thing. He was all alone.

Remembering the call for haste, Tavar left the small, dark room where he had been told to change and wandered back into the kitchen. Ahmed was nowhere to be seen. Most likely he was ensuring that preparations for the table were running smoothly. The three other servants for the evening stood together. Tavar felt a strange sense of relief at the worried expressions on their faces. He wasn't the only one struggling, though surely for different reasons.

"Tavar, isn't it?" One of them asked, scared eyes looking out under huge bushy eyebrows. Tavar nodded, his mouth tasting like he had swallowed a pile of sand. "I know your brother, Vandir. My name is Rashid."

Rashid placed a hand across his chest in welcome and Tavar mimicked the action with respect.

"This is Youssef," Rashid said, pointing at bearded young man to his side who repeated the respectful greeting. "And this here is Salim." Salim had a shaven head and wore a small ring in his left ear.

"Have you done this before?" Tavar asked, eager to continue the conversation and keep distracted from what he had been asked to do.

"Salim and I have done this twice before. Youssef once," Rashid answered. "It is an honour; praise be to God. Though, the Judges can be…" An elbow from Youssef shut him up mid-sentence.

Ahmed stormed into the room, interrupting the conversation and the four of them stood as one to attention.

"They are almost here. Rashid, dates on the table. Salim, pipes need to be ready for the Judges but his majesty will not partake this evening. Youssef, plates need to ready. And Tavar," Ahmed stared straight into his eyes, ensuring that he was listening and focused. "Water for all of them to be start. The wine can wait until the main course arrives. They will need a clear head for their meeting." He clapped his hands and raced away to greet the honourable guests.

The three servants raced away, each intent on their own individual tasks and all sense of teamwork and belonging flashed away from Tavar. "Water, water, water," he muttered to himself, looking around for the jug and cups.

The meeting room was unlike anything Tavar had

seen in his life. An unnecessarily long table stood in the centre of the ornately decorated room, covered with golden cloth that hung low from the edges, brushing against the crimson rug covering the stone floor. The ceiling was high; at least 30 paces high by his estimation and carved into the ceiling were various animals: elephants, tigers, lions and even a bear. Tavar thought he could spot a meaning within the carvings relating to an old fable Marek had once spoke of but he didn't have time to confirm his belief. He had a job to do.

Ignoring the urge to glance up at the table or stare at the four silver bull sculptures watching from each corner of the room, Tavar kept his eyes low, only looking up to pour water from his jug into the cups of the four powerful Judges seated around the table.

His actions allowed him to notice small details about the men. King Uhlad sat at the head of the table at the far end. He was dressed in a simple sand coloured robe and sat back in a large silver throne topped with a silver falcon that seemed to perch above his head. His arms sat on his thighs, his body rigid and uncomfortable as he listened to the words of the four men sat on either side of the table. Two on the left. Two on the right. He did not look like a man settled within his surroundings. He was more like a caged beast, looking for an exit.

The four Judges were more at ease in this environment than the king. They each wore navy turbans wrapped around their heads that sat above silver masks covering most of their face. Each had white beards that fell onto their silk black robes. At the end of their baggy sleeves, Tavar spotted that they wore golden bangles circled around their wrists. Only one of them could he get a good look at as he poured the water, it had green emerald stamped into the centre that shone as the candlelight fell upon it, casting a green light dancing across the wall to the side.

"The Emperor of Hondai sends his regards," the one with the green emerald said to the king. His voice was deep and controlled, booming through the room though the volume was low. "The troubles in Okada have settled down and trade has resumed as normal. The deals we have in place will continue as normal and there will be no interruption of supplies."

"Good. Good," the king replied almost absent-mindedly. Tavar risked a glance and saw the king nodding as though to himself before continuing. "At our last meeting you spoke of raiders in the desert; opportunistic bandits who were using our distracted gaze to take advantage and rob the merchants crossing the Undying Sands. How have things progressed?"

Tavar stood in the shadows of the room, as he had been told to do, eyes averted from the five men in the room as he listened to their conversations. He had wondered why the men would allow soldiers in the room to listen into an important discussion but Marcus had put his mind at ease. They were the most powerful men in the land; they believed beyond all doubt that any leaks would be deal with most severely. Most of the population worshipped the king as a god and respected the Judges above their own families. On top of all that, this was a preliminary meeting, the real business would be conducted the following day at dawn in the Closed Halls. Servants, including Ahmed, would be forbidden from such meetings.

"A small unit was sent earlier in the week to deal with these fleas bothering us." This time another Judge spoke. His voice dripped with honey as it sang through the room. "It won't be long before the raids end and our people will be able to make the passing across the sands with confidence once more."

The Judge next to him stroked his tidy, white beard and agreed. "As my esteemed brother has said, they are mere fleas annoying us, a pest we can finish with ease. The real issue is in stamping out the insects causing damage in Hartovan." Tavar noted with interest the way in which the king leaned forward onto the table and brought his hands up, pressing them together as he stared at the Judge.

The king cleared his throat and asked, "And how *is* the campaign progressing in the rebel land?" He drank from his cup, finishing the water in own long gulp before clicking his fingers. Tavar almost stumbled in his haste to refill the cup.

"We dispatched another unit following morning prayer today. The rebels are proving obstinate and appear determined to barricade the city until we give into their demands. I suggest we move from small skirmishes to an all-out attack on the city. They have defied us for long enough. We must show the strength and might we possess in the glory of the Izads and Alora Mazta. If we must send more units then so be it. It would be unwise to show any sign of weakness now that the eastern nations have called for an end to fighting. The Warmaster of Sarin gets itchy feet in times of peace. He will be looking for their next target. We need to ensure that it is not us and God willing it will not be."

"God willing," the other men repeated.

Tavar backed into the shadows as the king sat back in his chair, eyes on the glass of water in front of him.

"You have something else you wish to ask, your

majesty," the fourth Judge asked. His voice sounded like stone, hard and immovable. The Judge was broader than the others and his beard was not completely white but speckled still with bits of black from his youth. Seemingly younger than the other judges, Tavar still felt there was an aura of command that was almost palpable around the judge. "Speak."

The king scratched at his head and ran a hand through his black hair. He was the only one with uncovered hair in the room – perks of being an Izad.

"Hartovan always held a special place in my grandmother's heart. It would pain me to see the city destroyed when there may be other, less violent ways to solve the issue. Have all such options been exhausted thus far? Alora Mazta shall guide us, hopefully onto the righteous path."

"You have shown unusual affection for the city. As king, you cannot let that affection blind you," the commanding Judge snapped. Tavar caught himself, stopping a gasp from escaping. He never expected anyone to speak to the king in such a blunt manner. Even more shocking, was the way in which the king slumped into his chair, defeated. Like a dog, he was ready to roll over and accept defeat.

"You are right, Judge. As always. Send another two units at the end of this moon. I want this problem over with. It has pained me for too long."

Tavar dared a peek at the king and caught him looking exhausted, as though he had run the length of Market Street and twice round the bazaar. Sweat dripped down his brown skin and he stared at the table, lost in his own thoughts. Tavar pitied him. Marcus was right. He was a man without control. He would be rolled out and forced to play to crowds but there was nothing he could do. He was a puppet with no chance of cutting the strings.

"I believe I shall I have some wine," the king murmured. Tavar dropped his gaze to his own bare feet and listened for the click of fingers. "Wine, servant. Ahmed will know which one. I'll have it in my room. There is a foul shadow lingering over me this evening. Judges, I will meet with you at first prayer, God willing."

"God willing."

Tavar spun away at the click of the fingers and pushed past the door, heart beating fast enough that he could feel the blood booming around in his skull. He placed a hand on the scratched wooden table next to him, steadying himself as his head pounded.

"They're leaving already…" The blood drained from Rashid's face. "The food…"

"Ahmed!" One of the Judges called.

Ahmed rushed towards the meeting room at the sound of his name. "Tavar. Ready the wine for his majesty but do not take it through just yet. Wait for me. The rest of you, patience. I will see what our masters want us to do."

In all the commotion, Tavar grabbed the bottle of wine he had been told to use by Marcus. Checking to be certain no one was watching him, he unclasped the bottle top and lowered the wine beneath the table, hurriedly pouring the contents of the vial into the wine. His hands were clammy and sweat dripped into his eyes, burning them.

Tavar jumped with fright as Ahmed bowled back into the kitchen, hands rubbing furiously together as he struggled to keep to an air of elegant assurance.

"The Judges have left. The food we have

prepared is not needed. I suggest you help yourselves. An unexpected treat, I'm sure." The three soldiers cheered and clasped hands, amazed at their good fortune. No more pressure of serving and food better than they had ever had in their life. They were living a dream. "But not you." Ahmed pointed at Tavar, the smile dropping from his face.

"What shall I do?" Tavar asked, steeling himself for the response.

"His majesty has retreated to his chambers to rest. He has asked that you take him his wine and sit with him. This is not too unusual, though I have no idea why he has chosen you. Help him with anything he needs and do not embarrass me or yourself. God willing we can make it through the night without further incident."

The other soldiers were kind enough to look sheepishly at him. Tavar bid them farewell and calmed his breathing. Then he took the wine and walked through the meeting room, continuing through the now open door at the back of the room and into the king's chambers.

It took a while for Tavar to start breathing again. The room assaulted his senses with a wide mix of colours and scents, making him sway as he struggled to fix his eyes on any one thing. In front of him, the room guided his gaze to a large four poster bed with open sapphire-coloured curtains. At least six people could have lay in the bed with room to spare. Such decadence was befitting of a king and Tavar caught himself wondering who the king shared such a grand bed with. Surely sleeping alone in such a monstrosity would be a waste.

His mind flittered to thoughts of who he would share such a bed with and he was shocked by the image of Carver flashing first, that wicked smile of hers with the corner of her lips rising to greet and welcome him into the

215

comfort of...

No. He shook his head and ignored the scent of the perfumed oils attacking his senses. He placed the tray with the bottle of wine down on a round, oak table to his side and poured the deadly wine into the king's jewel encrusted goblet, hands shaking the whole time.

"Leave the wine for a moment." Tavar jumped, almost knocking the table over at the sound of the king's voice coming from a steam filled room to his side. "Join me in here. Speaking to oneself is ever so boring and slightly concerning. Ears to listen is all I ask for."

Tavar took a deep breath and peered through the steam, walking slowly and carefully as it blinded him. The smell reminded him of the public bathhouses in the city. The men would sit and bathe together and talk of whatever nonsense was on their minds. Tavar had a suspicion that most of them visited the bathhouses as an excuse to spend time away from their wives as men and women were separated upon entry.

The hot vapour settled on his skin as he entered the room. It was warm, almost unbearably so. Suddenly he became aware of the lack of water he had had that day; he'd been too busy worrying about his task that such things had seemed unimportant. How he wished he'd have taken just a small drink before leaving.

As his eyes adjusted, Tavar peered through the steam and saw that the floor had been lowered to enable access into a large bath similar to the ones in the city. It was rectangular in shape with circular holes cut into the edges which he assumed was for drainage. Most likely, there would be some kind of heating system beneath the bath to ensure the water was the correct temperature. The life of a king.

"Incredible, isn't it?" The king asked from the far side of the bath. His dark-haired chest sat above the lapping water as his slim but muscular body rested against the side, arms wide out and elbows leaning on the edge as he stared straight at Tavar.

Tavar averted his gaze, unable to decide on the best course of action. "Y-yes, your majesty," he stuttered.

Uhlad pushed back his wet hair and closed his eyes before dropping beneath the water. He stayed beneath the surface for such a time that Tavar felt uncomfortable, undecided over what he should be doing. Finally, the king broke the surface, his chest rising and falling quickly as he gasped for air. His brown skin had reddened with the heat of the water and he lay back against the side once more, staring over at Tavar.

"Join me." A command. From the king.

"Y-your majesty," Tavar stammered again, frantically searching for a way out of the situation.

"Cut the shit," the king snapped. "I'm your king. And I wasn't asking you a question."

Seeing no way around it, Tavar slowly slipped out of his robe, turning away from the king as he undressed before sliding into the warm water. He took a calming breath as his body adjusted to the heat and relaxed as he looked over at the King of Alfara. An Izad made flesh.

"Now. That wasn't so difficult was it?" Uhlad said, grinning.

"No, your majesty."

Uhlad's dark eyes scanned Tavar, searching for something. "Tell me, soldier. Where are you from? At first, I thought you from Alfara but there is something odd, something different that leads me to think otherwise. I know my people. Tell me your story."

Tavar tried to keep the suspicion from his face but was unsure of his success. He dipped his shoulders beneath the water and wondered what he should tell the king. Eventually, he felt lying would place him in a trap of which he could not escape. Use as much of the truth as you can without compromising yourself. That's what he had been taught by Oden when discussing interrogation techniques. Every solider needed to know that.

"My family were merchants. I was born on the road and brought to Alfara after my parents were… after they lost their lives."

"They were murdered," Uhlad bluntly added, stepping in. "There is no need for an elegant dance of words with me. I know the harsh realities of life, even sat up here in this palace of gold and silver, a king must be able to understand his people."

"Yes, they were murdered. By Alfaran soldiers," Tavar said, voice cracking at the memory, at the screams that echoed in his head.

Uhlad bristled as his cheeks ballooned with air before he blew out a long, hard breath, shaking his head. "You have my sympathy. What is your name?"

"Tavar. Tavar Farwan."

"Well, Tavar. Life can be cruel. Your parents were killed by soldiers of Alfara and now here you are, a soldier of Alfara. The irony of the divine never ceases to amaze me. Such humour is beyond most mortals, I'm afraid. Tell me, how do you feel about Alfara? This nation that has forced you to adopt it as your home."

Tavar looked away and thought. "I've never felt of it as my home," he answered honestly. "Cities are cramped, loud, stinking places of corruption and deceit. The road, the paths travelled by the merchants and the adventurers, that is my real home."

"A good answer. One that I would have assumed beyond your years. How do you feel living in *this* city?"

"Trapped. It isn't my choice to be here." Tavar paused, thinking about his time in Alfara. It wasn't all bad, just as Hashem had told him. "But I've made great friends and learnt a lot."

"Every scar is a lesson," Uhlad said, more to himself than to Tavar. "That's what my father used to love telling me, before he passed on." He seemed lost in a haze of old memories before snapping out of it and looking back at Tavar with a smile. "You said you felt trapped. Would it surprise you to know that I too, feel trapped?"

Tavar nodded, unable to keep himself from scanning the elaborate decorations and vibrant colours of the personal bath. Many people would kill to be trapped in such luxury.

"It is beautiful, I agree," Uhlad said, realising Tavar's thoughts by following his eyes. "Yet a bird in a golden cage is still in a cage. As comfortable as that bird's life is, he would still yearn for the freedom of the skies." The king sighed, dropping his gaze, and splashing a hand against the surface of the water. "Most people feel like I have the most power in the kingdom. It is a lie. You have friends, Tavar. People who cherish you and your company. People who you can laugh and play with. That is greater than all of the riches and power in the world."

The sad tone of the royal caught Tavar off guard and he found himself struggling to respond appropriately. "Surely you have friends, your majesty?"

"Bah! Friends are a weakness, apparently. I had one once…" Uhlad stuttered and Tavar's eyes narrowed as he noticed a change in the king, the shadow of a pain left in the wild to fester. "He was the greatest friend I could have ever wished for. When I drift off to sleep, I can still see his beautiful, dark eyes. Such eyes you could get lost into for hours without regret…"

"What happened? Tavar asked, eager to learn more.

Uhlad tensed, eyes lost in the distant memory as his lips quivered. "Such a friendship was forbidden for a king. He was banished. A heart-breaking choice but one that was better than the wall."

"Was there nothing that you could have done?"

"A king has a duty to his people, to his kingdom. This duty is more important than the whims of one man. I had no choice. Though, that is no comfort to me. If I could give you one piece of advice, Tavar Farwan, it would be this: either love so much that you never let it go, you fight for it until your dying day. Or don't love at all. Anything in between will just rip your heart out."

An uncomfortable silence hung in the steam around them as Tavar struggled for an appropriate response. However he had expected his night to turn out, it was a far cry from this.

"My apologies. You were sent here with orders to bring me wine. Yet, here you are, listening to the melancholic ramblings of your king. I appreciate the companionship. It is good to talk." Uhlad rubbed his eyes and regained his composure, pulling his shoulders back as an air of power, fake or not returned. "Now, how about we share some of that wine you brought me?" He pulled himself up from the edge of the bath, unashamedly naked and grabbed at a towel resting on a chair. "Come, Tavar. You have earned a drink as reward for listening to your king."

Unable to think of an excuse to turn down the invitation, Tavar lifted himself from the water and caught a towel thrown to him from Uhlad. He dried off and hurriedly changed back into his robe and carefully wrapped a headdress on, heart pounding the whole time.

Entering the next room, he saw that the king was dressed in a purple robe but with nothing to cover his dark and still damp hair. Uhlad sat in a chair, one leg crossed over the other and the goblet of wine in his hand, ready. He gestured towards an empty seat for Tavar.

Tavar begrudgingly took the seat, foot tapping against the floor nervously. He glanced at the other cup on the table, filled to the brim with red wine. Poisoned red wine.

"Shall we make a toast. It is customary in the east. The people of Albion do it at weddings and birthdays, I believe. Perhaps we can do one." Uhlad raised his goblet in the air. "To freedom, wherever we may find it."

Tavar raised his own cup, growing hot as Uhlad's unblinking gaze bore through him. He knew. He had to. Shit.

"It is customary in Alfara, for guests to take the first drink," Uhlad informed him, a smile appearing on his thin lips.

"I-I'm sorry," Tavar mumbled. "I can't. Alcohol doesn't sit well with me." It was the best he could do. A last throw of the dice.

Uhlad placed his goblet on the table and leant further forward, staring at Tavar with a measured gaze.

221

There was nothing sympathetic about him now. He'd replaced the morose suffering royal with a cunning, tricky bastard. Somehow he knew.

Faster than a falcon in flight, Uhlad slapped a hand across the table and sent the contents of the bottle and his goblet flying across the room. Tavar jumped up instinctively, throwing his own glass in the air as the adrenaline coursed through his body. Uhlad still sat on his seat, eyes now staring up at Tavar.

"Sit."

Tavar sat down, breathing heavily and keeping his own gaze on the king.

"It was poisoned, wasn't it?" Uhlad asked, though it didn't feel much of a question. "Do not lie to me."

"Yes." There was no use fighting it now. Give him as much truth as necessary without compromising the situation.

"You've got balls. I have to admit that," Uhlad said, impressed. "It seems that a promotion wasn't enough to stop Marcus trying to end my life again."

Tavar was taken aback by the revelation. "*Again?*" he asked before reprimanding himself for giving away too much information.

"You can relax, Tavar Farwan," Uhlad said, sitting back and offering a genuine smile that was in complete contrast to how Tavar was feeling right now. "I know what it feels like to be a puppet. Marcus and his allies can be convincing. Especially to soldiers who have a grudge against Alfara. I understand your desire for revenge, though I had no part to play in your parents' deaths."

"What will you do with me?" Tavar asked, unable to keep the fear from his voice. The faces of those suffering on the wall made his mouth run dry. An attempt on the king's life would surely bring a punishment even worse than that.

"I will give you an opportunity," Uhlad said.

Tavar nodded, willing to accept anything at this point to stay away from the wall.

"Alfara is a better place than you believe. There are nations that belittle women in the interest of men, nations who kill men if they dress in clothes not deemed acceptable for them, nations who kill people if you don't worship in the correct way. Alfara is not like this. We have our problems, problems which I have tried, in vain thus far, to resolve. I am one man and as I mentioned, I am trapped in the role of king."

"The Judges…" Tavar muttered, thinking back to what Marcus had told him.

Uhlad nodded. "They are the real power. Though, I have longed for a time where I can have real power, where I can make a real change to Alfara and its people. With your help, I may be able to make it happen."

"What can I do to help?"

"I need you to find someone for me, an ex-soldier of Alfara who is assisting Hartovan. He has evaded capture for years but if you could go as part of your unit, perhaps you will be able to secretly pass on a message to those hiding him."

"Who is he?" Tavar asked, shocked to find he was willing to help Uhlad.

"He is the reason for Marcus trying to kill me. His brother, the friend I was forced to banish. The one person I have ever loved. Pass on my message and together, perhaps we can take down these Judges and fly from the cages we are trapped in. Do this for me, and I will give you your freedom, Tavar Farwan."

Freedom. It's all he had ever wanted. There wasn't even a hint of hesitation.

"What message shall I pass on?

CHAPTER TWELVE: BREAKING POINT

His clothes stuck to his damp skin as Tavar jogged through the open land. His ankle buckled, almost throwing himself onto the stony ground but fortunately he managed to catch himself and continue his training. A close call.

The falcon run was one of the activities spoken of in hushed tones away from the trainers. Experienced soldiers would shake their heads and warn fresh recruits of what was to come. They'd look each other in the eyes and communicate without words as their minds flashed back to the shared trauma.

"How far have we gone now?" Adam asked him, breathing heavily and pausing to take some water from his flask. "Feels like we've been running for days!"

"Still about a third of the run left, I think," Tavar guessed, squinting to look around the rocky landscape for anything he could recognise. "Should be able to see the Falcon Tower once we've passed over that rock," he said, pointing out a large outcrop that stood above all others. His other hand shielded eyes from the sickening brightness of the midday sun.

"I think I need a lie down," Adam said, throwing his bag to the ground and falling next to it. "Why does it have to be so damn hot! Couldn't Oden have given us the run in the winter?"

"It's designed to break us," Tavar reasoned. "To make us give up. Come on. If we stop now then we'll not have the energy to make it. Just a bit further."

Adam groaned and dragged himself back onto his feet, muttering a string of curses. "I won't give up but I might pass out. My back is still killing me after carrying you for the first two hundred paces."

"Well, I'm carrying you for the last two hundred so you can't complain!"

Tavar put one dusty boot in from of the other, pulling his pack tight against his back and focused on each step. Oden had warned them that today's test would be the final one to pass before the unit left for Hartovan, and war. Any soldiers deemed unfit would be placed on a brutal regime to improve their endurance – something Oden claimed would be worse than any battle he had fought in. Needless to say, every soldier was giving it their all. They struggled through difficult terrain in the blaring sun in the hope that it would soon end. Many, like Qassim, were already licking their lips, eager to get their first taste of battle.

Tavar felt differently to them. He needed to journey to Hartovan. King Uhlad had commanded it and it meant seeing his brother, making sure that Vandir was still alive. That morning, Tavar had tried to find Marcus to inform him of the failed attempt on the king's life. Marcus was nowhere to be found. Desperate, he had even asked Oden if he knew where he was.

"Marcus is a busy man, soldier," Oden reminded him, "and in case you haven't noticed, we are a nation at war. Focus."

Focusing was proving to be more difficult than he could imagine right now. The muscles in his legs felt stretched and at breaking point, poised to snap at any moment. He soaked his turban in water from his flask and tied it back around his head, welcoming the refreshing, cool feeling on his forehead that allowed him time to regain his composure.

Standing atop the rocky hill, he looked down at the almost barren, beige landscape that greeted them.

"There," he said with relief, showing Adam the Falcon Tower stabbing the clear, blue sky. The circular tower had a single-entry point at its base and rose to a point like a spear. The tower, Oden had told them, was constructing by a wealthy merchant in the good books of the queen at the time. The merchant had earned his fortune and spent his later years training falcons to hunt for him, a hobby that had caught on with the rest of the Alfaran population. It was in this tower where he would retreat and feed his falcons and keep away from the world.

On the other side of the tower was a gorge with a drop steep enough to make the bravest of men dizzy. The gorge ran off towards the horizon to the north and beyond.

"Don't know about you," Adam said, wiping the sweat from his face and scratching his head. "But I thought it would be much more... well, grand. Why the hell would you want to stay in the middle of this rocky desert with a bunch of birds?"

"No idea," Tavar said, beginning his descent down the hill. "But there's shade. Any excuse to get out of this heat is a good one."

"Well, it's your turn," Adam said, stretching an arm across his chest and pulling it tight. "You ready?"

Tavar rolled his shoulders back a few times and cracked his neck to the side. "As ready as I'll ever be. Get on," he said, crouching to allow Adam an easier chance at leaning across his shoulders and back for the final part of the run.

Carrying Adam down the rocky path would have been difficult enough without the distraction of him poking him in the ear or attempting to make him laugh with a collection of strange and awkward jokes he had picked up from a few of the older soldiers during training exercises.

Reaching the tower, they collapsed and stared up at the blue expanse of the sky.

"If we ever get asked to do something like that again," Adam said through long, ragged breaths. "I'm gonna make sure I'm busy. Fake an injury or something."

"Think I might have a real injury…" Tavar muttered, wincing as he pressed his fingers against a burning calf, trying to ease the cramp. He pulled the edge of his boot away from his foot and sighed as he saw a huge bubble of a blister waiting to be popped. "Let's head inside."

"They better have camels or horses ready for us. I'm not walking back," Adam complained. "You'll have to carry my corpse back."

The tower loomed over them, tall, solitary and intimidating. Tavar knocked on the wooden door and looked around while he waited for the guard to welcome them. In the distance, he saw aurochs wandering ambling to the east. The closest body of water was that way, the river was the main source of life in the harsh land and one of the main reasons that Alfara thrived in the harsh climate.

They didn't have to wait long. The door creaked inward to allow them entry into a large, dark entrance hall. The room was sparse. A few portraits hung on the wall leading to a stone staircase that spiralled its way to the top of the tower. At the back of the room sat a lonely figure, his hood casting a shadow preventing Tavar from seeing his face.

"You've made it. Congratulations," the man said, voice weathered and beaten. "An Alfaran soldier needs to be physically fit, capable of traversing harsh land in a short amount of time. You have passed *this* part of the test."

"*This* part of the —" Tavar started before his world turned to darkness.

Rough hands knocked him onto his knees and placed a covering over his head, blocking out any source of light available. By the muffled yells at his side, Adam was dealing with a similar fate.

Tavar tried to stay calm, listening carefully for any information that could help him get out of the situation. From the footsteps around him, there were at least three assailants, maybe more. Oden had always impressed upon them the importance of being calm and thinking your way through capture. This was the next phase of the test. Shit.

"Being strong can mean many different things." Tavar recognised the figure's voice from before he had been thrown to his knees. "Anyone can become physically strong. Anyone can build enough stamina to run across the desert. But there is another type of strength we desire in Alfara. One that is more important than any of the others. Mental strength. Take a deep breath, men. Your test is just getting started. Show your strength and you will pass, God willing. Good luck."

The covering stayed over his head for the whole journey from the tower to a destination Tavar was unaware of. Camel skin, he thought, smelling the covering and holding back the urge to vomit. At first, Adam had tried speaking to their captors but by the sound of it, all he received in response was a thump on the head that shut him up. Tavar knew then that silence would be his ally.

He tried to use his senses but he was too disoriented with the lack of sight. He counted his steps as he was dragged along but there were too many and the heat scrambled his mind, making him question what number he was on. In the end, it was all he could do to muster the energy to place one aching foot in front of the other.

After what felt like a day's walk, Tavar felt a hand squeeze his shoulder, stopping him briefly. He heard a door opening and was pushed forward. Finally, he was knocked down and told to sit down and wait.

He sat, blind to his surroundings but relieved beyond belief that he could rest and take the weight from off his sore feet. The blister had popped halfway through his journey and each step had pressed the edge of his boot into the open wound. He heard footsteps leading away and a door slammed shut. There were no other sounds apart from heavy breathing next to him.

"Adam?" he asked after a moment's hesitation as he worked out the best path forward. "That you?"

"Yeah," Adam replied, voice exhausted and ragged. "That bastard Oden didn't tell us about this bit did he?"

"Just stay calm. They're testing us," Tavar said, trying to convince himself as much as his tired friend. "Don't break and we'll be back at the barracks before you know it."

"This is why those shits looked so horrified when they spoke of the Falcon Tower. They tried to warn us without actually saying anything. We should have known," Adam said, voice muffled.

The hours in darkness crawled by. The vacuum of activity was only interrupted by the sounds of dripping coming from somewhere nearby and every once in a while, Tavar would be prodded not too gently by what felt like the tip if a wooden blade against the side of his head. Any reaction brought with it a whack on the back of the head and angry curses.

The exhaustion, hunger and dehydration were taking its toll on him. He felt his body sway to the side, giving up and willing itself to sleep. Rough hands grabbed his shoulders and pulled him back to a sitting position. A searing pain shot up the muscles in his back, making him cry out in agony.

"Shut up!" a voice roared at him. "You think this is a game? We are just getting started, Farwan."

Tavar's eyes burned, the lack of sleep physically destroying him. Mentally, he just wanted it to end. He didn't know how much longer he could take sitting in the same position without food or water, unable to sleep. His head rolled across his shoulders and he heard Adam begin to sob.

"Take him."

He heard Adam's groans and a shuffling as of a body being pulled across the floor. A door opened and closed and Tavar was left in the void. He tried to steady himself, to remind himself that this was all part of their training but his whole body just ached so much!

What felt like a whole year later, the door opened

again and he was pulled to his feet. A strong hand clutched his wrist, pulling him forward. He stumbled, disorientated but the guard caught him with a curse and paused.

"One foot in front of the other, Farwan."

The guard led him for a while longer before pushing a hand against his chest, halting him and then pushing him down onto a hard seat. As terrifying as everything felt, Tavar had to hold back an audible sigh of relief at being able to sit in a more comfortable position. He promised himself that such a simple relief wouldn't be taken for granted for as long as he lived.

Without warning, the bag shot from his head. Even the minimal amount of candlelight in the sparse room pained his eyes at first. He squinted, trying to adjust to the light. After blinking a few times, his vision settled. Sitting opposite him were two men. Both wore the same black robes. Only their dark, suspicious eyes and hands were uncovered. One of them, a short, broad man stood, cracking his knuckles. The other, tall and slim, just sat there, staring.

"The Falcon Tower," the man standing said, scratching at the corner of his eyes and bending to push his face inches from Tavar's. "It is a monument revered by the desert warriors, a reminder of the peace of our land. You and your friend stepped into the tower and in doing so, disrespected me and my people. This is something I cannot allow." His voice was soft but Tavar caught the sinister hint that he was being played. A calm before a storm.

"Why are you here, Farwan?"

Tavar remembered his training. Speak slowly. Humanise yourself.

"It's difficult to think… I'm so tired, and thirsty. Please, do you have any water?" he croaked, breathing slowly and closing his eyes. It would have been a good act but, truthfully, he felt ready to pass out. The chance for water reenergised him.

The guard clapped and the second man stood from his seat and walked past Tavar, eyes still staring.

"My friend will get you water, as long as you answer my questions…" the shorter man said. "Now, tell me. Why did you come here?"

"We became lost and wandered towards the high ground, hoping to find our way back home. Our camels were tethered but broke free and we attempted to chase them down but it's too hot. We eventually found this tower and, God be praised, we found shade to protect us from the burning sun." It was a lie, but one with Tavar felt was realistic enough to be convincing.

"We sometimes find lost wanderers stumbling through our land, it is true." The guard nodded, seemingly pleased with the response. "But, your friend has already admitted the true reason for you being here. Perhaps you would like a second chance to tell me your story, Tavar Farwan."

Tavar's mind flipped and raced around, struggling to find the appropriate response. The second guard strolled back in, thrusting a cup of water into Tavar's hands before reclaiming his seat.

"My friend must be delusional." It was a stab in the dark but it was the best thing he could think of in his current state. "Sunstroke can have a terrible effect on people, especially the white ones, like my friend. His mind must be broken and he is imagining responses that you would prefer." He greedily gulped the water and licked his dry lips.

"Is that so?" Even with the lack of reference, Tavar felt he could see the hint of a smile reaching the guard's eyes, a small sign of acceptance that his answer had been played well. "We will call you again, and your friend. This isn't over."

He wanted to scream when the bag was placed back over his head but he didn't have the energy.

His second time in the interrogation room involved a new friend for Tavar. He had spent the time since the last session trying to hold his mind together, to remind himself this was all part of the test before being sent to war. He'd sobbed for what felt like hours as he silently admitted to himself that perhaps he was not up to it, the mental strength needed to be a soldier. That's when the new guard had arrived.

"You recognise his unit, don't you?" The short guard asked him, pointing at the new guard to his left. Dressed in gold, face impassive with cold eyes looking out from his dark face, it was clear to Tavar who he was. An Immortal. A member of the Royal Guard.

Tavar nodded, speechless as he wondered why an Immortal would be here, for his training. Surely they were above this kind of thing?

"You have done extremely well, Tavar Farwan," The guard said. His eyes were softer than before and he no longer covered his mouth. Instead he proudly displayed a bushy black beard as he spoke. "Unfortunately, there has been a change in our circumstances. You have a brother, Vandir, correct?"

Tavar nodded, unsure why they would bring up his brother.

"He has been captured in Hartovan by the enemy."

The words hit him like a hammer to the head. "Vandir…" His heart thumped faster an Okadan drummer as he bowed down, holding back the burning tears from his eyes.

"They have sent word that he is to be killed, a week today. Unless…" Tavar clung onto the pause as if his life depended. Anything. He would do anything to save his brother. "Unless we offer another, to take his place…"

It didn't take long for him to make up his mind. "Me. I will go. Save him, please." He stared at the impassive Immortal, praying for any support to save his brother.

"You would give your life to save your brother?" The guard asked, rubbing his beard and mulling over the suggestion.

"Yes. In an instant. He would do the same for me."

"It takes great strength to willingly die for another, family or not. Great courage. Guard!"

The door opened and the taller guard walked in, pulling a prisoner along. The guard's face was almost bored, as though this was just another day on the job for him. Maybe it was.

He took the bag from the prisoner's head and Tavar was relieved to see the pink face of his friend. Adam sobbed, allowing tears to freely fall down his face.

The short guard grinned as the two of them

greeted one another with a weary smile.

"Being a soldier means being part of a team, becoming greater than an individual. You have both passed."

The words didn't sink in at first. They fought through the cocktail of tiredness, hunger, and thirst before Tavar could process their meaning.

"We've passed?" he repeated, unsure of what was happening. "What about my brother?"

"He is fine, as far as I am aware. You made the correct decision. It allows us to choose where soldiers are deployed, to put them in the right units. You gave away too much information to be an elite soldier but this is just the beginning of the journey for you. Every soldier breaks the first time."

A harsh breath escaped Tavar as he finally understood what had happened. "My brother is alive. He is safe?" he said, ignoring the comment about breaking. That wasn't important right now.

"And my sister? Alice?"

"Both fine. Alice threatened to kill me if you came to any harm during her interrogation. She is strong, for an outsider," the guard laughed at the memory.

Relief overwhelmed both of them. Tavar broke into uncontrollable sobs as Adam hugged him. It was all a test. All a damned test.

"My name is Adnan ir Eladar. This is Masif ir Fularh," he motioned to the taller guard who just stared back. "You will be joining our unit as we march on Hartovan. It will be an honour to have you fighting alongside us. God willing, we shall make it out alive."

"It will be an honour for us, Adnan," Adam said,

sniffing and rubbing his eyes. "I have two questions left before this is all over."

"Ask away," Adnan said, beaming and clapping his hands together, all tension leaving his posture.

"Is he a real Immortal?" Adam pointed at the golden robed warrior.

"Salim Kingsworn is an Immortal. He aids in the training of candidates. It is useful for Immortals to scout the younger soldiers, to see which ones could be moulded into Immortals like them. You have another question?"

"Do you have any spare robes in this god-forsaken tower? It seems I've pissed myself."

CHAPTER THIRTEEN: GOODBYES

Passing through the courtyard, Tavar waved at a few of the older soldiers he now recognised as they went through their drills. All of them smiled and waved back. He was one of them now. They couldn't deny it. He had passed one of the most brutal tests and he was ready for war. Or at least that's what Oden had told them all as they returned from the Falcon Tower.

"The falcon run is designed to strip you down to your core; to reveal to us who you truly are. We can't afford to take soldiers into battle who lose their minds and become a problem for us. We have enough to focus on without having to mother fools who are in over your head," Oden had warned them. "I understand that some of you aren't from Alfara and you may not have chosen this path, given a choice. That kind of thinking stops now. You are an Alfaran soldier. Any hesitation will cost yourself, or your fellow soldiers their lives. You have been placed in your units. There will be familiar faces. There will be a mix of experience and youthful vigour! Become a family. Work together. Don't let me down."

It was a cool day. Well, cool for Alfara. Tavar remembered wandering through the northern pass with the caravan. His mother would wrap him up in around five layers and ensure every inch of him was covered. She'd warn him with tales of men and women whose fingers and toes would turn black and fall off with the severe weather and even made him sleep with three pairs of socks on when travelling through the northern regions.

He'd dismissed the warning as nothing more than a mother's way of forcing him to listen to her.

To hammer her point home, one day she had walked Tavar and a grumpy Vandir to one of the other merchants who sat in his wagon. He had a dagger in his hand and calmly sliced the tips of two of his fingers off in front of them. He proceeded to show the young boys three lost toes and that was all Tavar could handle. He'd puked in the snow and promised his mother that he would always wrap up in the cold. A cool day in Alfara meant you could still get away with one layer, you just might be a bit chilly. Finding shade was the issue in Alfara. Keeping his brown skin from burning was second nature to him. He laughed when Adam forgot to protect himself. His light-skinned friend would spend days with tight, pink skin that was sore to the touch. The first time it had happened, he'd barely managed to get any sleep as Adam tossed and turned in his bed, moaning with the pain.

The memory gave him an idea. Crossing the desert to Hartovan would be difficult at the best of times. Adam would most likely forget about his weak skin. The apothecary was close to the courtyard and Tavar knew the owner well, having to visit more than he would have liked over the years.

"Young Master Farwan!" The young apothecary greeted him with a wide smile and palms facing the heavens. She bid farewell to an elderly man hunched over so far that Tavar worried his nose would scrape against the floor if he wasn't careful. "See you soon, Saoud. Remember, twice a day after eating." Her intelligent green eyes turned back to Tavar and she placed her hands on her hips, searching for the reason for the visit. "What scrape have you gotten yourself into now, Tavar. I'm running out of herbs thanks to you."

"Or I'm keeping you in business," Tavar argued with a laugh. Yasmin had been one of the first adults to show Tavar that people in Alfara could be kind and gentle. "No scrapes for me today."

"That is good to hear," she said, relaxing and straightening her abaya. "That must mean you are here for Adam."

"Your skills of deduction never fail to impress me!"

"Alfaran women, Tavar: you will never find a people more intelligent than Alfaran women!" she mocked, fluttering her eyelashes and standing proud and confident. "Now, what does your friend need? Or shall I guess?"

"Guess." Tavar was happy to play the game. It would be a while before he would see Yasmin again, unless the war ended sooner than expected.

"Hmm…" She pressed a finger against her full, pursed lips and raised a perfectly plucked eyebrow. "He is a very pale young man. It is extremely hot outside. Has the fool burned himself again? I swear to the almighty, that boy will soon be able to hide with a flock of flamingos if he keeps this up! My father will never allow me to marry him if he looks like that!"

Tavar snorted and shook his head. She loved to laugh at Adam. She knew the boy had taken a shine to her and played up to it for both of their amusement. "Just a precaution! He is fine, for now. Though, we will be going away tomorrow and I'm not sure when we will be back…" He swallowed, a cold wave washing over him as he realised how much he would miss the apothecary. The way her face dropped told him that she knew what he meant and liked it as much as he did.

"You're going to Hartovan, aren't you?" her voice was low, as though speaking it out loud would only confirm her suspicions.

"At dawn. We'll be back when the war is over. Hopefully it won't be too long."

"I will pray every day for your safety, my young friend. I wish baba was in today, he has gone to the village to collect some herbs with mother. He would have liked to wish you farewell."

"Please pass on my apologies that I am unable to say goodbye in person. I'm sure he will miss my coin." Tavar pulled out three bronze coins from his pocket and placed them on the table. "For the herbs."

Yasmin stubbornly shook her head and wrapped his fingers over the coins. "Keep them. This batch is on the house. A gift for the brave soldiers fighting for us."

Tavar's mouth felt dry and he struggled to swallow down the lump rising in his throat. "I will be back as soon as I can. Look after the new recruits, like you've looked after me."

"Stay safe, Farwan. Your journey does not end here." Yasmin crossed an arm over her chest. "We'll meet again, God willing."

"God willing," Tavar repeated, mirroring the action as his eyes burned. Walking out of the apothecary, he thought about who else he needed to speak to. The enormity of heading off to war suddenly felt like carrying an aurochs over his shoulders.

He breathed out and took one step forward, away from the apothecary.

He knew who he needed to speak to.

"Tavar. It's been some time since I've seen you round here. What can I do for you?" Marek's dad had a warm smile that brought with it an ache in Tavar's heart, a reminder of what he had lost all those years ago.

"It's good to see you, sir. I'm actually looking for Marek and wondered if you knew where he might be."

Marek's father scrunched his face up and looked up into the clear sky, shading his eyes from the afternoon sun. "He should be in the fighting square now. He's been practising relentlessly since…" There was an uncomfortable pause as his eyes failed to meet Tavar's. "Well, since the test. He's been cutting those wooden dummies up so much there'll be nothing left of them by the time he joins the army. Just sawdust." He raised a finger to Tavar and busied himself with the produce laid out in front of him as Marek's uncle finished a sale for an impatient customer. "Take these. You have a big mission tomorrow, I heard." He threw a bag to Tavar who caught it with ease.

"Thanks," Tavar said, seeing the apples and vegetables in the bag. "Please, take some coin."

"Your money is no use here, Tavar. You are a soldier of Alfara and a friend of Marek's. Be safe." His arm gently crossed his chest. "And please tell Marek to relax. He is training himself into oblivion."

The fighting square was empty but for Marek. That pleased Tavar: it was for the best that no one else was here. It would allow them to be honest. No holding back.

Marek hadn't noticed him come in. His fighting robes were soaked with sweat but he kept going; dual blades snapping across the wooden body standing ahead of him, unmoving. Tavar was impressed to see the improvement with the speed of his strikes and movement. He certainly had been practising, just like his father had said.

"Two blades," Tavar said as Marek paused his attacks, breathing heavily. "Not standard instruction from Master Oden."

Marek dropped the blades and pulled a piece of cloth from his pocket, wiping the sweat from his brow and rubbing it over his reddening face. "Master Khedira has suggested we train with a variety of weapons. Anyway, after the way you embarrassed me, I thought it would be for the best if I train in every possible style, just in case. I have learned my lesson. Should thank you for it really. I won't."

Tavar controlled the heat rising to his cheeks at the unfair words. He wasn't here to argue. "You'll pass. I know this."

"What are you here for, Tavar? In case you haven't noticed, I'm busy."

There was no use dragging it out. He had to say what he had to and then it was up to Marek what would follow. Tavar looked around the room, thinking about how to word it. It hadn't been a long time since he had passed the tests in here but it somehow seemed smaller. He had been through so much since then, not lease of all the falcon run. No longer was it the intimidating square that scared him as a child. He was a man. A soldier. That meant he should be able to handle a conversation with an old friend, even one who now seemed to hate him.

"I know things haven't been good between us since the tests. You and I were friends, good friends before then. Tomorrow, I'm going to Hartovan. If I'm honest, I'm not sure if I'll be back. I didn't want to leave things like this…"

Marek ran a hand over his face and rubbed at his tired eyes. "Do you want to know why I'm so angry all the time? Why I am so pissed off with what happened?"

"I know it's because of the—"

"No you don't!" Marek interrupted him, screaming. His eyes grew wide as he stepped towards Tavar. "You think it's just because I failed because I was thrown off by your technique. Because I was humiliated. It's not just that…" As fast as the anger had risen, it faded, leaving behind only a sad and weary looking young man.

"What was it, Marek? Tell me," Tavar pleaded.

"You know how much this means to me. Born and raised in Alfara. My parents have struggled to make ends meet but they worked hard. Always have. All I wanted to do was join the army and show them how brave, how good I can be. Make them proud." Marek began to pace the square, rubbing at his forearm and looking anywhere but at Tavar.

"So I began to train. I was nervous but I finally felt that pride in myself. I was good with the tactics but needed to improve the other areas, which was fine. I could do that. Then my friend takes the same test, someone I care about: the son of peasants killed by Alfaran soldiers who still serve in the army today. I listened as you spoke of your hatred for my beloved country, the one who had given you the same chances given to me, a native Alfaran. It hurt, but you were my friend. I was happy for you. Then the test happened. You embarrassed me. I was beaten by my friend to a prize I had coveted all my life but one which you wouldn't give a shit about if you were given any other opportunity to leave this country. Having to train with a new batch of recruits while watching you swan about with my other friends as soldiers hurts like the hells. I envy you. The foreign peasant boy who lost his parents but became a soldier before me. Do you realise how much that eats away at me, the guilt I feel for hating my friend when all I wanted was to be happy for you?"

Tavar didn't know what to say.

Marek just stood there; eyes wet with tears he fought from falling.

"Marek… I'm sorry. I thought only of myself in that test. I've hated not being able to speak to you. I should have come here a long time ago."

Marek sniffed and wiped his face on his sleeve. "It's too late now. I feel different, more focused than before. I want no distractions, and that's what you and the others were. I need to be the best I can be and I can't do that whilst you're around. You're distractions."

The words hurt but they weren't unexpected. Tavar nodded.

"I understand. I might be in Hartovan for a while. No idea when I'll be back. When I do make it back, I'll come and see you. Hopefully things will be different then. Goodbye Marek."

Tavar made his way to the door, not trusting himself to look back, it felt like he had lost a friend forever. At the open door, Marek called his name out, making him pause.

"Tavar!" Tavar turned and saw a pained looking Marek staring after him, the tears finally running down his red cheeks. "Make sure you do come back. This isn't over."

"So it didn't go too badly then?" Hashem cautiously asked, brushing down Pan but looking at Tavar from out of the corner of his eyes.

"Could have gone worse," Tavar shrugged, thinking back to the conversation with Marek. "I don't think he hates me."

"Of course he doesn't hate you. You're friends. He's just hurting and doesn't know how to deal with it."

"How do you seem to know so much about people's feelings?" Tavar asked, genuinely curious about his good friend.

"I basically live with animals," Hashem answered, smiling. "Once you're able to work out how animals feel without them speaking, you get a kind of, understanding about things. I don't need someone to tell me how they feel to know it, just like I don't need Pan here to ask me for food when she's hungry. She'll let me know without words."

Tavar gave Pan a scratch and wondered why it was so much easier with animals than humans. If only humans were as easy at pleasing. A head scratch, a pat on the neck and an apple or two was all a horse needed. There were no games or unspoken rules necessary to follow to make them happy.

"He doesn't want me dead. I think that's the best I could get out of him if I'm honest."

"Good enough, for now," Hashem admitted. "You can sort things out properly when you return. He just needs time. He's emotional. Nothing wrong with that, it just means you need to be careful around him. He's like a wounded animal, just give him time to heal instead of forcing yourself near him."

It made sense. Enough for Tavar to agree with anyway. He would have to give Marek time now. Going to Hartovan meant he could give him as much time as he needed. That's the thing with war: there's no deadline. The end isn't predetermined and what you think could take weeks could end up taking years. He shuddered at the thought.

"How are you feeling about Hartovan?" Hashem asked, noticing his discomfort with that magical sense of his. "First real battle. Got to be tough on you."

"Shitting myself," Tavar said, eliciting infectious laughter from his friend. "Glad you're amused!"

"I have to laugh," Hashem replied. "It's that or burst into tears and I don't want to do that right now."

"I understand. It's difficult thinking about it. The years I've spent training for this very moment suddenly don't feel enough. Some of the others are excited and ready for fighting but every time I think about the possibility of taking a life, I feel nauseous. I'm not sure if I'm cut out for being a soldier." He'd felt it for a while but this was the first time Tavar had voiced his insecurities out loud. If anyone could advise him of what to do, then it was Hashem. The stable boy always knew what to say.

"It's a good thing. The nausea. Means you're a good person. I can't think of anyone I'd like to be friends with who looked forward to killing people. Still, you can't let it hold you back. It's a war. If you don't fight, you could get yourself killed, or your friends. You just need to find a way of blocking it all out in the moment. Afterwards, you can come back here and let it all out. The horses won't mind." Hashem nudged him and grinned. Tavar would miss him more than he cared to say.

"I'll hold you to that," was all he said, looking at Pan so that he could hold himself together. "Hashem…"

"Yeah?"

Tavar looked his friend in the eyes and composed himself, knowing that this could be the last time he saw his friend. "I've no idea what will happen from tomorrow. God willing I'll make it out alive but even if I do, I'm not sure if I'll be able to return to Alfara."

"I know." Hs friend sighed, nodding and biting his lip.

"That means that this could be the last time we see each other. I'd hate to leave without you knowing how much fun I've had with you. You've put up with me moaning and hating Alfara for a longer time than most people would but I haven't hated my whole time in this country. Looking for the light shining through the dark clouds, meeting you here has been one of the best things about life in Kessarine and I just wanted to say thank you."

Hashem allowed the tears to slowly roll down his face. Tavar fought back his own tears by taking a deep breath and swallowing what felt like a whole apple in his throat.

"Only God knows what will happen to us, Tavar Farwan," Hashem stammered, wiping his nose on his sleeve and trying to hold back the tears rather unsuccessfully. "But there is one thing I do know: whether it is here in Kessarine or a city on the other side of the world, we will meet again. Anyway, you'll need to see Pan. She's made it through too much for you to just leave her here with me!"

They shared a laugh together and hugged briefly, enjoying the bittersweet moment.

"You'll look after her, won't you?"

"You know I will, I've told you that before. She'll be pampered like a princess until you're ready for her," Hashem promised, finally winning the battle against his tears.

"Goodbye, Hashem."

"I prefer, see you soon." Hashem pulled him in for another hug and then released him. "I'll pray for you, Tavar. It may not mean much to you but I'll do it every day. Twice if I remember," he said with a wink and a smirk.

"I'll take anything I can get at the moment," Tavar admitted.

"Now go. You're late already. Tell the others I said to stay safe and I'll be thinking of them. Even Carver…"

"You have gone mad," Tavar laughed before sobering. "See you soon." He gave Hashem one last nod before pulling his horse in for a silent farewell. Then he left the stables with heavy steps.

From the hillside next to the riverbank, Tavar watched the sun dip below the horizon, casting an orange haze over the land. The silhouettes of palm trees and prayer towers spiked up from the in the distance past the small villages that lay scattered between the forest to the south and the desert in the east. It was one of his favourite places to come and think, to just sit and watch the world pass him by. He liked to pretend his life had turned out differently and imagined what it would have been like to sit on the hillside with his parents and brother and gaze out at the beautiful land before them. Just a dream.

"I hate the place but," Adam started, lying beside Tavar, "I can't deny it's a beautiful place. Shame it's full of pricks."

"Like us?" Tavar smirked.

"Exactly."

Tavar turned at the sound of footsteps. He was pleased to see Carver walking towards them. She smiled briefly as their eyes met. The golden robe she wore caught in the light evening breeze and wrapped around her. He felt the heat rise to his face as his eyes fell on the curves of her body. She wasn't the immature girl who bullied him in the fighting square. She was a woman. A warrior. A friend.

"Not interrupting anything am I?" she asked with a wink.

"We just got here," Tavar said, patting the ground next to him.

Carver sat carefully and pulled her knees up to her chest, wrapping her arms around them as she too took in the sight of the evening sunset.

"Haven't seen my sister or Cassie anywhere have you?" Adam asked her, "Thought they'd be here by now…"

Carver's eyes flashed to Tavar and he thought she held back a laugh before she answered Adam. "They were a bit, erm… busy when I saw them. They said they'd catch up in a bit though."

She caught Tavar's gaze again, willing him to read into her words but he was at a loss, unable to decipher whatever message she had for him.

"The last evening together before we march on Hartovan and they're late again. Typical. Don't know what's gotten into them lately," Adam complained as Carver snorted.

The three of them sat in silence, enjoying the company and the view, not wanting it spoiled. They knew that everything was about to change and needed this moment together. Tavar wished he could magic this moment into his mind forever. Just sitting with friends and washing any worries away, enjoying the moment for what it was and nothing more.

"Doubt I'll be getting any sleep tonight," Adam finally broke the silence. "Dawn will be here before we know it."

"It will be a few days before we see battle, perhaps longer," Carver reminded him. "Don't worry. We've trained for this very moment. We're prepared."

"Yeah…" Adam said, nodding to convince himself more than anything. "We're ready. We can do this. We're soldiers."

"Well, most of us are," Alice's voice called from behind them. "Not too sure what you are, brother."

Tavar turned to see Alice holding hands with Cassie and giggling as though they didn't have a care in the world. They beamed at each other, a smile that spoke of more than friendship. The cogs in his mind began to turn and he spun, staring at Carver.

"Finally caught up, have you?" she whispered to him with a deliberate raise of her eyebrows.

"Alice and Cassie…" he said back, the pieces of the puzzle finally slotting together.

"Sorry, we're late," Cassie said as she checked the ground for a suitable spot to sit. "Lost track of the time."

Alice grabbed Cassie's hand and dragged her down next to her, both falling in a pile and giggling together, lost in each other's embrace.

Tavar laughed as he watched Adam go through the same process he had only a moment earlier. The confused look on his face slowly changed to one of shock and finally amazement as he realised what he was witnessing.

"You two are... I mean you're... erm..." he stammered, struggling for the correct words.

"Yes, brother. We *are*," Alice confirmed to a further outbreak of laughter.

Adam's brow creased with further thought. "So that's why you..."

"Kept asking about your sister whenever we trained together?" Cassie finished, flicking her hair back and gazing into Alice's eyes.

"Yeah," Adam said with a satisfied grin. "That makes me feel better."

"The awareness of the average male is mind-blowing," Carver said, leaning back onto her hands and staring off into the horizon.

"You knew?" Adam sat up and stared at Carver, astonished.

"Anyone with a decent pair of eyes could tell!"

"It's good," Tavar said, smiling at Alice. She tore her gaze from her partner and grinned back. It warmed his heart to see his old friend so happy. So content. "Don't think I've ever seen you so happy."

"Thanks," Alice replied, eyes falling back on Cassie as she wrapped her arms around her and allowed her to lean back against her chest. "I'm glad we're all here together. Tomorrow is the start of something big. One last proper night together is what we need. Who knows what the future holds?"

All five of them sat in silence, lost in their thoughts; thoughts of the life ahead of them. Tavar hoped that this was not the end of something, just the beginning. Looking around at his friends, he wondered what his life would be like if he didn't have them by his side. They had grown up together, through the good and the bad. He felt it was a bond that could not be broken. Then he thought of Marek and dark cloud passed over his heart, casting a shadow upon him.

"Whatever happens in Hartovan," Tavar said. "It won't take anything away from the last few years. Some of us will be in a different unit over there but I promise, if there's anything I can do to have your back, I'll do it. Things may end up going south but I want you all to know that you're my family now. Something I didn't think I'd have again. You're my brothers and sisters, like Vandir."

"Here's me thinking we'd be able to make it through the evening without weepy little speeches," Adam chuckled, wrapping an arm around his shoulder and pulling him closer. "We are family. In all honesty, I don't completely hate Carver since she's stopped with the constant stream of insults and attacks."

"The feeling's mutual," Carver inclined her head towards him with a smirk. "Though the insults will continue, whether you like them or not, pale boy." She picked up a clump of dirt and chucked it at Adam's head. He dodged the blow with a cry of victory and released

Tavar from his brotherly embrace.

"In all seriousness, thanks. To all of you," Carver said, running her fingers across the dirt and staring at it, concentrating on anything other than the four people staring at her. "The last year has been tough; tougher than any other in my life. You've helped. All of you. Before we became friends, I craved glory and status. To be the greatest soldier meant being the fastest. The strongest. I thought it best to cut away the weak and that included anyone not from Alfara. For my whole life, I was raised believing this nation is the greatest in the world. Then my friends stabbed me in the back and the king hung my father from the wall."

Tavar's eyes darted nervously across to Adam who looked back with pursed lips, unsure how to respond. Carver had never wanted to speak about it before. She was a locked chest unwilling to share with any of them, no matter how close they got.

"Just so you all know, when we're in Hartovan, I'm not fighting for Alfara. I'm fighting for each of you. I'm fighting for my family name. I owe this country nothing and as soon as I have earned my name, I'm gone. Carver ir Edemer will walk away from Alfara and not look back."

"What will you do?" Tavar asked. She could leave whenever she wished. She was not held by the ten-year rule like outsiders. A disgraced Alfaran is still an Alfaran.

Carver finally looked up at them and shrugged. "I've been in Alfara all my life. I want to see the rest of the continent. To see the world. I could work as a hired sword and get as far away from here as possible."

The idea had promise. Life on the road as a hired

sword. Sleeping where they wanted, stopping only when they needed to. The dark cloud passed from Tavar and the light shone. For the first time in a long time, he could see a future, one that didn't seem too bad. Once his debt was paid to the king, he could get Vandir out of Hartovan and leave. Like Carver had suggested, there wouldn't be a backwards glance. His past was his past, but the future held endless possibilities.

"There's more to this world than Alfara," Tavar agreed as the last of the light faded from the horizon. Countless stars shone brightly in the night sky, each one representing a possible path for them. "I think after this campaign, it's time we explored that.

"I would love to return to my homeland," Cassie agreed, leaning her head back to look at Alice who nodded in agreement. "To see my people and remind myself of their ways."

"I wanna see the dwarves," Adam said. "Banished and outcast from Alfara. I feel we'd have something in common."

"Whatever we do. Let's promise that we'll do it together," Alice said, her hand hovering in the air next to her. "Promise?"

Cassie placed her hand on top of Alice's and waited for the others. Adam followed shortly after with another chuckle.

Tavar peered over at Carver who seemed drained from the conversation. "What do you say ir Edemer? You in?" Tavar shuffled over and put his own hand on top as they each stared over at Carver. She caught his eye and there was a flicker of the fire he recognised from when they had first met.

She sighed and crawled over, dropping her hand

on top of the pile. "You lot are a bunch of weirdos. But yeah, promise."

CHAPTER FOURTEEN: DAMNED IF YOU DO

In the barracks, the battle was in full flow and it was one that always played out for far too long. The battle to fall asleep before an early start.

Snoring from all four corners filled the room in an orchestra of the damned. Tavar recognised Adam's low, drawn out booming snore amongst the group. It was a much larger room than the one he had moved into when first entering the city. It was designed to aid in the bonding of roommates. Four soldiers in close quarters who were expected to eat, drink, and wash together; constantly watching each other's backs. Just like when they were on a campaign. They were a team. The four would become one, thinking as one. If a member of your team fell, it was on you, a burden you would have to carry for the rest of your life. As if he didn't already have enough weight to carry.

Adam, he knew like a brother. The other two were easy enough to get on with. Harun proudly introduced himself as the son of a whore and a gambler who had lost him in a poor game at an early age. His parents wouldn't miss him, he told them. With pride, he said that he had already surpassed any expectations set on his family just by joining the army. He walked around with an unceasing smile on his face. Even the barked insults of Master Oden failed to remove the curl upwards of his lips.

Bushy Bermudo was less of a positive figure in the room. His skin tone sat between Tavar's and Adam's:

a sign of his western heritage on his mother's side. Though a year younger than Tavar, the young man was a giant in comparison and had been able to grow a beard before many of the older soldiers. He braided the beard into a long tail that hung from his chin. Any soldiers looking to insult him would receive a glare from dark eyes that sat under two absolute monstrosities that passed as eyebrows. Bushy Bermudo indeed.

Tavar couldn't complain. Things could have been much worse. Aside from the snoring and Harun's willingness to talk loudly to him when he was taking a shit, they were a good enough group. He shuddered at the thought of what it would have been like being bunked up with Qassim or any of the other nobles. Here, they were equal, Alfaran or not.

All four of them were part of the same unit, led by Qassim, much to Tavar and Adam's disgust. The other two didn't care too much. But they'd never had any run-ins with the smug noble-born bastard. Soothing Tavar's anger at working in Qassim's unit was the fact that Adnan and Salim would be in charge overall, keeping a close eye on Qassim ir Alisson and the way he led the new soldiers. Other, more experienced soldiers would assist the group, ensuring there would be no issues with their first mission.

Tavar held back a laugh as Bushy cried out in his sleep. "But I don't know what to do with the babies! They don't have the right shoes…"

As the giant rolled over, his snoring once again joined the others. A slither of moonlight snuck in past the closed curtain, falling on a door slowly opening.

Tavar shot up to his feet just as a figure entered the room.

"Sorry to disturb you," a meek voice found its

way out of a thin man holding a small lantern covered with a black cloth, forcing any light forward. "There is a man here to speak to Tavar Farwan. He says it's urgent."

Eyes adjusting to the darkness, Tavar saw the man as one of the helpers from the north. *Assistants* was the phrase preferred by the nobles. Slaves would be a better fit in Tavar's thinking.

"He is waiting in the campaign room. I will ensure you are not disturbed." The assistant backed out of the room, allowing Tavar time to change into a loose robe.

The short walk to the campaign room allowed him enough time to panic over who would be meeting him at this time of night ahead of such an important day. The fresh air woke him up, clearing his head and sharpening his thoughts. In doing so, his mind landed on one name.

Uhlad.

Entering the room, he had convinced himself that the king would be sat next to the war table, waiting for him. He was wrong, but to his pride, not too far off.

"Ahmed," Tavar said, startled. "I wasn't expecting you."

"Why would you?" the head servant said, lowering his hood and crossing an arm across his chest. "I doubt you have many meetings in the dead of the night. I, on the other hand, have a wagon full of them. The perks of my role, unfortunately."

"How can I help you?"

"Take a seat. I am here, as you may have guessed, on behalf of the Godking, Uhlad Izad, the second of his name, and ruler of the greatest country in the world," Ahmed said, racing through the expected introduction. "At dawn, you leave for Hartovan. My king wishes to impress upon you the importance of this mission and its success. As mentioned previously, the success of this mission means your freedom, something I am sure you do not take lightly."

Tavar took the seat offered and waited for Ahmed to continue. The old servant paced around the room, pulling the curtain to the side and peering out of the window.

"One must be careful when dealing with such matters. I trust that you have kept your meeting with the king to yourself?"

"Of course. I know what will happen if I break his trust." The suffocating, tortured souls dying on the wall flashed into his head. He shook them away and focused again on the king's servant as the old man took a seat of his own, content that they were not being watched.

"Fadil will be somewhere in the heart of the city. We know this as we have surrounded the land around Hartovan and ensured that none could escape. The assault on the city will begin on the second sun from when you arrive. Ensure you are part of the team that enters the city once it is breached. Should you fail to enter the city, both you and your brother will not make it back alive…" he said the final threat with a cold detachment, barely even paying attention to Tavar, instead glancing at his fingernails and finding something to his distaste.

"How will I know Fadil when I find him? I've never seen him before."

"Marcus. Follow the traitor once inside the city and he will lead you to the brother. Do not allow Marcus to deduce your reason for following him. Inform him of your failure to kill the king and explain that you have since been sent to assist with the sacking of the city. Knowing the fool, he will take you under his wing and lead you straight to Fadil."

Ahmed strode over to Tavar and pulled a piece of rolled parchment from a deep pocket on his crimson robe. He pushed it into Tavar's open hand with a glare capable of paralysing the most courageous of men. And Tavar wasn't one of those.

"When you see him. Give him this note. He will know what to do. Under no circumstance do you read it. The seal involves and Okadan enchantment that will cause you harm if you open it. Understood?" Ahmed narrowed his eyes and loomed over Tavar, pinching his fingers and thumb around his shoulder, immobilising him.

Ahmed released his vice like grip and backed away, his meaning clear.

Tavar rubbed at the ache in his shoulder and nodded at Ahmed, letting him know the message was loud and clear.

"That is all. May God shadow your footsteps, Farwan. Do not disappoint."

Tavar rose from the chair and instinctively pressed his arm across his chest before backing out of the room. Weary from lack of sleep and the concentration from the meeting, he stumbled his way across the moonlit courtyard, stifling a yawn as he reached the door to the barracks. Even with the snoring, he felt that at last he would be able to sleep before the dawn rise and the long journey through the desert.

Although sleep deprived, his eyes were still able to make out a movement in the shadows under a balcony leading to the barracks. He thought nothing of it, perhaps there were others unable to sleep, their nerves spread thin at the thought of their duty upon the morning dawn. For the briefest of moments he thought he saw a hooded figure pass into the soft moonlight. He glanced again but there was nothing but shadow. He shook his head. Sleep was needed, his mind was already playing tricks on him and that wouldn't be beneficial come tomorrow. Crossing the desert would be enough of a struggle without the added curse of sleep deprivation.

He walked on, rubbing his forehead and attempting to shake away the sleep.

As his hand touched the handle, the hooded figure stepped out of the shadows. Tavar jumped back, mind whirling at the shock.

"Bit late for a stroll through the courtyard. Especially the night before leaving for battle…" The figure lowered her hood, revealing short, dark, cropped hair and a wicked smile. "That's how gossip starts in this city you know?"

"Lilian," Tavar breathed, holding his chest and slowing his breathing. "You gave me a fright."

"I have that effect on people," Lilian said, flashing her eyes and raising a single eyebrow. "Can we speak?"

Thrown off guard, Tavar struggled for an answer. It seemed he wasn't getting any sleep tonight. "Y-yeah. Sure."

"Weapons room. I doubt anyone will be training tonight."

With reluctance, Tavar followed Lillian into the weapons room. He wearily closed the door behind him and looked out across the vast space as Lillian walked along the walls lined with a collection of weapons that had taken his breath away when he had first entered it. The room was a bigger version of the training chamber where Tavar had taken his first steps to become a soldier. Its sheer size could intimidate those used to the cramped chamber but there was another aspect that made anyone entering for the first time stand up and realise that this was a room for true soldiers, for men and women who would be fighting in life and death battles soon enough. The weapons. No longer were they training with the wooden blades of the fighting chamber. Blades, lances, pikes, arrowheads, scimitars, falchions, throwing stars and more. All were sharpened to a deadly edge designed to tear flesh.

"I've always loved this room," Lilian said, running a gentle hand along a piece of navy scaled armour, her nails scraping the iron before she drew away and turned to face Tavar. "This is where soldiers are made. Fighters. Men and women born to spill blood and become heroes. The people we read about in books were forged in rooms like this, sharpened until ready to face their enemies."

"Not all become heroes," Tavar said, rubbing at his tired eyes. Already his body was aching, calling out for the sleep that seemed so intent on eluding him this night.

"Not all," Lillian agreed. "I used to break into this room when I was a girl and swing the swords around. The scimitar was my favourite." She spotted the curved sword and let out a small squeal of delight. "Humour me." She pulled two of the blades from their resting place and flung one at Tavar's feet. The crash against the stone floor pounded in his head.

He groaned and pinched the bridge of his nose,

not in the mood for such games. "Look, Lillian..."

"Ahmed visited you," she said bluntly, catching him off guard once again and stopping him in his tracks. "He can't be trusted. Neither can the man he serves. Whatever plan he has for you, ignore it. Run away."

Tavar scratched irritably at his head and cracked his neck to the side. "What do you mean? You know who he serves."

"I do. He wants something with Marcus's brother," Lilian said. The way her lips curled told him that he had been unable to keep the shock from his face at the statement. He was too tired for this and unable to play such games.

"I think it's best if I just head to bed, Lillian. I've a big day ahead of me, as everyone keeps reminding me."

As he turned his head, a rush of wind brushed his cheek followed by a thud as a throwing star slammed into the wall, embedding itself barely an inch away from his head. He spun towards Lilian, furious. She had always been kind to him and he had no idea why she would have done such a thing, risking his life with one throw.

"What do you think you're doing?" he screamed, heart racing.

"Pick up the blade. Then I'll explain," she replied, calmly turning her own weapon over in her head, checking the curved, silver hilt wrapped around her fist. "Not a poor design. I've seen better."

Tavar cursed to himself and did as she asked. It was lighter than he was used to. Designed to be wielded with one hand. He tested his swing a couple of times before stepping forward. Lilian smiled as though they were playing a child's game and not brandishing deadly weapons at one another.

"Much better. As we dance, keep your mouth shut, and ears open. It's time you listen to your better."

Without warning, she stabbed forward, feet moving unexpectedly fast. Tavar blocked a probing swipe of the blade and backed away, eyes fixed on the laughing woman.

"Very good!" she cried, pleased with the display. She crossed one foot over the other, circling Tavar with careful, trained steps. "One of the many times I came in here at night, I discovered that I wasn't alone. I was always fascinated with soldiers. They travelled the world and their actions inspired the songs sung in every tavern on the continent. Sadly, I didn't have your luck. I was sold to a whorehouse and not the army. No one wants to be in the songs about the whores. The swords I was being stabbed with every night were not the ones that inspired people, though my powers of deflection definitely improved.

"Most soldiers, upon finding a dirty, scruffy whore in the revered weapons room would have had me beaten, or worse. Luck was on my side for once that day. The soldier was kind, caring. He listened to me and we became friends. He trained me, taught me how to look after myself." Tavar listened but stayed on edge, watching carefully as Lilian slid her blade against his own, running it slowly up and down, scraping the edges together as she licked her lips.

"He was as good a man as I had ever met in my life. We would meet at night and talk, train and… do other things. He had a powerful friend. Very powerful. He arranged for me to escape the life of a whore, and so I became the head of the South House, looking after the new refugees from war and other issues. He saved me. Without him, I would have rotted away in the dungeons or have been sent to the wall. I owe him my life." Her voice cracked at the end and Tavar spotted a hint of weakness in her face for the first time. It was only for a moment. She scrunched up her face and launched herself forward.

Tavar blocked the first strike but fell for the feigned second. Lilian spotted the mistake and stepped to the right, striking upwards. He caught the blow but was sloppy. The edge of her blade nicked back of his hand. He winced and jumped back. Quickly checking the injury, he cursed again as blood dripped from a thin wound running from the top of his wrist to the knuckle on his little finger.

"You cut me."

"I have to make you understand, Tavar. I'm not messing around." She pushed forward and pressed her sword against his neck. He didn't try to fight back. He'd had enough of this madness.

"I don't know what you want but I'm not doing this. Kill me if you want but I want no part of this." He dropped the scimitar on the floor and stared her straight in the eyes, ready to accept his fate, whatever that may be. At least he'd finally get some sleep.

Lilian's eyes softened but she kept the blade kissing his skin beneath his dark beard.

"The soldier and I, we fell in love. He had my heart and I had his. There was one problem…"

"His powerful friend…" Tavar muttered, his tired mind finally starting to link together the fragments she had offered him.

"A very powerful friend. One who loved him as much as I did. One who was not keen on sharing."

"Fadil… Marcus's brother," Tavar said, realising

the implications.

"If Uhlad can't have him, then he will kill him. He is not used to not getting his way. I know you failed the task Marcus set you and now he too is in Hartovan. Find them both and get as far away from Alfara as you can. Cross the sea if you must. Just do not do what that monster and his servant have asked you to do." Her eyes sparkled with tears as she released Tavar. He wiped his hand across his neck and looked down at the blood on his hand.

"I will find him," Tavar said, overwhelmed with the revelation. "And I will get as far away from here as possible."

"One more thing," Lilian said, wiping the blood from her blade with her sleeve. "I'm as good as dead."

CHAPTER FIFTEEN: THE UNDYING

Tavar forced a smile and raised a hand to the rows of well-wishers who had gathered to wave the soldiers on their way to Hartovan. Many sat on the banks of the river and the top of the hill waving flags and singing the old songs of Alfara in support for the men and women on their way to risk their lives for the nation.

He watched a play fight break out in giggles between two young children playing with long sticks, green leaves still clinging to the wood. The adults next to them laughed along and clapped, enjoying the display. He wondered what type of person would encourage their children to aspire to become a soldier, to fight. He'd like to think his parents would have wished more for him than to be sent to a foreign land to fight and possibly die on a battlefield away from his family.

Then he remembered the times his parents caught Vandir fighting with the twins and how they would laugh and offer instruction, happy for the games to continue. Maybe they would have liked him to have become a soldier. Maybe they would have been proud if they were the ones standing on the banks of the river, teary-eyed as they watched their son march off to war. Of course, he had no idea of knowing how they would have felt. That's the problem with the dead. They're silent.

"Not a bad turn out," Adam said, leaning towards Tavar whilst waving back at the crowds and displaying his bright teeth to all looking his way. He soaked up the adulation like a sponge and was eager for more. "I didn't even think there were this many people in any of the villages around here. Why aren't we sending these folks off to war?"

Tavar's smile grew easier at the comment, a reminder that his friend wouldn't change. He would always be the same old Adam. "I doubt they have the skill to fight a war. They're better prepared for harvests and trade than landing killing blows."

"Have to admit, feels good to be seen off like this. Feels like we've accomplished something. I've actually found something I'm good at."

"What? Marching through a field?" Tavar snorted, gaining a scowl for his troubles.

"Nah, you fool," Adam smirked. "Being a soldier. Feels good to do something. And look at these people: they're proud of us. Haven't felt that in a long time…"

"Well, it'll feel even better making it out alive."

"Grim, mate." Adam shook his head but the smile didn't fade. "Very grim."

Led by General Abdulrahman, the soldiers pressed forward through the village, buoyed by the reception from the people of Alfara. One young woman broke from the crowd and flung her arms around one of more experienced soldiers and planted a long, passionate kiss on his lips, drawing raised eyebrows and a smatter of giggles from soldier and villager alike. The soldier released her with a wink, blowing her a kiss as tears began to stream down her face.

"Do we all get one of those?" Adam asked, rubbing his trimmed, blonde beard and staring at the girl who was now being consoled by an older couple, probably her parents.

"Only if you're likeable. You've no chance."

"Likeable? I'm more addictive than that special brand of haze they smoke in the western quarter. One hit and there's no turning back."

"Shame no one has made plans to take that first hit then!" Tavar mocked, accepting the light punch on his arm with good humour.

"Wish I'd had the chance to have been with a woman before we left. Just once," Adam said wistfully, scanning the crowd, his smile fading at last. "Even my sister beat me to that…"

"Maybe you should focus your attention on the one that like men," Tavar offered with a wink. "I thought you and Yasmin's sister were close after that night at the tavern. Very close."

Tavar held back his laughter as Adam's pale cheeks turned a shade of red that would put a rose to shame.

"We were close," Adam said, clearing his throat and coughing into a gloved fist. "Are close, I should say. Tasneem is a wonderful young woman."

"So…" Tavar pushed him, eager for more information. He'd been bursting to know how the night had finished for over a moon now and this may be his only shot at finding out.

"I fell asleep…" Adam muttered, turning his face away and staring off into the distance as though inspecting something vital at the front of the line.

"You what?" Tavar repeated, keeping his voice down so as not to offend his friend.

"I must have had too much of the red. She was good humoured about it. Too good humoured for me.

Said we will have another chance Though, thinking about it, that is not certain now, is it?"

"You'll see her again," Tavar said, his voice sounding more certain than he felt.

For the rest of the march through the village, they kept silent. Instead, they focused on the people around them, the villagers, the soldiers, the cavalry riding past them at a steady speed. Tavar took in every detail, unsure if he would ever return. The final group of villagers played on their kernai (made from goat horns), tanbur, and drums. The music followed them even as the land melted from rock to golden sand.

Tavar felt his sandals push against the soft, hot sand and he took a breath, gazing out at the vast desert in front of him. Layers of sand dunes met his gaze like still, golden waves. It was no wonder why the merchants often called this the sand sea. As far as the eye could see to the west, there was sand. Nothing more. The gold reached the horizon, mocking any who wished to pass, daring them to challenge it and see who would win. Most would turn back, daunted by the prospect. But he was a soldier. And there was a mission that needed to be completed. He thought of Vandir and placed another foot forward with a heavy breath.

Footsteps were heavier now, battling against the sand. The heat from the sun and pull of the sand creating a concoction potent enough to drain the energy from any but the strongest of soldiers. Tavar kept his head down, pushing forward and praying that soon there would be a chance to break and recuperate his energy.

"Your eyes are red," Adam said between heavy breaths of his own. "Not sleep well?"

"Not really. Too much snoring in the room."

"Harun and Bushy? Loud bastards, aren't they? Surprised I slept through it," Adam said, puzzled.

"A complete surprise. No idea how you managed it," Tavar replied, flashing his bloodshot eyes and laughing again. "Doubt I would have slept well anyway. Been dreading today for long enough. First time we've been away from the city since…" He couldn't finish the sentence but Adam knew what he meant. The first time they'd been outside of Kessarine since the murder of their parents. Tavar was shocked at how much the memory still pained it, jumping at him from the shadows when he least expected it. He thought he would've built some sort of shield to the pain now but here it was again, an open wound showing no sign of slowing.

"Yeah I know. Still have nightmares. I wake up in a pool of sweat looking for a weapon to defend them, or seek revenge," Adam said, voice at a steady, controlled level, as though he didn't want to lose control. "Then I realise that we've joined the very army that killed them and I become overwhelmed with guilt. Hate to think what they would say if they could see me here, today."

"They'd be proud." Tavar smiled softly and patted his friend on the back. "Proud of the man you've grown into. We've made difficult choices. Sometimes we've not even been given a choice. We're doing the best we can. I have to believe that," he said, though he wasn't too sure if he did.

"Yeah. Yeah we are. We won't be doing this forever will we?" Adam said, seeking reassurance.

"What do you want to do? When it's over."

"I dunno." Adam scratched his chin and stuck his tongue out of the corner of his mouth, thinking. "Always told father I wanted to be a blacksmith. I liked making things, still do. Could settle down in a little village somewhere with a wife and a few kids. Get fat and make shit for people. Wouldn't be too bad."

"It sounds perfect," Tavar agreed.

"What about you? Still thinking about being a mercenary with Carver?"

"Maybe. I just want to see things. For too long we've been cooped up in the city like caged lions, pacing the same small streets year after year. I want open space and freedom. I want to make my own choices, good and bad. Though, I'd like to do that with the friends I've made."

"Well, you can always visit me and the wife," Adam joked. "I'll make you the finest sword in the land and you can wander off and be a hero. Alice could write about it. She's always been good with her letters. Anyway, better check on the others." He looked over his shoulder and called back. "Bushy! Harun! Hanging in there?"

"Better than you, my pink friend!" Harun shouted back to laughter. Tavar looked back to see the pair of them forcing themselves over the dune but laughing together, at ease all things considered.

"Always has to be about my skin, doesn't it?" Adam cried, feigning injustice. If anything, he enjoyed standing out and being an object of attention. He knew he had friends and those who weren't didn't have an impact on him.

"You *are* a bit pink," Tavar said, inspecting Adam's pink cheeks above the line of his beard. His felt cap covered his head and kept the sun from his forehead, thankfully. "You been using the herbs from Yasmin's?"

"Yeah, of course. Tasneem reminded me close to

a thousand times. Ended up telling her that she had a choice: remind me one more time or cut my ears off because I was sick of hearing it."

"How did that play out?" Tavar asked, swatting a fly from his face and flinching away.

"She said if I spoke to that again then it wouldn't just be my ears she'd be cutting off." Adam winced at the memory, pulling at the trousers by his crotch. "As you'd expect following that, when she reminded me, I offered back a smile and a polite *thank you*. She seemed happier with that response so I've stuck with it."

Their amusement was cut short as Tavar peered over the caps of those in front and saw a proud man riding a camel with ease and heading in their direction. Adnan. Their unit leader.

"Heads up," he warned Adam, flicking his hand towards his friend to make sure he had his attention.

"God be with you, my young soldiers," Adnan said, slowing the camel and falling in line with the two of them. "How is the march treating you?"

"It's tough. Slogging through the sand in this heat isn't for the faint hearted," Tavar admitted, raising a hand to block the sunlight from his eyes as he looked up at the general.

"Indeed. Now, perhaps you understand how useful the falcon run is for us. It is a gruelling test but it weeds out those who would not survive such a journey. Our army is as strong as our weakest soldier."

"Must be easier on a beast, though," Adam said. Tavar coughed loudly as Adnan's eyes flashed at the insolence. Fortunately, the proud warrior decided to let it go.

"My role means I need to be able to move a great distance in a short time. I have soldiers to look after."

"I meant no offence." Adam bowed, realising his error. His cheeks seemed a slightly darker shade of pink than usual.

"I am here with a command. The Judges of Kessarine have been frustrated with the desert raiders attacking passing caravans in a region just a bit farther along. I plan to take a select group of soldiers and flesh them out. A strong, stark strike will warn others in the region that we mean business and their actions are not acceptable. A short detour for us could result in ending further misfortune for the innocent travellers passing through to Alfara."

"And you would like us to be a part of that team?" Tavar asked, baffled as to why he would have wanted them. There were much more experienced and worthy men and women more than ready and eager for battle, no matter how small.

"You showed strength in your test. Also, I spoke with your team leader, Qassim ir Alisson. He put your names forward and suggested that both of you would be willing to play your part in such a mission." Bastard. Qassim knew exactly what he was doing. At best this would weaken them. At worst they would be dead. But there was no way Tavar could turn down the offer. It would look weak and this wasn't a time to look weak.

"We'd be more than happy to assist in any way we can," Tavar said, trying not to laugh at Adam's slackened jaw and wide eyes. "I hope Qassim will be joining us, he is a great warrior and such a proud man would not be willing to miss out on an opportunity to lead his team. Or perhaps his sister. She too is a great fighter and it would be an honour to fight alongside her." This time it was Adam's turn to hold back a grin, catching onto Tavar's plan.

"Hmm… I shall think on it," Adnan replied after a moment. "It would be wise to see him lead before we enter Hartovan and face the heathens. Be ready for sundown. I shall inform the others in our little group and collect you as the last light fades."

"How did we get dragged into this again?" Harun moaned, lying down at the crest of a dune and peering out across the sands and looking out for any sign of movement. "Not that I'm not super excited to be out at this time of night, freezing my balls off in the middle of a desert looking out for raiders who have been known to skin their enemies alive. *Alive!*"

"Something about your tone makes it feel as though you're not actually excited," Adam whispered back. Harun laughed incredulously before Bushy dug an elbow into his side, silencing him.

"Qassim has a grudge against us and you two are unlucky enough to be in our unit," Tavar explained. As much as he didn't like the idea of this whole thing, he understood why Bushy and Harun would feel sour towards them. They would be asleep with the others now if they weren't connected to Tavar and Adam.

"Great. Some fucking noble's brat with a grudge in the middle of a war. Just what I've always wanted to get caught up in," Harun sarcastically spat. "Here they are. Took their damn time."

Tavar looked out and saw two dark shadows crossing the dune. Adnan led. Hot on his heels, Nahra followed with a scowl, eyes full of hate as they stared straight at Tavar. She knew it was his fault she was here. Adnan had eventually decided to keep Qassim with his unit so it was his sister who had been called to take part in this merry adventure. She wasn't best pleased with the decision. Tavar couldn't care less.

"One tent. Not too far from here, it won't take long," Adnan instructed. "There'll be three of them at the most. They'll have swords, possibly a bow and arrow but if we catch them whilst they are sleeping, then that won't be a problem. The perimeter is clear but we can't risk taking a chance that there are more close by. I will go in with Adam and Harun. Nahra, you, Tavar and Bermudo wait a short distance away where I showed you. Spread out and make sure there are no more coming to help. We must be swift and make as little noise as possible. Understood."

The five of them answered the affirmative and shared a solemn look with each other. Well, Nahra's was still just one of disdain for Tavar. Even faced with a fight ahead of her, she couldn't shake off her dislike for him.

"On me," Adnan said, content that they were ready. He slunk off down the dune, footsteps silently running across the sand. Harun followed with a curse. Adam turned and blew the air from his cheeks, flicking his eyebrows up in farewell at Tavar before racing off after them.

"On me. And don't take the piss. I'll leave you behind if you can't keep up," Nahra warned, eyes flashing from Tavar to Bushy and back again before heading back where she came from.

"She seems nice," Bushy said with a shrug, the hint of a smile crossing the lips hiding amongst a mass of dark hair. He ran off after her with a grace that belied his great size, leaving Tavar to chuckle to himself at the joke.

Nahra kept at great speed, her face turning from side to side, looking out for any sign of the raiders. After a hundred or so paces, she eased off, slowing down and holding a fist in the air, allowing Tavar and Bushy time to reach her.

"There." She pointed at a large tent that sat in a natural shield made from the surrounding dunes. Firelight burst through the material casting shadows of the three raiders pacing in the tent. "Bushy, go left. Circle the tent and make sure there are no outliers. Peasant," she said, turning to Tavar with a smirk. "Go right. Same thing."

"What are you going to do?" Tavar asked her, unable to keep his mouth shut.

"I'll wait here and keep watch over everything. Make sure you don't get a knife in your back..." Her tone made it clear that such a thing wouldn't be a great shame for her. "Usually I'd prefer rubbing nettles between my thighs than having to rely on you but this is my first proper mission. Don't fuck it up."

Tavar thought he caught a hint of pleading in her voice. This meant a lot to her. In that moment, she reminded him of Marek. She could be a stuck up, cruel, self-centred bitch but she was part of his team now. He couldn't let her down. The stakes were too high.

He stalked off into the night, fingers pressed against the hilt of his sword, gently kissing the leather grip. This wasn't a game now. This wasn't training. It was the real thing. He pushed his hate for Nahra from his mind and focused on the task at hand. This was life and death. No time to distractions.

He kept low as he made his way around the rim of the dunes circling the tent. The canopy of stars above him cast enough light for him to see before him but there was no noise. The silence of the desert would relax him at most times; now it just added to a sense of eerie foreboding bubbling away in the pit of his stomach. Something felt off but he couldn't place his finger on it.

He slowed his pace, taking care to look around him for anything that seemed out of place. Beneath him, he saw movement: three shadows carefully descending the dune towards the tent. He held his breath, watching as Adnan, Adam and Bushy drew their weapons.

The air grew thick with anticipation. He watched as the three of them spread out, surrounding the tent. Adnan took point, creeping to the front of the tent as the others made a triangle, scouting the structure. The shadows inside stilled and slowly lowered themselves to the ground as the light inside faded. Their day was over. Little did they know, their lives would soon be over.

Remembering his task as a lookout, Tavar turned – straight into his enemy.

Furious eyes full of surprise greeted him in a dark, pained face. Tavar had just enough time to notice the spiked hair lining the middle of the man's head before he instinctively reached for his weapon.

His enemy's eyes flashed towards the blade and he snatched at Tavar's wrist, preventing him from drawing the weapon.

Idiot, Tavar thought. Should have had it drawn and ready, just in case.

He pushed against the raider with all his force, throwing the two of them down the dune, rolling over the sand with grunts and groans. He was the first to stand, breathing heavily as he finally drew his sword and faced the recovering man.

The pause allowed Tavar to see the raider's face

clearly for the first time. Painted white with two red lines running vertically past each of his eyes. Though cold at night in the desert, he wore nothing but a piece of cloth running from his hips to his knees and a long scarf around his neck that fell to a point at the middle of his chest. It was the man's eyes that seared into Tavar's memory though. Bright and wild. Furious. Scared.

He was just as scared as Tavar was.

The raider picked up a weapon that had fallen during their scuffle in the sand. Tavar glanced at it nervously. Some kind of axe. Long, wooden handle with a loose flayed material hanging off one end whilst the other end glinted in the starlight. Straight iron made with one purpose. To slice open whatever was placed before it. Tavar made a promise to himself to make sure he wouldn't meet his end at the edge of that axe. It was a promise he wasn't certain that he was going to keep.

With an indecipherable roar, the raider lunged forward, axe raised high. Tavar rolled to the side to dodge the attack, tilting his blade. The edge nicked the ankle of the raider. He swiftly breathed in through his teeth, shocked eyes staring down at the blood slowly dripping from the scratch.

The next attack was faster than Tavar expected. He jumped back from a horizontal swipe, struggling to judge the unusual weapon as it cut through the air, barely missing his forearm. By the sound it made swiping through the air, it was heavy. The muscles straining in the raider's arms warned Tavar that the chances were he would be outmatched in strength. Speed was his ally in this fight.

He rushed forward, striking high. The wood of the axe pushed back against the blade as the effort sent vibrations racing through Tavar's hands and forearms.

Strong bastard. He attacked again, two strikes. High and low. He stepped to the side and the raider tried to match him but his right foot gave way, dropping him to his knee. Tavar instinctively took the advantage offered, just as he had countless times before in the fighting square.

His blade dropped down and across, catching his opponent across the neck, just next to his left shoulder. Tavar jumped back as the raider dropped his axe, clutching at the wound in his neck, attempting to staunch the flow of blood dripping down his torso. He felt a wave of nausea dizzy him as he watched the fear grow in the man's eyes, the realisation that he would die here in the desert, alone. This didn't happen in the fighting square.

Tavar stepped forward as the raider dropped back, his head resting in the sand, eyes still frantically moving, looking for any way out of his death. He pressed a hand against the raider's in a futile attempt to erase what he had done. As he did, he noticed that he too was bleeding from a wound on his forearm. In the heat of the battle, he hadn't even felt the strike. Still, it was nothing to worry about right now, a scratch compared to the fallen warrior's injuries.

"M-my brothers," the raider stammered, looking into Tavar's eyes and swallowing hard through the pain. "You have killed them too?"

Tavar nodded, not trusting himself to speak as he felt a lump in his own throat.

The raider nodded, accepting his fate. "We shall join our ancestors and become one with the land. It will be done."

"I-I'm sorry," Tavar uselessly muttered, knowing how stupid he sounded.

"You are from Alfara?" Tavar nodded, still

pressing against the wound. Dark blood poured over his hands and swamped the sleeves of his robe. "My people are growing in strength. It won't be long now."

Tavar paused, confused. "Your people? The desert raiders aren't growing in strength. Alfara has been sending soldiers to put down your people. More of us will come. Your people need to run, to hide. Or they will suffer your fate."

To Tavar's bemusement, the dying man laughed, followed by a cough that squirted blood onto his face.

"We are not desert raiders. We are the Blood Nation. The true rulers of the Undying Sands. For generations we have sat back and watched your people desecrate our land. You dismiss us as petty thieves and fools. You are wrong. The sands will drown in your blood before long. It is you who should hide." The warrior laughed again and moved his hand to his side, aware that his efforts were useless. This was the end. "Finish it. I deserve a warrior's death." He held a hand out for his axe.

Against his better judgement, Tavar stood and reached for the axe. He placed it in the warrior's hand and watched as he closed his eyes and held the axe against his chest.

"Are you ready?" Tavar asked, eyes burning with tears.

"Make it quick. The gods will welcome me with open arms."

Tavar stepped over the unmoving body and drove the point of his sword straight into his heart with a roar, releasing all his frustration and horror.

He stepped away from the corpse, exhaustion taking over. His sword dropped into the sand and he fell to his knees, staring at his blood-soaked hands.

He had taken a life.

"You look almost as pale as me. What happened?" Adam asked, as they returned to the camp. Adnan had allowed them to head back without it, wanting to stay behind and check the tent for any signs of other raiders. Nahra rushed on ahead, eager to leave behind the rest of them. Bushy and Harun walked on ahead, talking together and laughing, undisturbed by the night's events.

"There was another raider. He ambushed me," Tavar replied, still shaking. He could still see the look of fear in the man's eyes when he had realised that his fate was sealed. There was no chance of staying alive.

"What? Why didn't you tell Adnan?" Adam admonished him, pulling at his arm to stop him and glancing at the other two ahead of them, making sure they had not heard.

"I dunno," Tavar answered, kicking the sand at his feet and cursing himself. "It all just sort of… happened. It was so fast. He spoke to me. As he was dying."

"Shit, Tavar." Even in the low light, Tavar could see the blood drain from Adam's face as he realised what his friend had done. "You killed him. Your first blood. How does it feel? What did he say?" Adam asked, his speech racing as he wanted the details as soon as possible, his excitement taking over.

"I feel… empty," Tavar said, struggling to explain the feeling. He'd taken the life of someone. Someone who had a family. Someone who may have lived a long a loving life if he hadn't stumbled upon Tavar in the dark of the undying sands. "It was furious and there wasn't much time to think. After I wounded him, everything just slowed down again. He calmed and spoke to me. Told me that his brothers were in the tent and asked me if they were dead. Did you kill?"

"Didn't even head inside the tent. Adnan did it all. We were just to watch out in case any escaped." So it was only Tavar and Adnan who had killed that night. Adam hadn't even seen the warriors.

"He said they were part of Blood Nation. Warriors from across the sands. You ever heard of them? No mere desert raiders like Adnan had suggested." The words of the dead man swirled around his head as they walked back to the camp. He had thought he was doing something good, prevented raiders from attacking merchants crossing the sands. Now he wasn't so sure.

"Blood Nation? They're a band of rabble rats living like beggars in the west. Qassim used to throw shit at that guy in the class below ours. Forgot his name but his mother was part of the Blood Nation. Weird customs. Used to burn things to get rid of 'bad spirits' or some shit. Nice guy though. Dyami. That was it." Tavar remembered him. A sullen soldier but friendly enough whenever they had spoken. "If they are the ones raiding then it probably just means they're sick of living in their shitty homes in the desert. Nothing to worry about."

"Yeah, you're right." Even as Tavar said the words, he knew he didn't mean them. There was something off about the whole thing, something niggling at the back of his head that didn't sit well with him. Still, there was nothing he could do about it now and there was no use in disturbing Adam with it. Best to put on a happy face and keep his mouth closed.

They walked the rest of the way in silence, drained from journey. Every muscle in Tavar's body ached and he could feel the bags weighing down under his eyes. Yet, he still wondered if he would be able to sleep. For the second night in a row, it was a battle he would lose.

"Been for some fun in the dunes?" A familiar voice called out. Carver smile dropped as she they drew closer, seeing the night had taken its toll. "What have you been doing?"

"You go on," Tavar said to Adam, clasping his friend's forearm before turning to Carver. "Take a seat. You on lookout?"

"Yeah."

He sat down and told her everything. The story rolled out from his tongue as he sat there, unmoving. It was like he had been possessed and some other force had taken over to tell his story. There was no emotion in his voice, the events just seeping from him as his body swayed with the light breeze creeping across the desert. At any other time he would have worried about what Carver would have thought about him killing someone and leaving their body in the desert. He didn't have the capacity to feel anything but exhaustion and nausea right now though. Probably for the best, he thought.

As he finished, he felt a warm arm wrap around his waist and pull him closer.

"I remember the first time I killed," Carver said, her voice detached, like his had been. "First and only time, so far at least. My father and uncle were arguing. They always used to argue but this one was worse than most. Both were bloodied when I entered the room. I saw the dagger in my uncle's hand and the look of defeat on my father's face. Without thinking, I picked up my father's fallen weapon and stabbed his brother in the back. Five times I felt the blade enter and leave his body. Then I just sat there next to my father and watched my uncle die."

Tavar carefully placed his arm around her as she finished. She wasn't crying. She just stared out into the stillness of the desert, eyes blank and unseeing.

"What happened after?"

"My father claimed that a slave had attacked my uncle and then my father killed the slave. Easy to cover up. Most people in Alfara don't ask questions about the slaves. They are happy to believe that only slaves would be capable of such betrayal. No one cared that my father killed a slave over it. They saw it as acceptable revenge for the crime." Carver chuckled morosely at the memory. "Mad isn't it? My father had a slave killed to cover up the fact that I had killed my uncle."

"In all honesty, I've given up trying to make sense of this world. It amazes me that I can still remember a time when everything felt so warm and safe. Now I realise that was my parents doing. They sheltered me from the horrors around me. Without them, everything was clear and open for me to witness. There was no barrier to protect me from the blood and shit of the world." Tavar pulled his cap from his head and shook some of the sand from his head that had been lodged in since his fall down the dunes. "Does it go away?"

"Does what go away?" Carver asked, finally facing him, her beautiful eyes burning into his.

"The guilt. As soon as my blade flashed across his neck, I felt it. Like a weight in the pit of my stomach, dragging me down. It's all I can think about."

"My father used to say that time is the best healer. It helps, certainly. So does a few drinks. Though,

I've found it just numbs the pain before it comes rushing back. Like trying to hold back the seas, once you can't hold them back anymore, it hits you a thousand times worse than before." Carver sighed and pulled her hand back, sniffing and rubbing her eyes before standing up. "I better circle the perimeter. Make sure there's no more of these raiders, or Blood Nation warriors. Whatever they are."

"Sure," Tavar agreed, standing and brushing the sand from his legs. "Thanks. For listening. It means a lot. And you know if you ever need to talk about anything…"

"Don't make this weird, peasant," Carver, said, back to her normal self. She started to walk off as Tavar called her back, pulling at his cap nervously.

"Carver. He was going to kill your father. You had no other choice." He wasn't sure why he said it. Maybe it was just an exhaustion-induced action but he thought it was what she would have wanted to hear. What she *needed* to hear.

She stopped in her tracks but didn't turn, making it impossible for Tavar to see her reaction to his comment.

"The ones you kill aren't like the other dead," she said, voice strong as iron. Her fists clenched at her side. Her whole body tensed like an arrow waiting for release. "They don't go away. They live on in you. Every time you close your eyes or have a moment of silence to yourself. It's like you're never alone. They're watching you, always watching, making sure that their loss wasn't for nothing. Only thing we can do is keep living. And make sure that we live a life worth dying for."

Tavar stayed rooted to his spot and could only watch as she walked away. Even after her silhouette was lost to the darkness of the night, his eyes lingered on the sands.

CHAPTER SIXTEEN: DISTRACTIONS

To thank them for their help in dealing with the raiders, Adnan offered camels to the five of them, to ease their journey through the desert. All had accepted, of course. The only drawback from such acceptance were the looks of envy shot their way as they passed the struggling soldiers sweating and heaving heavy bags.

"I'm starting to think this wasn't the best of ideas," Adam called over to Tavar from his camel, catching a particularly venomous glance from a large, scarred warrior in the line. "Think we're making more enemies than we should."

Tavar returned the scarred warrior's stare, unflinching. He was a soldier now, just like the scarred man. There was no need for submission within the ranks. "Forget them. We've earned this. Whilst they slept, we dealt death. Let them stare."

"I suppose so," Adam responded, sounding unconvinced as he tried to avert his gaze from the warrior.

Riding a camel wasn't as comfortable as Tavar had thought. Being a lover of riding horses, he assumed it would be similar. Though happier on the beast than walking across the unforgiving sands, the constant instability of the humped animal kept him from being able to relax like he could with a horse. At any one time, he was either directly on top of the hump or forced at some strange angle. Still, through it all he made certain that he looked dignified, forcing himself to look down on the soldiers as the beast strode alongside them. War was no time for weakness. That's what Oden had warned him. The ride was bumpy but he would rather be up here than down there, that was certain.

Another perk of the ride was being able to look amongst the soldiers in the Alfaran army, even ones from different units. He smiled as he found Alice and Cassie marching together, bows wrapped over their shoulders and heavy bags strapped to their backs. Even through the difficult slog of the march, they found the energy to grin at Tavar and Adam and, after checking for signs of an officer and finding them lacking, they were able to strike up a short conversation.

"Who'd you have to kill to get one of those?" Cassie remarked, blocking the sun from her eyes with a forearm as Adam eased his mount towards them, Tavar hot on his heels.

"Top secret. We'd have to kill you if we told you," Adam said, looking over his shoulders for dramatic effect.

"Usually I'd take my chances but I wouldn't want to hurt such a beautiful creature," Alice said, rubbing the camel's side and smiling up at her brother. "Just to be clear, I'm on about the camel."

"We're twins…"

"You and the camel are twins?" Cassie asked, her laughter starting Alice off and in turn, Tavar.

"Very fucking funny," Adam said, voice soaked in sarcasm. "How you doing, anyway?"

"It's hot. Really fucking hot," Alice said, wiping an arm across her sweaty face and sighing. "Could do with a break but they're pushing us hard. They want us in Hartovan as soon as possible."

"A rebellion doesn't look good," Tavar said. "Makes the country look weak. Signs of weakness are usually followed by an invasion. Alfara can't risk such a sign. Not with the other kingdoms being so strong right now."

"If they keep pushing us this hard, we'll keel over before we can take the city back. There's your sign of weakness," Alice scoffed.

"*The need of the common soldier is always overlooked for the greed of the great*," Tavar said, remembering a line from one of his many history lessons.

"Malike ir Terrasil," Alice commented, a look of disbelief on her face as her eyes found Tavar's. "Are you seriously quoting Terrasil months after those lessons have ended? You spend too much time in those books."

"You don't spend enough time in them!" Cassie jumped in, reprimanding her partner before blowing her a kiss to calm her down.

"You are supposed to be on my side!"

"No. I'm supposed to make you a better person. That's what a partner is," Cassie said with a shrug. "Deal with it."

"She's got you there, sis," Adam chuckled along, happy to see his sister defeated for once.

"I feel attacked on all sides," Alice cried in mock frustration. "Sod you all. I'll read books whilst you're all out in the city fighting with the rebels. And don't come crying for my help when you need an archer to cover your back."

For the rest of journey, they stayed together,

sharing jokes and laughing together. Tavar was happy for the distraction. Whenever silence fell, his mind strayed to thoughts of the man he had killed. The man of the blood nation. He'd achieved some sleep the previous night but it was light and fitful. His dreams had been struck with images of the dying man, accepting his fate as his life faded away. Tavar had woken up covered in sweat, unable to keep thoughts of the man and the possibilities of life that he had cut short from his mind.

That night was just as difficult. Adnan had informed him that this would be the last night they slept in tents as he hoped that the following night they would be able to procure houses in some of the villages on the outskirts of the city. Tavar didn't know if this would help his restlessness. Every time his eyes fell upon the blade strapped at his waist, he remembered the damage it had done, the life it had taken. Just as Carver had said, the man was undying, living on in his dreams and waking thoughts.

There were no snores in the tent, though his three allies were lost in a deep sleep. Admitting defeat after only an hour of rest, Tavar exited the tent and crept across the camp. A crescent moon hung overheard surrounded by a swarm of pearl like stars sitting amongst the velvet sky. Without thinking, he found his feet carrying him across the camp, towards the tent he knew Carver was sleeping in. Out of anyone here, she would know what to say, just like she had last night.

There were a few lookouts but they didn't pay any heed to the young soldier wandering between the tents. One smiled and nodded, happy to see another friendly face instead of an enemy. Tavar smiled back and continued. Eventually, he found the crimson tent. It was small, just large enough for one occupant, as was expected for a unit leader, rookie or not.

"You know I can have you thrown into a cell for entering my tent unannounced at night?"

His heart quickened as his eyes adjusted to the low light thrown out by the lantern in the corner of the tent on top of a small wooden chest. They fell upon Carver's dark, alluring eyes framed by unusually long eyelashes that fluttered as she sat up from her bed. She covered a yawn with one hand, not bothering to cover herself properly as her thin nightdress fell seductively, exposing her cleavage.

Tavar tore his eyes away, aware of his lack of etiquette. "My apologies. I just needed... I just needed..."

"You needed someone to speak to?" Carver asked, eyes not judging him. She patted a hand next to her and sat up properly. "Come, join me."

He hesitated, suddenly aware of all the cultural rules he was breaking just by being here. Then again, what was one more rule to break? He was here now, why not break them all?

He crossed the tent and lowered himself awkwardly next to her, his eyes looking anywhere but at his friend.

"So, you've entered my tent in the middle of the night without being invited. We should be sleeping and we are a day or two away from battle. This must be important," Carver said with a jovial tone. She seemed to find the whole idea amusing, as though it was some kind of joke.

"I couldn't sleep," Tavar admitted.

"That much is obvious. Why aren't you sleeping is what I want to know. Judging by the frustrating number of snores I can hear surrounding me, the rest of the camp doesn't seem to be having such problems. So how can I help you?"

He slowly breathed out and turned to face her. Tired and defeated from the past few days, suddenly he felt all his guards fall from him, the shields he had put up to stop himself from being hurt like he had in the past. Lost in her deep, brown eyes, he realised what he wanted, what he needed. To tell her how he felt. How he felt about her.

The blood rushed through his body as she ran a hand through her dark, wavy hair and pushed it behind a delicate ear.

"Last night was…" he struggled to find the words, knowing how important this moment was. "Horrendous. But it made me realise something. We said that we've no idea what's going to happen once this is over. We don't know who will make it out of the city alive." He saw Carver's lips move but he stopped her, needing to get this out before she could stop him. "Please, let me finish, I need to finish or I'll break and this will have all been for nothing." Carver's face softened as she bit her bottom lip. Somehow it just made her look even more beautiful to him. "Last night, I could have died. I've no idea how I managed to survive but I did. Next time, there'll be loads more warriors fighting and I'm not sure that I'll be that lucky. You said it's important to live a life worth dying for, well I'm not sure I have, not yet anyway. There are so many things I want to do and one of them involves telling you exactly how I—"

Carver pushed a finger against his lips and hushed him, chuckling to herself. "Shut up."

He flinched back. Definitely not the response he was looking for.

"Last night was terrifying. The nights ahead will be just as terrifying," Carver said, eyes not leaving his. "We're going to be going through a lot of shit and just like Oden said, we can't have any distractions, no matter how anyone feels."

Tavar felt his breathing slow and the blood no longer rushed around his body. His brain kicked back into gear. How could he have been so stupid? She was right. They didn't need distractions. Not now.

He calmed himself down. Rational thought. That's what he needed.

Then she pulled him in by his collar and pressed her lips against his. His arms wrapped around her, pulling her body tight against his. Her flowery smell was like a drug to him, intoxicating. He parted his lips and felt her tongue twist around his in a wet embrace. It felt sloppy. It felt strange. It felt amazing.

The blood in his body rushed faster than the Dukhan Falls. Most of it felt as though it rushed towards his waist and he felt his cheeks redden as Carver pressed against him. He shuddered slightly as they parted for a moment, both breathing heavily with sweat dripping down their faces. Carver clutched at his hair and pulled him in once more, continuing the kiss with even more vigour and passion.

Tavar closed his eyes as he ran his hands over her body, feeling every line and curve. She pushed him back and he allowed himself to fall onto his back as she lay on top of him, one leg either side. His hand found the smooth, naked skin on her leg and he pushed up, feeling her dress ride up with his hand.

"Are you okay with this?" he asked, wanting to make sure she was comfortable.

Carver nodded silently and kissed him again, biting his lower lip and laughing as he cursed her with a grin. Suddenly she paused, jumping to the side.

"I'm sorry," Tavar said, frantically thinking about what he may have done to upset her.

She stood there, dishevelled and frowning, one hand resting on her head as she stared at the carpet on the floor. "No. It's not you. This is just, a distraction. Maybe you should go."

Tavar stood, confused. He checked his clothing, making sure he looked presentable. He passed Carver, brushing his hands against hers and feeling a jolt of excitement as she pulled at his finger.

"You know what," Carver said, turning to him and pulling him closer once more. "We could both do with a distraction…" She pulled her dress over her head and lay back, completely naked on the bed.

Tavar swallowed hard and unclasped the buttons on his robe. "Distractions can be good…"

CHAPTER SEVENTEEN: THE FACE OF WAR

It was messier than he had thought it would be. More blood too. No one had ever mentioned that. She'd managed to stifle her screams of joy by burying her head against his shoulder or kissing him passionately, once even drawing blood as she bit a bit too hard on his lip. It was after faster than he would have liked. His apology brought another laugh from Carver and a wicked smile that just made him want her again. Luckily enough, after a short pause, he was able to go again. Much to both of their enjoyment.

"You better leave before you fall asleep," Carver had warned him as she wrapped the sheet around her body. Tavar's eyes felt heavy and so he shook his head to keep from drifting into slumber. "Go. And don't say a word of this to anyone. I have a reputation as a hard bitch to uphold. Speak to anyone and I'll make sure you don't have the parts to ever do this again."

He'd practically floated through the campsite back to his tent. His skin tingled with a new energy that pulled him forward and it was impossible to wipe the grin from his face. The moon shone brighter than he had ever seen in the sky and sand at his feet felt softer and more welcoming than it had on his journey there. Even the snores that greeted him back at his tent sounded like a song the heavens sang just for him.

"You're smiling too much. It's scaring me," Adam said, staring at Tavar with a raised eyebrow from his camel the next day. "It's the look I'd expect if you'd just seen Qassim fall from a cliff. If that's what happened, then tell me. I need to know too."

"Qassim is alive," Tavar said with a roll of his eyes. "well, as far as I am aware."

"Then why the stupid grin?"

"We're almost in Hartovan. We are well rested. And we're alive. Life is good."

"Okay, now I *know* something is up," Adam mocked. "You've never said that in your life. You're a pessimist. It's one of your many qualities that make you my friend. Sure you didn't get hit on the head? Or maybe you were hit in the face? That would at least explain the swelling on your lip…" Adam's eyes narrowed as his voice lowered. He knew he was onto something.

"Maybe I was. I'll have the medic look at it later," Tavar replied, eager to move the conversation away before he spilled the truth of the matter. He had to visit the medic anyway, so it was a good answer. The wound he had acquired in the fight with the raider still pained him. He'd cleaned it often to keep infection away but he thought it would be best for an expert to take a look, just in case he was missing something. Too often had he heard tales of warriors who soaked the edges of their weapons in poison to add to the distress and stretch out the torment for their opponent. Even after death, the warrior could still have the last laugh. Undying indeed.

"It is good that we are nearing Hartovan," Adam admitted, not pressing the issue. "Not for the fighting. I'm just looking forward to seeing the end of the sands."

"We should be turning northeast shortly and out of the desert. If we were to continue, straight east, we would be able to continue across the desert for weeks." And at some point we would reach the Blood Nation,

Memories of Blood and Shadow

Tavar thought.

"Thank the Izads we don't need to do that. It's only been a few days but I miss trees. I miss rivers. I miss going to bed without having to play a game of 'what's the weirdest place you can find sand?'"

The soldiers turned north as they reach the Valley of the Dead, a pass flanked by two mighty red canyons.

"That is our sign to turn," Harun said to Tavar and Adam as they reached him. Bushy leant over the side of his camel and spat in the sand. "The living may not pass down the valley and return."

"Why not? Adam asked.

"They say the old gods wandered down the valley after a great war. They stumbled upon the pass and travelled along it until they found a place to die," Harun explained.

"Who's *they*?" Tavar scoffed. In all the vague stories, it was always some shadowy unnamed people who were passing on the tales, the messages.

Harun shrugged. "No idea. All I know is that people do not head down the valley."

"My people have heard of this valley," Bushy said, his face paler than usual amongst the mass of hair. "It leads to the Land of the Gods, supposedly."

"Well, whatever lies at the end, we're not finding out today," Adam said as he turned the camel to follow the others away from the valley. "And I'm not too keen on coming back either. Looks like the valley will remain a mystery. I reckon there's just a bunch of rocks and bones, anyway."

Before long, they spotted the first signs of life. The bits of green on the trees and plants they passed weren't much but after days in the desert, they brought smiles to the soldiers' faces.

"Really makes you appreciate the little things," Adam said, staring out at a cluster of spindly plants growing a few paces away. "A few days in the desert and I'm welling up at some ugly plants. Think the heat has got to me."

"Nah, you've always been this odd," Tavar joked. "If that small heap of green is getting to you, you're going to burst in a moment." The incline of the land allowed him to look far out across the world. No longer was there just sand and rock. In the distance, he could see the shimmer of a great body of water, a lake, as the sun shone down onto it. Beside the lake stood a cluster of wooden houses that Tavar recognised as more of a western style than he was used to seeing in Alfara.

"A lake…" Adam said, breathlessly as he stared out at the horizon. "We can bathe. I can finally get this bastard sand off me."

As they drew closer to the lake, Tavar had a better look at the houses scattered across the region. Wooden with straw roofs and a hole cut out at the top. The houses were very long, and each had various animals walking, eating or laying on the green that grew beside each building. Men and women came out of the houses at the sound of the marching army, worried looks on their faces. Some of the men pulled their family in closer, eyes not leaving the passing soldiers. In the distance, right at the edge of the horizon, Tavar thought he could see the outline of the city standing in front of the mountain range.

A horn blew at the front of the marching soldiers and was repeated three times further down the line. As one, the soldiers halted, waiting for their commands. Tavar pulled the reins on his camel and was pleased with the beast's quick reaction. He patted it on the side and waited with the others.

"Looks like we're here," Adam whispered over to Tavar, pointing to the houses in the east. "Look." The houses were covered in the colours of Alfara with flags waving in the gentle breeze on poles stuck down in the soil. The whole place was turning into one giant Alfaran camp site.

"I don't think these people will be very welcoming," Tavar said, glancing around at the scared and angry faces of the men and women clustered outside their home. "We're taking their homes. Their food. Their land. We're the invaders. They won't care why we're here. They just want to look after their families."

"That's war for you," Adam spat.

"Soldiers of Alfara!" a voice called out down the line. "You will stay in your units and wait until you have been designated a room to rest for the night. Food will be provided by our most welcoming hosts who wish for the speedy liberation of their city." Judging by the frowns and scowls on their faces, Tavar thought they wished for the whole army to just fuck right off. "Rest. Eat. Drink. Tomorrow, we shall fight."

"How did you acquire such a wound?" The medic scanned over the cut, pulling Tavar's arm closer to his face and staring into the wound as though it would be able to tell him all it knew.

"Sword practice," Tavar lied. "Got a bit too carried away."

"Hmm…" The medic didn't seem entirely

convinced but Tavar was thankful that the old man decided not to pursue that particular line of enquiry. "Save your energy for the real fighting tomorrow. Hurting each other will only lead to our downfall. An over eager soldier is poison to his unit. Remember that."

"I will."

"Here," the medic crushed up some herbs and swirled them into a cup of water. "Drink this." He watched Tavar drink the whole thing. It tasted minty but wasn't too unpleasant. Yasmin had forced much worse remedies upon him. "It should ease the pain by sundown. The wound itself is healing. It certainly won't hold you back in the fighting so don't even think of using it as an excuse to get out of it!"

"Do soldiers do that?" Tavar asked. He assumed that any punishment against those seeking ways to escape battle would be severe.

"You wouldn't believe what I've had to put up with, boy! A few years ago, I even saw a soldier cut off a finger the night before battle."

"What happened to him?" Tavar asked, shocked that anyone would go to such an extreme.

"His unit leader made him enter the battle first. Ended up with worse than a chopped finger, I can tell you that," the medic chuckled to himself. "God is watching at all times. The tricks and lies of humans are as clear as the blue sky to our Lord. Remember that as well."

Tavar exited the medic's tent and almost bumped straight into Master Oden. The master stopped and pulled his arm across his chest. "God be praised. Such perfect timing, Tavar Farwan."

"How may I help you, master?"

"The house you and your unit have been placed in currently has, how shall I put this? Frustrated occupants." Oden flashed a mischievous grin that instantly had the hairs on the back of Tavar's neck stand up. "I wish for you to speak to them. Advise them that they should leave their home for a few nights and we can give them a nice, little tent to stay in."

"I don't mind staying in the tent, if it helps matters. Been doing it in the desert so it's no problem, master." Tavar knew immediately that he had said something wrong by the frown on Oden's face.

"It does not help matters," he replied bluntly, rubbing his wrinkled forehead. "If we allow them to stay in their home, the other men and women will get restless. We must treat all the same. Remember, boy, there is a place for everyone. Make sure they know theirs. Come, I will show you which house."

Tavar trudged along behind Oden, cursing him silently. This was the last thing he needed. The villagers were already on edge. How would they feel once Tavar argued with a family so that he could sleep in their bed before killing people they might know?

Around him, he could see scared villagers led away from their homes by determined soldiers. Children were dragged along in tears by their parents, unable to comprehend what exactly was going on. For a moment, he saw one man step up to a soldier, fists balled and ready for a fight. Thankfully, at the last moment, the villager's shoulders sagged and all the fight faded from his body. Rational thought defeating the rush of emotions brought on by the soldiers' occupation.

"As you can see," Oden said, looking around at the disgruntled villagers. "We are not as welcome as we would have liked. Though here to liberate the city from the stench of the rebels, these people are having their lives changed, and in their foolish minds, not for the better. We need this battle over fast."

"I understand, master," Tavar said though deep down, he wondered why they didn't just stay in Kessarine. Hartovan had been its own kingdom once before. He didn't see a problem with it being one again. A small city on the edge of the undying sands, they weren't bothering anyone. Alfara was just trying to save face.

"I must admit, I needed a moment to talk to you alone. Your brother is in the city, a small unit led by Major Marcus managed to enter in darkness last night through a tunnel one of our informants revealed. Their mission was to capture a high ranked enemy for interrogation." Tavar's body tensed as he processed the information. His brother was already in the city, behind the gates of Hartovan in enemy territory.

"Have you heard from his unit?" he struggled to hold his voice together, biting his lip after it wobbled before remembering it was already swollen. He swore under his breath as his lip throbbed again.

Oden sighed and stopped in his tracks to face Tavar who did the same.

"No. We have had no word. At first light, there will be a full-scale attack. The plan is to take the city in one go."

"Why are you telling me this?" Tavar asked, curious why Oden would allow such information to be given to a lowly soldier.

"The rebels have been hanging soldiers they catch within the city. Their leader is claiming to be the King of Hartovan and his word is law. He is allowing no prisoners. Death to Alfara is his mantra. I'm telling you now so that you can compose yourself. You might see something tomorrow that strikes the fear of a demon through your bones. Ready yourself tonight, ready yourself for the worst."

Tavar nodded and rubbed at his beard, his body shaking. He thought of his brother, swinging from a rope... No. He'd be alive. This wasn't the end for him. He'd be somewhere in the city. He was a survivor; he'd proven that time and time again. They'd already been through so much.

"Now, let's deal with these peasants. I thought you would be able to relate to them and they to you."

By the time Tavar had reached the home, the family was ready to give up. They'd watched some of their friends dragged from their homes kicking and screaming. Arguing was an exercise in futility. They wanted to keep some of their dignity.

The husband and wife were young, a few years older than Tavar. Yet they had two small children: one looked three years old and clung to the hem of his mother's dress, whilst the other was a babe, tiny and cradled in his father's arms. Their dark skin reminded him of Cassie, a constant reminder of the difficult past endured by the people of Hartovan. A whole generation had been taken from their island home on the belt of the world and forced to serve others following the Desert War – a fifteen-year war still spoken of in Alfara with pride. Often omitted were the tales of murdered babes and homes set aflame. The victors could always choose the light they stood in once the war had been won. History had always been that way.

"We don't like it. But we'll go," the father had agreed after Tavar had briefly spoken to them. "I've worked all my life to build a home for my family. Please don't ruin it." The man had two vertical, white scars carved under his eyes that drew Tavar's gaze. He quickly realised how rude he was being and cleared his throat before anyone else noticed.

"I promise, you will have your home returned to the same standard as when you leave it," Tavar promised, giving the man a small smile that was only returned with a snort.

"Right. Just like that commander of yours promised this war would be over before the banishment. I'm used to the weak promises of soldiers. Still, I will pray that you are one of the good ones." The family left the house, the child weeping softly as his mother took him by the hand.

"You handled that well enough," Oden said, nodding his head as he paced around the room. "I wouldn't have made any promises but I suppose it helped grease the wheels that set their exit in motion. A good touch."

"They seem like good people," Tavar said, looking around the room. It was larger than his tent, almost twice as big. There were three beds at one end of the room. A hearth sat in the middle of the table, cool embers still softly burning away under a pot of water. The steam rose through the hole in the ceiling. A wooden partition separated the far end of the room beside a wooden table with four stools. They would be comfortable enough here. More so than the family staying in one of the smaller tents, especially with a baby.

"They do seem like good people. War is a bastard to good people. You'll do well to remember that," Oden advised, peering into the pot of water and sniffing before drawing back. "We grow up with tales and stories that give us the rose scented view of war. War stinks like shit and there's no escaping that fact. The face of war is not some hero smiling with perfect teeth. It is the starving, homeless farmer. The bloated corpse of a young boy. The terrified gaze of a daughter looking upon the motionless bodies of her parents. You have a soft heart, Tavar Farwan. The days ahead will turn it to stone or it will break. Up to you which one it is. I will send a messenger for another bed and for your colleagues to join you. Sleep well. It is the last one you will have before the whites of the enemy's eyes are boring holes into your very soul." The officer swept out of the room without a backward glance, leaving Tavar to his thoughts.

The silence hanging over the village was all consuming. Even the stars didn't want to come out that night.

Tavar crept between the wooden houses, keeping to the shadows as he made his way up the hill overlooking the city of Hartovan. It took him a while but eventually, he found what he was looking for.

"I hope you're not back for round two..." Carver said with a wicked smile that stopped his heart. She sat on the hill, legs crossed as she looked out at the city. "I would be flayed if I didn't do my job as a lookout. No distractions tonight."

Tavar grinned at the reminder of the night before. "Technically, I think it would be round three," he said with a cheeky smile of his own and watched as her eyes lit up as her thoughts also turned to the previous night. "But no. Just thought you might enjoy some company."

He sat down next to her and quickly felt in his pocket for the rolled-up parchment that Ahmed had given him before leaving Kessarine. His thoughts soured at the memory of what he had to do as the sun rose in the morning. Fighting a battle would be bad enough without having to search for both his brother and the king's lover.

"Sure, why not?" Carver said, eyes flicking to him before turning to the gated city. Though not as imposing as the wall of Kessarine, the city gate of Hartovan would still cause them trouble. Twenty paces high, the main gate at the front of the city would need to be battered down or else the soldiers would have to climb over with the ropes they had brought across the desert. They would be sitting ducks for enemy archers in that case.

"My brother is in the city," he said, wondering what Vandir was doing right now and praying that he was safe.

Carver frowned but she did not turn to him. There was still animosity between the two of them. "Captured?"

Tavar shrugged and exhaled. "Maybe. I don't know. His team was led by the major. They were supposed to capture someone important. Haven't heard from them since."

"I don't like your brother. Never did. Still, I hope he is alive. For your sake more than anything else." Tavar forced a smile and leaned back, looking up at the empty sky. He felt once again for the scroll in his pocket and bit his top lip, missing the one Carver had attacked in passion the night before.

"I can trust you, can't I?"

"Course you can. What's up?" Carver asked, tilting her head to the side and pursing her lips at the change in conversation.

"I have something to do in that city tomorrow. An important mission that no one can know about. It's the king's business. Truth be told, I'm shitting myself. Talking about it might help, with someone I trust."

Carver placed a hand on his as he sat up. "You can tell me."

"The king wants me to pass on a message to Major Marcus's brother. Someone he fell in love with years ago. I'm to find him and give him this parchment." He pulled the small scroll of parchment from his pocket and watched as Carver's eyes lit up at the sight.

"That's enchanted!" she exclaimed, reaching out and grabbing the scroll. She cupped it in her hands, peering down at it and searching every bit of the paper and the gold rod showing on either side. "Okadan script. This must be really fucking important, Tavar. The message will light up in flames after it has been read. This is old magic. Djinn magic. I didn't know it still existed."

Tavar smirked at her excitement, pleased she was so happy with the discovery. She snapped out of the moment, suddenly connecting what Tavar had said. She handed the parchment back and stared at him, her face worried.

"I remember Marcus's brother. He was a deserter. Went missing not long before we became recruits. I can help you find him but if we mess this up, we're in big fucking trouble."

"We're storming a city tomorrow; I think we're in enough trouble as it is." He exhaled, relieved at being able to share his worry. "I just need to find him and hand this over. That's it. Mission over."

"Back to the fighting then. Great," Carver said with more than a hint of sarcasm.

"Uhlad said he would give me my freedom when I succeed," Tavar said, watching as Carver's body tensed. "I could finally leave Kessarine. Travel the world like we said."

"And you trust him?" Her eyes were fixed on his, questioning and alert. Tavar felt anger bubbling in his stomach, angry that she wasn't happy for him. His freedom was all he had ever wanted. He struggled for words, stuttering over them as a cloud of confusion covered his mind.

"Y-yeah. Why shouldn't I? I'm doing him a favour."

"He's a king. He would have manipulated lesser men than you, Tavar Farwan," Carver warned.

Tavar felt the rage rise in him. He stood to his feet, breathing heavily and running a hand through his hair. "I—"

"Shut up," Carver said, interrupting him and jumping to her feet. He followed her gaze and saw what had distracted her. The gates of the city were opening.

Carver grabbed for her horn and blew loud and long. A moment later, the camp was awake with soldiers rushing around, weapons drawn and eager for battle.

"Find your unit. Looks like the battle will be coming to us…"

Alfaran soldiers marched into place, each unit standing together as one as the thousand strong enemy steadily made their way across the fields towards them. Tavar stood next to Adam and Harun, craning his neck to catch a glimpse of the enemy. Torches on both sides had been lit, lighting up the land between the campsite and the city, giving it a haunting, orange glow.

"Why would they leave the city?" Adam asked. "Stupid decision if you ask me."

"No one is asking you, boy!" One of the more experienced soldiers spat back, shutting Adam up instantly. "Fucking rookies need to know their place."

Adam looked sheepishly over to Tavar and pressed his lips together to stifle his laughter. Even at the break of battle his friend was still able to make light of the situation. Tavar was thankful for it. Adam always helped put him at ease.

Seconds passed by like years as Tavar waited for the enemy to reach them. The sounds of heavy boots stomping on the ground grew steadily louder until, at once, they fell silent.

The whole place fell silent, waiting for the next move. It was like a deep breath before a plunge into icy water. A few coughs broke out amongst the soldiers but nothing more. Tavar could hear the wind catch the flags waving at the top of long poles held in each unit. The more experienced of the soldiers stood upright and facing forward, like statues watching in the night. The rookies were different. Their eyes flickered around, looking for any reassurance of what was about to happen. Their hands slackened on their spears and their boots shifted uneasily on the mud.

"You picked a beautiful evening to visit our humble home." Tavar stepped slightly into Adam, trying to see through a gap in his unit. He saw at the front of the thousand soldiers dressed in chain mail and spiked helmets, a tall, thin man who for some reason made Tavar think of spiders. The man was not wearing any armour. Instead he wore a long, flowing deep purple robe speckled with dashes of silver that complemented his rich, black skin. He was smiling with a row of bright, white teeth at the huge number of soldiers facing him with weapons, as though they were mere children holding toys past their bedtime. "I am the voice of the lion, chosen to speak on behalf of our king. If you do wish to visit, I do ask that you lay down your weapons. Such draconic things are not needed. The nation of Hartovan will welcome our neighbours from Alfara but fighting is unseemly in such progressive times, wouldn't you say?"

The spider-like man held out his long hands as though he was just asking for a simple gift. Commander Grey marched forward, dressed in all his fine, silver armour, chainmail falling either side of his horned helmet. He stopped barely twenty paces from the man before turning back to his army with his own hands out wide, laughing to his men. A few chuckles broke out in line with the commander's own amusement.

"Unseemly?" the commander repeated, loud enough for his own men to hear as well. "Fighting can be unseemly. Especially when a city starts fighting against the reason it is thriving. Hartovan is a part of the Alfaran kingdom. Your allegiance is to the king. King Uhlad the Second will accept nothing but your complete surrender and an oath that no Hartovan citizen will raise a weapon in anger to our great nation ever again. Your so-called king must stand before the people of Alfara, humble and apologetic. It is treason and blasphemy to call oneself a king. Such profanity in the face of God and the Izads must be punished."

"King Uhlad is gracious with his offer. However,

I am afraid we must decline. For over a generation Alfara has ruled our great city with an iron fist, stifling its people and ramming their idea of culture down our throats until we choked. We were dragged from our homeland against our will and told to be grateful and say thanks to our new masters. No more. Our king is just and worthy of the title, unlike so many claiming to be of the Izads. We will live free and we will die free. This is my promise." His voice was deep and rich, singing through the air and coursing through Tavar's bones. It had a magical quality to it.

"Then you will all die tomorrow," Grey barked back. Even with his back turned on Tavar, he could sense the anger emanating from the leader of the army.

The man laughed, just as he would if he had been told a warm joke by a friend sitting in a tavern. "Some will. And I'm sure Uhlad and his judges have many pawns to throw at us over the coming days. It is sad that it has come to this, but so be it." The unarmoured man gave a sigh that made Tavar truly believe that he was sorry for how things were unfolding. "Bring forth the prisoners." After clicking his fingers, five of his heavily armoured soldiers stepped out from the mass of men and women, dragging with them a prisoner each, all with hands tied behind them and a dark bag on their heads. The soldiers pushed the captured figures to their knees with a smirk before fading back into their unit.

"What is this?" Grey asked, a hint of unease cracking into his voice.

"You probably don't recognise them with the bags over their heads," the voice of the lion said, looking almost bored with the conversation now but obviously enjoying playing with the commander. "Thirty men and women. Thirty. That's how many we found trying to sneak into our great city to cause chaos and deal death."

A collective intake of breath could be heard through the forces, rookie and experienced alike. The connotations were obvious. Thirty soldiers had attempted to sneak into the city. Only five were here.

"Vandir," Tavar muttered to himself. "Please be one of those lucky souls in the hoods." The odds were not in his favour, but his brother was a survivor.

"Twenty-five were killed by order of our king, the merciful King of Hartovan. Beheaded. A swift death for all, unlike how your king dishes out punishments. Their bodies have been given to the flames. But we offer you a slither of hope. Take the five we saved for you. Hear their words and leave this new kingdom. Or suffer the consequences. I am Sett al-Ra'yaan, the Voice of the Lion. Hear me." With that, Sett al-Ra'yaan turned and marched back towards the city, the army turning together and following. None looked back.

Grey raised a hand and flicked his fingers forward in the air. On command, five soldiers left their posts and raced over to the hooded captives. At once, the hoods were pulled away, showing the faces of five beaten and bruised men and women. All had their head shaved and swayed with dizziness. One woman was missing an ear.

Tavar released an audible gasp as his eyes fell on the face of his brother through swollen and black eyes. Vandir was alive, thank the heavens. Adam nudged him and gripped his wrist tight, letting him know that he too had spotted Vandir.

"Major Marcus," Grey said, sounding relieved as he stepped in front of the captive at the end. Out of the five, he seemed to be the one suffering the most. Supported by the soldier at his side to stop from falling to the earth, Marcus's face was a mess of cuts and bruises.

His jaw on the one side was swollen and the top of his right ear had been clipped by a blade, slicing off its curve. "It seems God has not finished with you, yet."

"God be praised," Marcus managed to mumble before finally falling to the floor.

"Clean them. Give them food and drink," Grey told the soldiers closest to him before turning to face his army. "This changes nothing," he cried. "At first light, Hartovan will crumble."

CHAPTER EIGHTEEN: THE SONG OF THE DYING

He was woken by the sound of thuds and screams.

Rushing from his tent ahead of the other four and drawing his weapon, he found a chaotic scene. Soldiers screamed curses so vile they took the breath from Tavar. He looked past the nearest tent and saw a soldier on his knees in the mud. In his hands was something round but unevenly shaped. It took a moment for him to realise what it was. A head. A human head.

Fighting the urge to vomit, Tavar looked away, only to be met by another head. This one stared up at him with unseeing eyes. He heard the whip of a catapult and another one landed in the distance, met with more screams, raised voices and curses on Hartovan and its people.

Under the dark cloak of night, Hartovan played their hand well, letting chaos and confusion blossom amongst their enemy. They knew exactly what they were doing. Expecting attack at first light, they wouldn't let the Alfaran soldiers rest.

Adam finally emerged from the tent, hair a complete mess and his blanket falling at his feet. "What the fuck is going on?"

"A gift from Hartovan," Bushy said, spitting on the ground and nodding over at the head next to Tavar. "They expect us to falter. To break. A scared enemy defeats itself."

"Quoting *The History of Warfare* might seem clever most of the time but this means the battle is upon us," Harun warned them. "Armour on. I expect Grey will want us to take the fight to them now. First light be damned."

They raced into the tent and hastily attached their greaves, gauntlets and placed their horned helmets onto their heads before tightening the clasps. Thankfully, they had slept in their chainmail, just in case. Tavar tied the waist band around his hips and checked that both his sword and dagger were attached correctly. He picked up his shield and exhaled. This was it. He could still hear screams and shouts from outside along with the sound of three thousand soldiers' boots pacing across the field.

Exiting the tent, he found more of a controlled chaos than before. Horses and camels rushed to their places at the sides of the infantry. Tavar jumped out the way as one member of the cavalry raced past to join with his unit.

"Stand with your men and women! Battle! To battle! For our king!" Tavar heard an unfamiliar voice cry between blows of a horn. He looked up and found a blue flag waving with a black falcon in the centre.

"There!" he pointed, checking that the others were following. "Adnan's flag."

They joined up with the unit, standing in line, chins raised and heels together as Adnan paced at the front on his camel, peering out over the men and women he was about to lead into battle. He looked surprisingly calm, a relaxing presence in the chaos surrounding him as more heads fell from the night sky.

"A little earlier than expected, but war waits for

no man. Or woman," Adnan added with a smile. "Once the gate is broken. I will lead our cavalry through and into the city. Infantry, you will follow under the guidance of Salim."

The silent giant nodded, seemingly unimpressed and bored with everything going on around him. He may have been watching a tame play by the way he stood, sleepy eyes looking out over the crowd of soldiers.

Another head dropped next to him. Some soldiers jumped at the thud, Tavar included, but Salim just stood there, not even looking at what had caused the commotion. "Archers, you will march behind and begin firing when in range. Break when Nasser commands and do not loose until he says. We do not need our own arrows killing Alfaran soldiers. Hartovan will be happy enough to do that for us. We wait for the signal and then we fight for our king, for our God, for our lives and most importantly, for the brave people either side of you. We are not separate soldiers now, my friends, we are one unit. A collective. Show me what that means and make it out alive. For Alfara!"

"For Alfara!" Every soldier raised their sword to the heavens and screamed the response. Tavar's adrenaline shot through his body, his blood thumping faster than a predator chasing its prey as his skin prickled under the starlight. This was it. War.

"God be with you, my friends," Harun said, touching his heart three times as he looked across at them. "I pray we see each other on the other side."

Tavar and Adam copied the gesture with a smile. "God be with you."

Bushy tapped his heart, eyes straight ahead at the city lit in starlight and torchlight. In the distance, Tavar could just make out the soldiers gathered around the city gate, guarding the battering ram as it smashed against the gate, attempting to force its way through. A rain of arrows fell from the wall around the city onto the soldiers who raised their shields. Most blocked the death from above but a few of the arrows made it through, taking down soldiers. At last, there was a huge crack like thunder followed by a roar from the Alfaran soldiers. The gate was open. The city would be breached. A deep, ominous horn blew across the night and the cavalry began their descent down the hill towards the defending city.

"Cavalry! On me!" Adnan roared; sword raised to the moon as he led his beast towards the city. "We enter the city as one hundred. We leave the city as one hundred!" he declared to another roar from the unit.

Sweat unrelated to the night's warmth dripped into Tavar's eyes as a second horn sounded. Salim turned without a word and marched forward. The infantry, Tavar included, followed.

"Stay with me," Adam said, brushing his shoulder against Tavar's.

"To the very end," Tavar agreed, offering a morose smile. Adam grinned back but he had no more words. No jokes. They both realised what they were about to do. What they were about to face.

Hooves of the cavalry battered the ground, deafening Tavar as they picked up the pace, racing to the city and to battle. The infantry marched as one. Spears at the front. Swordsmen behind followed by the archers. Tavar wondered where Alice and Cassie were amongst the mass of soldiers and how they were feeling.

"One hundred paces away!" Tavar heard Qassim yell in front of him, repeating Oden's words as the master called back further ahead. "Shield wall!"

Standing in the middle of the unit, Tavar raised his shield above his head, playing his part in ensuring the protection of the unit and praying that those around him were doing the same. Unable to see through the shields and the mass of soldiers, the sounds of battle hit him hard. The unit crept forward as one under the shadow of the city as cries of battle and death rang out around them. The clang of metal on metal as swords met was joined by the crackling of flames and the stomp of running boots.

"I don't wanna be here, Tavar. I want to be home," Adam said through broken sobs. Tavar turned his head under his shield and looked at his friend, offering him strength.

"Me too, mate. But we can get through this. As long as we stay together. I promise."

Adam nodded and steadied his breathing. "Together."

The *thwack* of an arrow smashing against his shield made Tavar almost jump from his armour. He gave a silent prayer to the heavens and whichever god was watching over him at that moment before sharing a relieved look with Adam.

The line of soldiers in front of Tavar suddenly broke and he remembered his training. Lowering his shield and twisting his body, he raised drew his sword and slid it over the top of his shield. The city was alight with flames and chaos. Wooden buildings burned down the two roads that lead further into the city on either side of a large, stone fountain. Soldiers in the red of Hartovan backed behind crude spear walls and debris as the Alfaran soldiers in blue and silver advanced. A wild eyed soldier rushed at Tavar and on instinct, he blocked the surprising attack and sliced his sword upwards from his hip, riding up the man's armour and finishing at his unprotecting neck. The soldier dropped with a strange gurgling sound.

All sense of unity disappeared in a flash as madness descended upon the soldiers in the heat of the battle. Some of the more experienced fighters yelled for calm and structure but such words fell upon deaf ears as the blood flowed.

Tavar watched as Adam stabbed wildly, thrusting his sword into the gut of the nearest enemy. Adam released the weapon, leaving it impaled in the dying soldier's stomach as he watched him fall to his knees. Tavar pulled the blade from the man with a noise like slicing fruit and handed it back to his shocked friend.

"You'll need this. Come on," he said, pulling Adam along as Bushy and Harun charged into a skirmish breaking out at the back of the fountain. The pair of them attacked with grace, turning their backs to each other and swiping at any enemy that came within range.

The heat of flames enveloping the buildings to Tavar's right burned against his skin. Smoke rose to the heavens as soldiers of Alfara kicked in doors to search for any enemies hiding from the unrelenting fighting. He fought down the tightness in the pit of his stomach and marched down the road to his right, thrusting his blade into the back of another unsuspecting enemy. There was no time for mercy.

"I killed him. He died right in front of me," Adam muttered to himself as he followed Tavar. Tavar turned to see his friend staring at the blood dripping from his weapon. He grabbed Adam by his creased collar and looked him in the eyes.

"Stay with me, Adam. We can do this."

Adam nodded, still trembling. He swallowed hard and composed himself with a slow breath. Tavar turned with a nod and stomped forward, eyes darting in all directions.

Soldiers and horses scrambled about the burning city as Tavar swung his sword. A would-be attacker fell to his right, cleaved from shoulder to the bottom of his rib cage. Tavar looked away from the damage he had done and stared forward. There was no time for guilt.

The invading Alfaran army pressed ahead, winning, to Tavar's eye. The blue and silver wave crushed against the red wall, forcing the Hartovan defenders back down the roads and into the centre of the city. Unarmed citizens fled from their homes and struggled to contain the growing flames dancing through the city at an alarming rate. Tavar winced as he watched an Alfaran soldier cut down one of the innocent citizens from the seat of his horse. The soldier cackled as the poor man fell to the ground, pleased with his ruthlessness.

"This is war," Tavar whispered to himself, barely able to hear his own words as the blood thumped around his body, making his ears throb. He deflected an attack from a soldier with no helmet and a bleeding wound just above his right eye. As his attacker's sword snapped to the side, Adam pounced, stabbing his blade straight through the man's heart.

"Thanks," Tavar said, nodding at his friend.

"Don't mention it."

Tavar stepped over the body and glanced around. Surrounded him, the scene was repeated over and over. Bodies falling to the ground with grunts and blood staining the stone street. Soldiers grimaced and took lives with barely a thought, their own survival was the most important thing right now. Through it all, the screams, the horns, the orders, the crackling of flames and the cries of the innocent rang out as a sickening song of the dying.

He did his best to ignore the wailing and focus on his goal. He had to find Marcus's brother and to do that, he needed Carver. He searched the battlefield, deflecting strikes and dodging what would have been killing blows before striking his own. Adam followed suit, blocking out the fear, guilt, and horror as he became the soldier he had trained to be.

Tavar scanned the mass of axe-scarred doors hanging from their frames and glanced up at the broken shutters smattered with arrows. The city was falling apart. Corpses lined the streets as both sides clashed in the light of the flames. One soldier passed Tavar, clutching at the bloodied stump at the end of his arm, staring at the place where he should have had a hand. His eyes were wide and white with confusion. He'd dropped his weapon and stumbled along the street, oblivious to the battle raging on.

As they pressed on through the city, Tavar heard a cry and paused, looking down an alley between two buildings: an apothecary and a butchers. A moment later, a familiar horn sounded from the alleyway.

"Adnan..." Tavar said, recognising the horn and rushing to the aid of the warrior.

The alley was cramped. Adnan stood, blade drawn and blood dripping from a wound that had swollen his left eye socket, helmet nowhere to be seen as his eyes glanced between the six soldiers pressing on him. To his left was Qassim, hair matted with blood. He held his sword weakly in his right hand whilst his left hung loosely at his side. A last stand for the two of them, unless help came soon.

Putting all thoughts of his own safety to one side, Tavar jumped into the shadows, forcing his sword into the back of the closest soldier. The soldier arched his shoulders back with a surprised grunt and fell to his knees, dropping his spear. Both Adnan and Qassim's faces lit up as Adam cried and swung his blade across the neck of the next soldier who had turned at the sound of his ally's death.

The element of surprise gone, the two of the remaining soldiers spun and attacked with abandon. Qassim and Adnan leapt into the fight, reenergised with the hope of victory. The largest of the four swung a mighty hammer, slow but powerful. Tavar pulled up his shield and blocked the blow but the force knocked it from his grip, sending the shield flying into the wooden building and leaving Tavar with only his sword and a throbbing hand, possibly broken.

The hammer rose in the air again but this time Tavar was ready for it. He dived low, ducking beneath the strike and coming out of a roll with his sword thrust straight up, straight through his opponent's stomach. The body fell onto the sword and gravity did the rest. The hammer fell with a deep thud before Tavar pushed his boot against the now motionless body and pulled his sword free. With no time to lose, he looked up to see Adnan slamming his shield on the back of the head of a soldier looming over a fallen Qassim. The soldier fell next to Qassim and turned onto his back, just in time to meet Adnan's blade with his throat.

A moment's peace fell in the alleyway as Tavar searched for the next enemy. There were none left.

Adam leant against the wall, helmet forgotten on the floor and his left eye half closed as his chest rose and fell with heavy breaths. Tavar walked over to Qassim and offered a hand. There was hesitation at first, as though Qassim was waiting for some trick. But there was no trick, no deception. Finally, he took Tavar's hand and welcomed the help to his feet, wincing and pulling his limp arm in tight to his chest. He wouldn't be much use for the rest of the battle, that was certain.

"Thank you," Qassim said, inclining his head ever so slightly but keeping his eyes fixed on Tavar.

"We would be meat for the worms had you not arrived when you did. You have my thanks," Adnan said, crouching low over one of the bodies and cursing.

Adam did the same before jumping up and shaking his head at Tavar. "Two of these men are Alfaran soldiers. Traitors."

"Shit," Adnan spat. "It's a civil war. We're not putting down a rebellion anymore. We're fighting for survival. Eyes everywhere, trust no one. We need to break through to the Hall of Justice. It's in the centre of the city. It's where the so-called King of Hartovan will be. If we cut the head off the snake, the rest will fall. Most of the citizens have left anyway, escaping across the sea to the Arrow Islands according to our spies. That means if anyone stands in your way, don't think twice. No matter what colour they are wearing, we take them down." He wiped his sword against his sleeve and turned to Qassim, his eyes landing on his useless arm. "You gonna be okay?"

"I can still fight," Qassim argued, a bit too much fight in his voice, as though he was trying to convince himself more than anyone else.

"You'll have a chance to prove it. Let's go."

They kept to the backstreets, sneaking past much of the bloodshed and keeping out of sight of the archers perched on the roofs across the city. Adnan led with Qassim close behind. Tavar brought up the rear, constantly checking that they weren't being followed as he kept close to Adam's heels.

The tight streets amplified the clang of swords and the last screams of dying men and women. Tavar tried to block it all out, scanning for any sign of Carver. The four of them weaved in and out of the narrow streets, trusting that Adnan remembered the correct path to the Hall of Justice. Thankfully, the city had been designed in such a way it was difficult to get lost.

"Get down," Adnan warned, crouching and pulling his body tight against a door swinging off its hinge. The road ahead was wider than the previous ones. Flags waved from tall buildings either side leading to a huge structure at the end of the road. The building had six marble columns at the front and a tall iron door closed shut. In front of it, the battle was fierce. There was no way around. They would have to go straight through. Tavar looked at the cluster of warriors and wondered if Carver was there, amongst all the blood and chaos.

"There's no hiding now," Adnan said, watching the battle, the light of flames flickering in his brown eyes. "God be with you. Shields up."

Tavar looked to his left and right, at the soldiers on either side. One a best friend, the other someone who he had viewed more as an enemy up until moments ago. Now he was willing to put his life on the line for him. Funny that. How things can change when the blood was flowing. They nodded to each other, knowing this could be the end and placed their shields up high, building a shield wall and advancing forward.

As they neared the mess of a melee, soldiers in red spotted them and broke from the chaos to rush their way, screaming into the night and holding their weapons high. From either side, warriors in blue turned as Adnan blew into his war horn, calling for support. They cheered and joined the line, shields connecting as one as they continued the march, meeting the attack head on.

Tavar braced as the first wave of red crunched into the shields. He pulled his sword back and lunged over the barrier, feeling his blade connect with the nearest enemy. The wall slowed but kept advancing, stepping over the dead. More warriors joined as Adnan continued to blow the horn, knowing they were near the target as the Hall of Justice loomed large in front of them. The next wave was almost too much. The door of the hall opened and another hundred soldiers poured out, fresh and ready for battle with painted faces and spears gleaming in the torch light.

"There's too many of them to hold!" Adnan roared. "On my signal, break."

"Stay behind me," Tavar turned to Qassim.

"What?"

"Stay behind me. You can't fight with one hand."

Qassim scowled but only grunted in response. Not wanted to answer properly. Tavar knew that he understood. Every move looked painful for him. He'd done well to last this far.

"Break!"

The Alfaran soldiers spread out on the signal, confusing the rushing attackers. Tavar slipped inside a thrust of the blade and swung his own weapon out, knocking an enemy's shield to the side. Qassim finished the unbalanced soldier off, his blade stabbing through his eye. Tavar had no time to admire the work. He raced forward into the cluster of enemies, sword dancing wildly, deflecting attacks with his shield and stabbing at any opening offered.

The bodies piled up and soon, his arms began to ache. He struggled to keep his weapon up, barely blocking the attacks of the fresher soldiers who had stormed out from the hall. He roared, calling for a last burst of energy, willing himself forward. Out of the corner of his eye, he spotted the flash of a blade and swiped wildly with his own to meet it.

"You've improved. Much faster. I'm impressed."

"Carver…" Tavar sighed in relief, almost hugging her before realising where he was. Both of her sleeves were frayed and bore scorch marks. Her dark hair stuck to her head, glued with dried blood and her eyes were bloodshot. "You look a mess."

"Not looking so hot yourself," she said with a wink. "Come on. Whilst they're fighting." She pointed to the open door leading into the Hall of Justice.

"Is he in there? Marcus's brother?" Tavar asked, eager to finish his mission.

"You saw him earlier. Calls himself Sett now. The Voice of the Lion. He'll be in there."

Tavar frowned and pulled some wax from a ringing ear. "Sett…" The Voice of the Lion was Marcus's brother and the man who King Uhlad had loved. The man Tavar needed to pass his message to. He checked his pocket for the scroll and was relieved to feel that it was untainted by the battle. "Let's go." He followed Carver, pausing only for a moment to look for Qassim and Adam but they were lost amongst the madness.

The entrance way was in pristine condition, in contrast to the rest of the fallen city. A cavernous room was flanked with two sets of stairs leading up to a balcony on which hung a huge painting of a black-skinned woman dressed in the traditional clothing of the western islands, the same place where many of the citizens of Hartovan had been dragged from over a generation ago. Marble busts lined the room standing on small columns. Tavar read the plaque on the nearest one:

Hassan Bast – First blood of the true Hartovan people. Killed standing up for his brother and sister by Alfaran soldier.

The next one had a similar, sad tale written beneath it:

Zuri Emem: Last Queen of the Western Isles. Died with her family under a rain of Alfaran arrows. Her death shall not be forgotten.

"Come on," Carver said, pulling on Tavar's sleeve to drag him away. "We don't have much time."

They followed a red carpet spotted with black and entered an even larger room. Tavar cursed and bent over, retching. Hanging from the ceiling around a chandelier were ten lifeless bodies stripped naked, the cuts and bruises a patchwork of evidence of the abuse they had suffered before being hung as ornaments in the grand room. He tore his eyes from the decaying bodies and followed the marble columns lining either side of the room as they ran up along a golden floor to a simple, black throne with a carved black lion looking to leap from the head of the seat. On the throne sat the Voice of the Lion.

Sett's shoulders slumped. He no longer looked like the dignified man who had mocked an entire army at the gates of the city. He looked defeated. Still, Tavar had to give him credit as he smiled as Tavar and Carver walked towards him, blades drawn and ready.

"Two victors carrying blades of destiny," Sett said, sitting up in the throne and shaking away the defeated attitude. Once again he had that aura of authority, of control. "It is fitting. Like in the old stories. Two young warriors working against adversity to rise to a challenge, a foe that must be defeated. I love the poetry of it. The drama. Reminds me of the plays I used to watch in Alfara as a young boy. Seems like a lifetime ago," he sighed. "So, what are the names of my angels of death come to take me down the red river of the boatman?"

"We're no angels of death," Tavar said, stopping at the stone steps leading up to the throne. "Just two soldiers. With a message."

"Where is the king?" Carver asked, looking around the empty room.

Sett leaned back and laughed, a true, honest laugh that echoed around the room. "No one speaks for the lion but the lion himself. You are looking at the King of Hartovan." He stood and gave a dramatic bow, spinning his hands in the air to the side before falling back onto his throne. "The people of Hartovan came to trust me after I deserted the army. I am one of them, a lost soul looking for their place in the world. Alfara is right, there is a place for everyone They are just often wrong about the correct place. I learned that after being torn from my rightful place in Alfara by old men who knew nothing about life."

"Your rightful place? Alongside Uhlad?" Tavar pressed, remembering what the king had told him.

"At first. Yes," Sett replied, not missing a beat. "Once that was taken from me, I tried to start a new life. I had a child who was taken from me. So I fled, living in the wilderness before finding my place here."

"But you've caused the death of so many. The

citizens of Hartovan will curse your name," Tavar argued, thinking of how few people he had seen in the city and the villages outside the gates.

"The people of Hartovan have escaped. I will not tell you where. They have freedom. They are able to find their place, to choose their destiny. There is no one left to tell them what to do or when to do it. Their heart shall decide, as it should be."

"This is why you've been goading Alfara," Carver said, smiling at the brilliance. "Distracting them whilst your people fled to the mountains or the islands nearby.

Sett grinned at his own wisdom. "Took some convincing. They didn't want to leave me. I had many volunteers to die in the city but I couldn't allow too many. Then it would have been pointless. I needed my people to start a new life. Begin their own journeys. Not end them. Uhlad knew what I was planning, of course. I've had people in his court ever since I left…"

"Your brother tried to kill Uhlad," Tavar said, confused. "Why?"

Sett frowned and looked down at his bare feet. "I love my brother. But from time to time, we have… disagreements. My relationship with Uhlad strained things with us. I had to flee the kingdom ad Marcus always blamed Uhlad. He felt the king was too weak and that he should have done more. Marcus always knew how this would play out, unless Uhlad was killed, of course."

"And how was it going to play out?"

"With my death, of course. It is the only way Uhlad will ever have the strength to kill the vermin who control him."

Tavar rubbed his fingers over the scroll before

pulling it out and holding it before Sett. The man's eyes fell on the scroll and flashed with recognition.

"Uhlad wanted you to have this."

Sett's fingers shook as they clutched at the scroll. He stared at it in silence for a while, unmoving. Then in a quick motion, he twisted the gold clasps and unrolled the message. Tears welled in his eyes as he chuckled to himself, raising a hand over his parted lips and laughing as the parchment burst into flames.

"Thank you for the message, angels. In another life, we may have been good friends. Alas, life doesn't always work out the way we would have liked. Still, Hartovan lives on. My child is safe and I can take my place in the gardens of my ancestors. When you see my brother, tell him I forgive him."

Tavar caught the flash of a blade as Sett drew a dagger from his waist and slashed it across his throat. Crimson blood poured from the wound and soaked his purple robe. He crashed forward from the throne and fell down the steps, falling at Tavar's feet in a pool of his own blood.

CHAPTER NINETEEN: THE LIGHT IN DARKNESS

The courtyard had been taken by the Alfaran soldiers. Battered, bruised but victorious, the soldiers hoisted their flags and danced around the courtyard of corpses, singing songs from the old days and giving each other hearty pats on the back and even a kiss on a cheek or two. Some of the less jubilant soldiers had sunk into the shadows, curling up into themselves and staring at something that wasn't there, trying to process what they had just been through. Battles were a damned thing and Tavar didn't think they were worth the pain and suffering. What had really been accomplished here?

He stumbled from into the courtyard with Carver at his side. His whole body felt drained, as though he had run for days with no rest, not even to eat or sleep. This day had cut years off his life, he knew it there and then. He scoured the crowd of signing soldiers, sighing as they poured from nearby taverns to raucous applause, holding barrels full of ale and mead. There would be fun, dancing and drink tonight. So much drink. That's how many coped. Fight back the horrors of war by forgetting they even happened. That way you'd be ready for the next one, with only the shadow of a memory waiting in the back of the mind waiting to pounce at some inopportune moment.

He returned the smiles and pressed his hand to his heart, accepting the greetings from his fellow soldiers, hiding his distaste at the whole thing. He scanned the crowd, looking for any sign of his friends, praying to the heavens that they had survived.

"Where the fuck did you get off to?" Adam almost bundled him over from the side, grabbing him in a bear hug and kissing him on the cheek. "I thought you were dead! Been turning over corpses wondering if they were you…" The smile faded as he shuddered at the memory.

"I'm alive." Tavar smiled weakly, pushing Adam back and taking a good look at him. "And so are you, it seems."

Adam pointed his thumbs at himself and grinned. "Better than ever. Alice is safe too. Cassie took a blow to the head but she's fine. They're in the medic's tent. Come, let's grab a drink and you can tell me where you buggered off to." He glanced at Carver and the corner of his lips curled into a wicked smile. "Though, I understand if you don't want to give me all of the details…"

"Seriously?" Carver scoffed, hands on her hips and tongue running past her lips. "In the middle of a battlefield."

"Nothing gets the blood flowing like the chance of your life ending any second." Adam shrugged before bursting into relieved laughter. "We're alive!"

The colonels were rushing around the desecrated city now, barking orders at their men and women, flushing out any enemy soldiers who may be in hiding and passing messages where needed. The majority of soldiers sat around, resting in the starlight and accepting the cups passed to them by their allies. A few were in tears, kneeling by fallen friends. One soldier pushed against her friend's lifeless body, willing it to come back to life and screaming into the night when it did not. Tavar saw another soldier crouched beside her, wrapping his arms gently around her shoulders and reasoning with her to walk away. The woman rocked and leant forward, pressing her head against the dead soldier's chest which muffled her cries. The fusion of joy and horror drained Tavar. He clutched at his chest, wincing with the physical pain it caused.

"You okay?" Carver asked, looking concerned.

"I'm fine. Just shattered." He meant it in every sense of the word but she didn't need to know that.

Half the city had been consumed by flames. Wood blackened and turned to crisp, destroying buildings that had stood for centuries. Tavar couldn't help but reflect on the waste. This city had been a diamond in the rough; a thriving city of displaced people living on the edge of one of the most unforgiving and harsh deserts on the continent. Now it was little more than a pile of rubble and ash. No one was taking charge of putting out the fires. He couldn't help but think this was it for Hartovan.

Alfara would prefer it forgotten, a stain covered up and never spoken of. *At least the people had survived,* he told himself. A city can be rebuilt, wherever it is. People cannot be brought back from the dead, except in the old tales of djinn and magic. Looking at the piles of bodies around him, he wondered if any of them would want to come back. They were at peace now, away from the horrors of war.

"What are they doing?" Adam stared desperately at one of the buildings that had survived the fires. A huddle of Alfaran soldiers were shouting and laughing, evil cackles that shot through the night. They had captives, four men and women of Hartovan who had their hands tied and were stripped of their armour. They were pulled and pushed amongst the crowd in only their underwear, the bruises and cuts on their bodies easy for all to see. One of the Alfaran soldiers had climbed to the upper level of the building and swung a rope over the flagpole that loomed over the street, the intention clear to see.

Tavar had seen enough death for one night.

"That's enough," he cried, voice cracking with the effort."

The soldiers all turned to face him. The nearest one smiled at Tavar before sticking his tongue into his cheek as he nodded, surveying Tavar. He had a neatly trimmed beard and the badge stitched onto the breast of his tunic proved that he was a major.

The others just chuckled at each other, eager for their friend to dish out more punishment. One soldier, a female with wild hair and a swollen lip called out to him. "Don't be too harsh on him, Saad. He's just a little kid. Could be useful…" The look she gave Tavar as she licked her lips unnerved him more than the major.

"Enough? Was it enough when they flung the heads of our brothers and sisters into our camp?" Saad asked, his voice breathy and low as he stepped towards Tavar, scratching his cheek and spitting on the ground. "Was it enough when they burned their own city to stop us advancing? I watched a dear friend die. Engulfed by flames that *they* started. I decide when it's enough," he roared, spit flying from his mouth as his eyes bulged mad and wild.

"They're prisoners. This is murder." Tavar stood his ground, feeling the air shift behind him as Adam and Carver closed in on him.

"Murder? There will be murder if you don't run along with the other children," Saad said, flicking his dagger from its sheathe and glancing at Adam and

Carver. "Be a shame for me to kill such young, fresh bastards but I've done worse. You argue again and we'll call it disrespecting a senior officer. Two years in the dungeons for that if I push hard enough…"

"It's not worth it," Carver muttered, pulling him away.

Tavar allowed Carver and Adam to pull him away, turning him from the frightened, defenceless Hartovan soldiers. It sickened him. The battle had been won. There was no need for such brutality.

"This is war," Carver said, her thoughts aligned with his. "This is what happens. Doesn't matter what you're fighting for, the victors get the spoils. And that usually means a free reign to do whatever the fuck they like to the losing side. That's just the way it is."

"Well it shouldn't be," Tavar said through gritted teeth. Just because that's how things had always been, that didn't mean it always had to be the way. "Someone needs to change it."

"Who?" Carver asked, voice suddenly more tense and aggressive. "You? If you think you can change the way things have been done for generations then be my guest. I'm telling you though, the only thing that will change is that you'll be the one swinging from the noose."

Maybe she was right. Didn't mean he had to like it. He grunted and carried on through the city, averting his gaze from the soldiers revelling in their victory and the ones stumbling despondent through the streets.

"I thought winning would bring a sense of happiness," Adam said, watching a young woman with what looked like a broken nose, blood spattered across her face as she was dragged by her hair through the street by a laughing woman of Alfara. "And I did at first. Now I just feel sick. It doesn't feel right. They're people just like us. Imagine if that was Alice…"

They marched through the city together in silence, heads down as they ignored the continued cries and laughter, the heat of the flames and spilling of ale. They just wanted to get home. To sleep and forget all about the madness. Unfortunately, the campsite wasn't much better.

The drink was flowing and voices rang out loud and proud. Songs of the old days and a couple that spoke of the future. Vulgar, crass lyrics sang to old, familiar tunes that spoke of the sacking of Hartovan and its fallen people. None of the villagers were out. They stayed in the tents, wanting none of the chaos and knowing that it was too dangerous. This wasn't a night for the people of Hartovan. He thought of the children and how scared they would have been. He remembered the little boy trapped in a wagon and forced to do nothing as he heard the sounds of soldiers attacking his family and friends. Now he was part of that same army and a part of the same system of destruction and horror.

"Lieutenant Salim," Tavar said, pressing a tired hand to his heart as the tall, grim-faced man approached him.

The lieutenant did the same with a curt tip of his head. There were no scratches on his face. No cuts or bruises. To Tavar, the lieutenant looked just as he had when he had entered the battle.

"Oden is looking for you," Salim said before pointing at the cut on Tavar's jawline. "Best get that stitched up first. I will tell the colonel that you are in the medic tent and he will find you there." The lieutenant shuffled away, helmet held in one hand as he glided through the night, seemingly unaffected by the madness around him.

"Strange one, he is," Adam said, inspecting his own helmet and catching his reflection in it. He rubbed at a patch of filth on his chin and checked again. "Barely looks like he's been in a fight. You do, though." Adam motioned at the wound on Tavar's jaw. "Better do as he said. I'll go with you. Be good to see Alice and Cassie again."

"Yeah," Tavar said absent-mindedly before turning to Carver. "You coming?"

"I'll meet you after. Going to head back to collect my things, make sure none of these fools have had the dumb idea to take something that isn't theirs. Never know who you can trust at times like this…" Carver muttered darkly as she walked off with a wave.

The medic's tent was the biggest one on the campsite. A thousand paces long and two hundred wide; it had been raised for this very purpose, expecting the huge influx of injured soldiers. Hastily built beds were full of bloodied soldiers. Some cried out in pain whilst others sobbed quietly. An unfortunate few stared at the space on their body where a limb had once been but no more. A couple of despondent soldiers had to be restrained by friends and allies as they made to rush from their beds, wanting to leave the horrors behind them, not wanting to admit that this was the place they had to be right now. Doctors and nurses raced from bed to bed, doing their best to help the men and women where they could.

All were stained in dark blood, their faces ashen and haggard. Tavar saw one doctor check a motionless soldier and press his face close to the man's blue lips. He stood straight and shook his head to the soldier holding a limp hand and offered a gentle squeeze of the shoulder as he gave news that he didn't want to give. News that would be more common as the night wore on. Specially designated soldiers combed the rows of beds and helped to carry the bodies of the dead out the back of the tent where they could be burned. Disease would spread and fester if they were left for too long and that could cause more damage than the battle had.

Tavar caught the attention of one of the exhausted doctors. Sheepishly, he pointed to the wound on his jaw, trying not to look at the soldier staring into nothing, ignoring the missing right leg. "Was told to get this stitched up."

The doctor gave it a quick look before frowning. "Fifty paces up. Keep to the right. One of the nurses will be able to sort you out," he said before checking on the soldier with the missing leg. Tavar watched as the soldier broke from his daze and smiled sadly up at the doctor. His eyes watered but he didn't cry. He merely nodded at whatever the doctor was saying and touched a shaking hand against his breast as he looked up to the heavens. The doctor left him alone and the soldier sighed, looking sadly at what had once been his right leg. His left leg lay there, bent at the knee, almost mockingly. He looked up and caught Tavar's gaze.

"I guess that's why I was blessed with two legs. Always handy to have a spare. God is indeed good," he chuckled.

Tavar laughed back, doing his best to fight the lump in his throat as he marvelled at the courage of the soldier. "God is good," he replied, though, looking around the room, Tavar wondered how anyone could possibly think that at a time like this.

"Shit," Adam whispered as they carried on

through the tent of the injured and dead. "Lost his bloody leg and he still sits there with a smile on his face. That's incredible."

"Tears won't help the leg grow back," Tavar said. "That must be what he's thinking right now. Better to smile about something than to cry. I think I'd be asking for as many sleeping herbs as possible if I was him. And I'd be screaming my head off."

They passed more dying and injured. Nurses with the light blue sash of their profession spoke soft words to comfort those who needed it. Tavar was amazed at how they managed to do it without breaking down into floods of tears. They were silent heroes. Heroes who were never mentioned in the tales he had read. Stabbing a sword into the gut of someone trying to kill you wasn't bravery. It was an act built of self-preservation, on the fear of dying. To be able to sit there with men and women, knowing they would be dead by dawn and having to find the right words to comfort them without falling apart; that was true bravery.

"Stitches?" one of the nurses asked, wiping her hands on a bloodied piece of cloth and exhaling heavily as she spotted Tavar walk over to her. He nodded and pointed at his jaw.

"I'm going to look for Alice and Cassie," Adam said, slapping Tavar on the back. "Catch you back in our room when you're done."

"You're one of the lucky ones," the nurse said, threading the animal hair through the needle and tapping her hand on the edge of a free bed for Tavar to sit on. He did as he was told and sat, staring at the tent of the roof as the nurse leant over him, pressing a hand against his jaw as she pressed the sharp needle closer. "Shouldn't take too long."

Tavar grit his teeth as he felt the needle pierce his skin. Wincing and crying out didn't seem like the right thing to do as he remembered he was sitting in a room full of soldiers with much worse injuries than his.

Still, it hurt like hell. He kept his chin up and tried to sing a song in his head, one his mother had sung to him as a young boy. Before he knew it, the nurse had cut the stitch at the end and leant back to admire her work.

"Not gonna score you any pretty points but they won't be in for too long. Have a medic check them in three days' time and we'll see how it's progressing. Shouldn't have any problems and you'll end up with a cute scar more than likely," she smiled and sucked her teeth in. "Try not to get hit in the face again."

"Great advice," Tavar said, grinning at first before realising how painful it was. "Definitely something I should be aiming for. Thanks. I really mean that."

"You're welcome. Now go and drink and dance and do whatever it is that you soldiers do after all the killing."

Tavar strode off back through the aisle in between the rows of beds. He caught sight of the wounded soldier he had spoken with earlier. An empty chair sat next to the soldier, inviting Tavar.

"Hope you don't mind me taking this seat for a while," Tavar said as the soldier sat up and grinned.

"Of course not. I see you've had stitches," the soldier said, rubbing at his bushy beard and smirking. "Must have been painful."

"You have no idea," Tavar responded as they laughed together.

"My name is Sultan. Sultan ir Nair."

"Tavar Farwan."

"It is a pleasure to meet you Tavar Farwan. I would stand with respect but it seems that I have misplaced a leg…"

"Understandable. My own grave injury has caused a dizziness that threatens to overwhelm me if I stand for too long," Tavar said in a mocking tone. Sultan laughed. A warm honest laugh. "How did it happen? If you don't mind me asking."

Sultan blew out a few breaths between his tightly pressed lips and pushed his head back against his hands. "My unit chased down a retreating squad through a darkened alley. When we came out onto a new street, we were ambushed by a greater number of enemies than we had anticipated. I fell to the ground but kept swinging my sword. When I looked down, I noticed a wide gash in my leg, deep enough to see white bone sticking out. Drifted in and out of consciousness for a bit, saw enough to know that one of my unit had dragged me with all of her strength back into the alley. She left me in the shadows and went back to fighting the bastards. I just lay there, trying not to scream too loudly until I passed out with the pain. I woke up in here and the surgeon had taken the leg. Said there was no chance of saving it and I was lucky to be alive. Not sure if I agree with that last bit yet but I can't complain. The dead don't appreciate the moaning of the living."

"The dead aren't listening," Tavar said.

"They are, Farwan. The dead are always listening. What else would they be doing?"

"Sleeping. That's what I'd be doing!"

"Yes, I guess so. What will you do once we

return to Alfara? I sense you are not one for drinking and dancing in the wake of such an occasion?"

Tavar shrugged his shoulders and tapped a foot on the floor, thinking. "I'm not sure. Master Oden will want us training again. There's always another battle around the corner. Drinking may help one day but I've never been good at dancing."

"I'd offer to teach you but for some reason I feel as though my dancing days may be behind me!"

"I'm not so sure!" Tavar snorted. "Even on one leg, I think you may be able to teach me a thing or two."

"You are kind. If our paths do cross in Kessarine, we shall share a drink and discuss dancing. Perhaps I could start a new hopping craze that the nobles will come to love." Sultan smiled sadly.

"Perhaps." Tavar stood and placed an easy hand on Sultan's wrist as he saw tears begin to glisten in his eyes. "I wish you well, Sultan ir Nair. I pray that our paths do indeed cross again."

"And you Tavar Farwan. Though I am certain whatever path we are on, you shall journey faster than I am capable of. God willing, we will meet again."

There was a chill in the night air as Tavar stepped out of the tent. Hands on hips, he scanned the campsite, surveying the scene with tired, aching eyes. The singing and merriment rolled on across the camp. The colonels were satisfied that any enemies worth hunting down had been dealt with; any who escaped were gone now and their lives were their own. There's only so much one could do.

He turned and looked at the burning city of Hartovan. The smoke filled his nostrils, even from this distance. A couple of young soldiers passed by coughing but smiling as they stumbled, arm in arm and looking for a private place to continue their celebration.

A chill wind picked up and Tavar bristled, wrapping his arms around himself and stalked across the camp, looking for his place for the night.

"Tavar," he heard a voice call from the darkness of the shadows. Qassim walked into the torchlight. His arm had been bound with a sling wrapped around his shoulder and heavy bags sat beneath his eyes. His felt cap replaced the helmet that had been knocked off in the fighting, covering his trimmed hair. "A word, if possible."

"Sure," Tavar replied. The animosity during training seemed like a world away now, paling in insignificance compared to the horrors of the day.

"I thought I was a goner today. Said my final prayers and everything," Qassim admitted, sheepishly laughing and rubbing an eye, unable to look at Tavar properly. "We've never exactly been on the same page."

"Quite the understatement."

"Yeah, exactly. If I'm honest, with the boot on the other foot, I'm not sure what I would have done if it had been you needing the help. Looking back, it hurts me to admit that but I feel you deserve the truth. You didn't even think about leaving me though. You rushed in and saved my life. I owe you a debt and saying a mere thanks doesn't cover it."

"You don't owe me a thing. We were in the middle of a battle and I attacked the enemies. Nothing more."

"Humble of you to say that but it ain't the truth and you know it."

"Well, we can call it even if you agree not to beat the shit out of me or my mates ever again. And I'll make sure my brother stays away, wherever he is in this damn camp."

"He's in the tent next to Oden's room. With Major Marcus," Qassim said, happy to help in any way he could.

"Thanks Qassim. Hope your arm heals quickly," Tavar said, clapping his hand on his chest and walking off into the direction of Vandir's tent as Qassim bowed.

CHAPTER TWENTY: FLAMES OF BROTHERHOOD BURN BRIGHTEST

"You look like shit."

"Still more likely to get a woman than you are," Vandir smirked through a swollen lip, one eye half closed and turned an unnatural purple. He sat up in the bed at the sight of Tavar, one arm pulled protectively across his ribs.

"They must have hit you really hard in the head," Tavar laughed as he marched over to his brother before pulling him closer and kissing him on each cheek in greeting. "Good to see you brother, even like this."

The other bed was occupied with the major. Marcus looked better than Vandir. A few bruises but he stood with ease and splashed some cold water onto his face from the bucket in the corner and stretched before facing Tavar, eyes fiery and intense.

"You saw my brother." Tavar nodded. There was no use denying it. "Tell me what happened. Please." Marcus sat on the edge of the bed, elbows resting on his knees and head dropped into his hands. His eyes stayed fixed on Tavar, as though he didn't want to miss a thing.

"Your brother is dead," Tavar stated. "He took his own life."

Marcus nodded, furiously tapping his foot against the floor and pulling at his wild beard. "He said this would be the end, before he took us from the city. I wanted to get him out, get him away but he wouldn't listen. In the end, he cared more for these people than he did about me."

"Uhlad passed a message onto him," Tavar said, noting with interest the way in which Marcus's eyes flashed at this new piece of information. "Told him that he would look after Fadil - *Sett's* son."

Marcus stood and paced the room, rubbing his knuckles and muttering to himself before turning on Tavar, a finger pointed in the air. "Look after... Uhlad doesn't know how to look after himself. He doesn't let Lilian see the child and keeps him locked away. The boy needs a woman's touch. He needs his mother. Uhlad is just being petty and immature, to the surprise of no one."

"Uhlad knows you tried to kill him."

Marcus calmed at this. He breathed long and heavy and sat down once more. His eyes darted around the room as he bit the nails at the tips of his fingers. "I thought as much. Sett arranged for a ship to wait for me on the coast. I could slip away, no one will notice, not tonight. You could come, both of you. And your friends. Start a new life away from Alfara."

Tavar's heart leapt at the thought. This was what he had always wanted. A chance to be free. A new life away from the iron fist of Alfara. Away from the people who had taken him from the warm embrace of his parents and thrown him into the cold, harsh world full of blood and death and missing limbs.

He glanced at Vandir who was smiling, even through the pain.

"It makes sense, little brother," Vandir said. "Lock these memories away and do some good. I could even start my own farm."

"Not with a face like that. You'll scare the animals."

The three of them laughed together. Tavar ran his tongue over the roof of his mouth and then across the sharp spike of a chipped tooth. He looked at Marcus and a question popped into his tired mind.

"Why do you want to help us?"

"What do you mean?" Marcus frowned, pulling his finger away from his mouth.

"You were good to us from the beginning. You're wanting to help us escape now. I want to know why."

Marcus's eyes fell to the carpet at his feet. He breathed in deeply and then began, not looking at either of them. "You were there when your parents were murdered. When all those people were murdered. They were innocent, all of them. A rabble of travellers, merchants and entertainers passing through the land with no ill will to Alfara, no ill will towards anyone as far as I know.

"I'd been on patrol the day before. I was nervous. Practically shitting myself and praying to God with every breath and thought I had in me. You see, my brother had decided to flee Kessarine. The Judges were onto him and Uhlad could offer no protection, curse his name," Marcus spat. "Sett told only me and Lilian that he was to leave. Uhlad knew nothing.

"I helped him flee the camp, distracting the lookouts. A few others left with him. The army is full of soldiers who want out. Especially those who were forced into servitude, like yourselves. Sett had a plan. Sadly, a storm hit and he couldn't get far. He broke from his fellow soldiers and fled into the wilderness. When Grey found out what had happened, he ordered us to search for the deserters. He found a couple of them, shaking and scared in a cave near where you and your family were sheltering from the storm."

Tavar's heart shot with pain at the memory of the frightened men he had seen that day, shivering and hiding from the storm.

"What are you saying, Marcus?" Vandir's voice quivered. A useless question. He knew what it meant. Just as Tavar did.

Tavar's fists balled as a storm of emotion raged from the pit of his stomach up to his chest. Every nerve burned as he stared at Marcus, head slumped into his hands as he started to sob.

"They all died because I led Grey to those caves, knowing my brother would have fled to the forest. Your parents died because of me. Forgive me."

Tavar shook, allowing the hot tears to roll down his cheeks. He knew Marcus hadn't meant it, but the fact was, if Marcus hadn't led them to the caves, Grey wouldn't have killed their parents. His life would have been so much different.

"You can make it up to us. We will go with you to the ship and you can get us the hell away from here. Then you leave us and never see us again," Tavar glared at Marcus. "Agreed?"

The major lifted his head and nodded to Tavar before turning to Vandir who just sat there, a hand covering his mouth as he stared at the corner of his bed, lost in memories.

"I'll go and get the others who will want to come. One hour and I'll meet you at the back of the medic's tent."

Tavar spun and fled from the room, suddenly feeling too hot and needing air. He struggled for breath, pushing the flap to the exit and opening his mouth wide in the hope that the cool night air would chill the hot hatred rising in him.

He stomped in the direction of the longhouse, fingernails digging into the palms of his hands. His eyes widened in horror as he spotted it. It was hard to miss, standing out amongst the others in the darkness as flames licked the roof and grew with each passing moment. Out the front, a crowd had gathered around a soldier who was shouting and laughing, a soldier with a familiar snarl. Saad. The murderer.

"Tavar!" The villager whose house was alight rushed over, nearly bowling Tavar to the floor as he clutched at his collar, tears streaming down his face as he fell to his knees. Tavar looked behind him and saw his wife being held back by some of the soldiers. "My children are in there. We went in to grab some of our things, hoping the battle was over. They dragged us out but my children are still in there. They will burn alive!" he tore his robe as he dropped to the ground, sobbing. "Please help me. I will do anything!"

Tavar ran towards the flames, already feeling their heat attacking his skin. Spotting a bucket of water nearby, he tore his sleeves and submerged the pieces of cloth before wrapping them around his face and head. As he neared the front of the longhouse, Saad stepped in his way. None of the other soldiers were laughing now. Only him.

"Look who it is," Saad snarled, licking his lips as he looked down at Tavar. "Best be leaving, boy. This isn't your business."

"There are children in there."

"Hartovan peasants. Not like real children. Let them burn."

Tavar noticed the uneasy glances of the soldiers watching as Saad's words reached them. It seemed not all of them were so heartless. Just cowards.

"One way or another, I'm getting into that house," Tavar warned, drawing his blade to cries of enjoyment. Some were eager for more blood.

"Do you really want to be doing that, boy?" Saad ripped his own blade from its scabbard as the flames continued to rise. There wasn't much time. Tavar would have to end it quickly.

He lunged forward with his blade low, ready to slice upwards. He saw Saad's elbow twitch just before he slashed forward, blocking the strike. Tavar rocked backwards with the force of the block. He swung just as his opponent lunged. Tavar was faster but Saad had the experience, he twisted his sword at the last second, diverting what could have been a deadly blow.

Tavar tried to block out the shouts and screams of the audience baying for blood but they were so loud. He had to focus, otherwise he'd be just another body burning behind the medic's tent.

Saad flashed forward. Tavar raised his sword but he wasn't quick enough. Thankfully, the blade caught the edge of his greaves, rolling down before nicking the skin on his forearm and drawing blood.

"You know what? This is fun," Saad said, raising his hands in the air to the cheering crowd. "I'll make sure you have a quick death."

Their weapons clashed as Tavar roared. He flicked the edge of his blade down his enemy's sword but Saad moved just in time. They pulled apart, both panting and watchful. The smile faded from Saad's face as he raised a gloved finger and wiped at the new blood dripping down the cut on his face. That was close.

Tavar dodged a furious thrust and parried two strikes before launching his own attack, only managing to catch the edge of his blade on the elbow guard with a clang. Saad recovered and swung his sword which Tavar caught with ease, expecting such a strike. What he hadn't expected was the gauntleted fist that followed, slamming him straight into the nose.

He fell back as the world spun and the stars danced in front of his eyes. He felt the warm blood cover his face and drip into his mouth with the taste of iron. His vision blurred as he lamely raised his sword, seeing double as Saad stalked forward like a predator watching his prey, victorious.

Tavar watched in defeat as Saad swatted his weapon away and placed a huge boot on his chest. "I promised you a quick death, boy. I never break my promises."

Tavar looked up at his conqueror before glancing at the flames. All he could think of was the two children stuck in the heat, possibly fallen due to the smoke filling their house. He could hear the screams of their parents as they saw their only hope fall.

Then he heard the twang of a bow immediately followed by a thud and silence.

He gazed up at Saad who frowned, his mouth opening and closing in an odd silence. His eyes fell, staring at the arrow haft stuck in his neck. A figure stepped forward next to Tavar and raised their sword, driving the blade straight through Saad's throat with one hand. Blood rushed from the wound and fell onto Tavar before Saad stumbled back and dropped to the ground, gurgling and twitching.

His vision cleared as the figure offered him a hand and pulled him to his feet.

"That should go some way to making us even," Qassim grinned. "Though I can't take all the credit." His eyes glanced to the side where Alice stood with Cassie, bow in hand and glaring at Saad's fallen body.

Tavar nodded his thanks and ran towards the flames, pushing past Qassim as he tried to grab him back.

"It's too late!"

Ignoring the warning, he kicked the door down, coughing as the wave of smoke engulfed him. He squinted, trying to peer through the smoke and flames. On the floor, under a table, he spotted one of the children, lying unconscious. The older one. He ran over and scooped up the limp body, holding it close to his chest. He ignored the heat and rushed out of the house, falling to the ground as others rushed around him.

His lungs were close to failing as Alice leant over him. The father grabbed at his child and held him close as his mother ran over, both parents crying as they attempted to wake their son.

Tavar coughed, rolling onto his back and pointing at the longhouse. Adam knelt next to him, holding his hand. "There's another child in there. I have to go back in," Tavar said through more coughs. Without a word, Adam bolted into the longhouse. Alice's scream pierced the air as she helplessly watched her brother charge towards the house and leap through the flames.

Cassie and Qassim pulled Tavar to a seated position. His chest was tight and he struggled to move. All he could do was watch as the flames leapt higher and higher, consuming the wooden longhouse. The whole scene dragged on, feeling like a year in itself.

"Adam..." Tavar managed to utter through another bout of coughing.

Tavar felt Qassim's good arm pressing on him, preventing him from moving as Cassie fought against Alice who was trying to follow her brother into the burning house. Everyone else just stared in morbid silence, all thoughts of the battle lost in the dancing flames.

After what felt like an eternity, Adam crashed out from the house, his robes alight. He staggered towards them before dropping onto his back.

In his arms was a small child, motionless. A wave of men and women rushed forward. Cassie pulled the child away as its parents rushed over, rivers of tears still flowing down their faces as they checked on their child. Alice leant over her brother as other soldiers ripped his burning clothes from his body and attempted to keep him awake. Tavar felt Qassim's guard soften and so he took the opportunity to move, crawling over through his painful coughs to reach Adam.

His skin was a mess.

One side of his face had already blistered over pink skin. Part of his torso and right arm were a deep, raw red. Tavar could see a further patchwork of blisters bubbling away. What scared him the most was the way in which Adam's body just lay there. His eyes were closed. Lips still as the stars.

"Wake up, Adam. Please, wake up. For me, please. Don't leave me." Alice rocked back and forth, her tears falling onto his blackened face.

"He needs medics. Give me a hand." One of the

soldiers, motioned for those closest to him to help lift Adam and they steadily carried him to the medics' tent, careful to not touch his burned skin. Alice followed, joined by Cassie.

"You and your friend saved our family. I don't think I can ever repay you," the farmer said, cradling his coughing child with care as his wife did the same with their older child. "Thank you. I hope he makes it. He is a hero." The farmer watched sadly as Adam was carried away.

"He is. I should have saved them both. He didn't have to go in…"

"Don't think like that, Tavar," Qassim said, helping him to his feet.

"I've got to go. I need to speak with my brother." Tavar ignored whatever Qassim was saying, stumbling through the camp site, his chest heavy as though crushed with a giant rock. He crashed through the swaying flap leading to his brother's tent, coughing furiously.

"What's happened to you?" Vandir rushed over to him, catching him as he fell. Marcus jumped to his feet, already dressed and ready to leave, sword tied firmly to his waist belt.

"There was a fire. Adam's in the medics' tent. Vandir… I don't know if he'll…" Vandir didn't wait for Tavar to finish. He ran from the tent and into the night. Marcus slung a bag over his shoulder and picked up Vandir's waterskin, left forgotten on the bedside table.

"Do the others know we're leaving?" Marcus asked.

"Not yet."

"We'll have to grab them on the way. There's not

much time. You grab them. I'll meet you at the back of the tent. Go."

Tavar stepped back out into the night. The smell of burning flesh still clung to his nostrils, forcing him to fight the urge to puke with every breath he took. Cassie was holding a crying Alice outside of the tent. Vandir was arguing with Qassim who was rocking backwards, his good arm outstretched with palm facing the angry Vandir whose voice grew steadily louder.

"You're lying! How can I trust you!" Adam roared, hand on the hilt of his sword.

"I'm sorry. The smoke…" Vandir punched a fist into Qassim's shoulder as the tears started to roll down his face. Qassim just tightened his face and bit his lip, resisting the urge to fight back.

"He's dead. Isn't he?" Tavar muttered, almost to himself as he reached Cassie and Alice. He knew it. He'd known it since he had seen his friend hit the ground as the flames rose behind him. He'd known it since he saw him bravely leap into the flames, making up for Tavar's mistake.

Cassie shifted to allow Alice a chance to look at Tavar. Her eyes were red and her body shook with volatile sobs. She had no words. She threw herself at him, falling onto him like a dead weight, her arms wrapped around his shoulders as Cassie patiently rubbed her back, ignoring her own tears.

The world fell silent as Tavar closed his eyes. He felt the wetness of Alice's face on his neck but nothing else. This was his fault. This complete sadness was all his fault. Adam wouldn't have been in there if he had done what he was meant to do. He bit his lip, breaking his skin and welcoming the blood dripping into his mouth. He deserved this pain. Deserved everything he was feeling. He opened his eyes and looked at the grief pouring from his friends. They didn't deserve this.

Vandir dropped to his knees, face lost in his palms as his body rocked back and forth. Tavar backed away from Alice with an apology. Cassie welcomed her back into her arms as Qassim looked on, awkwardly lost in their shared grief.

"He died a hero. More than most can say," Qassim offered, looking down at the earth.

"He shouldn't have died at all!" Vandir roared. "Who started the fire?"

Tavar blinked and shook his head, fighting off the memory as the back of his throat burned with vomit.

"Sister," Qassim called out, looking past Tavar. "What's wrong?"

Tavar turned to see Nahra striding towards them. He blinked again, unsure of what he was seeing as Carver kept in step beside the woman she hated.

"Word is you killed a colonel," Nahra said, staring accusingly at them all. "They're sending soldiers this way to arrest you. He has powerful allies. You can't escape this brother, and we can't fight. Not with your arm…" Her dark eyes glanced at the sling with regret.

"He was burning the villagers alive!" Tavar cried, pounding a fist into his palm and turning away as his rage threatened to consume him.

"They won't care about that," Carver said, her eyes begging forgiveness. Tavar felt her hand on his shoulder, calming him instantly as he looked into her soft, brown eyes. "Killing a colonel has consequences. Undeserved or not."

"Then we need to go," Tavar, staring around at their confused faces.

"Where?" Cassie asked. "There's nowhere to go."

"There's a ship, waiting on the coast just past the city. If we go now, we can make it, get away from all of this. We need to go now," Tavar urged, realising this was their only way out.

"Adam…" Alice whispered, biting her sleeve and looking back at the medics' tent where her brother's body would be waiting.

"Adam wanted us to be free," Tavar said, his heart skipping a beat as he realised he would never hear his friend's laugh ever again. "This is our chance. He would prefer that than to have us rot in a dungeon or suffocate on the wall."

The warning had the desired effect. He could see the steel return to their faces as Vandir snapped into action, leading them away. They all followed, knowing that this was the one chance they had for freedom.

"No, sister," Qassim pleaded, stopping as he saw his sister following him. "This is not your fight. I wouldn't be able to live with myself if you left Alfara for this."

Nahra sucked her teeth and gave her brother a few soft pats on his cheek. "Brother. You are such a fool sometimes. Try to keep up." She ran after Vandir, Alice and Cassie, daring her brother to catch up.

Tavar stood still, eyes falling on Carver. "This is our chance to live that life you wanted. Freedom." He smiled as he saw the others fade into the darkness of the night. The soldiers wouldn't find them. Not once they made it to the ship.

"Freedom," Carver repeated with a smile. "That's all I want. For myself, and for my mother." She nodded herself, readying her mind for what she was about to do. "She is trapped in Alfara, the widow of a traitor. The Judges and Uhlad would need a good reason to allow her freedom."

"What are you saying?" Tavar asked, perplexed with what this had to do with anything. Did Carver want to stay in Alfara with her mother?

"Providing them with a traitor who killed a colonel might be a good start."

Tavar's eyes flashed as he realised what she was saying. "Carver, n—" She was too fast and he was too tired. The weight of her gauntleted fist whipped across his jaw, knocking him off his feet. He coughed, too weak to get to his feet as Carver stood over him.

"Must be a familiar sight," she said, no humour on her face. "Been a while, though. For what it's worth, I've always been honest with you. You're a good friend and I wish things could have been different. At least I let your friends go. You can thank me for that at least."

"You fucking bitch..." Tavar spat, staring up at her as she unstrapped the horn hanging from her waist.

"I deserve that. I'm sorry Tavar. Family comes first. Surely you understand that." She pressed the horn to her lips and blew long and hard, informing the soldiers that the traitor had been found. She raised her foot and dropped her boot directly onto his face.

Tavar's head swam and he welcomed the silent darkness that took him completely.

PART THREE: THE EYES OF THE MAN

"The eyes of the man fall back to the past. They are weighed down with bags of regret and shot with lines of guilt. Though tired, they sparkle with a wisdom gained through pain and suffering and yearn for the innocence of the past; an innocence they will never again attain..."

-Malike ir Terrasil – author of "Life in the Shadow of the Godking"

CHAPTER TWENTY-ONE: DEAL WITH THE DEVIL

"The storm's cleared the air. Has that crisp feel to it that always makes me feel like the world has reset, readying itself to start afresh. Storms have an odd place in my memory. Always take me back to that day in the forest by the mountain pass. The last day I saw my parents alive."

Tavar dropped the seed on the wet path and grinned at the flurry of robins descending and hurriedly pecking away at the expected meal. A bright sun shone down on his fields as he meandered through the paths and crops alongside a cautious Jassim. The wounded warrior winced with each step but he wasn't complaining. The walk would do him good, whether he liked it or not.

"Did you ever go back there?" Jassim asked, rubbing a hand across his torso and stretching to the side with a quick exhale. "Where they died?"

Tavar watched the birds flittering around the seeds, full of energy and life as they jumped back and forth on the muddy path, careful not to get too close to one another. "Yes. Once or twice." He let the words fall alone in the space between them.

The land looked well fed and watered. Tavar cast his mind back to the times he used to dance in the storms with his family, laughing together and splashing in the puddles before rushing for cover as the lightning and thunder arrived. For a second, he felt like the young, innocent boy he had been, unburdened by guilt and reality; just lost in the beauty around him.

"That Carver girl," Jassim said, prodding for more information, not content to wait for its arrival. The haste of youth. "She warned you. You said so yourself. She warned you not to trust anyone. Should have seen that coming, whether you fucked or not," Jassim said with a knowing grin.

Tavar scoffed and lifted the bag he was carrying higher, catching it in the nook inside his elbow. "I was a fool. No one is denying that. With innocence and youth comes a huge space for mistakes and regret. You see the best in people. You expect the people you care about to care for you. You want them to follow the same path you are on. It's only when you grow a little that you realise that things can't work like that; everyone has their own path to go on, one they decide for themselves. Pain and suffering are, unfortunately, inevitable. Carver taught me a lesson that day. One I have never forgotten."

"The farmers," Jassim said as he cleared his throat, thumping one hand against his chest. "The children. The ones you and Adam saved…"

Tavar laughed. They had finally got to this bit. A slice of understanding between the two of them. "Your father and uncle if I'm not mistaken."

Jassim only grunted and nodded, staring at the birds as they flew away, seeds all gone.

"You have his eyes. It's been a while since I've seen Youssef but I don't forget a face. He must have been just past fifteen years when I last saw him. Found himself a pretty dressmaker from a city in the west."

"My mother."

"Your grandparents buried Adam for me. They

were allowed in to see the soldier who had died for them. All the soldiers were being burned out the back of the tent in one huge, unglamorous pile. No respect. No privacy to mourn. They asked for his body and with Alice gone and I having been taken as a prisoner, there was no one else to argue against it.

"They buried him on a hill overlooking the coast and with a great view of the waves. Adam would rest with a view of where his sister and friends had found freedom. Well, most of them, anyway." Tavar smiled at Jassim and stepped forward. "It's not too much farther. Bit of an incline but it's worth it."

"Lead the way."

They walked in silence. Waves of green fields shone with morning dew. A wall of beech trees clustered together to the east, offering shade for the animals sheltering from the growing heat as the sun made its way to its highest point of the day. Horses paced around the field, their tails absently swatting away the flies that gathered too close. Cowslip covered the patch of fields to the right to the delight of many of the animals casually grazing, happy that the storm was over.

Tavar was just beginning to feel the burn in his legs as the tough walk took its toll on his aged body when they reached the top of the hill. Standing alone in the centre of the hill was a weeping willow, its branches stretched out wide like arms to shelter any passing by in its grand, elegant embrace.

He walked over to the old tree and ran a hand against its trunk. He pressed his head against the bark and closed his eyes, lost in memories of the past.

"This tree mean something to you?" Jassim asked, looking up at the tall tree and shielding his eyes from the midday sun.

"This tree means everything to me," Tavar murmured. He backed away and pulled the bag from his shoulder, setting it down on the grass and opening the top. He grabbed at the blanket inside and threw it on the ground. "Take a seat. It's time you hear the rest of the story. Of my story."

He hadn't known true darkness. Not like this.

Tavar had marched in the middle of the blackest of nights but even then he had a glimmer of moonlight or a few scattered stars to guide his way. He'd drawn thick curtains in the barracks to block out any source of light in order to get to sleep but even that didn't come close to this. He closed his eyes for moment and breathed in. Once. Twice. Three times. He opened them again but nothing had changed. Just an all-consuming blackness. The absence of light.

The darkness suffocated him. It caught in his throat and tightened his chest, threatening to take his life. As a result of his complete lack of sight, there came a creeping paranoia. Sounds and smells were heightened, compensating for his lost sense of sight. It made it all so much fucking worse than it would have been. Every scratch was the sound of rats scuttling past him. Every drip was a flood about to break into the cell. Every bolt slide was his inevitable death entering the door to take his life.

It was hell.

At first, he tried sleeping as much as possible. How long he was out for, he had no idea. The lack of light threw him completely. He had no idea how long he had been there since he had been thrown in by rough Alfaran soldiers. It made him miss the journey across the desert on the way back. He'd been beaten and tied up by soldiers he didn't recognise. At one point, he'd spotted Adnan riding past. The colonel just looked away and hurried his mount forwards, unable to meet his eye.

He prayed to the heavens that his friends had made it to the ship. He'd listened to every hushed conversation in the vicinity, hoping that what he heard wasn't anything to do with their capture. He'd heard nothing of importance. Most conversations were bland and uninteresting. Soldiers complaining about the chafing on their thighs or their problems passing shit.

He'd heard no conversations since being thrown into the darkness. No voices at all. He'd wake up to the sound of a tray slamming against the floor next to him and every meal placed upon it was the same. Stale bread and water. Nothing more. Part of him wondered if starving would be better but then his stomach would constrict in agony and his throat would burn with thirst. He'd take what was given and be thankful for it.

Migraines assaulted his head and sweat dripped from his every pore, soaking his skin and the small piece of cloth covering his dignity. Not that he had much dignity in the moment. In the blackness of his cell, it didn't really matter at all. Nothing really mattered at all. The only thing keeping him sane as he rocked in the darkness was the thought that one day he might escape this hell. His friends would be waiting; Alice, Cassie, Vandir. Even Qassim. Then he thought of Adam and a crushing wave of doom overwhelmed him, dragging him further into a pit of despair.

Tavar was ready to jump at any glimmer of hope. Any glimmer of anything different at all. Anything to break up the unending feeling of doom and darkness taking over. That's why he tried desperately to stare at the light that entered his cell one day, ignoring how it burnt his eyes and blinded him.

It had been so long since he had light. Since he had been able to see anything. He blinked and finally shielded his eyes from the torchlight as three figures entered the room. The light bounced off the golden uniforms of two men who placed chairs down opposite each other in what Tavar could see was a grubby, decaying, and sparse room. A rat scuttled from the light and back into its corner, hiding from the strange new thing.

The final figure pushed a purple robe from under himself as he sat on one of the plain wooden chairs and waved the Immortals from the room. They left with curt bows; lighting torches ensconced in the wall to fill the room with light. Then they left, slamming the iron door shut and pushing a bolt to the side. Tavar didn't see the point in locking it. He didn't have the energy for escape. Not now.

"Makes even your old barracks look fit for a king," the figure on the chair said, crinkling his nose and scanning the place. "But I suppose that's the purpose of places such as this. They are meant to punish; to destroy the souls of their inhabitants and teach them that there is a greater power and justice will always be served."

"Ahmed…" Tavar finally recognised the king's slave, peering at him in the light bathing the room in a golden glow. It was much smaller than he had even thought. Barely six paces in any direction and you would crash into one of the grey walls splashed with damp.

"Take a seat." Ahmed flicked a wrist casually to the empty chair opposite him. Tavar pushed himself up from the floor, muscles aching with that small movement and he crept over to the chair, slowly lowering himself onto it and pressing his back against the wood. He groaned, twisting the sore muscles in his back and shoulders.

"The Judges wanted you dead. Killing a colonel, especially one as well liked as Colonel Saad, wasn't the best move you could have made," Ahmed argued, tutting and rubbing his hands together. "Doing it in front of so many witnesses with your friends and then helping them escape punishment really upset a *lot* of people. Uhlad had plans to give Marcus pride of place on the wall. He was most displeased to have that moment taken away from him."

"You can tell him that I am sorry for denying him such pleasure," Tavar snapped, not regretting what he had done. "Saad was a monster. He was burning children alive and everyone just stood there and watched. As for my friends, I hope they are as far away from here as possible."

"People stood there and watched as they knew the chain of command. They knew their place. As it should be in Alfara. You acted out of turn and so you are being punished," Ahmed explained, as though discussing with a child why they were being kept in and away from their friends after a minor infringement. "Commander Grey is leading the hunt for the deserters. He will find them. They will be punished accordingly."

"Like he found Sett?" Tavar asked, unable to help himself. He noticed a slight twitch in Ahmed's eye at the name and felt a smug sense of satisfaction.

"Sett was a… delicate situation. He had people helping him in our own army. We have purged that particular plague and are more aware of the possibility of such foolish acts."

Tavar rubbed at his wild, itchy beard and stared at Ahmed. The slave was dressed immaculately, two ringed gems sparkled in the light bouncing toward the fingers on his right hand. A well-paid slave.

"You have a good life, Ahmed," Tavar said, sighing and leaning forward, pressing his elbows into his legs and resting his chin in his palms. "Why come and see me here in this hell when you could be up there, barking orders."

Ahmed smirked, a soft, appreciative smile like Tavar had said something that he had wanted him to say.

"As I said, the Judges wanted you dead. So many people wanted you dead. The information gathered and passed onto the king by your friend, Carver—"

"She's not my friend!" Tavar screamed as the blood rushed to his face.

"Well, she claims otherwise. She told us how you managed to pass the message onto Sett for Uhlad. You did what the king wanted you to do and for that, he is grateful. And so he chose to give you your life. He is mercy personified."

Tavar scoffed and looked around, opening his arms wide and laughing long and hard until his throat was sore with the effort. "You must pass on my thanks to his majesty!" he mocked. "Tell him that I said thank you for trapping me in darkness and leaving me to rot in this shithole." Tavar stood and pointed a finger at Ahmed. The slave sat motionless, unaffected by the sudden outburst. "If he had even a slither of mercy, he would have killed me and be done with this whole mess. *This* isn't life. This is just a slow death, torture. You know this."

"I do," Ahmed agreed, nodding. "Please, sit. I know this isn't life. That's why I have come here with a proposition. A deal. One which I believe you will find leads to an improvement in your circumstances, should you agree to the terms."

Falling back into his chair, Tavar ignored the flutter of his heart. Hope could be a dangerous thing. Clutching to false hope could destroy a man more completely than if he had none at all. It wasn't a path he thought himself ready for.

"Of course, I could just leave you in here to see out the rest of your days with the rats. Your mind will go before your body, I assure you. I've seen it all too often, down here." Ahmed's eyes flickered to bloody scratches etched on the wall and Tavar suddenly longed for the darkness.

"What kind of deal?"

"The Alfaran Arena is on schedule to be completed in three moons time. King Uhlad wishes to take his people's minds off the war and fighting and betrayal. He wants to give them something to cheer for, something that will excite them. Hand to hand combat. Warriors, beasts, slaves, nobles, and prisoners..." Ahmed smirked as Tavar sat up at the final word, listening closely. "The prisoners will live in rooms beneath the arena, to ensure no escape. Nobles will be able to pay the crown to enter the contests to pit themselves against the desperate and violent. Some contests will be first blood, others, to the death. Uhlad has decided that any warrior who wins one hundred battles to the death will be granted their release. Freedom on the condition that they never return to Alfara."

Tavar rolled his tongue across his cheek and chewed Ahmed's words over. Hope for release. For freedom from the darkness and from Alfara. But one hundred matches.

The likelihood of surviving was low and Uhlad knew it. The catch in his gift. The odds were stacked against the prisoners, of course. Designed to ensure no one made it out alive. But there would still be the chance that someone would do it. That thrill would force the prisoners to take risk and in turn it would produce a spectacle that drew thousands to the arena. Exactly what Uhlad and the Judges needed now. A distraction to ensure the people of Alfara did not get restless.

"When can you get me out of here?" Tavar said, eyes locked on Ahmed as the slave smiled wide and manic. It unnerved him. This was not a man to trust. But did he have a choice? He glanced at the bloody scratches and shivered.

"Half a moon," Ahmed answered, standing up and banging on the door. The bolt shifted and an Immortal opened the door. "I will send someone to collect you when the time is ready. You will need to regain your strength. In half a moon, you'll have a new room, and a new cell mate. One different from the rats…"

The door slammed shut, leaving Tavar with the torchlight and one thought running through his head. He had a chance to get out of here. Away from Alfara. Out of the darkness.

CHAPTER TWENTY-TWO: WISHES IN THE DARK

His final days in darkness went faster than he had expected. Even the smallest hint of hope gave Tavar focus and kept his mind alive, failing to succumb to the madness that so many had before him. Even the meals tasted better. The bread fresher and the water pure and clean. Every other day, he would be given fish or meat in addition to the bread and water. He assumed this was Ahmed's way of ensuring he stayed alive and didn't just wither away and die.

Guards came in each day to light the torches in the corners of the room. Tavar was undecided as to whether that helped. The darkness threatened to steal his mind but in the flickering of the flames, his cell took on a whole new threat. In darkness, it was his mind tormenting him but in the light he had the true horrors to deal with. Messages left in blood from the previous occupants, reminders that this room meant death and nothing else.

In the morning of his move, three guards entered, pikes in hand. One had handed over a small bundle of grey clothes. He changed happily, relieved to be wearing new, fresh clothes again. The material felt like magic against his skin though he knew it to be coarse, rough cloth. Wearing the robe and placing his keffiyeh on correctly, he felt human again for the first time since Carver had placed him in darkness. He took a deep breath in and closed his eyes. When he opened them, he was ready.

They covered his head on the journey to his new home. Bundled into a wagon, he sat in silence and listened to the sounds of life on the streets outside. The calls of merchants and the laughter of men and women sharing a joke or two together. He thought he would have welcomed the sounds but after so long sitting with only his thought to accompany him, but they overwhelmed him. His heart thumped a painful beat against his chest and he struggled for breath. A piercing, ringing noise pierced his head and he tightened his eyes shut, trying to push it away. Relief swarmed him as the wagon neared its destination and the noises stopped.

Hands tied with rope and head still covered, he took careful steps forward as the guards led him to his new home.

"Steps," one of the guards grunted, warning him and pushing a hand against his chest to slow his walk. Tavar cautiously walked down hard steps, wobbling once or twice as his foot slipped on an edge of the step. The guards were either side of him, catching up when he made an error.

The ground eventually flattened and his walk grew more comfortable. Or as comfortable as it can be when you're shrouded in darkness and being led by armed guards to an unknown destination.

Then again, maybe he was just overreacting.

"Wait," a gruff voice said as the bag was pulled from his head. Stabbing light burned his eyes, catching him unaware. He blinked rapidly as he rocked backwards, knocking into a stone wall. His eyes adjusted and he took in his surroundings unhindered.

The corridor was wide enough for three chariots to ride along. Torches lined the stone walls lighting the path for one of the guards as he marched away. At the end of the corridor, Tavar thought he could see a statue of a lion carved in marble, though, he didn't exactly trust his eyes at the moment. Nor his mind.

A whistle from the first guard signalled the next part of the journey. The remaining guard grabbed Tavar's tied wrists and pulled him along.

Tavar's eyes burnt and he struggled to trust what he was seeing after so long in the darkness. Seemed they were working just fine, though. The room was circular and opened down six different pathways.

"The way you have just entered is the only way in and out of these cells," the first guard said, voice droning as though he was already bored. Maybe he had done this for countless others already. "For prisoners, anyway." He pointed to Tavar's left. "The two paths this side are for cleaning and health. There is a bathhouse, toilets, and an infirmary. At all times, there will be a doctor in the infirmary. Fighting in the arena will lead to injuries and in many cases death. The doctor's role is to patch you up as best as they can, where possible. The nobles will be placing a lot of money on the fights, they will want you in prime condition at all times."

Tavar craned his neck to look down the paths the guard was pointed towards. They weren't as wide as the one he had just walked down but they were lit up well and the idea of a soaking himself in hot water was like he had died and gone to heaven. Such luxuries had seemed beyond him only minutes ago. Saying that, just staying alive seemed beyond him not so long ago.

"The pathway behind me leads the training square." The guard continued, scratching his lip and looking at his fingernails before he carried on. "To enter the square, you must be accompanied by at least two guards who will monitor your actions with a bow and arrow to hand. The slightest sign of insolence and they have been told to kill without hesitation. This is the only warning you will have."

"Understood," Tavar replied, pressing his tongue against his own lips and standing on the tips of his toes to get a better look past the roaring lion. It was a wide corridor, like the first one.

"There will be a rotation of trainers paid for by nobles who wish to have you as their champion. These trainers will hone your skills to make certain you are ready before we send you in front of a crowd. King Uhlad will not want to be disappointed. There will be a variety of weapons for you to become accustomed to. Up to ten warriors may enter the training room at any one time."

"How many warriors will be… erm… staying here?"

"Eighty." Tavar blew air through his lips and chuckled.

"Eighty warriors fighting to survive housed underground together?"

"Any problems and you can share it with the cell manager," the guard snapped, infuriated that he was having to answer questions. Why didn't everyone naturally know everything? Then his life would be so much easier.

The guard sighed and marched to Tavar's right, to where the two final corridors lay waiting for them.

"These corridors are homes to the cells where prisoners and slaves whose hopes of fighting their way to freedom and glory will reside. You will share your cell with one other, a warrior who will be your partner for any team games that take place in the arena above. If there are any problems with your cell mate…"

"Cell manager," Tavar said with a smile, knowing where that was going. "I'm sure there will be no problems."

"Warriors from each corridor will be separated at all times unless needing to use the infirmary," the guard explained. "This is due to the fact that King Uhlad may wish to pit large scales battles in the arena with many soldiers taking part. In such an event, we shall split the teams up according to which corridor they stay in." He pointed to the corridor closest to the training room. "Warriors of the Falcon corridor." He pointed at the final corridor with an open palm and sighed. "Warriors of the Snake corridor. You will be part of the snake. Follow."

The snake corridor was thin but lit well. Carved into the stone were small rooms behind iron barred gates. There would be no privacy. As Tavar walked along the snake, a few of his new teammates came to greet him, leering with smiles that displayed missing teeth and showing off the size of their biceps as though it would impress or intimidate him. In all honesty, it did both.

"New Meat!" one of them called out, clicking his tongue and pressing his lips together to blow a kiss. "A pretty one too! God be praised!" he shouted, leaning against the bars.

The guard slapped the flat of his dagger against the prisoner's knuckles in warning. "Get back into your cell, Zaif! Next time, I'll take those fingers."

"And what would you do with them, I wonder?" Zaif laughed maniacally and fell back onto the thin mattress in the corner of his room, rubbing his hands wildly across his shaven head and down his unwashed face. "I do so love our talks. Looking forward to speaking to you, New Meat! See you in the training room." The laughter unnerved Tavar. He looked away, hoping to find a friendlier face in the other cells. No luck. What did he expect, really?

The prisoners mostly shied away as Tavar walked past them, flanked by the watchful guards. A couple called out insults but nothing like Zaif. About halfway down the corridor, the guards stopped Tavar and held his wrists up. One swipe of the dagger later and his hands were free. He stretched them and pulled the cut strands of rope away, rubbing at the raw, red skin where the rope had been tightened too much.

"This is your cell. Say hello to your new home," the first guard smirked whilst the second just chuckled along, most likely to curry favour with his more esteemed colleague. "Settle in and make yourself at home. Who knows how long your stay will be?"

The second guard brought out some black keys hanging from a circular chain. He unlocked the gate and moved out the way.

Tavar walked timidly into the room. The first thing he spotted was that there were no bloody scratches on any of the walls. Things were looking up.

The gate closed behind him and without another word, the guards left. Tavar just stood there. To his right lay a thin, skeletal figure snoring. Always with the snoring! The man's hair was long and white, though there was a large bald patch in the middle of his head. He rolled over, smacking his lips together and displaying a wrinkled, weathered face with thin eyes and a long, wispy white beard that draped over his shoulder. On the plus side, his clothes looked new and comfortable – a deep blue robe lined with dashes of snow white at the edges.

He wanted to greet him but thought it best to leave the man sleeping. He looked like he needed it. This was his partner – an old, tired, balding man. Wonderful.

Tavar wondered what their battles would be like if they were forced into a team fight and he shuddered at the thought. Surely this was some sort of joke by Ahmed. A way of preventing him from ever escaping. A final punishment. That was it. He shook his head and walked over to his bed, past the bucket half full of yellow piss. He sniffed in the air and regretted it instantly. The bucket probably hadn't been moved in days. He lied down on the bed. Time to focus on the positive: he had a bed, thin as it was; he had light; and he had someone to talk to. That's more than he had yesterday.

The snoring stopped and Tavar worried for a moment that the man had died. A loud fart followed by a sleepy smile put Tavar at ease as he rolled his eyes and lowered himself onto the bed. He stared up at the ceiling and smiled. No bloody scratches. Life was good.

Life was very much not good.

Tavar snapped up, sweating all over and breathing heavily. His eyes burned with tears. Dreams filled with Adam's pale corpse animated and chasing him, questioning why he left him to die. Blaming Tavar for his death. Dream Tavar had ran away, doing everything he could to escape but his legs had failed him as he stumbled through a stone maze as lions roared around him.

"Night terrors?" Tavar had forgotten that he was not the only one in the room. "I can help with that. They are the sign of an overactive mind. You need to relax before you sleep. Clear your mind of any thoughts that may trouble it."

The old man was sitting up and leaning against the back wall, his hair blocking his face from Tavar.

"Troubling thoughts?" Tavar scoffed. "Why would anyone stuck in a cell beneath an arena where they will soon fight to death have troubling thoughts?"

The old man chuckled. The sound eased Tavar and helped him to steady his breaths.

"Humour is a gift from the Gods. There aren't many places where it does not belong," the old man said. "Kenji. My name is Kenji."

"Tavar. How long have you been here Kenji?"

"Fifth day. The food isn't too bad," Kenji tilted his head and Tavar could see milky orbs. "But the views aren't the best."

"You're blind…" Tavar murmured. He'd been paired with a blind, old man. God really did have a sense of humour.

"Such insight and clarity of vision you have," Kenji chuckled darkly. "Yes I am blind. Though, guessing by the smell and sounds of this place, and the fact we are underground, sight isn't something I can say I truly miss at this moment in time."

"You're going to be fighting in the arena," Tavar said, aware of the panic in his voice, mainly for himself but also slightly for the old man. "You must have pissed someone off."

"Pissed a lot of people off. And not at the same time. Forty years have passed since my vision was taken from me. I'm still breathing. I wonder if you will be able to say the same when you are my age?" Kenji stroked his beard and laughed again, musical this time. Tavar eased up again and relaxed. He liked the old man, strange though he seemed.

"My aim in to make it through the day alive. Forty years is a long time."

"You don't need to tell me that, kid. Food should be here in a bit. If I were you, I'd start sculpting that frame of yours. The crowd will love the tale of a muscly prisoner rising from the depths of death to his freedom. They use their eyes more than any other sense. Fools."

"The crowd will hate me," Tavar said, a bitter taste filling his mouth. "I killed a colonel of Alfara and helped my friends desert the army for a new life, away from this cursed kingdom."

Kenji stood with creaking bones and a few moans. He walked the short distance over to Tavar and slumped onto the bed beside him. "That definitely makes things a little more interesting. I believe you and I are going to make an excellent team, young Tavar."

"So, how did you end up here?"

A mischievous smile broke out on the old man's face. "I will tell you when I'm ready and not a moment earlier. Now, time to work out."

"Sure," Tavar said, standing and stretching the aching muscles in his back and legs. "You joining me?"

"I'm old!" cackled Kenji, milky eyes staring up at the ceiling. "Rest is more important for me. Muscles won't make a difference. My mind needs to be honed more than my muscles. Now, shall we say one-hundred push ups?"

Tavar shrugged and fell to the ground. What else was there to do? "One. Two. Three…"

The training square was like the first one Tavar had used in Kessarine. The weapons perched on a wooden rack at the back of the room and the square was filled with soft soil. The stone walls were covered with paintings of various scenes of combat.

Tavar's eyes fell upon a one large piece on the eastern wall. An impossibly muscled warrior stood on top of a pile of corpses with blood staining his ripped, bare torso and dripping from his dual blades. His mouth was wide open in a roar of triumph as an adoring crowd looked down from the safety of their seats around him. The painting was meant to inspire but Tavar wondered how that warrior really felt. Carving such a path of destruction and death would take its toll on anyone. Tavar had almost buckled after his first battle. How would he cope if he was standing on top of that pile of death?

Marble busts of famous soldiers from Alfaran history filled the room, staring at the prisoners as they sweat and bled. The largest bust was reserved for King Uhlad. It was a good likeness but there was something different about the eyes. The marble gave him a hardened look that Uhlad didn't often have on display. Here he looked like a war master, not a politician.

Four soldiers stood at attention, each manning a wall. They were alert with fingers caressing the bone bow and arrows ready in their grasp. The soldiers were outnumbered by the prisoners. Tavar could see the others coming to the same realisation that he had. If they wanted to, they could clear the room with relative ease. He waited for the next thought to enter their minds. What would happen next? They all knew what would happen. Back to their dark, solitary cells or placed on the wall. Their only chance for freedom was to play along and kill when told to do so.

"Grab a weapon. I'll be sitting over here," Kenji said to Tavar, shifting over to a seat next to one of the guards.

"Are you not training?" Tavar asked, puzzled by the old man. "You could use the practice and I'd like to see what you can do!"

"I'm sure you would, kid," Kenji groaned as he tapped his stick against the chair and turned, slowly lowering himself onto the seat and resting his hands against the small staff. "Train with one of the others. I'll be listening closely. I can give you some assistance to help you improve."

"Help *me* improve?" Tavar said, stomach hurting from laughter as he strode over to the weapons rack. "By listening?"

"Smell, too. The sweat of a warrior is a stench that can be easily traced. It will be as though I've been handed a new set of eyes. Trust me."

Tavar's face tightened. The last time he'd given his trust it hadn't ended too well. Now he was living underground with criminals who had done the worst of the worst. The well of trust had almost run dry and the drops he had would not be given up lightly.

"What weapon you using?" a woman beside him asked, nonchalantly flipping a spear in her hands. She looked a few years older than Tavar. Soft, brown skin lit up in the light of the flickering torches. Her hair was shaved on both sides but what remained was long, dark and spiked. She reminded him of the man he had killed in the desert. The warrior claiming to be from Blood Nation.

"Dual swords," Tavar answered, his eyes drifting to the two falchions lined up in front of him. Seems the painting had inspired him after all. He pulled the weapons from their berth, testing their weight and nodding with satisfaction. He pushed a finger against the edge of one of the blades and bit his lip. Blood dripped from his fingertip. Sharp enough to kill in the right hands. Or the wrong ones.

"You must be fast to deal death with two short blades," the strange woman said. "Need to get in tight to your enemy and see the light fade from his eyes."

"Or hers," Tavar smirked.

"Or hers," she agreed with a smile of her own and a tilt of the head. "Care to fight? I'll be gentle. It's been a while." She winked and stepped into the middle of the square easing past two other warriors who stood and watched with anticipation, eyeing up the competition.

She attacked without warning, not even allowing Tavar time to get his feet properly set. He rocked back onto his heels and slapped the point of the spear away just as the deadly point lunged towards his chest.

"You could have killed me!" Tavar screeched as he paced across the square, keeping his eyes on the smirking woman.

"Could have. Didn't though. That's the important bit."

"Always be ready to defend yourself, Tavar," Kenji shouted from behind him, comfortable in his seat. "Your heart is beating fast. Calm down."

"If you could have seen how close that spear was to stabbing my heart then you would understand, old man," Tavar bit back, annoyed at Kenji's lack of sympathy.

"Anticipate the attack. Focus."

The next attack cut low, sweeping for Tavar's feet. He anticipated the attack and jumped, dodging the spear and slicing his falchion across the air, pulling the strike at the last second to ensure he didn't cut her neck. She only licked her lips in response and pressed her neck against the blade until Tavar pulled back, confused.

"Excellent control," she said to him, impressed. "You could have had my head then, but you stopped. Mercy is a weakness here though. You won't make it through one fight, let alone one hundred if you show such weakness."

"I'm not going to kill you in here. Up there is a different matter," Tavar warned, glancing up above him.

She raised her eyebrows and sucked air in through her teeth. "We shall see."

Tavar pushed his feet forward and cut high, dropping low as the first blade hit the shaft of the spear and swiping at her knees. The spear twisted to snap against the stack and flicked forward, the blunt end of the weapon almost catching Tavar between the legs. He jumped back and circled his opponent, aware now of her speed. She had been trained well. Not in the Alfaran style but she was no novice.

"Move your feet," Kenji advised him. "You need to get closer if you're going to cause any damage with those."

"He's blind, right?" the woman asked Tavar, frowning at the old man.

"Yep," Tavar said. "Tongue works well enough though. Apparently, he's listening and smelling for movement."

"I heard that!"

"I know you did, Kenji!" Tavar laughed.

He continued to circle within the square, momentarily glancing at the two silent men watching intently, bulging biceps on show with arms folded across their chests. They looked Alfaran. Cool, brown skin and dark, wild beards. One of them had braided his beard so that two tails fell low down past his nipples.

"Concentrate!" Kenji bellowed.

How the hell did he know? Tavar cleared his head and breathed slow and long, focusing on his opponent. He decided to be patient, wait for her to move and slip into the space she leaves as she attacks. Then he would need to make her yield.

She was patient. Her eyes flickered to his feet, looking for any sign that he wasn't ready for the attack. Tavar thought he would give her an opening, or at least make her assume there was one. He crossed his right foot over a quarter pace too far, brushing the ball of his foot against the soil instead of planting it.

She flashed forward but Tavar was ready. He spun, twisting to his left as the spear whipped past his right shoulder. He slapped the flat of his blade against her knuckles and she released a hand from the weapon with a cry. He kicked at the inside of her leg and threw an elbow into her face, following her fall as she dropped her weapon. He pressed a knee against her chest and pointed a falchion at her throat.

"Yield?" he asked, pleased with himself.

"I was just about to ask you the same question," she smirked.

Tavar cursed in disbelief as he felt the cold steel of a curved dagger kiss his neck.

"You had a concealed weapon," he said, furious with himself. "There is no honour in such an attack."

"Fuck your honour. My aim is to kill and stay alive. I don't give a shit how it gets done, and neither should you. There are different rules down here."

"She's right," Kenji added, eager to not be forgotten. "I could hear that dagger with each movement she took. Right hip. Loose catch ready for easy drawing. Am I right?"

"You have a talent, old man! Mind letting me up?"

Tavar felt the dagger pull away from his neck so he stood up with a groan and begrudgingly helped his opponent to her feet.

"Name's Medda. This is Faisal and Bilal. New friends of mine." The two men grunted and nodded their heads. Talkative bunch…

"Tavar Farwan. This is Kenji."

"A blind prisoner from Okada," Medda called over to the old man who bowed and pressed a hand on his chest. "I bet you have an interesting tale to tell."

"Not from Okada exactly but close enough. My city was just a small way out of the empire. In the small state of Hiroshoya."

"Bit far from home, then?"

"Yes. Your Alfaran is excellent but there's a hint of a Coreland accent that I detect," Kenji said, frowning in concentration.

"Impressive ear, Kenji. Spent some time in Coreland but my people are not from there. Not really." Medda offered no more, clearly wanting to change the conversation. "Bit of blood there, I see." She pointed at

Tavar's neck. He wiped a hand across it and cursed at the small drops of blood that had appeared.

"How's the hand?" Tavar glanced at Medda's swollen, grazed knuckles on her right hand.

"Had worse," she shrugged. "How about a little two on two? Us two against these Alfaran meatheads?"

"Bring it on."

The bathhouse was simple. Three small rooms, each with different temperatures of water. A northern slave had met Tavar and Kenji at the entrance and given them a fairly uninspiring tour of the three rooms and showed them where they could change and who to call if there was an issue.

Each room had a circular hole cut into the ground with three layers. The holes were large enough to swim across if needed and deep enough to completely submerge oneself. A collection of shells decorated the walls of each room, the variety of colours used displayed scenes of Alfaran history from Queen Tamira to King Uhlad. Tavar spotted familiar scenes such as the Banishment of the Dwarves and the Great War with Albion. All the scenes showed Alfara as the pious, righteous heroes defeating their hateful, evil enemies.

Tavar slipped off his clothes and dropped carefully onto the first edge in the warm pool. His sore muscles relaxed and he leant his head back against the edge of the pool and moaned with pleasure. Not many feelings were better than relaxing in warm water after a hard day's training. His thoughts flashed to Carver and her body on top of his in a dark tent. He pushed it away, cursing as his body tensed again.

A slave led a naked Kenji over to the pool and supported him as he sat next to Tavar. Tavar looked away, eager to give his new ally some dignity, though Kenji didn't seem to care. He couldn't help but notice the scars patterned all over the old man's thin frame.

Kenji thanked the slave as he relaxed, comfortable in the large bath. The slave bowed and walked away, leaving them alone.

"Not a bad day, all in all," the blind man said, kicking his feet gently under the water. "You fought well. I'm confident that we will succeed in the arena. A bit more ruthless aggression wouldn't go amiss though, if you don't mind me saying."

"Are you going to shout orders and advice to me when we are up there as well?" Tavar asked, unable to keep himself from grinning.

"Of course! My mind and your body. That's how you make it out of here."

For a while, the pair of them just sat there, letting the water lap against them, content in the silence of each other's company.

"What did you mean when you said that's how *I* get out of here?" Tavar asked, thinking on Kenji's words. "You not planning on making it out?"

Kenji leant back and blew out a few quick breaths from his pursed lips. "I'm an old, blind man, Tavar. I've lived a full life and enjoyed most of it. The imprisoned part of my life hasn't been the most fun, if I'm honest, but I've loved and I've certainly laughed. I can feel the wrinkles around these eyes of mine that are proof of that. It would be amazing to hold my daughter in my arms again and hear what she has done but I know she is safe and happy. My time is coming to an end. It would be a waste for me to make it out of here at the expense of someone who has their whole life to live. I've made my mistakes and learnt from them, there's not much more I have left to do, apart from help others live their own lives. Like you."

"If you help me get outta here, Kenji, I'll owe you more than my life."

"You will owe me," Kenji agreed. "And you will pay back that debt by getting as far away as possible and living a life where you can be happy. Settle down with a lover and if you'd like, surround yourself with little bouncing babies. Or puppies. I loved the puppies we had back on my farm. Most affectionate beasts in the world."

"Was that in Hiroshoya?" Tavar asked, recalling the name from earlier.

"Close enough that we could travel into the city after a few days' riding. I liked the quiet of the farm. We were close enough to the world to not feel left out but far enough away to feel as though we had a little slice of the world to ourselves. Perfect."

Tavar kept quiet, understanding that how tough it must be for Kenji to talk about such a pleasant past whilst stuck down here, away from it all.

"My mother was Okadan. She loved her homeland. Father was a deserter from the Alfaran army," Kenji said, swallowing hard and licking his cracked lips. "They fell in love after she sheltered him whilst he was wounded. She took care of him and they eventually married and had children. Two were lost in childbirth. Then my brother was born. I followed not long after. My father became a blacksmith and we moved to a town near the coast. My mother loved the sound of the waves crashing against the rocks. I used to sit with her on the cliffs and just watch as the day passed us by. When I was around eighteen years, they came looking for him. Well, they stumbled upon him. Fifteen Alfaran soldiers.

"It was a hard-fought battle but the four of us fought with a fury they did not expect. We'd been trained from birth, me and my brother. More soldiers arrived two nights later. Too many this time.

"They forced my mother to watch as they cut my father into pieces and threw what was left over the cliffs before they slit her throat. A young soldier took pity on us, or maybe he was just terrified after the way he had seen us fight. He succeeded in getting the commander to take mercy on us, to spare our lives. So they took our vision instead. Couple swipes of the blade." Kenji motioned with a straight palm across the scars on his eyes and made a whooshing noise. "That was the last thing I saw. Every time I closed my eyes for the next two years, all I saw was what they did to my parents and then the steel slicing down my face. My brother's screams pierced every dream I had, ensuring sleep wasn't an escape from the horrors."

"Kenji..." Tavar shook his head, raising a hand before hesitating and dropping it back below the waves, thinking better of consoling the old warrior.

"Meeting my wife changed me. She showed me there was still something to live for. She gave me a purpose. My brother continued my father's work. He was a pretty good smith, better than I ever was. It runs in my family's blood. My grandparents on both sides made swords that people from distant lands would cherish. We were content. I had a beautiful daughter, Mako. She was a warm, happy child. The only time I had to wipe tears from her face was when the sickness took her mother from us."

"I'm sorry Kenji," Tavar said. "It hurts to lose someone close to you. Hurts like the hells."

"Ain't that true. She married and her husband is a good man. He agreed to move to the farm as Mako didn't want to leave me all alone. We were happy, I even had two granddaughters. Then, one day, word reached me that the commander who had killed my parents and maimed me and my brother had been found. He'd retired to the countryside and was living alone, save for the collection of slaves he had around him.

"Without thinking, I took a sword and followed the instructions I had been given. I'd paid a local mercenary to help me on my way, travelling isn't so easy for someone like me. I left him with the horses outside the estate whilst I snuck in. He was asleep, I could hear his breathing and the beat of his heart. I cut his throat, like he had done to my mother.

"Revenge is a strange thing. You can spend so long desiring it but when it arrives it's often a disappointment; a waste of energy more than anything. The mercenary had worked out what was going on and made some coin by tipping off the Alfaran soldiers nearby. Took a few down but there's only so much one blind, old man can do. That's how I ended up here, having this conversation with you."

"Your family…"

Kenji smiled as tears dropped from his milky eyes to be lost in the bath water. "I had left them a note. Didn't expect to make it back home, anyway. I'd kissed my granddaughters and hugged them all like it was the last time I would be with them. By the time they would have discovered I had left, it would have been too late to stop me."

"Do you wish they had been able to?"

"With every single nerve in this old body. But they can live their lives now; happy lives without me as a burden. I only wish for them to be happy. What do you wish for, Tavar Fawan?"

Tavar thought about it for a moment. "I wish to see my brother again. To see my friends. If it means fighting a thousand times, then I'll do it, or I'll die trying."

"I do not wish to see you die, young man. So let's make sure you succeed. We need to work together, an old, blind man and young, foolish man. I believe we can do it."

Tavar pushed himself from the edge and dunked his head underwater, embracing the echoing of the water.

"You know what, Kenji? I know we can do it."

CHAPTER TWENTY-THREE: BLOOD, SWEAT, AND FEAR

"Three moons of training and today is the day," Kenji said, unable to keep the excitement from his voice: completely at odds with Tavar's anxious nausea about the whole thing. "How are you feeling? Excited? Nervous?"

"Like I'm about to paint the walls with last night's stew." Tavar held his breath and clenched his stomach muscles, praying that what he said wouldn't come true.

His time under the arena had passed by in haze of blood and sweat. More prisoners had been brought in to fill up the numerous cells, all eager to showcase their skills in the hope of making their way out of the shackles of Alfara.

Kenji had been with Tavar every step of the way. The old man sometimes leaned on Tavar, taking his arm and asking for support to guide him to the baths or to the training room. It wasn't long before Tavar noticed that this only happened when there were others near to them; close enough to listen and to see the weak Okadan. Before long, Tavar felt he had enough evidence that suggested the Kenji wasn't quite the frail, old man he loved to portray. Tavar didn't bring it up though. If that's what his friend wanted to do then he wasn't going to stop him. He'd listened to the blind man's advice and often found himself swelling with pride as Kenji cheered and clapped as he sat in on Tavar's daily training exercises.

Blind though he was, Kenji could sense movement better than most predators in the wild. Still, Kenji had not even touched a weapon since Tavar had arrived. Some of the newer prisoners had laughed and mocked him, thinking it was a joke that the blind man would be a part of such an event. Openly, with loud voices, they discussed how long Kenji would last in the arena and bet food and time in the training room against the seconds and rarely, minutes, that they thought he would survive.

"New meat!" Zaif called out as Tavar helped Kenji past the arrogant prisoner's cell. The brute had taken a liking to Tavar since his first day, speaking to him whenever they passed one another and mocking his friendship with Kenji. "How long do you have the blind fool lasting? I said two minutes. Reckon you can keep him alive that long for me? I'll make sure your death is swift when we meet in the arena if you do this for me..."

"As great as an offer that is, I think I'll pass. Kenji and I are making it until the end." Tavar watched the tall brute lick his lips and thump a fist against his chest.

"Oooohhh, I love that confidence. A romance for the ages! We're gonna have a lot of fun up there one day, New Meat. You'll see."

Ignoring the creepy stare and wave, Tavar pressed forward with the line of prisoners chosen for combat. Heavily armed guards surrounded them, leading them up the stairs and out to the next level of the arena.

The noise was deafening.

The first fight had already started. A mix of cheers, screams, curses and one horrified collective intake of breath reached the prisoners. Tavar caught Medda's eyes as she blew out a quick breath, trying to ignore the disturbing sounds coming from the arena.

"As this is your first battle, you may choose whichever weapon you wish," the guard said as he led them into a curved room with a similar range of weapons displayed in the training room. "It is team combat and to the death. Ten on ten. Last team standing wins. Fairly simple, even for you idiots." The guard chewed on a tobacco leaf and spat some dark liquid at Medda's feet.

The warrior tightened and glared at the guard but restrained herself from any further response. "Watching you dogs tear each other apart will be fun, When the gate opens, you enter. Commander Grey is our guest of honour for today's battles. Wait for his signal before starting. Understood?"

Happy with the grunts of affirmation, the guard left the room and slammed the door shut behind him.

"I would like to see that guard in the arena," a huge, broad-shouldered and pale warrior said to the room as he stomped over to the weapons and pulled a mighty hammer from the shelf.

He swung it through the air and placed it over his shoulder with the same ease as Tavar would throw a shirt. He smiled at the rest of them through a trimmed, fiery beard and flicked back his long, blonde hair. "I'd crush his skull within seconds." He feigned slamming the hammer against the ground and laughed, completely at ease. "I will have to make do with fellow prisoners today, it seems. I do hope you stay alive," he said, eyes looking Medda up and down as though noticing her for the first time. There was a lot of skin on display for all the warriors. The crowd wanted to see blood so minimal armour was allowed. Just a sleeveless leather covering for the torso, skirt or shorts and a helmet. "You look strong. I love strong women."

"Will you love it if I crush your balls with that hammer of yours?" Medda replied, her own eyes falling down the warrior's incredible body.

"You certainly are one to keep an eye on. No offence blind man."

"None taken," Kenji said, walking over to the weapon rack. "I can almost smell the energy in the air. I hope you are all ready for this. Now is not my time to die."

"That smell might not be the energy. Think I just shit myself." A thin, lean woman was looking out through the horizontal gap in the wall, watching the fight as the crowd roared its approval. "Some poor bastard just lost their head."

"It will be difficult to stay calm in such an environment," another prisoner, an Alfaran by Tavar's guess, said as he tested one of the spears.

"No. I mean actually lost their head," the woman explained. "Three hacks with a scimitar. Sick fucker is holding the head up to the crowd."

"That explains the cheers," Medda said, taking a spear of her own and inspecting it closely.

The pale warrior ignored everything else in the room; he was making his own inspections of Medda.

"Where are you from? Are all women like you from there?" he asked her.

"None of your fucking business."

"I'm a Naviqing from Naviqand. I killed Helgath the Eternal in the battle of white peaks. Halfor is my name. What can I call you?"

"Wasn't so eternal then, was he? Keep us alive and I'll give you my name."

"Success!" the Naviqing pumped a fist and danced away, smiling to himself.

The room fell silent as they tested their weapons. A good weapon could be the difference between life and death today. Everything needed to be checked.

"I'm intrigued to see what you choose, Kenji. Spear, sword, or whatever this is?" Tavar asked as he walked along the row of weapons, stopping at an unusual rope coiled up tight with a sharp iron blade tied at its end. He'd never seen its like before.

"Okadan whipblade," Kenji informed him, running his coarse hands over the weapon. "Extremely difficult to use properly but, in the right hands, extremely deadly and difficult to predict."

Tavar grabbed the twin falchions and spun them in his hands until he was comfortable with their movement. The amount of time he had spent with them over the past few moons meant they were almost an extension of his body. Kenji thought that was the only way he would make it out alive. Make the blades become one with you.

"There is only one weapon that I will ever use," Kenji walked beside the weapons and gently ran only the tips of his fingers against them, breathing slow and even. He stopped as he reached a thin sword lying on top of two iron hooks. He lifted the weapon from its resting place and slowly twisted the rough and battered leather hilt with one hand pulled the crimson scabbard decorated with a golden dragon with the other. The blade sang as it escaped its prison. "A kyushira. Okadan sword meant only for the finest of warriors. My people have never forgiven outsiders for stealing them from our land and making cheap imitations such as this. Still, a beggar must not cry for gold when offered silver. It will do."

Tavar looked around at the prisoners waiting for their time to fight. They were nervous. All of them. Even the Naviqing now sat in a corner, cross legged and eyes closed with his hammer lying across the front of him as he muttered a prayer to whatever gods he believed in.

Tavar cleared his throat and walked into the middle of the room. "Should we be coming up with some kind of plan?" The others all looked up at him and then glanced around at each other, no one knowing who should respond.

"My plan is to stay away from the blind man with the sword," one of them said, bringing most of the others to laughter. She had wild, red hair that fell in curls past her shoulders. Her pale face was freckled, and she had a small, curved scar next to her left eye. She'd seen battle, that was certain. "He'll be the one to worry about," she said pointing at Kenji. "Giving the blind, old man such a sharp blade is a death wish for anyone who gets close to him. My plan is to give him a wide berth or an *accidental* knife in the back."

"Say that again." Tavar rushed forward, feeling his nerves and anger tip him over the edge. Kenji pulled at his leather top and wrapped an arm around his chest as the red-haired woman laughed and joined two others watching the display in the arena.

"Not worth it, kid," Kenji warned. "Let's focus that energy on the ones we need to kill."

"She threatened to kill you."

"Not the first one to do that and she sure as hell won't be the last. Let it go. Such energy is wasted on fools. Save it."

"My people have a ritual before any battle," Halfor said, standing and marching over to Tavar. He scratched his red beard and licked his lips, drawing Tavar in close with a huge, meaty hand. "To dispel any bad energy that there may be amongst our warriors, we hold a fight. First blood. First one to cut the other wins and everything is good. Releases the bad spirits that can sometimes swirl around a camp before a big fight. Of course, often I have seen the warriors get carried away with the bloodlust and end up killing their opponent." The big man shrugged his massive shoulders and chuckled. "That is life, I suppose. Or death." He frowned. "The gods work in strange ways, do they not?" He clapped a monster of a hand on Tavar's back, nearly flooring him before walking away, winking at Medda who just gave him an icy stare.

"He's not all there, that one," Medda said as she joined Tavar and Kenji with her two silent allies, eyes not leaving the Naviqing. "Those barbarians are odd. Must be mad to live up there in the mountains with all the snow and ice. People aren't meant to be around such cold. Not good for the mind."

"I sense you're thinking something important, my Coreland friend. What do you need?" Kenji asked as Medda finally turned her gaze away from the large warrior.

"You're right about a plan. If we just rush out there swinging wildly then we can just get picked off with ease."

"What do you suggest?" Tavar asked. "Doesn't seem like the others want any part of it."

"There's five of us. Three spears and two with swords. We stay close to each other and defend one another. Think of us like a mini shield wall."

"So you three defend whilst Kenji and I attack?"

Tavar thought out loud, picturing how they would go in his head and not liking it. "Great plan."

"You got anything better?" Medda spat, obviously annoyed with the rebuke.

Tavar pulled at his growing beard and scanned the room, carefully analysing each warrior they would be fighting beside. He'd seen most of them in the training room; all had strengths and weakness, like him. How to use the strengths and hide the weakness; that was the art of being a leader.

"Follow him." Tavar nodded towards Halfor who was now flexing his biceps to a rather uninterested Alfaran male.

"That it?" Medda mocked.

"Follow him. He's the biggest. The others will go for him, wanting to take him down first. We can use that to our advantage. We stay together and pick off any of his scraps. He'll kill at least a couple, look at him." Their eyes turned as one to Halfor as he re-enacted some scene from a previous battle, picking up the poor Alfaran soldier and feigned throwing him into an oncoming horde of enemies. He placed the shaking man down with a hearty laugh and picked his giant warhammer back up. "Whilst they waste energy on him, we cut them down. Pick them off like vultures."

"I like it. Impressive," Kenji said as Medda mulled over the plan.

"I don't have anything better," Medda agreed, just as the black gate began to rise, opening the arena floor to them.

Sunlight poured into the small room as Tavar stared out at the full arena. A mass of people had gathered in the circular stadium, all roaring and cheering together as the warriors stepped out tentatively.

"This is it," Kenji said, tilting his ear to the cheers of the crowd and placing an arm around Tavar's as he led him out into the bright light of the sun.

"Don't die old man."

"Like I said before, today is not the day I die."

Halfor rushed forward, basking in the adoration of the crowd as they stared at the massive Naviqing. "Your hero has arrived, people of Alfara! Halfor the Bloody is here to entertain you! A red battle is upon us, and songs will be sung for the ages!"

"He seems keen," Tavar muttered to Medda as she nervously looked around at the screaming fans.

"He wants to know my name. He'll survive. Men have killed for less."

"Here they come," Tavar warned as their ten opponents strode out in a line as one, marching together with a mix of swords, spears and shields in hand.

"How you feeling, kid?" Kenji asked, squeezing his arm gently.

"Like shitting myself."

"That's a good sign. Use the fear. Use everything you can."

The crowd fell silent as Commander Grey stood from his seat with two slaves next to him holding high waving falcon flags. All eyes fixed on Grey as he smirked and held his hand high in the air. He waited a moment, enjoying the power before slicing his hand swiftly down to the sound of trumpets and the lowering of the falcon flags.

"Let battle commence!" Halfor roared, rushing forward with his warhammer.

"You heard the guy," Kenji said, letting Tavar go and offering a wicked grin. "Time to have some fun."

Halfor yelled something over his shoulder but amidst the screams and shouts from the excited crowd, Tavar couldn't hear a word of it. He pulled one of his falchions from the gut of the unfortunate bastard who had been knocked to the ground, shield smashed to pieces by the great warhammer Halfor swung with such ease and enjoyment. The Naviqing looked in his element. Tavar wouldn't have been surprised to find out that the warrior had requested to be here and wasn't actually a prisoner, such was the look of hellish joy upon his bearded face as he sent any who crossed his path to the floor with abandon.

So far, the plan was working. Four dead to one in Tavar's team's favour. The first moments had been manic as his targets focused upon Halfor before realising that attacking the strong monster was akin to smashing your head against a stone wall repeatedly. The battle had calmed slightly since then as the two sides took their time, judging the opposition before making more intelligent forays into enemy territory.

"Gonna have to change the plan up, I think," Medda said, creeping up next to Tavar, spear pointed at a particularly gruesome looking fellow with no teeth. "Any other good ideas?"

"Nine on six," Tavar said, counting the remaining warriors. "Spread out and choose your attacks carefully. We have the advantage and we don't want to lose it." Tavar had barely finished his sentence when he cursed, watching with fury as the red-haired woman charged into a group of enemies, alone. She fought well, blocking attacks from two of them with her wooden shield and landing a spinning strike with her scimitar that sliced the third from the hip up to his shoulder. The crowd roared in appreciation as she checked her strike and snapped her shield into her fallen foe's face.

Tavar couldn't do anything but watch as her first opponent returned with her axe and chopped wildly. With a thud, the axe fell deep into the red-haired woman's neck. Her weapon and shield fell before she did. Her feet wobbled to the side and she stumbled to her knees, eyes darting around in desperation. She fell on her front, axe still buried in her neck as her adversary cackled and picked up the fallen scimitar before racing away towards the next opponent.

"Eight on five," Tavar corrected himself.

"Better off without her," Medda said, spitting on the ground. "Faisal. Bilal. On me." Her two allies snapped their shields next to Medda and pushed their spears forward as they marched forward as one. "Stay alive, Tavar. You too, old man."

"I think our numbers have dropped…" Kenji poked the hilt of his sword against Tavar's back, grabbing his attention.

"Shit." A small but swift fighter wiped the blood from his two curved daggers. The intricate silver handles wrapped around the small warrior's fists like gloves. Two bodies dropped simultaneously either side of him and he just stood there, barely a bead of sweat on show from his shaved head to his toes peeking out from his sandals.

"Shadow warrior," Kenji said as though the name was a curse.

"What?" Tavar had never heard the name before.

"He doesn't come from this continent. Past the wastelands, there's a group of warriors trained as assassins, hired to fight for whoever has the most coin. Best killers on the planet, some say. His heart has barely changed its pace since the fight started. Best leave this one to me, kid."

"You're joking. Right? Now is the moment you decide to do something. When a deadly assassin kills two of our guys."

"Patience, young Tavar. Now, go and fight some of the others. I'll handle this." Kenji waved him away and raised his sword to his face in a loving embrace.

"I'm not leaving you."

"Do as you're told."

Tavar glanced over his shoulder. The fight had turned. Faisal lay motionless in the sand as Bilal bled next to him from a nasty looking wound to his chest. They had the advantage now. Medda fought with fury, twisting her body and spinning her spear in ways Tavar thought were impossible. She fought off two attackers but she was on her heels, unable to launch an attack of her own.

Halfor fared only slightly better. Two of the larger members of the opposing team circled him, bodies coiled like snakes waiting to spring as they aimed their own spears at him, not letting the frustrated Naviqing get close enough to do any real damage to either of them.

Time was of the essence and he couldn't be in three places at once. With a last look at Kenji who stood facing the still shadow warrior, he ran towards Medda, swearing at himself along the way and praying that his blind friend would survive long enough for him to help.

Medda dropped and rolled to the side, drawing

her two attackers towards Tavar with their backs now turned on him. He thanked her under his breath and jumped high into the air, driving his falchions into the necks of both enemies as he fell, taking both of them with him. Medda leapt like a lion towards her prey, spear smashing through the skull to end the fight for one of them as Tavar withdrew his blade and finished the other off with quick slice along his neck. Ignoring the blood splashed upon him, he accepted Medda's nod of thanks and followed her as she raced towards Halfor.

The huge warrior was slowing now, his large body tiring as he chased shadows. His attacks still rung with power but they were easily dodged by the pair of intelligent warriors he chased. They both moved forward as the Naviqing missed another swing and dropped to a knee with the momentum. They pulled back their spears and lunged forward, keen to finish him and take the glory.

The cheer of the crowd sent vibrations through the arena, shaking Tavar as he blocked the attack with one blade and stabbed up through the gut of the shocked warrior with the other. He pulled the blade free and thrust it back in. Once. Twice. Three times. Had to make sure. The body fell with a thud and Halfor stood, breathing heavily as Medda stepped on her opponent's chest, casually driving her spear through his neck and pulling it free with a squelch.

"Had them right where I wanted them," Halfor panted.

"We know, big guy," Medda agreed with a pat on his large back. "One left."

"What is he doing?" Tavar asked, staring over incredulously as Kenji stood still as a statue, waiting whilst the shadow warrior circled him, eyeing him up with a measured gaze.

"Don't even think about it!" Kenji called over his shoulder to the three of them. "This is my fight. Not yours."

"The bastard is gonna get himself killed!" Medda shook her head and slapped the back of her hand against Tavar's shoulder. "You gonna let him?"

"It's his fight," Tavar muttered weakly. He wanted to help. With every bone in his body, he wanted to help. But something held him back. Respect for his friend, perhaps? The blind man hadn't done much up until now but he had asked for this. Live or die, this is what he wanted.

"Crazy bastard!" Halfor roared, shaking his own head and licking blood from his stained hands. "I like him. Hope he survives."

"He's a fool. Between you, you'd have one whole brain," Medda said, eyes fixed on the pair of warriors patiently waiting for the first strike. A hush fell over the entire arena. No more screams. No more yells of horror or excitement. Thousands of people joined as one in anticipation for the fight between the shadow warrior and the blind swordsman. Tavar scanned the crowd and spotted Commander Grey. Even he leant forward, barely touching his seat as he held his breath, consumed by the scene before him.

"Come on, Kenji…" Tavar prayed to all the gods he had ever heard of, making deals he knew he couldn't keep but making them anyway in case any one of them led to his friend's survival.

The shadow warrior paused his stalking. He leapt forward, twin daggers flashing in the sunlight. Tavar inhaled so fast he choked on his saliva. At the last second, Kenji snapped his blade up, diverting the path of both daggers and forcing his opponent wide.

The crowd cheered as one at the speed of the display, knowing they were in for a treat.

"Bastard's been tricking us this whole time," Medda said, shaking her head in disbelief.

Tavar balled his fist and cheered to himself, willing his friend to victory.

The next attack was just as swift. The daggers flashed towards Kenji but the blind man spun of the balls of his feet, wrists twisting frantically to halt each strike before they could land. This time, Kenji flashed the blade diagonally, striking low and missing the shadow warrior's thigh by the barest of fractions.

The shadow warrior backed off, smiling to himself as Kenji returned to his statue like stance. A flurry of furious attacks followed, heightened with annoyance as the shadow warrior tried to kill off the blind swordsman. The daggers snapped and twisted in all directions but the kyushira met them at each point. Kenji moved like the wind, whipping from side to side, jerking back and lunging forward like a man a third of his age. His snow-white hair and beard whirled with the motion as the two of them danced together to the flow of the crowd's adoration.

Tavar's energy drained from him just watching the two of them trade blows. He gasped as the kyushira drew blood, a meagre cut to the shadow warrior's ankle promptly followed by a dagger slashing wildly across Kenji's cheek. Blood splattered on the sand but the fight continued, each warrior ignoring their own injuries and limitations, focusing all their energy on ending the other.

Tiredness didn't seem a factor as the pace quickened, the two warriors moving as one in a blur of motion so fast that Tavar's eyes struggled to keep up with the flashes of steel and red spray. They broke apart suddenly and the crowd exhaled together. Tavar scanned the scene for what had happened and his eyes found Kenji's hand soaked in blood and pressed hard against his neck.

"No!" Tavar rushed forward as the shadow warrior marched toward his prey. He picked up a shield and kept running, ignoring the calls from behind him, intent only on saving his friend.

Kenji's kyushira shook in his hand as his legs buckled, dragging him to his knees. Tavar ignored the ache in his legs as he launched himself past his friend, shield flashing forward. He caught the first dagger square on the shield but there was nothing he could do about the second. He felt a burning sensation accompanied by the wetness of blood dripping from his ribs down to his hip. The shadow warrior grinned over the shield and pulled both blades away as Halfor and Medda joined them, weapons raised and ready to strike.

"Stop!" All eyes turned to Commander Grey who stood with both flags raised beside him. "Drop your weapons. The fight is over. Alfara, I give you, your champions!"

The crowd lapped it up, overjoyed to see such worthy fighters survive the hellish combat. Tavar spotted some frowns and angry looks from the audience. Some had come for blood and guts and the disappointment over missing out on one more death seemed too much for them. Tavar wasn't sorry that they felt hard done by.

"You fool," Kenji whispered to Tavar, pulling his cloak to the side to reveal a hidden dagger ready to strike. "Did I teach you nothing?"

"You can be a right bastard sometimes, you know that?" Tavar laughed, though it pained him. He pushed his hand against the wound and swore as more blood seeped out.

"I do. Looking forward to the next one?"

"You have more to learn. I can't wait."

CHAPTER TWENTY-FOUR: FRIENDS

"Four years of fighting side by side and becoming the toast of the Alfaran people. I'd say that means we drink!" Halfor raised a jug of ale to the cheers of the fellow warriors of the snake and pulled a reluctant Medda in for a one-armed hug, sloshing some of the drink over her shoulder, much to her disgust. "Four years of drawing blood together and fighting as a fearsome unit. Long may it continue!" More cheers and bawdy cries as drinks were passed around the winner's circle.

A year into the arena games, the just King Uhlad in his unending benevolence granted the building of an extension for the warriors. A whole room for the winners following a victory where they could drink and socialise with guards watching them through barred doors away from the losing team. The alcohol had been welcomed with tears of joy from even the biggest bastards in the corridor. A just reward, they claimed, for their service to Alfara. Many had forgotten the crimes that had brought them there. Murderers and cutthroats feigning innocence and expecting a reward for more murder, just this time it was in front of a paying audience.

"Nasty cut you've got there," Medda said as she made her way over to Tavar and pointed at the wound on his bicep. She sniffed at the stickiness on her shoulder and rolled her eyes.

"I'll get it looked at soon enough. You stink of ale."

"Halfor is having his fun. You know what he's like."

"So he should. Did you see the way that guy's head crunched under the weight of his strike today?" Tavar cocked his head to the side and chuckled darkly. "That's when I knew we'd be fine. When he's on form, the other team basically begs for death."

"That arena reeks of death thanks to the big guy," Kenji agreed, sipping his cup of shinmiz. The liquid looked, smelled, and tasted like piss but the old man loved the stuff. Reminded him of home apparently. If there was anything that put Tavar off ever visiting the blind warrior's homeland then it was that comment.

"Stinks better than that," Medda said, crinkling her nose and backing away from him.

"It takes a fine intellect to enjoy something so refined," Kenji said before knocking the horrific drink back and opening his mouth wide to exhale, breathing the stench onto the pair of them.

"Shit…" Tavar waved a hand in front of his face to blow the fumes away, coughing but unable to keep a smile from his face.

The four of them had spent the last four years together. They were a second family. Well, maybe a third for Tavar. They knew each other better than they knew themselves. He knew all about the way Kenji would sleep with a blade and wake up at the break of dawn to train with his family. He knew how Medda had lived on the edge of the Undying Sands and thieved and killed to survive. He knew that Halfor was afraid of the dark…

They were more than friends. Four years had passed with many fights as a team in addition to the fifty Tavar had fought alone, many to the death. As the moons and years passed, their bond grew stronger. But so too did the shadow hovering over them. The realisation that to escape this world, only one of them could survive. There was an unspoken rule between them. Whenever talk would shift to their freedom, the conversation would change. None of them could think of ending the life of another, hardened warriors as they were. They had saved each other's lives a countless number of times and debts were owed. When the time came, they would deal with it. Until then, some things were better left unsaid.

"I better get this cleaned up," Tavar said. Ignoring the wound in his arm would only cause problems in the morning. Best to get something done and finished than sit and cry about it. That's what Kenji always told him. "I'll catch you both once it's sorted. The four of us can share some of that shit Kenji loves."

"That a threat?" Medda said.

"Less of that cheek, girl. You'll learn to love it," Kenji replied, grabbing her arm and leading her away. "I'll settle for some of the red wine you so love for the moment."

The infirmary was empty. One of the perks of killing the opposition was that they didn't need any recovery time. Straight into the fires at the far side of the stadium beneath the north stand. The smell alone brought a burning sensation in the throat and nostrils but the tickets for each combat were cheaper on that side of the stadium, according to one of the warriors who had gotten friendly with a guard.

"Back again," the lone doctor said, placing his book down on the table at his side and turning to the bed next to him.

"You know me, Abu. Can't keep out of trouble."

Tavar had spent enough time with the doctor to know that he liked him. He was down to earth and kind, unlike most of the people who crossed paths with the warriors down here. The guards were mainly pretentious fucks who'd spit on them before saying a word.

The only other people who spent any time beneath the arena were the nobles rich enough to pay for 'time' with the combatants. Tavar had his first visitor after a year fighting in the arena. He left the dedicated room for such meetings feeling more drained and exhausted than after he had been in battle. He had no idea the more mature ladies of the city were so full of life! He'd been visited by a few others after that. Some just wanted to talk and tell him of their troubles, safe in the knowledge that their words wouldn't leave the arena. Both men and women enjoyed his company, eager to escape the frantic pace of the world above. Halfor was the most popular though. The Naviqing was busy most weeks with various visitors, often drawing a raised eyebrow from Medda, not that she would admit that it had anything to do with him.

"Doesn't look too bad." Abu peered over his eyeglasses at the cut as he pulled on his gloves. "I'll clean it up for you and then I'll stitch you up for what feels like the millionth time."

"You're exaggerating. It's closer to a thousand," Tavar said, looking down at the cut. It had been his own fault. Too busy looking out for Kenji. Not that the blind man needed it. If anything, he seemed to be getting faster with each year, as though he had just been warming up in the beginning. The crowd loved him. "Be much easier if I wasn't doing this forced combat thing…"

"Yeah, unpleasant that," Abu agreed, pressing a hot, wet cloth along the cut and dabbing it, ignoring

Tavar's wincing. "How are you not used to this yet?"

"It stings!"

"*It stings!* You big baby."

"Well how about we swap places next time? You seem talented with sharp weapons." Tavar watched as Abu grinned and brought the needle closer.

"The city of Kessarine is not ready for the brilliance of Abu Sharif ir Zawarwi! One day perhaps."

As much as he hated the injuries, he enjoyed his time with the doctor. It was good to speak to someone whose life wasn't spent under the city trying to survive by killing others. Any conversation they had warmed him.

"How's the family?"

"Little Salim began to walk last week. Amira was so proud, God be praised. It won't be long before we are having to chase him around the house and make sure he doesn't get up to mischief. He is a blessing from God. Praise him."

"Praise him," Tavar muttered instinctively. "He is growing up fast. I remember the smile you had stuck on that stupid face of yours for moons after you and Amira announced the news."

"He is growing up too fast. Time really does fly by." Abu looked up from his work and frowned. "I'm sorry Tavar. Sometimes I forget that you are stuck down here."

"There is no need to apologise. Time does fly by, even when one is stuck down here. Each passing day is one closer to my day of freedom, so I can't complain."

Abu finished the stitches and gave them a proud smile. "Not my best work but you'll be fine. No training or heavy lifting this week. Though, I'll give you clearance to lift those mad jugs of ale Halfor enjoys so much."

"Much appreciated, Doc. I'm sure I'll be seeing you soon." Tavar jumped to his feet and stretched his arm, checking for any signs of stiffness.

"Not too soon I hope. Earn your freedom and get out of here. Then we can have a conversation where I'm not trying to piece you together."

"Nah. That would be too strange. See you, Abu."

Tavar could still hear the revelry and partying through the stone walls as he left the infirmary. The night would last well into the morning as the warriors made good use of the relative freedom afforded to them by their victory.

"Tavar Farwan." A guard stepped in his way; spear pointed towards the ceiling.

"Yes." Tavar felt his fingers twitch on instinct as he looked at the sharpened point of the weapon. He had to remind himself that not everything was a battle.

"You have a visitor. I'm to escort you to the Closed Room."

"I need to shower first."

"The lady was very specific that you came with all haste. The usual expectations are to be set aside for this meeting."

Tavar frowned, puzzled. All meetings followed a strict protocol. The change in expectations unnerved him, putting him on edge. "Who has asked for this meeting?"

"She made it through an intermediary. The woman said that she is an old friend."

"Lead the way." Tavar marched behind the guard with all haste, keen to discover who this old friend may be and why they wanted to speak to him down here, of all places.

"So how does this go? You take all of your clothes off and I just ravage you? Or shall I undress and play the damsel in distress? This is all so new to me…"

"Lilian…" She'd grown her hair out, tying it into two bunches at the top of her head that gave her more of a playful look than he had ever seen on her before. Her dark eyes flashed with the same sparkle of mischief that he had first seen in them all those years ago on his first day in Kessarine. The low torchlight in the room danced against her skin as she walked towards to him looking like midnight made flesh.

"It's been a long time, Tavar," she dropped the playful swagger and relaxed with a smile that reached those sparkling eyes and drew him in for a hug before pushing him away to get a better look at him. "You've grown into a man, and some man might I add!" she giggled and pressed a gentle hand against his toned bicep.

"Why are you here?" he asked, trying to ignore the sweet perfume emanating from her as she strode to the wine waiting for them on the bedside table.

"Take a seat," she said, pouring the wine into a silver cup for him and nodding to one of the chairs. Tavar did as he was told, eyes flickering to the scarlet sheets hanging from each of the four corners of the large bed in the centre of the room. "Unless you would prefer that first?" Tavar froze in the chair, not knowing where to look. Lilian broke into a high laugh that ended with a snort. "You're cute. I'm joking Tavar. It's taken me years to have this opportunity to speak to you. We can't waste it with such base actions. Not this time, anyway," she added with a wink.

She handed him a cup and sat opposite him with her own, folding her long legs and staring him in the eyes as he greedily gulped the wine. It was sweet and fruity. Not his favourite but it would do. He didn't have the chance to be picky down here.

Lilin sipped her wine and licked her painted lips before shrugging. "Not bad. Can't expect too much, I guess." She placed her cup down and patted the creases of her dress that ran down her thighs. "I wanted to see you when they brought you back from Hartovan. With Sett dead and Marcus missing, I panicked. Tried to leave the city. Uhlad stopped me. He kept me in one of the cells to the east of the palace, noble prisoners, not like the hell you stayed in. After two moons, he brought my son to me and told me to leave. He claimed that he had no need for Sett's son anymore and that I wasn't to step foot in Kessarine again."

"Yet, here you are," Tavar said, gasping as he downed the rest of his wine and placed the empty cup on the carpeted floor.

"Here I am," Lillian agreed, throwing her arms wide and making a clicking sound with her tongue as she winked. "I'm sure word eventually reached you down here; the joyous news regarding King Uhlad the Great?"

"He had a son," Tavar said, remembering the celebrations from the crowds in the arena and the banners and flags they had waved in honour of their ruler's joy. "A healthy prince."

"Yes!" Lilian's eyes flashed as she leant forward, dragging her chair with her as she grew closer to him. "A little bouncing baby boy for the king who would rather cut his own cock off than lie with a woman. God really had blessed the bastard. When the news reached me, I was shocked, but I knew that this is why he had let me leave, with my own son. He had his heir."

"What did you do when you left the city?"

"Breathed in the fresh air. Spent time with my son and travelled to cities I'd only heard of from soldiers and passing merchants. Every new place we visited it felt like our strength was growing, along with the true bond of mother and son. Eventually, I headed home. The islands are healing following Alfara's cruel treatment. Some of the lost people of Hartovan have secretly returned and made homes with their people. They have pride and the smiles on their faces are no longer forced. They can be themselves without fear of a king blocking out their light like a cruel shadow focusing only on its own amusement."

"I am glad for them. They did not deserve what happened to them," Tavar said, lost in thoughts of the farmers of Hartovan. He saw again the flames that had consumed Adam and he bit his lip, closing his eyes to stop the burning in them. They needed to be buried deep, those thoughts, buried and never be released. They were too painful. "We all deserve freedom. A chance to make our own mistakes."

"Couldn't agree more. It was interesting on the islands. I enjoyed my time there with my son but after a while, I longed for the freedom of the road, just as you had once said to me. It's funny, I ran as far away from Alfara as possible and yet, I bumped into some old faces…"

Tavar's chair creaked as he shifted, trying to keep his breathing steady. "Which old faces?"

"In Albion, I heard tales of a crew of deserters

riding the eastern waves on a new ship that struck fear into the hearts of even the meanest of sailors. A young pirate queen and her friends attacking the murderers and cutthroats of the five seas and sharing their wealth with the poor and needy. I travelled to the coast and followed the whispers of this new queen. I found her, eventually, hanging out with her wife in a tavern overlooking a white, sandy beach facing the old continent."

"Her wife?"

"Alice and Cassie married a couple of years after fleeing Hartovan. Qassim was with them, Marcus too, though he didn't look as good as the others."

"Vandir. What about Vandir?" Tavar asked, growing increasingly urgent as he fought against his racing heart and the dizziness brought on by the drink.

Lilian's eyes dropped to her lap and Tavar saw the edge of her teeth dig into her bottom lip. "Your brother wasn't with them. He had been at first, but he left before I caught up with them."

"Where is my brother, Lilian?" Tavar asked sternly, his face growing hot.

"He tried to rescue you. Your brother is being held by King Uhlad. I'm so sorry, Tavar." The sparkle in her eyes faded as she looked up at Tavar, lips slightly parted. Her fingers twitched but she kept them on her lap as she watched him dig his own into the arms of the check. Tavar heard the wood break beneath them, snapping him from his trance.

"He's in Kessarine."

"Yes. But I don't know where. I can't even promise that he's alive. The Judges are merciless when it comes to deserters and Vandir was well liked by those in power. Commander Grey took the desertion personally, so I heard."

"Lilian, you need to help me escape. I need a plan to get out of this shit hole before he dies. I can't wait another four years in the hope that I can kill my way to freedom."

"I don't know…"

Tavar moved forward and fell to his knees in front of her, almost losing himself in her eyes as he looked up at her. "You would have done anything to be with the last member of your family. I understand that. I would do anything to save Vandir. Please, help me."

Lilian sighed, taking his hands in hers and patting them gently. "Can't say I didn't prepare for that question. I knew how you'd respond. There's not much I can do at the moment. This place is well-guarded and there's only one way in or out. Rumours are, that's soon to change, and when it does, we'll need to be ready. I have a friend in here, a guard. He will be able to pass on any messages I have for you. It will be too risky for me to visit in person again. Stay alive and keep hope. You'll see your brother again, Tavar."

"Thank you."

"Don't mention it. Now," Lilian stood, wiping away the tears forming in her eyes as she walked over to the wine bottle. "I've paid for another hour. Let's enjoy it."

He stumbled back to his room, giggling like a child as Kenji fell against the wall, both victims of too much revelry. Tavar couldn't call the room a cell now, not really. There were bars to prevent him exiting without consent and he was trapped in here unless one of the guards permitted it. But the room was three times the size of his original cell, a reward granted from one of the anonymous benefactors of the arena games. Winning certainly had its advantages. He fell against the welcoming sheets on his bed and chuckled into his pillow as Kenji stumbled towards the toilet in the corner: another perk of success.

The sound of a staggered stream hitting the metal and a few groans brought more laughter from Tavar as he rolled onto his back, the room swimming around him. It wasn't the best of feelings but it sure as shit wasn't the worst either. That would come in the morning.

"A man of his size shouldn't be dancing around on tables. It was bound to break," Kenji mumbled, swaying on the seat and stifling a burp. "Excuse me. Halfor is lucky he didn't break his damned neck. Medda looked furious with him."

"I'm sure she'll be releasing all of that anger out on him as we speak, Tavar said, wiping away warm dribble from the corner of his lip and scratching his beard. "That's just who they are."

Kenji fell into his own bed, moaning with pleasure as his old frame slammed against the soft mattress. "Today was a good day. You going to tell me how that little meeting went?"

"Just like all the others," Tavar lied. Guilt stabbed at his chest as he said the words. He never liked lying to the old man and he always regretted it.

"You know I hate it when you treat me like a fool. I'm old and blind but not stupid, kid," Kenji barked at the ceiling.

"What do you mean?" Tavar said, cursing the quiver in his voice that betrayed him.

"I could smell the wine and a bit of perfume on you when you returned but there was no way you did anything more exciting than a little chat. Must have been important, you weren't yourself after. Took a few more cups until you began to enjoy yourself again. I'm a friend, Tavar. No matter what has gone on before, we've spent four years putting our lives on the line for each other. Doesn't that count for something?"

The stab of guilt swelled at the pain in Kenji's voice. He was right. Four years of blood sweat and tears. It meant something. It meant a lot.

"She was an old friend. Though, friend might not be the right word. She helped me when I first arrived."

"What did she want?"

"She's seen some of my friends, the ones I helped to desert. She gave me news on my brother."

Kenji sat up; head tilted to Tavar. "And…"

"He came to rescue me. A while ago. Last she heard, he'd been captured and is in a cell somewhere in the eastern quarter of the city. He's locked up because of me. I need to save him, Kenji. I can't stay here."

"Well if you have any ideas of getting out, then let me know. As much as you know I love you, I'd enjoy somewhere that doesn't always stink of piss. My own space wouldn't be a problem either. Any ideas?" Kenji asked, still swaying with the drink.

"An ember of an idea. Less than that. A spark." Tavar felt the room steady itself as everything came together in his head. "We're making it out of here, Kenji. All of us. This isn't just me now. I'll see Vandir. Halfor and Medda can argue in another city. You can be with Mako again."

"That's a lovely thought, Tav," Kenji said, settling back against his bed and breathing in softly. "My aim is to get you out of here. Any else is just a bonus. All you need to do is tell me what to do and I'll do it."

"That's the drink speaking."

"Maybe, if so, it's making a lot of sense. The drink should speak more," Kenji snorted. "Perhaps I will sleep on it. Night Tavar."

"Night Kenji."

CHAPTER TWENTY-FIVE: IMMORTAL

Tavar pushed the weights up with both arms. The strain on his muscles warned him that he could be pushing too far but he ignored it, as he often did. One more push, then he'd stop. He pushed up and relaxed as Halfor took the weights from him and took them to the side, carrying them with ease, as he always did.

There wasn't a weight in the room that the mountain of a man struggled with. He'd taken to lifting other people whilst they held weights just to challenge himself. Tavar groaned and let his body relax against the bench. Sweat stung his eyes and the taste the salt sat on his lips as his tongue rubbed against them.

He sat up and rolled his shoulder, pressing a hand against his chest to soothe the sore muscle. Hell, it was hard work training with the Naviqing. He pushed Tavar more than anyone else would or could. Halfor wouldn't accept defeat; the very word was anathema to him. In the six years they had trained together, Tavar had sculpted his body into that of an elite warrior. Halfor had helped him to train muscles he hadn't even been aware of. He'd hurt in ways he hadn't known possible and when he caught his reflection in the mirrors of the bath house, he felt a sense of pride in what he had achieved with such effort. He truly was a man now; strong and powerful. One of the few perks of having nothing to do but train.

"You pushed harder today," Halfor said, smacking his mighty hand against Tavar's sweaty back. He frowned at his hand and wiped it against his shirt.

That winning smile of his soon returned. "You should be proud. We should celebrate with a drink."

"That's what you say after every session."

"And that is how I feel after every session."

"Fair enough," Tavar said through another groan, twisting his torso and rolling his wrists to ease out the stiffness in his body. "This is going to hurt tomorrow."

"That's the good thing about tomorrow: it's not today," Halfor said, his grin growing wider.

"Can't argue with Naviqing logic, can I?"

"You can. But it would be foolish. Many have lost their lives for less." Halfor passed Tavar a cup of water and motioned for the guard that their session had come to an end. "That Naviqing logic tells me that a good soak in warm water would help ease the strain on our glorious muscles. What do you say?"

"I'd say that's more logic I can't ignore."

The bath house was empty. Just as Tavar liked it. He sank into the water with moans of pleasure and closed his eyes, letting his head bob just above the lapping warm water. He felt the water rise and escape as Halfor's huge frame joined him.

Tavar opened his eyes to see the Naviqing dip his head beneath the water and return with his mass of long hair soaked and darkened, draped around his face and sticking to his colossal chest.

"You ever going to cut that mess?" Tavar mocked as the warrior pushed the hair to the side of his face and spat water from his mouth like a courtyard fountain.

"I'll cut it when I'm a free man. That's the promise I made to myself and to my Gods. A promise is not easily broken, even by one as strong as me."

"You're a mad bastard, you know that?"

"I've been told many times! Often by you…"

Well, it's true. Glad you're always on my side though. Would hate to fight you. Couldn't live with the guilt of having to kill you," Tavar smirked, knowing his friend would rise to the bait, as he always did.

"I would crush you like a snail beneath my boot, though the act would cut my soul into pieces. I would have to spend moons drinking and fighting to get over such an experience." Halford scratched his chin, thinking hard. "Might be worth it just for that actually…"

"I'm glad my death would be reason to drink and have fun!"

"Purely to deal with such tragedy," Halfor laughed. "You must be able to understand that."

"I understand you take any opportunity to drink and fight! I'm tempted to visit Naviqand one day just to see if there are others like you. I bet the parties are the best in the world," Tavar said, smiling at his large friend as he watched a glossy sheen fall over his eyes at the thought of his homeland.

"There is much drink and revelry in my homeland. Fighting too. We are a passionate people. We love hard and we hate harder. We are proud. The tribes are constantly at war with one another, that's why it was so easy for us to be defeated. We were too busy fighting ourselves to see sense and join up to defeat the outsiders. Naviqing slaves can be found in many parts of the continent because we were too violent for our own good. Too proud to sit down and join forces and see who the true enemy to our kind was. We brought about our own downfall. That's why I left. I needed to discover more, to learn more for my people. One day I shall return and teach them all I have learned on my journey."

"And what will that be?" Tavar asked.

"That friendships can be found in the unlikeliest of places. That it doesn't matter what the shade of your skin is. I've seen Naviqing men crumble in the heat of battle as Albion women fought to defend their children with a ferocity I would be proud of. I've seen a tribe of women rebel against men in the south and defy their oppressors with a unity most nations thirst for. I've seen an old, blind man wield a kyushira with a proficiency like no other." Halfor stared at Tavar and met his eyes, making sure he was listening as his voice dropped. "And I've found friendships worth dying for with people from distant lands, lands of Naviqand's greatest enemies. I have much to teach my people and I long for the chance to push them forward to a better world, a better life."

"Will they listen?"

"Look how strong I am, Tavar," he curled his arms and pouted his lips, jokingly displaying his enormous biceps. "Would you argue with me?"

"When you put it that way…" They laughed together as the mighty biceps fell into the water and splashed them both.

"What about you? Do you see where our home will lie when we are free?"

Tavar took a deep breath in and blew out against the water. "I'm not sure. There's so much of the world I haven't seen. It's too soon to think about a home. I'm focused on leaving this one first. My friends are travelling the seas, according to Lilian. I'll join them and see where the waves take me."

"My people are sea lovers. I shall go with you.

Then perhaps the waves will take you to my home. My people will have sore jaws when they drop at the sight of a brown man embracing me as a friend! It will do them good to see such a pairing."

"And Medda?" Tavar teased, eager for more information. The pair of them were as keen to talk about their relationship as a starving dog would be to share food.

"She has her own path," Halfor grumbled, raising a knowing eyebrow. "I can see her path as clearly as Kenji can see his own feet." The Naviqing fell silent for a moment, thinking. "I would like her path to join with mine, one day. It will be her own decision though. It is not something I can press upon her."

"I don't think you'll have to press. She likes arguing with you."

"That she does..." Halford leaned back on the water with his hands behind his head. "And the making up would shake the highest mountains of Naviqand..."

The whine of a gate swinging open alerted Tavar of a newcomer to the baths. A guard in full armour, face covered by the silver of his elite soldier helmet. Green eyes stared out from the slit running across the helmet, gazing straight at Tavar as he marched forward, a folded parchment in his gloved hand.

"Tavar Farwan," the guard said, voice deep and rich. This was no random guard. He stood to attention, heels clipping one another, and chest puffed out as he pressed a hand against it before relaxing as Tavar nodded.

"Yes. And your name is?"

"Unimportant. I have a message for you." The guard's hand twitched forward with the parchment before he thought better of it as though he had only just noticed the perils of handing it over surrounded by water.

"I'll dry off. Give me a moment." Tavar pulled himself from the bath and grabbed his towel from the bench. He dried his hands thoroughly before wrapping the towel around his waist, covering his modesty before nodding to the guard and accepting the parchment.

"A chosen ally will be meeting you this time in two moons. Be ready with your answer." The guard saluted once more and spun in his heels, marching off and out of the room without a backward glance.

"You have such interesting friends…" Halfor muttered from the water as Tavar opened the sealed parchment.

Tavar ripped open the blue seal and pulled the parchment open, devouring the smartly written letter as quickly as he could.

Vandir was moved three moons ago. I do not know his current location, but he is still in the city. My informant claims that Vandir has struck some kind of deal with Commander Grey to lessen his sentence. My advice to you is to keep fighting and try not to think about your brother. I will work on getting the both of you out of this city as soon as possible but there is only so much I can do. There have been talks regarding a special contest of great warriors where the winner will be given a great gift. I have two allies searching for Alice and the others in the hope of finding them soon enough to gain their support in your escape but no luck so far. Keep fighting and stay alive. You have come so far. Just a bit further…

L

"Good news?" Halfor asked.

"I'm unsure. We should know soon enough. There is to be a special battle; one with great reward."

Halfor splashed the water and his laugh echoed around the cavernous bath house. "Battles we can do! We haven't lost yet, have we? The Gods are on our side, Tavar. Have hope!"

Tavar nodded as he scanned the letter one more time, searching for any hidden message or something that he may have missed. Happy that he had read it all, he strode over to the nearest torch and lit the parchment, allowing the flames to consume the letter.

"Pray to your Gods, Halfor. We need as much help as we can get."

The Naviqing rose from the water like a god, shaking the water from his hair as he marched over to Tavar, placing a hefty, muscular arm around him and letting his manhood swing freely, leaving his towel on the bench. No shame.

"The four of us could take on the Gods themselves if needed. Together, we are unstoppable."

Only one moon passed before Tavar found out the big news. The prisoners were pulled from their training in selected groups and gathered in the training room to be told the exciting news. A herald of King Uhlad himself passed on the word to the prisoners. In two moons time, there would be a contest of champions in honour of the king's birthday. Uhlad himself would be in the crowd to watch the spectacle and something special was needed for such an important occasion. It had been decided that one warrior would win their freedom in front of a full stadium and the king himself.

Needless to say, an excited energy burst through the prisoners at this news. The training room buzzed with energy at all times of day and night as all of the prisoners worked to hone their skills in the hope of winning their way out of their incarceration. Tavar and his friends were just like the others.

"I can feel their muscles burning with the effort," Kenji muttered to Tavar as he placed his weights on the ground, motioning to a group of prisoners pushing themselves hard and wincing with pain. "Half this place will be disappointed when they carry injuries into that arena. They'll be too weak to put up a decent fight. Desperation does terrible things to men and women. Terrible things."

"Yet here we are," Tavar said, not seeing the difference.

"Here we are, doing our usual training. Nothing more, nothing less. A routine, that's what a warrior needs."

"They want to be at their best. I understand that."

"Understanding is fine. But if any of these fools get placed on our team then they can drag us down. Remember that guy who blew his knee and was too stubborn to sit out? I heard it pop within three minutes of that fight and for once, I'm glad my eyes no longer work."

Tavar had to agree with the old man. Seeing the knee spin to face backwards as the poor bastard screamed and fell into the sand was a horrible sight. The entire crowd had gasped as one. His eventual killer was seen as a merciful warrior as he walked up to him and put him out of his misery with one swing of an axe through his throat.

"We'll be fine. The four of us can make up for any deficiencies."

"Arrogance sits closely beside confidence Tavar. Do not confuse the two. We have not fought every warrior yet. The ones who live have proven themselves in that arena. We have no idea who we may face."

The night before the contest, Tavar felt the usual nerves hit as his stomach twisted with anxiety like snakes slithering in his gut. The familiar evasion of sleep attacked and he didn't fight it. In his mind, he ran through every scenario possible, everything he knew about fighting in the arena, as a team and on his own. As Kenji had warned him, they needed to be prepared for anything.

"Can't sleep?" Kenji called out.

"Nope. Nothing new."

"It's gonna be okay, tomorrow. You'll make it out of here."

"And you'll come with me. I haven't forgotten my promise," Tavar reminded him. He heard Kenji shuffle to a sitting position on his bed.

"Look, I appreciate you saying you'll help me escape but… you can't think like that. If there's a chance for you to get out there, then you take it and you don't look back. This isn't about being the hero. You don't want to spend your whole life stuck in a place like this, or worse. If you can see your brother and your friends again then you sure as shit better do it. I won't accept anything else."

"Kenji. You, Halfor and Medda have kept me going in here. Without you three, I'd be dead. We leave as a team or we don't leave at all."

"You know how stupid you sound?"

Tavar frowned at the insult, feeling the anger rise inside. "Stupid? I'm loyal. Nothing wrong with that."

"But there is!" Kenji jumped from his bed and rushed over to him, placing a hand on Tavar's as he sat next to him. "Loyalty is all wonderful and flowery but all it gets you is a dagger in your back. You should know this by now, after what you've been through. I'd be offended if you didn't leave me here. I told you before, I've lived my life. Now it's time to live yours. Tomorrow, you fight until you are the only one standing and you go. If you even glance back at me I'll know and I'll stab you myself, in the chest, not the back so you can see how fucking stupid you are."

"I love our talks Kenji."

"I know you do. You can think about them when you have your own farm in the country with a family. That's what I want."

"Can't always get what you want," Tavar warned with a smirk.

"No. But I'll kill every last person in this place for you to make it out of here. Don't piss on that by trying to be the hero. If you're going to get out of here, you need a ruthless streak. Killing is for men, not boys."

"If your plan is to bore me to sleep, then it's working, old man."

"Ah, fuck you," Kenji playfully slapped his hand as he rose. He shuffled across the room and climbed into bed, grumbling to himself. "You know what I'm saying is true. I love you as family, like you are my own son. I'm proud of you and I can't have you waste your life in here."

Tavar smiled at the kind words. "I love you too, old man. Get some sleep. There'll be blood tomorrow."

Every seat had been filled in the arena. There was a spark in the air that was almost tangible as Tavar stepped out with fourteen other Snake warriors, spinning his falchions for the crowd and surveying the fifteen enemies that stood in their way to victory. He peered up at what was usually an empty seat in the middle of the western stand and almost dropped his blades in the sand. King Uhlad waved to his adoring people. He'd put on some weight since Tavar had last seemed him. Looked as though being a father had relaxed him. But it was the woman standing next to him that caused his alarm. Her face was stony, arms folded. Even after all these years, he knew that scowl even from this distance. Carver ir Edemer.

"What the fuck is she doing here?"

"Who?" Medda asked, following his gaze.

"Carver..."

"She's the one who—" Kenji started.

"Knocked me out when I was *this* close to escaping. She's the reason I'm stuck here and not with my brother and friends," Tavar answered, his whole body shaking. For a moment, their eyes met, but just briefly. Carver played with her collar and averted her gaze, looking across at the opposing team. How could she stand there and look him in the eye after what she had done?

"Focus," Kenji said, ignoring Halfor as he danced to the front of the line, bowing to all sides of the arena and swinging his hammer around to thundering applause. "You need your head here, in this battle. Now is not the time to get distracted by her. By anything."

"She's the reason you got to meet us. You should

be thanking her," Medda added with a wink, hoping to put him at ease. All it did was make the bile in his throat burn ever more.

Tavar bit his tongue, tasting the blood swirl in his mouth as Uhlad calmed the crowd into silence with a single wave of his hand.

"This day is a special day. My thirtieth birthday has me in a merciful mood. People of Alfara, today we shall witness greatness in this grand arena!" The crowd roared and Uhlad flashed his white teeth before calming them once more. "One warrior, a gladiator of immense skill, will escape the confines of the dungeons beneath this famous arena. Through skill, determination and bloodlust, they will fight and kill for the chance to breathe the free air once more. All of these warriors have countless victories under their belts, today one of them will fight for you one last time. Our fist battle is a team battle, Falcon versus Snake. Let the battle commence!" The crowd cheered as a horn boomed through the arena. Tavar slowed his heavy breathing and thought of Vandir. And Alice. He would see them again, all he had to do was focus.

They fought furiously. Tavar's rage sharpened his focus, dodging attacks left and right and rolling under a huge swing of an axe before twisting his hips and lashing out with a falchion across the back of an enemy. His other blade swung methodically around his opponent's shoulders and caught him across the neck, spraying blood all over the sand as a roar erupted from the crowd that shook the ground.

He barely broke his stride, allowing Kenji and Medda to finish off the other two either side of the fallen warrior. To his side, Halfor was having his usual fun, smashing his hammer into his enemies with reckless abandon. Tavar pushed on, spotting two cautious warriors. One wielding an axe whilst the other lowered a spear as she spotted Tavar marching towards them.

He grinned and sped up, spinning the falchions and releasing a roar of his own. His blades crashed against the shaft of the axe and swatted a strike of the spear. He dipped under the attacks and danced between his enemies, sliding his falchions towards defenceless torsos.

One of the attacks landed and he heard the thud of the spear fall to the ground with a groan. He twisted as an axe rushed towards his face and moved just in time to deflect the attack.

Slashing his sword sideways, his blade tore through the leather cuirass just as a fist smashed straight into his face, rocking him back. The arena blurred as he stumbled, struggling to regain his footing. He instinctively raised his weapons and caught a vicious blow of the axe but he wasn't strong enough. The block barely kept the axe at bay. He felt the edge of the weapon crush his own armour and dig into the left side of his chest. He pushed back with his weapon, forcing it back before it could bury itself any deeper. With a scream, he felt the weapon tear from his skin and he rolled to the side and stood shaking his head, trying to regain his composure. He met the next attack with a low block and snapped his elbow forward as he spun past his enemy's defence. He felt the nose break with his attack and twisted his sword in his hand and flicked his blade back, stabbing it straight through his enemy's gut and smiling at the groan of pain and surprise that met the killing blow. Turning quickly, he flashed his free falchion with controlled rage, taking off the head to the approval of the baying crowd.

Tavar breathed heavily as the blood dripped down from his nose into his mouth. Could be broken. No time for that now. He moved on, stalking his next prey.

"Kid!" Kenji called from behind him. Tavar turned to see the old man covered in blood. By the look of him, none of it was his own. He carried his bloodied kyushira with the usual reverence and he marched towards Tavar. "Slow down. You're making mistakes."

"I killed them, didn't I?" Tavar bit back sharper than he meant to.

"Yes. But there's more There's always more. One mistake is all it takes. No more sloppiness."

Tavar took the rebuke with a sigh and controlled his heavy breathing. "They have four left. We can finish this quickly."

"And we have eight left. They're slow, too many injuries like I warned. Patience, kid. We got this."

The remaining four fell quickly as Tavar's team lost only two others. He took off his helmet as the spectators chanted and waved, content with another display of brutality. He dropped the helmet and walked over to the king's seat in the crowd, looking up at the ruler and averting his gaze from Carver.

"Today is a celebration! Tavar shouted as the noise died down.

"What are you doing, kid?" Kenji scolded him from ten paces away.

Tavar ignored his blind friend and marched closer to Uhlad, making sure that he would be heard. "A celebration of your birthday. Give me your best warrior. I'll cut through him like I have done with anyone else placed before me. Let me put on a display worthy of celebrating such a revered monarch."

Uhlad stared back, his uncertain eyes darting across the battlefield and back to Commander Grey, struggling for a response. Grey tilted his head to something Tavar could not see and a smile grew on Uhlad's face. Against his better judgement, Tavar's eyes flicked towards Carver as her own face dropped and the blood drained from her beautiful features.

"You have fought valiantly! All of you," Uhlad called out so that the whole of the arena could hear him. "Blood has been spilled in my honour and you have all displayed the strength that Alfara possesses. A strength that even the lowest of our people can possess!" he smirked. "But today is a special day. And we need a special event. Tavar Farwan, you ask for a challenge. You ask for a great warrior. And so you are asking for your name to echo throughout our people's history. You are asking for songs to be sung in taverns around these lands for generations." Uhlad paused and stared unblinking at Tavar before he nodded and sat back in his seat. "You are asking… for *immortality*."

Uhlad inclined his head to Grey and the commander raised a hand in the air. Tavar's attention turned to an iron door opening on the western side of the arena. Sunlight hit a lone warrior as they stepped out from the shadows, their golden robes shimmering in the afternoon sun, their face covered apart from their eyes as they marched steadily forward: an Immortal. One of the elite warriors of Uhlad's kingdom.

"To become immortal, you must kill one," Uhlad said with thinly veiled delight. The crowd whispered in shock and awe as the warrior stopped and revealed a small dagger like blade at his waist. They pulled the dagger away from their body and with it came a rope that had been tied around the warrior. A weapon Tavar had never seen used before in the arena. A weapon Kenji had warned him to never use. "One on one combat, Tavar Farwan. The gladiator versus the Immortal. This is an event for the ages!"

The people watching erupted with maniacal screams and shouts. Fists pumped in the air and tears flew down red faces of shock. They were going to witness an Immortal in action. True history being made in front of their eyes.

"You really did it this time, Tavar!" Kenji screeched. "An Immortal!"

Tavar bit back his retort and stared at his sole opponent.

"You can do it." Halfor raised a bloodied hand and squeezed Tavar's shoulder, his smile more of a grimace than he may have intended. Tavar appreciated it, nonetheless.

"Keep your focus," Medda added as she strolled over, her eyes fixed on the Immortal. "They're fast but they're mortal. They can't live forever. They bleed just like you and me." She clasped his forearm and nodded before following Halfor to the side where the rest of the warriors were waiting with anticipation. Only Kenji stayed.

"Don't give the bastard an inch. The girl's right. They bleed and die just like us. Dressing shit in gold doesn't make it any different from other shit. Just looks better." The old man grabbed the back of Tavar's neck and pulled their foreheads together. "Kill the bastard." He kissed Tavar's forehead and marched away, sheathing his kyushira.

The Immortal wore no armour. Just a golden

hooded robe to match the scarf that wrapped around the lower part of their face. A silver band tied around their waist matching the rope they were spinning around their fist, the dagger glistening threateningly on the end.

Tavar gulped and took a breath, reminding himself that this was not an immortal being, and the whole arena would know that before the day was over. He clapped his falchions together and pushed his chest out. Kenji had always told him to show courage on the battlefield. Combat could be won in the opening seconds if you display courage and confidence. The opponent may sometimes question why they are there and then falter. He didn't think it applied much in this situation, but he was willing to try anything.

A horn sounded and the Immortal jerked a hand forward, flicking his wrist with shockingly fast speed. Tavar had to twist on instinct to dodge the flying blade as it headed towards him, unable to even raise his falchions in time to parry the attack. The metal sliced the skin on his cheekbone as he rolled back, cursing himself. He lifted the back of his hand and brushed it against his face. Pulling it away, he saw that it was covered it blood. Shit.

The Immortal whipped the rope back and was now spinning the weapon along as he strode patiently towards him, looking for more blood.

Tavar stumbled back as the dagger snapped forward. He was better prepared this time, even if his parry was still clumsy. The clang of metal was lost with the roar of the bloodthirsty crowd. He looked for some way to counterattack but it was no good. There were no openings for him when the weapon he was defending against had such a long reach and could be wielded so swiftly. It was unnatural.

"Cut the rope, Tavar!" screeched Kenji.

"Snap forward!" screamed Medda.

"Kill the bastard!" yelled Halfor.

All great advice. All so difficult for him to achieve.

Tavar dodged the next three strikes by the barest of margins. He laughed nervously at the gasps of the crowd after the last one as the blade whistled past his ear. His breathing grew heavy. There was no way he could keep this up for a long time. The Immortal just stood patiently, swinging the rope with ease and spinning his body to add to the power of the next attack.

Tavar rolled forward, cutting their distance in half. He heard the rope whip back and dodged its return to the side, urging himself to press forward whilst he was inside the enemy's defences. He jerked away from the blade once more but then felt the burn of a rope tie around his wrist and snap it to the side. With a cry of pain, he dropped the falchion in his left hand and hacked at the rope with his remaining weapon. The rope dragged him forward before he could do any damage and the Immortal's boot slammed into his gut, forcing him down to his knees.

The arena rang out with a mixture of boos and screams and whoops of delight and horror. Helpless, the rope wrapped around his neck and dragged his head up so that he was staring into the stony, dead, unflinching eyes of the Immortal who nimbly danced around behind him, tightening his grip on the rope, choking Tavar and forcing him to drop the falchion on the ground as he clutched at the rope around his neck.

He struggled hopelessly for breath and pushed his body forward attempting to alleviate some of the pressure. The Immortal could have killed him by now but this was meant to be a spectacle; a performance for the crowd and a warning to the warriors hoping for freedom. There was only one ruler in all of Alfara and he wanted everyone to know one thing. There is a place for everyone, and that place would not be decided by individuals. The Godking Uhlad would decide.

The Immortal kicked the falchions further away in the sand and landed a punch on the back of Tavar's head. He felt his energy drain as his eyes lost focus and the arena swam in front of him. He'd been a fool. There was no chance of escaping this shithole. Uhlad and the Judges would always make certain of that. His eyes drifted shut lazily. He forced them open but didn't know why. There was no escape. No chance of overcoming this challenge. He was alone in this fight and he had come up short.

The rope tightened and his head rolled back. Tavar heard an indecipherable call behind him and saw the Immortal's head snap to the side. Sounded like Halfor and Medda.

"Tavar! Tavar! This way, kid!" From the other side, he could recognise a voice, Kenji. He struggled against the rope and twisted his head so that he could see the old man. His friend motioned to the kyushira in his hand and flung it towards Tavar with all his might. With the last sparks of his strength, Tavar caught the hilt of the blade and roared, twisting his body just as the Immortal turned back to face him. And welcome the kyushira under his chin.

Tavar thrust the weapon straight up as far as he could. The end of the blade carved through skin and bone, popping out of the Immortal's dead eye. He felt the rope loosen around his neck and fell forward before his enemy, coughing and wheezing as he pulled at the rope.

A hushed, shocked silence fell over the arena as everyone inhaled at once before releasing the greatest sound Tavar had heard in his whole life. Flags waved, horns blew and people flung themselves together in tight embraces of joy and surprise. An Immortal had been defeated.

Tavar rubbed his sore neck and coughed as a hand helped him cautiously to his feet.

"I did tell you that I wasn't going to let you die," Kenji chuckled.

"That's a good fucking blade," Tavar said with a weak smile, turning the kyushira over in his hand and ignoring the bloody mess of his opponent lying motionless next to him.

"I'll make you a better one."

"You're alive!" Halfor roared, clapping his hands together as he jogged over to them, followed by a beaming Medda. "I knew it. I knew you would win!"

"That's not what you said to me…" Medda laughed.

The smile on Halfor's face dropped as he scratched his head and nudged his friend. "That was me jesting. I always knew he would do it. An Immortal! What I would give to face one…"

"I would be dead if wasn't for the three of you," Tavar croaked. It felt like a thousand daggers had embedded themselves in his throat when spoke.

"We'll chalk it up as you owe us. Call it a life debt," Medda winked at him.

The eruption of the crowd faded away and Tavar turned to face Uhlad who stood with an arm raised and a face like thunder. A storm was coming and he knew it was heading his way.

"A great fight. It takes cunning, skill and bravery to defeat an Immortal in one-on-one combat," Uhlad said to the anxious crowd. "But, it wasn't one on one, was it? You were ready to die and if it was not for the blind man's assist, you would be dead in the middle of the arena. For that, I cannot let you just walk away to your freedom."

Violent shouts and curses flew in the king's direction and Tavar spotted a scuffle break out as guards rushed towards the commotion. The crowd had their champion and they weren't ready for Uhlad to go back on his word. Judging by his scowl, the king knew that he was walking a dangerous tightrope with them.

"So I suggest a token of your regret at how you won your victory, Tavar Farwan. You have ended many lives in the years you have fought in the arena. I ask you, to end one more. A prisoner to be sacrificed for my honour, on this most glorious of days in *my* kingdom." Uhlad clicked his fingers and Grey disappeared down the steps leading into the arena. Cautious whispers ran around the arena as they all waited for clarification of Uhlad's words.

"This can't be good," Kenji said.

Tavar handed him back his kyushira and picked up his fallen falchions. "I know. I have a bad feeling about this…"

Grey marched out with a devilish grin on his face, dragging behind him a prisoner with wrists tied together and a black bag covering his head. The skeleton-thin prisoner stumbled along in the sand, the brown skin visible covered in bruises, burns and scars. Their thin clothes were ripped and ragged and as they drew closer to

Tavar, the stench of piss greeting those around him.

"This scum betrayed Alfara and the city of Kessarine that had done so much for him. Kill him, and you may leave this city and go wherever you wish," Uhlad called out to gasps from the crowd. Grey pushed the prisoner to his knees and walked to the side, still holding the rope attached to the wrists.

Tavar had dreamt of leaving the arena a free man for so long, but the defenceless prisoner dropped at his feet left a bitter taste in his mouth. Killing warriors fighting for their survival and clashing in combat was one thing, executing a defenceless prisoner who couldn't even see the blade coming was quite another.

He looked around at his friends, at the waiting crowd and at last, on Carver. She shook her head ever so slightly. Uhlad beside her didn't notice.

Tavar sighed and cursed himself, throwing the falchions down beside the prisoner. "I can't do it. I'm not going to kill a random prisoner tied up at my feet."

"Your freedom…" Kenji reminded him unnecessarily. "It means *everything*…"

"Yeah," Tavar agreed. "But it's not worth this. I can't do it."

"He must die, if you are to walk free from this arena!" Uhlad called, feigning sorrow to the watching crowd. "Such a pity…"

Kenji stepped between the prisoner and Tavar and held the kyushira up, pulling Tavar's hand against it. "I can't let you waste this opportunity."

Before Tavar could do more than frown, the blind man snapped the blade back, dragging Tavar forward and slicing the point of the blade straight through the prisoner's neck.

Tavar screamed in horror as he watched the body fall, pushing past Kenji.

"I'm sorry, kid. I couldn't have you just stay in here with a fossil like me. You have to live your life, no matter what."

Tavar dropped to his knees, his body heating up as Grey stepped over the bleeding, unmoving body.

"There's always a price, Farwan," Grey muttered to him as his fingers gripped the edge of the hood and pulled it away, revealing a face familiar to Tavar.

There was swelling around both eyes and the jaw looked broken but he knew that face. Hot tears streamed down his cheeks as his body shook with despair. He pressed his head against the body of his kill, muffling his scream as he ignored the open wound on his neck where blood continued to pour from.

"Vandir... my brother."

"Brother..." Kenji repeated, voice shaking with shock. "Tavar..."

Tavar kissed his brother's cheeks and pushed the dark hair out of his icy eyes. His chest felt as though it was ripping apart, threatening to pull two sides of him away from each other like an earthquake as his heart doubled in speed. He whipped his head around and stared at Kenji, his best friend of the last six years, a man he would have died for. All that was obscured by hate and rage.

"You killed him," Tavar said, his voice low and venomous. "You killed the last member of my family that I had. I dropped my swords Kenji! Then you killed him!" he roared, screaming into the open air.

"I'm so sorry, my friend," Kenji said, falling to his knees and ripping a patch of his shirt in frustration. "I failed you." The blind warrior took his sword in both hands and plunged it straight into his stomach and twisted. He fell as blood seeped from his mouth and stained his snow-white beard.

Tavar's screams were covered by the sound of horns blaring out from each side of the stadium.

Then the fighting began.

CHAPTER TWENTY-SIX: ESCAPING THE STORM

Chaos reigned in the stands as steel shone in the sunlight. Civilians drew weapons and clashed with guards as King Uhlad hastily made his exit surrounded by his men and three Immortals. As the crowd pushed for the exits, several of them fell over the small barriers into the stadium with screams as no one knew what to do.

Tavar stayed on his knees, shielding his brother's body and refusing to look over at what he knew was Kenji's corpse. He had lost two of the closest people he had in one moment once again. He was cursed. There was no other explanation.

"This is for Uhlad. Now you can join your waste of a brother," Grey said, drawing his own great sword and raising it high. Tavar bent his neck, offering it to the commander. He just wanted it over.

An almighty crunch caused Tavar to lift his head and witness a furious Halfor standing over the twitching body of Grey. The Naviqing warrior lifted his warhammer and slammed it back down, cracking the commander's skull like an egg and spraying blood in all directions.

"People you love are dead!" he roared, grabbing Tavar's collar and lifting him with one hand to his feet. "Tough shit. I'm not losing you as well as the old man. Pick those fucking weapons up and cut your way out of this madness. We're leaving and I ain't taking no for an answer!"

Madness had truly gripped the arena tightly and refused to let go. Guards fought with civilians and prisoners as people of all kinds ran away in all directions. Steel met steel and blood stained both the sands and the stone as screams of fear and anger mixed for an unholy song. Dark clouds loomed overhead, blocking the light of the day from the cursed city as Tavar picked up his bloodied falchions and took one last look at Vandir and Kenji, silently apologising to them for what he had done and begging them for forgiveness.

"Block it out, Tavar. Now isn't the time," Medda warned, reading his mind and heading for the exit. The guards were too distracted with staying alive and controlling the crowds to care about prisoners heading back towards the cells. They reached the shadows of the familiar corridors with ease but it looked different to when they had last walked through it.

Blood stained the walls and floors. The bodies of guards and prisoners alike lay at awkward angles on the ground. One guard had his head twisted all the way around so that it was facing backwards. A battle had been fought here and it had not been one for the light-hearted. Tavar spotted a prisoner still breathing faintly, though his eyes were closed and the hole in his gut said that he wasn't making it out of the corridor.

"What in the five hells happened here?" Halfor said in awe.

A huge, blood-soaked warrior stepped out at the end of the corridor at the sound of Halfor's booming voice, axe in hand. Zaif.

"New Meat!" Zaif spread his arms wide and

cackled. He marched towards them; weapon lowered. Without looking, he snapped the axe into the dying prisoner's throat and continued his stride. "We've had a bit of fun down here. Good of you to join us!"

Tavar dropped into his fighting stance, holding one of his blades horizontally in warning to the big man. A shocked and hurt look passed the big warrior's face as he froze and stared at the weapon.

"What are you doing?"

"You've promised to kill me every week for the past six years," Tavar reminded him. "What do you think I'm doing?"

"Yeah. I promised to kill you when we were prisoners fighting to get out of this shit pit. Now we're on the same side. Let's get the fuck outta here!"

"You first," Medda said, jabbing her spear in the direction of the end of the corridor.

Zaif shrugged and did as she said, bounding away.

Shouts and screams echoed down the bloodied corridors but the wherever they ran, the fighting was over. Every gate was open and clear for them and eventually, they reached the steps leading out of the arena. They had to climb over the pile of corpses to make it to the top of the steps, just as rain began to descend from the heavens. Tavar faced up and let the water fall upon his face, cleansing him.

He shook his wet hair and opened his eyes to be greeted with an older, fuller but no less welcome face.

"Long time, no see." Hashem ran a hand through his curly hair and laughed awkwardly, unable to meet Tavar's gaze. The stable boy had grown since their last meeting, both upwards and outwards. His emerald-green robes looked fit to burst and they were covered in patches of sweat. Tavar almost bowled him over with a hug, allowing himself a moment to fall against his old friend.

"Good to see I've been missed!" Hashem said. "But you have to leave, now."

"Where do we go?" Tavar asked, pulling away from Hashem to see a group of horses tied to a nearby gate, including a familiar palomino.

"Eastern gate. The path may not be completely clear but there are guards sympathetic to getting you out of here," Hashem informed them. "Now go!"

Tavar quickly kissed his forward and smiled at the look of amazement on his allies' faces as they ran for the horses. He buried his face into the palomino and laughed as the horse lowered its head, ears facing forward as she whinnied. "I've missed you too, girl."

He jumped on the saddle and urged her away from Hashem, waving at his friend and smiling through tears before racing away to the east of the city beside his three allies. The look of Halfor and Zaif on the beasts brought a tired laugh from his stomach. The horses didn't seem too much happier at having to carry such large bastards. Medda was more at ease. She made a clicking noise with the side of her mouth and her horse rushed forward, leading them all.

The chaos of the arena spread throughout Kessarine, infecting the city as soldiers struggled to work out who was friend and who was foe. Fires erupted and violent clashes broke out wherever they rode but they kept on, ignoring it all. The eastern gate was the least used of the four gates of Kessarine.

The gate loomed over them angrily, daring them

to leave the city. The drawbridge had been lowered and a few corpses lay next to a single guard, sword in hand and covered in blood.

"Took your time. Lilian said you would get here earlier," the guard said, taking off his helmet to show a handsome warrior with short hair and a neatly trimmed beard. His dark, knowing eyes sparkled at Tavar with sadness and joy both at once.

"Marek…" Tavar said, jumping from his horse and embracing the soldier.

"You won't have long before the army collects itself and stomps this small rebellion out. There are only a few people who were willing to aid in this madness. Mainly those who fought with you in Hartovan. A few villagers from New Hartovan have put their lives on the line for you too. Don't go wasting their sacrifice."

"Thank you, Marek." Tavar didn't know what else to say. The day had drained him of words and rendered him almost speechless.

Marek looked around at the other three and frowned. "Where is Vandir?"

Tavar opened his mouth but the words wouldn't come. His body shook with the effort. He wanted to explain. It was an accident. Vandir shouldn't be…

"It's okay," Marek said, placing gloved hands on Tavar's shoulders and squeezed. "You don't need to say anything. Just go. And don't come back. This won't happen again. Next time, they'll make sure you are dead. Lilian is waiting at the next farm along. Abandoned stables. It's a long ride and you'll want to make it by nightfall. She'll be burning a blue flame. You can't miss it."

Tavar returned to his horse and beat his fist to his

chest three times in farewell.

"Say hi to the others for me. I've missed them," Marek said, voice breaking as he struggled to control his emotion.

Tavar nodded and rode off into the storm.

There wasn't much Tavar had missed more than the wind whipping past his face as he urged a horse on through the open lands. But, the cold wind, lashing rain and threat of being captured definitely soured the moment somewhat. He kept his thoughts away from the arena and what had happened and decided to focus on the moment: he had friends riding by his side; he had friends who had helped him escape Kessarine; he had friends waiting for him, ready to embrace freedom for the first time since his parents' deaths. He pushed the stab of guilt from his chest as his mind tried to turn to Kenji and Vandir. Now wasn't the time for that. He had to reach freedom before he could deal with the loss. He had others counting on him, people who had put their own lives on the line. He wouldn't let them down.

Only when night fell over the lands did the four of them risk slowing down and easing the strain on their mounts. The land grew greener as the light faded. Tavar worried that they wouldn't find the abandoned stables but then, in the distance, a blue light caught his eye.

"There!" he shouted over the storm to the others, pointing at the small light and urging his horse on. "Last leg of the journey; then you can rest, I promise," he whispered to his old horse.

On the approach, Tavar could see a huge farmhouse behind the worn and beaten stable. The land around looked good and fertile but not cared for as well as it should have been. The stable itself looked to be falling apart with wooden panels broken and bent. The farmhouse looked little better.

"Place looks like it's seen better days," Halfor said from under his soaked hood, leaping from his horse and grabbing the reins to pull the horse closer to the stable.

"We've lived for years in a dungeon," Medda reasoned, copying the Naviqing. "This stable looks like a palace in comparison."

Zaif spat from his horse and looked up at the carved, wooden falcon sitting on top of the wooden beam at the top of the stable. "Can't stay long. Half a day's ride from Kessarine. They'll be searching places like this by dawn."

"We need food and rest. Wouldn't hurt if we waited out the storm," Tavar argued. "But I agree. We can't stay long. Best to get as far away as we can."

"Any chance you know where that may be?" Medda asked, looking to Tavar for answers. He didn't have any. Sleep first. Answers after.

"My friend should be able to help. Let's hope she's here." He jumped from Pan and walked over to the stable. He knocked three times on the stable door with his fist and waited. The door creaked open and Lilian's warm smile greeted him before she looked nervously over his shoulder at the others.

"It's a long story," Tavar mumbled, just loud enough for her to hear.

Lilian's smile dropped as she looked at the pain on Tavar's face and then back at his three allies, making note of who was missing. "Come in. There's a bit of food and enough hay to get comfortable. We have much to discuss."

Tavar led his allies into the stable as Lilian moved past them with a bag of sand. He turned to see her throw the sand of the blue flame before closing the door behind them. A single, small lantern sat in the centre of the stable on a stone floor. Hay lined the walls and the horses eagerly strolled over to a space at the far end of the stable to munch on whatever they could. Tavar spotted a bag of fruit and vegetables hanging from a rusty nail punched into one of the wooden beams. He pulled out a few carrots and apples and threw them towards the horses who greedily ate the treats before lying down to rest from the hard ride.

Halfor jumped into a pile of hay after laying his warhammer down against the stone. The back of his head lay against his saucepan like hands and his eyes followed Medda as she circled the room, looking out for anything untoward. Satisfied, she took a seat next to him with a stony expression in contrast to the warm smile that appeared on his face.

Zaif stretched the muscles in his back and arms and unbuckled his waist strap, carefully placing it down with his axe before sitting on his own pile of hay.

Tavar hung his own waist strap and falchions up on another nail and gently fell into the hay next to him. He closed his eyes and breathed, trying to calm himself. It had been a long day. A long, horrible fucking day.

Lilian bolted the door and shook her wet hair before sitting down the rest of them. Her eyes were only for Tavar, though. They pierced him more than any weapon had that day as he knew exactly what she must be thinking. He'd lost once again. He may have survived and escaped the city, but this was no victory. Only a fool would say otherwise.

"I'd call that a victory!" Zaif said, eyeing the bag of fruit and smacking his lips together. "Finally got the hell outta that cursed dungeon. Always thought I'd do it by killing the lot of ya but this ain't too bad. A man alone is cursed to darkness and allies together will build a light greater than the sun. Can't remember who said that. Some fucking idiot from the past most likely. Definitely wouldn't have made it here without the three of ya, so…" Zaif grabbed an apple and looked in turn to each of them. His face still bore the dried blood that had splattered onto him from in the dungeons. "Just wanted to say thanks." His crooked teeth tore into the apple and he relaxed back into the hay with a smile on his misshapen face,

"What happened?" Lilian asked, eyes still boring into Tavar. "Where is your brother?"

He sat staring at the lantern for a while, absorbed in the dance of the flame whilst the others let him have the moment of silence and contemplation. He appreciated it. More than he could put into words there and then. They knew he was in pain, even Zaif who barely knew him.

"Uhlad. It was some sick display of power of his. One final play," Tavar spat as the scenes played in his head. He closed his eyes and it was like he was back there again, in the arena. The smell of blood and sweat filled his nostrils and wretched, struggling against the rising vomit in his throat. "He sent out an Immortal. I killed him, with help," Tavar said, glancing at Halfor and Medda who had shuffled closer towards each other as they listened. "Uhlad couldn't have that, not in front of his people. He wanted me to kill an unarmed prisoner. A token gesture he called it. I wouldn't do it but Kenji couldn't bear to see me stay in that stinking place. He pressed my hand to the hilt of the blade and drove it into the prisoner's throat. It was Vandir," Tavar croaked. He pressed a fist into his mouth and bit his knuckles as a wave of nausea and grief threatened to overpower him. "I killed Vandir. My own brother."

"Tavar…" Lilian moved next to him and pulled him close as he fought back the ears. He pushed her away with a shake of the head and held out his arm, keeping her out of reach. He was sick of grieving for those he cared about. Sick of feeling so shit all the time.

"Alfara has been a curse on me and my family. I want out. I'm not waiting for dawn. I'm heading to the Emerald Coast to find my friends. You can join me if you want but I wouldn't recommend it. Everyone close to me ends up dead," Tavar said bitterly.

"We all end up dead at some point. Better to do it next to a friend than alone. I'll follow you. Then perhaps you can join me for some time in my homeland. One feast with my people will have a smile on your face. We can drink for those we've lost. For your brother. And for Kenji…" Halfor said, smiling at Tavar before placing a soft kiss on Medda's head. She leant towards him, accepting his unusual open display of affection.

"I'm with you. We've made it this far. This isn't where our journey ends. That's what the old man would say and he seemed to see more than the rest of us; blind or not," Medda chuckled sadly.

"This is where we'll part ways then!" Zaif said with a sigh.

"Weren't you just saying how it's important to not be alone?" Medda frowned, confused.

"Maybe," Zaif grinned and scratched his dark shaved head. "But I got business in the opposite direction to the old Emerald Coast. Some debts need to be paid on the Arrow Islands and I've been patient enough stuck in that dungeon. Time to go back home and see how much the world have changed in the years I've been away. I expect eating, sleeping, killing, and fucking are all still high priorities on folk's list? Time to find out!"

"Then you won't be alone," Lilian said, grinning. "My son is on the Arrow Islands with a dear friend. I will travel with you."

"Always good to have the company of a beautiful woman," Zaif said with a nod whilst displaying his yellowing teeth, or what was left of them anyway.

"Even think about touching me and I'll chop it off…" Lilian slid her dress high up to her thigh to display a sharp dagger tied tightly to a long leg. If her aim was to discourage Zaif then she was doing it all wrong.

The escaped convict licked his lips but kept his mouth closed for once. "If you want the Emerald Coast. You need to keep heading east. This farm is the only thing for miles in that direction. Old Omari hasn't kept it in good condition so the surrounding areas aren't too populated. There's a small village just before you get to the coast but they'll be sympathetic to those with grudges against Kessarine. The people out there are forgotten and prefer their own company away from the *city folk*. Keep your heads down and you'll be fine. I've passed on a message as best as I could to Alice and the others. With any luck, she'll be waiting for you."

"Thank you, Lilian. For all of this," Tavar said, knowing how paltry mere words seemed after all she had risked. "You've done so much for me. I wish I could thank you properly."

She blushed and averted her eyes from him

before speaking. "I don't deserve your thanks. Just get the hell away from Alfara and never come back." She shuffled towards him and took his face in two gentle hands, ensuring that he was looking into her dark, brown eyes. "Trust me. This kingdom will only bring you misery."

CHAPTER TWENTY-SEVEN: YOU CAN RUN

They said their goodbyes with a midnight sky above and a storm fading around them. There were no tears. They had shed too many for that. Promises had been shared to meet again away from Alfara and Lilian planted a kiss on Tavar's head when he mentioned seeing her son on the Arrow Islands. Zaif clasped forearms with them all and even called Tavar by his actual name for the first time.

They were still exhausted and hungry but resting wasn't an option. The three of them saddled the horses and rode east to a new adventure and the hope of a better life. The heavy burden of grief and guilt lay on Tavar's shoulders as he rode through the storm but he promised himself that he would not let it drag him to the ground and bury him. Vandir and Kenji had done so much to keep him alive. Adam too. He had to live on, as much as it pained him, for them.

Four days heavy riding with only short rests for the horses and chances to piss and replenish their energy with the increasing amounts of fruit and vegetables growing around the land. To the south, they could see the Undying Sands, an unforgiving and hostile land that Tavar had tried to forget. To the east and the north – away from Alfara – lush fields and rows of trees and plants covered the hills and valleys around them. On one of the clearer days, Tavar swore to Medda that he could see a row of mountains in the distance to the north. It had been so long since he had seen such marvels that it caught his breath as he took a moment to burn the image into his mind.

"If it's mountains you want," Halfor said, laughing at Tavar's incredulous look to the north, "then you must visit my homeland. Naviqand is full of the cold bastards. When a child is ten years, they take on the mountain with a trusted elder of their family. They come back down the mountain with great pride and a better understanding of who they are. We should do that together."

Tavar loved the thought of climbing the mountain. Tackling such a force of nature appealed to him in a way not many other things had since his life had been consumed with the idea of escape. "We should go together. You're the closest I have to family now." He continued to stare off into the distance but didn't miss the warm smile his two friends shared with one another out of the corner of his eye.

At last, as the horses slowed down, eager for their next break, a small village stood on the horizon. They passed through fields full of crops and lazy animals, riding at a slow pace and smiling at the few farmers and villagers who stared out at them with suspicious eyes. Most of the glares were aimed at Halfor. Tavar had spent so much time with the pale Naviqing that it shocked him to see how amazed and wary the people were of seeing such a large, pale-skinned warrior riding through their homeland. A couple of small children stared, mouths wide open as Halfor greeted them before an older woman cursed and grabbed the children, pulling them away into a small wooden house with a slanted roof.

An old man with weathered brown skin whistled loud and clear as he jumped from his wagon. A smell of fish wafted towards Tavar as the man drew closer and he looked beyond the wagon to see the sparkling water of a river running in the distance, heading out towards the sea. They were close to the coast.

"Greetings, outsiders!" The old man called, licking his lips and staring at them with narrowed eyes. He scratched at the patch of white hair sticking out around his lips and planed his feet on the ground in front of the three of them, stopping them from progressing further into the village. "May I ask what your business is? Not used to outsiders here, you see. Folk get creeped out easy and when they do, they come to me with their complaints. I get 'nough of that from the wife, it's why I enjoy sitting out on the water, surrounded by the fish."

"We're merely passing through," Tavar said to the elder man whose eyes didn't leave Halfor. "A bed for the night and some warm food and ale would put us in your debt. We'll be gone by dawn. Heading to the coast and a ship."

"Hmm… I suppose we can sort something out for weary travellers," the man said. "Name's Omar. I'm kind of in charge of the village. Don't mean much, but I do what I can to keep these folk happy and safe. Good people they are."

"My name is Tavar. This is Halfor and Medda."

"Friends or foes to King Uhlad?"

"Do we have to be one or the other?"

"To stay in my village, I like things to be clearer than the shimmering seas. Friend or foe."

Tavar glanced at his two allies. Halfor shrugged.

Medda frowned and pushed her chest out. "If Uhlad was here right now, I'd cut him down where he stood and spit on his corpse."

Omar's lips twitched in amusement at her words. "That's clear enough to me. Welcome to the village of Tuhail."

The first gulp of ale after cleansing in warm water felt like heaven. Tavar nearly drowned with his first drink. The second nearly choked him. He slowed down for the third. Instead, he amused himself by watching the stares of the locals as they all congregated around Halfor, poking his unusual skin and asking how he kept it so light.

"It's not usually this pink," the Naviqing insisted. "But it's hot in this part of the world and I get caught unprepared. The sun is one foe I have yet to defeat. In fact, it is an endless enemy that will outlast all of us, I feel. Burning us pale skinned people until we head back to the mountains in the north where we belong!"

The villagers laughed and prodded each other, pointing at the warrior and enjoying his accent and unusual ways.

"He's settled in well, hasn't he?" Medda said, watching him with a warmth in her eyes.

"People gravitate towards him. At least away from the battlefield. Strange how such a powerful fighter can be such a softie at heart," Tavar said shaking his head at the incredulity of it.

"That's exactly why I care for him."

"You finally admitting it?" Tavar prodded.

"I admitted it with my actions. Words are too easy at times. I like to leave them until the end."

"Think he knows that?" Tavar asked, watching

Halfor pick up a small boy and girl and sit them on each knee as he shared a story of one of the fights from the arena, edited in places for the audience of course.

"He knows."

"I hope so. You two make each other happy. That's good."

"You make us happy, too. Never forget that."

"Kenji—"

"—Loved you. He did what he did for you. Wallowing in your own sea of grief and frantically trying to keep your head above the water isn't what he would have wanted for you. Be happy. For him."

Tavar nodded. He wished the old man was here with them, but he wasn't. And there was nothing he could do to change that. It had been the same after Adam had died. The past can't be changed. You have to move on, as hard as that may be.

"I'm really sorry to disturb you." Omar knelt next to Tavar's seat and looked around to ensure no one but the two of them could hear him. Satisfied that the rest of the room was distracted by Halfor, he continued. "There is a man outside who is causing a small amount of distress to some of the villagers. He is standing alone on the edge of the village. I've sent scouts out to look for others but it appears to be just him and his horse. Usually it wouldn't be an issue but he's given my people the creeps. Young Asho was brave enough to call out to the man and ask him what he wanted."

"What did he say?"

"He wants you."

Tavar exchanged an unnerved glance with Medda. "Has to be from Alfara. I'll go out. Don't worry,

Omar. I'll deal with this."

"I'll go too," Medda said, standing with him.

"No. Stay with Halfor. I'll be back. If this stranger wanted trouble, he'd have entered the village. I'll see what he wants." He didn't need anyone else getting hurt on his behalf.

By the time Tavar had marched out to the edge of the village, the stranger had taken a seat on a log beside newly cut firewood. Only a couple of villagers stood nearby, watching him nervously. Tavar smiled at them to ease their nerves and they inclined their heads towards him in response before backing off towards their own houses and families. He peered at the man, dressed all in black. A wide hat sat next to him and he had his black shirt pulled up, exposing rows upon rows of scars that gleamed white in the firelight. In his hand, he held a small, curved dagger. The stranger pressed the point of the blade against his ribs and slid down, drawing a line of blood to add to the collection of scars.

Tavar didn't even wince. He'd seen worse.

The stranger tilted his head up as he heard Tavar's footsteps draw closer. Dark eyes flickered towards Tavar and a white smile flashed. Dagger like teeth gleamed in the fire, sharpened to points in four places, designed for biting and to instil fear into enemies. Tavar knew this man. He had seen him before. He had seen him fight, watched as Kenji's kyushira danced with his twin daggers.

The shadow warrior.

"There's no need for that," the warrior said as his eye's watched Tavar's hand flash to the hilt of his blade. "My killing is done for this night." The shadow warrior wiped the two fresh lines of blood from his chest and pulled down his shirt. "Please, sit."

Tavar walked cautiously closer to the warrior, sitting out of reach of those deadly daggers. He could pride himself on speed but the death he had seen this warrior wreak was unnatural. He remembered Kenji's warnings with a stab of pain.

"What do you want?" he asked, eager to get this over with so they could both part ways.

"To warn you. And to pay my respects." His voice was low and careful, barely reaching Tavar but he heard every word. The hair all over his body stood up on end as the warrior spoke, like some long-forgotten instinct begging him to be careful and get as far away from this creature as possible.

"Your people are dealers of death," Tavar said bitterly. "Why would you wish to warn me of anything?"

"We are dealers of death," the warrior admitted. "I come from another continent. My brothers and sisters are raised in darkness and taught nothing but blood and war. I made my first kill at the age of seven. Every assignment I have been given, every task involving my experience has been completed to the utmost satisfaction of those who employ me. When I fight, I fight to kill, and I always win." There was a fire in his eyes as his voice grew steadily louder and more bitter.

"Good for you."

"Except for one time." The warrior relaxed and smiled to himself. "An old, blind man from Okada with a kyushira in his hand. The one fight I wasn't able to finish."

"Kenji…"

"I prayed to the Gods for another chance to cross

blades with him but then I saw him in the arena. The opportunity to finish our battle has passed me by. I am bound by my code to offer assistance to his family or seek an honourable death of my own. If I was back home, I would seek hand to hand combat with a brother or sister with more kills than me. That is not possible right now, so I need to find his family."

"What's your name?" Tavar asked, unsure whether to believe the words of the assassin.

"You wouldn't be able to pronounce it. In your tongue, I am called Tajira Amwat."

"What's with all the scars, Tajira? Kind of an unhealthy obsession."

"One scar for each kill."

"And the two new ones?" Tavar wasn't sure he wanted to know the answer.

"You were being followed by Alfaran scouts sent by Uhlad," Tajira explained calmly.

"Just two?"

"There'll be more. You need to reach a ship before they catch up."

Tavar rubbed his beard and looked around at the quaint village. It wasn't fair on these people to stay here and wait for the scouts. It wasn't necessary for them to see death. Making for the coast as soon as possible seemed like the best idea.

"Why were you in the dungeons? If you're such a good fighter, how did you end up there?"

"That was my assignment. The Court of Shadows has begun its infiltration of this continent. My assignment was from someone high up in my organisation who has a place of power in Kessarine."

"And what did they want you to do?"

"Use my skills for entertainment..." Tajira cursed and spat on the ground. "I cannot refuse a member of the court, no matter how debased their request is."

"But now you want to find Kenji's family."

"Then I will continue my mission."

"Then let's make a deal. I owe Kenji. He died for me and if we go to his family, I can break the news and pay my respects. You can travel with us if you promise your blades to us."

Tajira mulled over the words and gently nodded. "The Okadan Empire does not look too fondly on my people. Travelling with others would be beneficial to me. We have a deal." He held out a gloved hand and Tavar briefly shook it. "I will rest away from the village. The people will not want me entering. Be ready in three hours. I will sound a horn if any more scouts head this way."

Tavar agreed and turned away to return to the village.

"One more thing," Tajira called out to him from the log pile, stopping Tavar in his tracks. "Do you have a ship?"

"No. But I know someone who does." Tavar let it hang in the air and strode under a welcome sign carved against a wooden archway.

Omar was waiting for him in the shadows of the entranceway to the tavern, fingers hanging close to the axe stabbed into the mud. "Any trouble?"

"We should be fine. Plans have changed. We'll be going before midnight. Alfara has sent scouts this way. It's best if we go by then, just in case," Tavar explained.

"We can hide you if needed. Done it before,"

Omar grunted. "Not that one though," he said, pushing his forehead towards the edge of the village where Tajira had stayed.

"He'll stay out of the village until we head to the coast."

"You taking him with you?" Omar snorted, an incredulous look on his face.

"For a while. We can help each other."

"Well, just be careful. There's something about him. It's unnerving. Makes everything around him seem cold and empty." Omar shivered even though there was a roaring fire nearby.

"We may need to use that coldness. It's been a long time since I've been away from Alfara." Tavar rubbed his wrists where he had so often had rope or iron tied against the skin.

"Just make sure it doesn't start to use you. The world is a big place. Danger lies behind every shrub and in every shadow. Watch yourself."

"Thanks," Tavar said, holding out his hand in appreciation for the warning. "Thanks for everything. I wish we could have stayed longer."

The village elder shook his hand with a sad smile. "Perhaps another time. The kids love the big man. Gives us a rest from running around after them so I'm sure you'd have friends if you ever came back this way. I'll get some packs ready for you to take on your travels. Some fruit and meat we can spare and some new waterskins for the three of you." He paused, looking out at the darkness of the early night. "Four. I'll get four packs ready," he said, changing his mind.

They rode at an easy pace. Medda led them, knowing the way to the sleepy, coastal town of Fisher's Landing. Halfor and Tavar rode beside each other, keeping their eyes on Tajira as he kept pace just behind Medda. The two warriors had taken the news of Tajira joining them better than he had expected yet they still harboured an air of caution, as they should.

No more scouts had been seen since Tajira had disposed of the earlier two. More would come; Tavar was certain of that, but once they had managed to reach water, tracking them would be much more difficult.

Light from the crescent moon gleamed through a thin layer of cloud and shone down upon a motley rabble of small stone buildings. Tavar had read of Fisher's Landing in his lessons growing up in Alfara. The quaint coastal town had the dubious honour of being chosen by the fleeing dwarves as their escape route following The Banishment. Alfaran nobles in the recruit pool had loved to joke about how the sea around the town had risen as the dwarves fled Kessarine, their tears changing the world as they cried their way from the continent. Tavar had always found the tale to be dumb and ignorant but he had kept his mouth shut, knowing what would happen if he annoyed one of the others.

They slowed their horses down as they reached the town. A few curious glances came their way but nothing more than expected. Being a coastal town, Tavar thought they must have had their fair share of unusual travellers. Unconscious men lay slumped against stone buildings that lined a muddy path through the centre of the town. They stank of stale alcohol. Must be a tavern nearby. The low buildings allowed Tavar to look past the town to see a collection of wooden ships bobbing beside the harbour. His heart leapt as he spotted the largest of the collection, a wooden galleon: black sails with a red arrow sitting in a white circle printed on the flag waving on the mast. The ship Lilian had told them to look out for. Alice. She was here.

"That's the one," he said in awe, thoughts running through his head as he wondered where she would be.

"Tavern," Halfor said as he watched the change in Tavar's demeanour. "They're pirates. Where else would they be?"

A cool sea breeze breathed against them as Tavar took over in front of Medda, eyes darting in all directions for any sign of the tavern.

"Follow the path of drunken men. Always works. Also lanterns. Taverns don't sleep, unlike the rest of the town," Medda suggested with a shrug.

Tavar followed the advice and grinned as they passed a couple more of the sleeping drunks and saw on man lean against a wall as he stumbled towards them, clearly inebriated.

"Where's the nearest tavern?" Tavar called to him.

"Why in the—" the man paused to burp and excused himself. "—shitting hells would I tell you that. It's my lovely tavern. All mine. To meself. You stay away or there'll be trouble." He put his fists up and fell back onto his arse. A look of puzzled resignation crossed his face as he accepted his new position on the floor.

Halfor jumped from his saddle and stood over the man, a look of violence etched on his warrior features. The man quaked beneath him. "Tell me now. And I'll let you live."

"A Naviqing," the drunk muttered. "Hundred paces that way. Turn left at the end. The Golden Serpent." The man pointed a quivering finger down the path and Halfor ruffled his hair, smiling before turning away.

"Thanks for the help," the Naviqing said as he followed the three others down the path, laughing as the man shuffled onto his side, unwilling to move from his new spot.

The Golden Serpent was a small wooden building erected in the middle of the town. Two lanterns hung outside the swinging saloon doors and a small, wild haired old man pushed a hand against the front of the tavern and continued pissing against the wood with no shame. He looked up at the sight of the four travellers and grinned, showing his gums before staring back down the puddle of piss and the steam rising from it.

Stepping over the mess, Tavar entered the gloomy tavern. A few torches sat in sconces on the decaying walls. A couple of paintings of large fish and proud looking fishermen had been hung up around the room but there wasn't much else. Behind a wide bar, a man stood wiping glasses with a dirty rag. He didn't seem to care about the cleanliness. Just seemed like something for him to do. A few patrons sat huddled in the shadows, hoods obscuring their faces. A lone drunk sat on a table next to the wall, his dark hair fell in waves to his shoulders and his beard reached the disgustingly sticky table as he swayed in his seat. Tavar looked at the man's hazy eyes and screamed with joy.

"Marcus!" He ran to the weary soldier and nearly knocked him from his seat as he embraced him. It took a moment for the confused warrior to focus his eyes on Tavar. His fingers slowly gripped Tavar's shoulders as he recognised him

"Tavar Farwan," his voice was low and full of surprise. It also nearly knocked Tavar out with a heavy air of alcohol. His face had aged, wrinkles lined his once sparkling eyes and his beard was a ragged mess full of crumbs and other things Tavar was uncertain of. "You made it out. Just like she said…" Marcus leapt from his seat with a roar and clapped his hands together before running them through his dark, lank hair. "Drinks, more drinks!"

Tavar grabbed Marcus again, calming him down as Halfor and Medda watched from behind him, cautiously keeping an eye on the drunk soldier. Tajira slunk off into the shadows, eyes scanning the room for trouble.

"Marcus, where is Alice? We need her ship. We need to go as soon as possible. Alfaran scouts will soon be here. Where is she?"

His whole body tensed as the steel of a dagger pressed against his throat.

"You told us to go. To run away. Adam had just died and you told us to leave him. But you stayed…"

Tavar turned his eyes to see a woman dressed in black leather trousers and a white shirt with a gold trim. She had a black, wide-brimmed hat hiding most of her golden hair that was tied up behind her in a bunch. A collection of daggers hung from a belt across her thin waist and she wore her bow around her as it hung loosely at her back. Her eyes were just as he had remembered: as blue as the ocean and as fiery as an erupting volcano. Beneath her left eye was a hooked scar that she hadn't had the last time he had seen her. Nor the golden ring glimmering in her right ear. Her right hand was gloved and balled into a fist. He looked at her left and his shoulders slumped. From her left elbow there was only steel. It ran all the way to where her hand should have been, ending in a dagger that was still pressed against his throat.

"Alice... what happened?"

"Lost an arm," she shrugged as though it was the most normal thing in the world. "Others have lost more. Could say I am one of the lucky ones."

Tavar braved a look behind him and saw Halfor and Medda with their palms raised as three pirates held thing, deadly swords towards them, faces covered with a thin black cloth. Only Tajira had managed to draw his weapon in time. He held his own curved dagger to the neck of the remaining pirate who had dropped his own weapon in surrender. Marcus just watched the whole thing with a grin on his drunk face, cheeks redder than a summer's evening sky.

"Made some interesting friends," Alice said, scanning the others.

"I could say the same to you."

"We have a lot to discuss."

"We do."

Alice lowered her unusual weapon and the shadow of a smile lit up her face. "I've missed you, Tav." She grabbed his shirt and pulled him close. Tavar fell into her hug and relaxed, wrapping his arms around her.

"I've missed you too. And I'm so sorry."

She pushed him away and nodded to her followers. They lowered their weapons though Halfor and Medda kept their icy glares upon them, not willing to trust the newcomers yet. "They'll be time for tears and talk. Let's take to the seas; you need to get your sea legs."

"Sea legs?"

"Don't worry," Alice threw a wicked smirk at him and looked at the blade on her arm. "Sea legs are nothing like a dagger arm. Less literal." She clicked a finger and thumb and the pirates marched from the tavern, all except the one Tajira held, still unwilling to release him.

"It's fine, Tajira," Tavar argued.

The shadow warrior reluctantly released the pirate who took his hat off and pulled down his face covering with a sigh. "Thanks, Tavar. I should be used to you saving my life by now." He flashed a blindingly bright set of teeth and clasped his hand around Tavar's forearm.

"You can return the favour now, Qassim," Tavar chuckled at the sight of his old foe.

"I'll see what I can do."

CHAPTER TWENTY-EIGHT: HERE THERE BE MONSTERS

"He's like that most of the time, if I'm honest," Alice said, stepping over Marcus's slumped and snoring body. An empty bottle rolled next to him as the ship rode another wave, making its way further from the coastal town and to true freedom. "Too used to the life of a soldier: the routine; the rules. You need to be adaptable out here. That's how you survive."

Tavar just nodded as he kept a hand on the side of the ship, swaying with the waves and praying that his sickness had abated. Alice said it was normal but the other seafarers continued to laugh whenever they passed him on the deck. Medda had struggled too, at first. Now she stayed beneath deck in a room she shared with Halfor, though the Naviqing spent much of his time above deck, watching the waves with a huge grin on his increasingly bearded face. "This is real freedom!" he had said to Tavar when they had finally reached open water, a cool wind slapping against his skin as he breathed in heavily. "Reminds me of home. Heading out on the deep blue to test yourself against nature itself. There's not much better." It was good to see the warrior enjoying himself. Not everyone else was as fortunate.

"I tried to stop Vandir when he left." Alice said as Tavar slid down to sit on a wooden crate of food. She had unscrewed the dagger from her interesting arm and in its place was what looked like a metal hand, though none of the fingers would ever move. "The plan was to always go back and get you. We wanted to recruit soldiers and mercenaries and get you out of there. But the people of Hartovan didn't want any more deaths; understandable really. A few offered to help but it wasn't enough for what we had planned. Albion was busy with the skirmishes breaking out in Solerra and Dolmund. So that whole region was off limits for us for the first few years. Had to find food and coin somewhere so we ended up working with mercenaries on the coast. Vandir got restless and moaned that we were forgetting about you. We were just surviving. Nothing more."

"I don't blame you," Tavar said. "I would have done the same."

"He had had enough. Stormed off and paid for passage from a small town on the edge of Okada and that was the last I saw of him. The final words we had were heated. I wish I could change that now. But I can't…"

"He knew how much you cared about him."

"Yeah, I know. Still, wish I could change it. Wish I could change a lot of things." She frowned at her metal hand, turning it over and watching the way the sunlight danced against the silver.

"We all do. He'd be happy we're together again. Adam too. Bet they're having a right laugh at the two of us, wherever they are!"

"Yeah! Just the two of them, they used to always be running off when we were younger and fighting with each other. Got nothing to stop them now."

Tavar relaxed with the rhythm of the sea as he fell back onto those warm memories on the road, letting them wrap around him life a blanket, comforting him. "What happened with Cassie?" he eventually asked. He'd been careful not to push the issue. Alice hadn't been too keen on spilling the details when he had brought up her name before. Her face hardened once more but she breathed slowly and took a seat next to him, watching her people busying themselves over her ship.

"I took a job that she didn't want me to take. We were offered a huge reward by some warlord in the west who claimed he had travelled to the three continents and amassed a great fortune. He asked us to sail to a small island in the southwest. The ruins had diamonds the size of your head." Alice held her hands out wide, both metal and flesh, to accentuate her point. "Thought we were in for a huge payday. Unfortunately, the ruins also had a tribe who were not friendly to people stealing their possessions. Lost half my crew and a hand. Lucky to escape with what I did, looking back. Cassie patched me up and staunched the blood flow. She saved my life. I don't remember much after that. She kissed me and left a note in my breast pocket explaining that she had had enough. The shadow of death loomed over us constantly and she couldn't handle it. She fled to the islands and last I heard, she was a nurse, helping those who needed it. I'm happy for her. She's safe."

"Do you miss her?"

"More than I miss my fucking hand," Alice laughed, looking at the metal limb. "I keep meaning to head over there and see her, but I always find a reason not to. You don't become a pirate queen without working your ass off. Always busy."

"Be good to see her though," Tavar let the suggestion hang in the air. "I'm sure we can do some jobs on the way."

"Let's find your friend's family first. One step at a time," Alice said, though Tavar knew that the seed had been planted. He could see the fire growing in her blue eyes, the yearning to see her love again.

Carver's face flashed into his own head, unwanted and painful. Even after all she had done and the years that had passed, he still remembered their time in the tent in Hartovan, the night before the battle. He remembered the look she had given him in the arena. She knew what Uhlad was doing and she tried to warn Tavar. There was some good in her. Perhaps she still cared for him? No. That was another path he dared not tread. That bridge had been burned long ago. Now all that remained was ash and smoke.

"So, what do you call her?" Tavar asked, patting a hand on the ship's wooden deck as Alice looked questioningly at him. "Every pirate ship needs a cool name, you know that!"

"Don't laugh…" Alice warned, already her brows had creased as she expected scorn. "*The Queen's Wrath.*"

"*The Queen's Wrath?*" Tavar repeated, choking back his laughter but not well enough to escape a punch on the arm from Alice; thankfully not one from the metal hand. "What?"

"I remembered it from one of the stories we used to read. Adam loved it. Anyway, whenever people hear the name now, they shake in their boots."

"Sure they're not shaking with laughter?" Tavar snorted, enjoying their playful conversation. Speaking with Alice felt like being young again, like he was that same child who had run through the woods and watched as she played with sticks and pretended to be a knight.

"I have a ship capable of instilling fear and dread into people who don't know me. What have you done?" Alice mocked, folding her arms and raising an eyebrow, clearing feeling victorious.

"Killed an Immortal," Tavar answered rather bluntly.

The frown returned to Alice's face. "Fine, you win that one. You're still not allowed to laugh though. Now, tell me about this Immortal. We have a long journey ahead of us."

Rain crashed against the deck of *The Queen's Wrath* as it sped across the Sunrise Sea. Not typical weather for this time of year but when had anything been typical for him.

Medda strode across the deck, refusing to be defeated by the nausea that attacked her every time she left her cabin. Tavar watched with a smile as Halfor tore off his own coat and wrapped it around his shivering lover. The Naviqing was used to the madness of the sea weather but Medda had been raised with a warm climate and the heat of a blistering sun, the rain only added to her foul mood.

He walked over to his friends and greeted them enthusiastically. Halfor beamed in response but Medda could only offer up a scowl.

"Enjoying the fresh air?" he asked them both, knowing the reaction he would get in return.

"Nothing has ever tasted so sweet!" Halfor said, nostrils flaring as he took in as much as the salty air as he could, his already huge barrel-like chest swelling to an obscene size.

"I never thought I would miss being in a dungeon," Medda bit back. "We are not meant for the sea. And when will this god cursed rain stop! It's been two days now!"

"I remember a season in my youth where the rain fell for five moons with no break. The rivers overflowed and then froze. We loved to skate and slide against the ice, daring each other to go further and test its strength and our bravery at the same time." Halfor paused and frowned to himself. "I remember shivering for days after I fell in. Had to sit next to a fire and stay there for the whole time until my mother was satisfied that I wasn't to be taken to the Gods. Good memories."

"Whenever you tell me tales like that, it puts me off ever visiting your homeland," Medda muttered, shaking and wet.

Halfor rubbed her arms with his calloused but gentle hands. "You will love it." He turned back to Tavar following a kiss on Medda's wet hair. "How long until we near Okada?"

"Alice said it will be a day or two, depending on the seas. All other ships recognise our flag so they've been keeping away, so we shouldn't encounter any problems. You two coming to shore when we get there?"

Medda nodded frantically. "You'd need a thousand swords to stop me."

"We want to pay our respects to the old man. The passage to the gods is clearer when friends are there to guide them. Our time speaking with his family will only help that," Halfor said. The big man was unusually spiritual for a warrior his size. Most fought and killed with no thought to what would happen after it all ended. Halfor was different. He claimed to live and fight in the thought of impressing his ancestors and impressing them enough to start his next life in their hallowed Hall of Heroes – a place he claimed all great warriors would be able to enter if they fought with heart.

Tavar nodded at a passing seaman who tipped his hat and muttered, "Immortal." Ever since word had got around about him killing the Immortal in the arena, the pirates had looked at him with a newfound respect and taken to calling him Tavar the Immortal, something Tavar had tried to stop but Qassim had fanned the flames enough for them to ignore any attempts he made at stopping it. The Alfaran had eagerly given Tavar a tour of the ship, showing him all the parts and explaining their significance. He seemed comfortable on the waves and happier out here than he ever had in Kessarine. He'd spoken with joy of his sister and how she had married a governor in Albion and was expecting a child. The pirate life hadn't been for her apparently. "She likes comfort and luxury. It's what we were used to, after all. She'll be happier when the kid is born, it's been difficult not being able to speak to our parents since we left... Didn't want them getting hurt on account of us."

Out of all of them, Tavar realised that Qassim and his sister had perhaps given up the most. Born into noble families in Alfara, their lives had been set and mapped out for them. They would spend five years in the army and then be awarded some easy post and a named position in the army. They'd choose a partner and marry and have kids and most likely grow fat whilst living out the remainder of their days in some huge house out in the country. Still, the look on Qassim's face was not one of regret.

"I'm sorry I dragged you into this, Qassim."

Qassim bristled at the apology. "You're joking, aren't you? You saved my life. Literally. And anyway, this ship has given me the chance to see the world. You know, we stayed on a small island west of Okada a couple of years ago. Slept in a tent and woke up in the middle of the night. Thought I'd go for a walk. Do you know what I saw? A wingless dragon. Fast bastard. Ran away on its four legs before I could grab anyone else. No one would believe me, but I saw it. A dragon."

A huge wave crashed against the side of the ship and snapped Tavar to reality.

"Funny how you get called Immortal and yet they don't even go near Tajira," Medda said to him. "They give him a wide berth."

"Can you blame them?" Tavar said. He'd made a deal with the warrior but even he didn't feel comfortable around the shadow warrior. "Have you had one fun conversation with him since he joined us?"

"We spoke of our favourite weapons only last week," Halfor offered. "He mocked you for wielding two falchions. Told me you were a fool for doing such a thing. It's the happiest I've seen him."

"Well, he won't be with us for much longer. We'll do what we need to do with Kenji's family and then he's moving on," Tavar told them.

"Where to?" Medda asked.

"Back to the shadows I suppose. As long as I don't become another scar on that body, I don't care."

As sudden as it had begun, the rain stopped. He looked up to see the hint of sunshine breaking through the dark clouds. In the distance, another ship floated on the gentle waves.

"Looks like the weather is improving," he said, bringing a smile to Medda's face.

"About damn time."

Halfor released her, a dark shadow passing over his own face as he rushed forward across the deck, his heavy boots bounded against the wood. He leapt onto the prow of the ship with unnerving grace considering his size.

"Halfor!" Tavar called to his friend. "What do you see?"

The Naviqing turned his head, his expression concerned and frantic as he roared across the ship. "Leviathan! Turn the ship! Leviathan!"

Bells rang out throughout the ship and horns blew as chaos took over. All hands rushed to the deck as fast as they could at the sound, panicked and confused looks on all their faces. Alice only strode up, a stern and determined as she stepped up next to the large, wooden wheel, barking commands to any she passed.

Tajira crept up from his room, curved daggers already in hand.

"Not sure they are going to help you here," Tavar said, eyeing the blades.

"They'll help me more than if I didn't have them." The warrior shrugged. "And more than two damn falchions…"

Ignoring the jibe, Tavar rushed up the steps to Alice and found Qassim standing next to her. Both of them stared towards the horizon, a look of steely determination matched on their faces.

"Ever fought one of these before?" he asked, praying that they had.

"Twice," Alice answered, her expression unchanged.

"Good." Tavar nodded, feeling slightly reassured.

"Lost the ship and most of the crew both times," Alice added before her eyes flickered at Tavar's concerned look. "Third time lucky, right?

The beast broke the water and tore straight through the ship in the distance, sending splinters of wood and screaming seamen flying through the air and into the unforgiving blue jaws of the sea. Alice's crew rushed around with experienced determination, all preparing the ship for defence as it lurched to the side, knocking Tavar to the ground just as Halfor caught Medda and prevented her from the same fate.

He grabbed a hand offered by a calm Tajira and thanked him.

"You seen any of these before?" he asked the unperturbed shadow warrior.

"A few. They are mighty beasts. The land and seas south of here are full of residual magic left from the Ancient Ages. The sea serpents are leftovers of those times. Our safety depends on making it to the nearest shore."

Tavar watched as the Leviathan broke the surface once more. Even from this distance he could see that the beast was longer than the size of the Alfaran Arena. Her scales were an emerald green that shone in the sun light and two horns stabbed out from her forehead like two giant pikes promising death and destruction to any who got in her way. A row of blood-red plates stuck out along her spine and ran all the way down to its thinning tail that slapped against the water as she dived once more beneath the waves and out of sight.

He had never seen anything as magnificent and frightening. The serpent moved with a grace and majesty that surpassed anything else on land or in sea. She leapt from the waves and for a moment looked capable of flight before crashing down against the remains of the sinking ship, sealing its fate and that of the passengers on board.

Tavar could only stand and watch the scene unfold before him as Alice barked orders to her crew who silently obeyed her, trusting her commands. The ship crashed through the waves, furiously racing towards the nearest strip of land. The coast grew closer but it was still too far away for any thoughts of safety.

"She is heading this way…" Halfor said. His voice shook with fear and his arms tightened around Medda protectively. She pushed his arms away and marched towards the steps heading down to the lower deck. "Where are you going?"

"I need my weapon. Those bulging biceps aren't going to keep me safe against that thing," Medda argued, her eyes flickering to the harpoon being readied by the crew. "If I'm going down with the ship, I want my spear with me. I'll take the bitch's eye before I leave this world."

Halfor gave her a wicked smile and roared, following her down to grab his own warhammer. Though what that weapon would be able to do against such a monstrosity, Tavar had no clue. Perhaps he felt like Medda, happier to go down with a weapon in hand than none at all.

Tajira walked calmly up the steps to stand next to Alice. She ignored him at first, focusing instead on the instructions she needed to send to all of her crew. At last her eyes turned to him. "Yes? I'm kinda busy here."

Tajira motioned to the harpoon. "What's that thing made from?"

Alice's eyes lit up at the question, her whole-body language changing instantly. "Okadan chimteki. Smuggled it out myself a couple of years ago. They were not happy about that, let me tell you."

"The only metal that has any chance of piercing its armour," Tajira nodded, obviously impressed. "You know what you're doing."

"I guess I do," Alice answered with a grin.

"That's the same metal Kenji spoke of. Said his family used it for their swords. True Okadan metal, he said," Tavar added, his eyes still on the water as mist rose from the surface of the beast's trail. "He said that's what true Kyushira blades need."

"Rarest metal in the world..." Alice said, her voice tailing off as she watched the incoming monster.

Tavar held his breath just as Halfor and Medda returned to the deck, weapons in hand and grim looks on their faces. Silence swept over the crew, a collective intake of breath before the attack. The Leviathan rose from the sea, displaying its cold, blue eyes and sharp teeth deadlier than any sword in the world. Her red belly splashed back against the surface and sent a tidal wave rushing towards the ship just as Qassim let fly with the first harpoon strike.

Then, chaos ensued.

A mighty wave slapped against the ship with the strength of a giant's punch. The ship lurched to the side with the impact as Tavar held on tight to the rope next to him. Screams were cut off as two of the crew fell overboard, unable to cling to safety as they were lost to a watery grave. As the ship steadied itself, the crew looked over the side, frantically searching for any sign of the beast.

"Load the harpoon!" Qassim called before

cursing to himself. "At least three paces off. Should have shot sooner."

Tavar cautiously peered over the side and saw a dark shadow circling the ship, readying itself for the next attack. It struck without warning. Tavar was close enough to see the slitted pupils staring hungrily at him just as its jaws widened and ripped into the side of the ship, dragging wood and part of the sail into the water with her. Tavar fell to the ground as the ship tilted with the attack. Cries of the men and women sliding down the deck and into the sea along with the beast filled the air around him.

Tavar swore as he clung onto a wooden beam, watching helplessly as Qassim's harpoon broke from its base and fell onto the main deck, catching against the netting at the bottom of the ship's mast.

Water engulfed one side of the ship, threatening to drag the rest along with it into the dark, foreboding water. Ominous streaks of red inked the sea around the ship as the dark shadow of the beast returned to its route, enjoying the fruits of its labour and preparing itself for the next attack, one that Tavar feared would be the last.

"Naviqing!" Alice roared over the howls and screams of her fearful crew. "The harpoon!"

Halfor clung desperately to the netting on the side of the ship, his boots slipping on the tilted, wet deck. Medda lay feet away, caught up against a wooden beam and holding on for her life.

The Naviqing stretched a boot out as far as he could, attempting to drag the harpoon back towards him. His boot pressed against the weapon uselessly as his body strained, his pale skin turning purple with the effort. At last, it brushed against the weapon, freeing it from the netting. With a cry of horror, Tavar saw the harpoon slip away and slide down the deck, away from the warrior. Barely registering the movement, he launched himself away from safety and clasped a hand against the sliding weapon allowing himself to fall into the water.

Beneath the waves he could feel the vibrations of the Leviathan cutting through the water as parts of the ship and the crew floating around him. He gripped the large harpoon as tightly as he could and kicked his feet in an effort to get to the surface. His chest felt close to bursting as he broke the surface, mouth open as he gulped in the air. He felt a hand pull at the shirt on his back and drag him onto the ship.

"Tajira..." was all he managed to say before coughing out the sea water from his lungs as he swatted the wet hair sticking to his face out the way from his eyes and saw the grim-faced warrior staring blankly at him.

"The serpent returns!" a cry came from below Tavar on the deck.

Ignoring the black spots flashing in his vision, Tavar crawled onto his feet, never releasing the harpoon. The shadow rushed forward for the final blow as the decimated ship continued to sink beneath the waves. From the corner of his eye, Tavar saw Halfor slide down the deck to Medda, grabbing her spear and placing it into her hand as she clung against the beam keeping her from the depths of the sea. They kissed as the monster reared up from the water, mouth wide open and large enough to swallow three warriors whole.

Tavar stared into its malevolent eyes and roared in defiance. With every last drop of energy, he threw the harpoon towards the beast, praying for it to strike his target and save his friends from the jaw of the monster.

Time seemed to stand still. The missile twisted in

the air as the Leviathan's scaled body blocked out the sun, casting a shadow on the remains on the ship. A piercing cry deafened Tavar and he clasped his hands to his ears to block out the bloodcurdling sound as the spearpoint buried itself into the roof of the monster's mouth. Its body twisted in the air and fell with an almighty crash against the prow of the ship. Tavar fell with the impact of the creature's landing and groaned as the back of his head slammed against a wooden crate. Dazed and disorientated, his vision blurred as he fell again below the surface of the water.

His body slammed into the water and the air burst from his chest. He wanted to open his mouth to breathe but he didn't have the energy. The sea welcomed him fully and Tavar caved in, accepting its embrace.

CHAPTER TWENTY-NINE: OKADAN HOSPITALITY

He immediately regretted opening his eyes. The torchlight in the room brought on the feeling of a thousand pins stabbing at the back of his eyes, trying to force their way out of his head. He groaned and covered his face with his hands. The back of his head throbbed and his entire body was aching and sore.

"Ah, you are awake!" a voice croaked from somewhere nearby. "I thought you'd be dead by now, but the big man said you were made of sterner stuff."

Tavar struggled to open his eyes again, slowly this time. He peered through half shut eyes and smiled weakly as the blurred form of an old, white-haired figure shuffled over to him, bowl in hand.

"Drink this. Tastes like dragon piss but it will help you regain your strength."

"You ever tasted dragon piss?" Tavar asked with a chuckle.

"Nope. You ever jumped from a cliff headfirst?"

"No."

"But you know it would hurt like a bastard?" the old man said with a chuckle of his own.

"I get you."

"Drink up, kid. The others will be happy to see you up and awake."

"Thanks Kenji."

The old man's smile faded at the name. Tavar took the bowl and sipped the hot broth, forcing himself to keep it down even though every nerve in his body yelled at him to spit it back out. His vision cleared and in the low torchlight, he could see the old man more clearly. Receding white hair was tied back into a ponytail and he had those scars covering both of his eyes. His beard was shorter though, only surrounding his lips and chin. This wasn't Kenji, but the likeness was uncanny.

"I'm sorry…"

The old man waved away the apology. "We look alike, my brother and me. He always liked to tell me that he was the pretty one, though. My name is Keito. It is good to meet you, Tavar the Immortal."

"Tavar, please. I'm no Immortal."

"I don't know. Killing one of those golden warriors and injuring a Leviathan. Not bad for a mere mortal."

"Flukes. I had help with both."

Keito smiled again. It was a smile so like Kenji's that Tavar felt his heart stop for a moment with grief at the reminder of the loss of his old friend. It was like having him back.

"I can see why he liked you. Humble. Kenji was never one for arrogance and bravado. "Arrogance blinds folk more than any impairment we have, my brother." That's what he used to say to me. Old fool." Keito chuckled again, sadly this time.

Tavar finished the bowl of broth and placed it on the small wooden table beside his bed. "You were right. Dragon piss," he said as he glanced around the room. It was simple. Just a bed and a table. A sapphire blue curtain with golden embroidery had been pulled across a window. Moonlight fought to enter the room but the curtain was thick enough to have aided in Tavar's sleep, not that he had probably needed it. The fight flooded back into his head and he sat up too quickly, wincing and pressing a hand to the back of his head.

"Not so fast! You need time to recover," Keito warned.

"My friends, are they safe?"

"Lost a lot of people out in the sea. Couple more fell on the way here. A fair few survived though. I'll take you to them as soon as I'm happy that you're out of the woods. Knife hand and the Naviqing have been threatening me when I don't let them in here but the soul needs to rest after such damage and the soul rests only in a deep sleep. Their voices would have dragged you back here before you were ready and I wasn't going to let that happen."

"Keito, your brother…"

"I know the main points of what happened, kid. No need to say any more today. Just rest. Kenji will be watching over you. How else would you have taken down that beast?"

Tavar lay back down, embracing the comfort of the thin sheets and let himself fall back into a restful sleep.

By the time he woke up, sun light had crept through a gap in the curtains and the torches had been extinguished. Ignoring the aches and pains, Tavar pulled the sheets from off himself and stood up, stretching his arms and wincing as his neck clicked with the little movement he attempted. His head no longer hurt so bad; the throbbing had abated at least.

At the bottom of his bed and neatly folded was a pile of clothes. He pulled on the white knee length undershorts and then a thin black vest top. Next was a black, silk jacket with wide, open sleeves. It was comfortable against his skin and allowed easy movement as he stretched. He picked up a tasselled golden rope and tied it around his waist. Finally, he stepped into two wooden sandals. Traditional Okadan clothing. He liked it.

He crossed the room and pulled the door across, sliding it to his left. Different to the doors back in Alfara. The next room was just as simple. It was rectangular and bright. Paintings covered the walls. Mainly of the region's animals. He recognised a crane, a macaque and stunning koi fish, all painted with colours that popped from the walls and shot out towards the watcher. Around the animals were paintings of trees with thin branches and beautiful, small pink blossoms. In the centre of the room was a low, rectangular table but there were no seats, just a thick red carpet. More of the sliding doors were closed to his left and right but he headed to the one opposite, sliding a door open and relaxing as he was greeted to a gentle breeze, the fresh air smacking him in the face.

It was a clear day and Tavar could see all the way towards the row of snow-peaked mountains on the horizon. He stepped forward and looked around at the new landscape. A forest of spruce and fir trees stood watch to his left and a to his right, the sun glistened against a large, calm lake. He felt as far away from Alfara as possible as he stared at the beauty of nature around him.

"Not too shabby, is it?" Medda clasped his forearm and gave a small smile. She was wearing Okadan clothes of her own: a navy blue robe trimmed with silver that shimmered in the light as she moved. She'd fashioned a harness around her shoulders that held her spear in place behind her. Even here she was ready for a fight.

"I've seen worse," Tavar admitted.

"How's the head?"

"Better."

"Two weeks of sleep will do that to a guy," she laughed. "We thought you were dead. We thought all of us would be dead, to be honest."

"What happened?" Tavar asked, trying to process the information that the world had kept turning whilst he was none the wiser.

"Here he is!" Tavar turned to see Halfor striding towards him, pulling along a huge net that stank of fish. The net would have taken around five men to carry but Halfor wasn't a normal man. "The Leviathan-defeating, Immortal-slaying, forever-sleeping friend of mine!" Halfor dropped the fish and spread his arms wide, ignoring Tavar's mild protests to pull him in for a hug, taking him from his feet and swinging him with ease as his laughter bellowed in Tavar's ears. "It is wonderful to see you on your feet, my friend!"

"He's not actually on his feet at the moment," Medda pointed out before Halfor lowered him back to the ground and took a good look at him.

"Been fishing."

"I can see that," Tavar said, looking at the large, bulging net."

495

"Another reminder of home, though I must say, this land is growing on me. The lake, the air, the mountains. Not bad."

"Where are the others?" Tavar glanced around but couldn't see any sign of anyone else.

"Alice, Qassim and that drunkard took what was left with the crew after the attack and travelled to the nearest village. We'll need a ship at some point and they have enough coin left to get one. They shouldn't be too long. Tajira is wandering the woods. Strange one, that shadow warrior." Halfor frowned and pushed his long hair from his eyes.

"What about Keito?"

"The old man is away in his little hut," Medda said, pointing to the left of the lake. Tavar could just see a small building in the distance. Smoke slowly rose towards the thin, white clouds lazily drifting over them. "He said he didn't want to be disturbed. He's a lot like Kenji. We spent the first night with him out here around a fire and told him everything. Keito spoke to Tajira alone after that. They said some words together and that was it. He's spent most of his time in that hut or checking up on you."

"Best go see him and say thanks."

The smell of smoke and burning invaded his nostrils as Tavar neared the small, wooden hut on the edge of the lake. The air rang with a sound Tavar knew well from his time in Alfara, the clang of hammer on iron. He remembered Kenji's tales of sword-making and knew instantly what the old man's brother was up to. There was no door to the hut, just an open space leading into the building with three walls enclosing it. A wide selection of weapons was strewn about the place: cluttering shelves and filling up the space on the stone floor. Axes, sledgehammers, chisels, arrows, shields, helmets, armour, and swords of every kind were scattered around the room. There were weapons in here that he hadn't seen before even in the training rooms of Alfara. In the centre of it all, covered in a leather apron and mask, Keito hammered at the glowing, orange steel on top of the forge, beating the metal with a controlled precision and ignoring the hot sparks flying off towards him.

"Kenji said that you were the best swordsmith in this region."

Keito raised his mask and dropped the sword at Tavar's words. He grinned proudly and Tavar felt that familiar pain in his chest at the memory of his dead friend.

"Full of compliments, was my brother. Not often to my face but it seems his silver tongue worked wonders away from home. I may be better at making them but he was a damn sight better at wielding them, as you saw yourself, according to the words of your allies. My grandfather was the one with the true gift though. Mohan Al-Taabi. Greatest of his generation. My father Tamir wasn't half bad either."

Tavar glanced at the weapon on the anvil and inclined his head uselessly at it. "That a kyushira?" It glimmered and shone in an unnatural way, reflecting something more than the light peeking in from the sun outside.

"A *true* kyushira," Keito corrected him. "Not like the bastard model you would have seen my brother wield. I am one of the few remaining smiths capable of imbuing the blade with the magic needed to call it a true kyushira."

"Magic?"

"Old magic. Only specks of it are left since the Ayurdava left these lands. Ancient magic, the kind that used to be seen across this whole continent in days long gone. The Leviathan is reminder of those times, a fallen giant left swimming amongst its lessers, forgotten by the very people who had created it. A pity."

"So, this sword will be magic?" Tavar was unable to keep the cynicism from his voice, try as he might.

"You will see. This blade will be yours." Tavar opened his mouth to protest but Keito cut him off. "You were close with my brother and you've come all this way to pay your respects. The least I can do is give you this one last gift. The last Al-Taabi ever to be made, I believe."

"Why the last?"

"I don't have the energy for this anymore. To sense the magic, you must shut yourself off from all distractions and embrace the silence, embrace the world around you, becoming one with the flow of water, the song of the birds, the deep rumble of the mountains. Even then, it is a struggle to catch the voice that will sing in your blade. Some claimed that it was dark magic, they saw it as trapping a soul inside a weapon. But it's not. It is the voice of the world around you, guided to support you in battle. There is a beauty to it." The old man sounded like he was speaking of a lover.

"I'm not sure I want to use weapons anymore," Tavar admitted, sheepishly scratching at his itchy beard and sighing. "Every time I fight, it's not just my enemies who die, but friends. People I love."

Keito walked over to him, taking his gloves off before placing his hard, calloused and blackened hands on

Tavar's face, forcing him to close his eyes.

"You fought in Hartovan. And your friends found freedom. You fought in the Arena and your friends found new life. You fought the Leviathan and your friends found a new belief in themselves." Keito released his hands from Tavar's eyes and smiled widely at him, showing his crooked teeth and chuckling softly.

"Every time you fight there will be loss. Loss is inevitable, it is a part of the journey of life. But every time *you* fight," he poked Tavar roughly in the chest. "People's lives are changed for the better. That is why I am forging this sword. Taking lives will cause you to bear a burden that will weigh you down and have you doubting yourself. But if you don't bear that burden, many more innocent lives will be lost and why? Because you didn't feel up to it. Because you were afraid. My brother hated killing. Loved fighting, mind you, but hated killing. But he understood that protecting people sometimes meant drawing a sword. Do you understand that?"

Tavar nodded. He had no more words left for the sword maker, just a lot to think about. Since being torn from his parents, every part of his life had pulled him towards fighting and bloodshed. He'd thought nothing good had come of it. It was draining and he could feel the strain on his still young but weary body. The bags under his eyes weighed down like two anvils of their own and each step he took came with a dull thud throbbing in his legs. Worse than all the physical pain was the mental anguish. Every time he looked at Halfor or Medda all he could think about was how long they had left. When would he drag them into a battle that they could not win? How many rolls of the dice did they have left before he was looking down at their corpses?

"There's evil in this world," Keito said, picking his gloves back up. "A darkness that spreads like a plague and consumes all around it. That assassin will be able to tell you all about it, his people understand darkness better than any. The thing about darkness is, it can only be defeated by light. Even one small light can hold back a wave of darkness. You can either take this sword and choose to be the light, or you can sit back and watch until the darkness blinds you more than me and Kenji. It may be difficult being the light but you've got good people around you, really good people. They'll help you shine brighter than you ever could on your own, even if their own light flickers and dies on the way. Your choice, kid."

Keito pulled his mask down and slid his hands into the gloves. He returned to the weapon and continued his hammering.

Each clang felt like a wake-up call from a long slumber for Tavar.

Three more days passed with no sign of Alice and the others. Keito told them not to worry, the closest village was quite a distance away and they would be lucky to acquire a ship even there. He continued to work on the sword day and night, the hammering of the blade filled the land until it blended in with the bird song and even the howls of the wolves in the forest at night. Tavar had taken to hiking through the thick forest with Halfor and Medda, hunting with bows and spears. The three of them enjoyed the sense of calm that the forest bestowed upon them. It was a world away from the tension in the dungeons of Kessarine. Tajira kept to himself, mostly. He would join them at night to feast over the campfire, but his words were minimal and, in the end, even the inquisitive Halfor had stopped asking the strange warrior any questions.

This night, the log Tajira usually sat upon was empty.

"Reckon he's got sick of your questions," Medda ribbed Halfor who only frowned, looking upset at the thought.

"Don't think he's used to spending time with people," Tavar suggested. "This must be bizarre for him."

The fire cackled as Halfor leaned across and twisted the hand-crafted spit, hungrily eyeing the meat he had stripped from his earlier hunt. They had offered Keito some of their food but he had declined, as always. Tavar had only seen the blind swordsmith eating fruit and vegetables. He didn't seem to eat meat at all. That would explain his lean frame.

Halfor pulled the pole from over the flames and without waiting, his teeth tore into the meat, ripping pieces away like an animal and swallowing. Then came the heavy blowing as he realised too late, as usual, that his mouth was not designed for such heat.

"We warn you every single night!" Medda screeched as the Naviqing rushed for his water and swilled the drink around his mouth in a futile attempt to ease the burning. "You won't be able to taste a thing for the next week. When will you learn?" she laughed and shook her head playfully as she watched the big man struggle with the pain.

"I'm jutht tho hungry…" he moaned with a lisp, looking like a berated child as his shoulders slumped and he sat back down next to Medda.

"Letting it cool for a bit before chucking it in your mouth might be advisable," Tavar said, unable to keep from laughing at his friend. He dodged a piece of meat flung his way and blew a cheeky kiss to Halfor which brought a smile to his friend's face as the pain abated.

"It's a good job I love the two of you…" Halfor muttered, the corner of his lips rising.

"Or what?" Medda asked, pulling her brows together, intrigued. "You'd eat us?"

"Want me to answer that?" Halfor said, voice low as his own brows flexed up and down.

"Your head is always in the gutter!" Medda screamed in fake shock, slapping the big man away before drawing him in for a kiss. Tavar averted his eyes, happy enough to watch the dance of the flames as his friends folded into each other, content with the company.

The trio sat together with the heat of the flames, lost in the warmth of their companionship. They had been through so much together. The atrocities of the arena had forged a bond that Tavar knew was unbreakable. Halfor and Medda could go to the other end of the world and he would still feel the loss if anything happened to them. They were bound by something even greater than blood. Kenji had been a part of that too. The old man had loved them like family and though his loss pained Tavar, he was comforted by Keito's previous words. Perhaps the old man really was watching from wherever he had ventured to after death. Hopefully Adam and Vandir were up there with him, and his parents. They could be sitting in some giant hall sharing their stories and feasting like Halfor always liked to believe.

Tavar snapped out of his thoughts as a dark shadow stumbled towards him from across the fire. He jumped up, eyes peering into the gloomy shadows of the night. Halfor and Medda reacted similarly, each reaching for their weapons. Tavar cursed as his fingers automatically reached for his falchions, only to find nothing there. He'd gotten sloppy. Too distracted by the comfort and freedom that he wasn't used to.

The figure stumbled into the light of the fire. Brown skin like Tavar's, fresh wounds on the torso and arms seen through a ripped grey robe, most likely made with a curved blade. The figure dropped next to the fire, a look of absolute terror on his face. His hands had been tied and the restriction of blood turned them a nightmarish blue. Part of his robe had been torn and tied around his mouth. His cries were muffled and tears were rolling freely down his face as his body shook. Behind him, Tajira strolled into the light, casually watching the beaten man and swinging a bag in his right hand whilst holding onto the rope attached to the man's hands in his left.

"Tajira, what the fuck are you doing?" Tavar asked, looking from the shadow warrior to the prisoner and back again. Tajira just rolled his tongue and launched a ball of saliva directly onto the fallen man's hair, sticking in his dark, blood-matted hair. Disgusting.

"Caught him in the forest. Had a bow and arrow and was watching the three of you with interest," Tajira answered, as though that cleared up the matter.

"That's no reason to beat him to within an inch of his life!" Tavar's eyes flickered to the sobbing man on the floor and wondered what horrors the shadow warrior had subjected him to before being brought to them.

"He also had this little note…" Tajira dropped the bag with a thud and placed a hand in his pocket, pulling out a scrunched-up parchment and aiming it towards Tavar.

Tavar cursed and walked around the fire, tearing the parchment from Tajira's hand and staring at the well-written but short note.

Bring Tavar Farwan back alive. He will die with those who helped him escape. Kill whoever else is with him. A payment of 10,000 crowns will be handed to any who completes this mission.

Signed in the name of the Godking Uhlad of Alfara

He crunched the paper up in a trembling fist and stared at the mercenary lying at his feet. Without Tajira, this man would have killed Tavar's friends and taken him back to Kessarine. The wall was waiting for him. He didn't care about what Uhlad had planned for him. What bothered him was the line in the middle of the note. *He will die with those who helped him escape.* Marek. Hashem. The people of Hartovan Islands.

"What does this mean? Who is Uhlad preparing to kill?" Tavar bent down and grabbed what was left of the man's shirt, pulling him up so that his face was close enough for Tavar to see his bleeding gums.

"He's putting them to the wall. For the Banishment. A celebration," the mercenary said through heavy breaths.

Tavar dropped his head to the ground and stood, brushing down the specks of saliva and blood that had landed on his robe. Halfor and Medda twisted their weapons in their hands, knowing what must be done.

Tajira picked up the bag and tipped its contents onto the ground. "He wasn't the only one." Two severed heads rolled across the grass, one hitting against Tavar's foot and staring up at him with cold, dead eyes.

"Looks like you need a weapon…"

Tavar whipped around to see Keito standing on the edge of the fire light. In his hand was an intricately cut bone scabbard with a leather band hanging loosely around it. The hilt of the blade shone emerald green and the guard had a golden dragon snaking its way around the it.

The blind man cautiously stepped towards Tavar, holding the weapon with the reverence and respect of a holy relic. Keito tilted the scabbard so that the hilt pointed at Tavar. Whispers broke out in Tavar's head, a longing, an unquenchable thirst.

His fingers shook as they reached out for the blade, the whispers growing louder, scratching at the walls of his mind. He wrapped his hand around the hilt and felt a power coursing through his body, a union of weapon and wielder that cut straight through him. A True Kyushira. Just as Keito had said.

He slid the sword from its sheathe and twisted. In one motion, the mercenary's head lopped off and spun onto the grass next to Tajira. A moment later, the rest of his body dropped to the floor as though confused by the attack and not knowing how to respond without its head.

Halfor and Medda's faces bore looks of grim resignation. Tajira just looked bored.

Keito nodded and smiled. "My brother would be pleased. He lives on through this blade. Use it sparingly. Once drawn, it must be bloodied."

"We wait for four days. Then we go looking for Alice and the others. Tavar sighed and glanced at Halfor and Medda, pleading with them to forgive him. He knew what this meant. Blood. "We're heading back to

Kessarine. Let's finish what we're started."

"We'll need an army…" Halfor said, blowing out his cheeks.

Medda shuffled uncomfortably and rubbed her forearms, unable to meet any of their eyes. "I think I might know where to get one. Though, it won't be easy…"

"Where? Who?" Tavar asked, wondering why she had kept this information to herself.

"My people," Medda responded, staring at the dying flames with cold eyes. "The Blood Nation."

CHAPTER THIRTY: THE TROUBLE WITH PARADISE

"We're gone for a week and you kill three people and Tavar has some weird shiny sword that speaks to him?" Alice asked incredulously, eyes dropping again to the kyushira strapped to his belt. "And now we're going back to the place you fought so hard to leave. Did I get that right?"

"I can't have them die for me, Alice. I can't have anyone else die for me."

"Well... shit. Guess we're going back then. And I've heard a bit of this Blood Nation. Secret bunch. You sure we can trust them?"

"We can trust them. I'll make sure they do as we ask," Medda said, staring out at the sea.

Tavar frowned. Medda had spoken even less than was usual since they had departed on Alice's new ship, a much smaller one but cheaper, and available, which was the most important quality. She had withdrawn into herself, only telling them what they needed to know. She had been raised in the Undying Sands as a member of the Blood Nation. They wanted vengeance on Alfara and they would provide an army. When asked any further questions, she had snapped, even storming away from Halfor who threw his arms up in frustration and watched her leave.

Thoughts of his first kill had come to mind, the warrior who had attacked him in the sands. That man may have known Medda growing up. They could have been friends...

Tavar rubbed nervously at the stitching on his sleeves. Keito had bid them all farewell with new clothes and weapons. He'd even offered to fashion a new tool for Alice's arm but she had declined, knowing time was of the essence. Tavar would be lying if he said he didn't have tears burning in the back of his eyes as they left the old man. But for once he was leaving a friend in the knowledge that they were safe and unharmed. How many times could he say that in his life?

"You sure that heading to the islands is the best idea right now?" Alice asked him. "Might be wasting valuable time. Heading to the Blood City might be the best course of action."

Tavar shook his head. He'd rolled the ideas over and over again, weighing up the pros and cons of both paths laid before him. This way was the right one. "I want as much information about what is happening in the city as possible. The people on the islands will be able to help us, Lilian especially. She knows Kessarine like the back of her hand," he explained. "Anyway, we might find more people willing to fight beside us. If there's anyone with a hatred of Kessarine and Alfara that matches our own, then they will be the people who fled Hartovan. Any allies right now will be useful." The plan made sense. He wanted to stop the deaths of his friends but he remembered the looks on the faces of those in Hartovan. The farmer who had almost watched his children burn to death for no reason other than the amusement of one sick bastard. This was their chance to pay back that debt if they wanted to.

"And what happens if Uhlad kills them before we get there?"

"He won't."

"How can you be sure?"

"He sent mercenaries after us. He wants us. I killed one of his Immortals. He wants to make a display of me, show his kingdom that this is what happens to those who cross him. He'll do anything to have me in his city. So I'll send *him* a message." Tavar turned to face his childhood friend. The weariness and sadness in her face pierced his chest in that moment. She was so different to the girl who he had laughed and played with in the woods all those years ago. "I'll give myself up. Uhlad will welcome me into Kessarine with the promise that any prisoners he has lined up for the wall go free."

"You know that's the craziest fucking idea I've ever heard," Alice snorted, banging a metal fist against the side of the ship and taking a swig from her waterskin. She swilled the water around her mouth and spat it out into the sea. For good luck, she had told him when he had asked her why the first time she did it. "And I've had Qassim pitch an idea to steal from the Empress of Okada and propose to a married milkmaid in Yorkland *after* bedding her. Uhlad could just cut your head off and that will be it."

"He's not that ruthless. He's dramatic. We'll need to time things right; I don't want to spend any time on the wall if it can be helped."

"That's a life goal right there," Alice laughed, turning from him and stepping over a sleeping Marcus on the deck. "Grab some water. We can wake this fool up. We need every sword we can get if we're going to keep you alive. And if I remember correctly, he isn't too bad when his blood to alcohol ratio is at a reasonable level. Though, he'll have one hell of a hangover. A decade of heavy drinking don't look pretty." She kicked Marcus in the gut and he groaned and rolled over. The snoring continued.

The Arrow Islands were a group of three main stretches of land and over a hundred smaller islands, most of which were only inhabited by unique animals and wildlife. They sat in the Smoking Sea, known for the continuous eruptions of the numerous volcanoes both above and below the sea. Smoke always danced somewhere around the islands. A fourth large island had been lost to the water a generation ago following a colossal eruption and wave that had swallowed it whole, killing all life in one dark day. The surviving inhabitants on the remaining islands never ran away. They knew their life was one of hardship but it was their home. They would only leave if they were dragged and forced. Unfortunately, Alfara had only been happy to oblige with this notion.

"Beautiful, isn't it?" Qasssim said out loud as he stared at one of the islands coming into view. Crystal blue sea, white sand beaches, and green as far as the eye could see. Tavar had to agree. Beautiful.

"Hot though," Halfor added, waving his hand up and down in front of his increasingly pink and sweaty face. "I remember why I cut the beard off when I ventured this far south now. The face doesn't need such a coat in places like this. Don't know how you brown folk do it," he said, pointing at Tavar's own dark mass of hair trimmed around his chin. 'But yes, it is a land of beauty."

"It would be more beautiful if I had a drink in my hand…" Marcus stepped between Qassim and Halfor, an arm around each of them as he followed their gaze, licking his lips.

He looked a mess. Wild, ragged beard and hair down to the middle of his back, he hadn't washed for days and stank like the hells. The rest of the crew were giving him a wide berth, tutting and frowning whenever they passed, not even bothering to hide their disgust.

"I think you've probably had enough," Qassim told him, peeling a hand from his shoulder and sneering at his old boss.

"I've barely touched a drop!" Marcus screeched, looking thoroughly aghast with the accusation. The stumble backwards and catch by Halfor only added to his dismay. It also added to everyone else's view that the man was a drunk loose cannon.

"The waters are still deep enough to drown him if we push him over," Qassim said, leaning over to Tavar and covering his mouth with a hand. "Wouldn't be the first time it's been suggested."

Tavar pressed his lips together but was unable to stifle a laugh at the idea. "No. Alice was right. Every man or woman who can wield a sword is needed." He peered over his shoulder at the clear blue water. "Maybe wait until it's a bit shallower. He could do with a wash at the very least."

The feeling of warm, soft sand and gentle waves of water slapping against his feet as he walked along the beach brought a sense of calm to Tavar. Whilst Qassim stayed with the ship and argued with the harbour master over docking fees and positioning, Tavar enjoyed the light breeze and the rejuvenating heat of the sun with Alice and a grumpy, dishevelled Marcus. Halfor had pressed on ahead, keen to get into the shade of the trees or, even better, a welcoming tavern overlooking the crystal waters. Medda followed him, more silent than ever, her boots stomping into the sand as she strived to keep up with the big man's steps.

"I wanna go with them," Marcus scowled, scrunching up his face and pointing wearily in the direction of Halfor and Medda. "Wine. Ale. Cider." His head whipped around as one of the locals passed him, swigging from a water skin. "Rum…"

"Wind your neck in Marcus," Alice growled. "I don't want to have to drag your bloated body out of yet another tavern. We're here to find out what's happening in Alfara. Not to get wasted and pass out in a pool of piss."

"That happened the one time…"

"That you can remember. Seven, by my count."

The buildings on the island were simple but full of character. Built into the many trees scattered across the island, they were a mix of wood and stone and painted with every colour under the sun. There was no system that Tavar could recognise, it was as though the people did whatever made them happy. A yellow stone house stood next to a small, wooden shack. The front of the shack had no wall, allowing Tavar to see straight into the building. A relaxed man lay across a gently rocking hammock. His hair hung down low, almost touching the ground, tightly wound into black ropes. He took a long drag from his rolled leaf and blew a smoke ring out before letting his hand drop to his side as he hummed a tune to himself. Hanging on the wall behind him were rows of colourful pictures, most depicting a sunset. Every now and then, he would call out to a passer-by with a smile, asking them to take a closer look at his work.

Women stopped each other on the beachfront, complimenting each other's colourful dresses and running a hand against their individual headdresses. Their skin was the same shade as he remembered Cassie's, slightly darker than Marcus's; a beautiful ebony that glistened in the light. The whole island was full of colour, flavour and life. The people beamed at each other and walked with their chests out and backs straight. They were proud to be who they were. They had lived through some of the worst events in history and came through the fires like a weapon forged by a smith.

"They are a strong people," Alice said, noticing Tavar's searching looks and grinning as two friends spotted one another and ran across the beach, hugging tightly and planting two kisses on each cheek. "The things they have been through mean they have come together more than any other nation. Alfara threatened to take their soul but it didn't happen. They've been able to rise from the ashes of those wars and come out stronger than ever."

"So there is hope for all of us," Tavar said, walking under a coconut tree and spotting a young boy sitting in the shade, enjoying the milk from the cracked fruit. The boy looked up at Tavar, the white milk on his lips dripping down his dark chin as he spotted the newcomers to the island. He bared his bright white teeth and giggled at the three of them. Tavar smiled back and Alice waved with her metal hand, delighting the young boy whose eyes widened with joy.

"Where's his parents?" Marcus snarled. "Just left here on the beach, in the sun to burn. Typical."

"He's drinking milk in the shade," Tavar argued, unhappy with the man's gloomy view of the situation.

"Don't defend them. They were better off when

Alfara was in charge. We gave them order, structure, a civilized way to live. Now look at them. What do you see?"

"Happy and free people," Tavar answered truthfully.

"Bah! They're lucky Alfara doesn't head back here and finish the job."

"I thought you hated Alfara, Marcus? These are your people." Alice queried, raising an eyebrow as they headed deeper into the village. The crowds grew larger as the number of market stalls increased. The sounds and smells of the market swarmed them: animals bleating and calling to each other, tradesmen shouting out prices and drawing customers in with their best deals. A vibrant island blossoming before his eyes.

"I love Alfara," Marcus answered, curling his lip up as he inched through a group of amused women. "It's the king I hated. Take him away and I'd go back in a heartbeat. These are not my people. Sett loved them; he embraced their lifestyle. He was the one who wanted to fight and die for them. It's not for me. There's too much of the Alfaran soldier in me."

"Bet you miss the taverns the most."

"You know me so well, Alice. I'd drain the place in a day. It would be drier than the Undying Sands."

Tavar paused, eyes falling on some peculiar red bananas. The merchant saw the look and grinned, strolling over to him and winking, obviously spotting an easy sale.

"Easy, my new friend. These succulent, sweet red bananas have fallen from the heavens just for you!"

Another merchant heard the usual speech and

snorted. "By heavens, you must mean the trees over there?" he pointed over to some trees in the distance and cackled, showing the gaps in his teeth and clapping his hands together. "Gotta love your pitch, brother."

The merchant selling to Tavar was unaffected. "That's right! My island is heaven to me. Look around, can you deny such a beautiful paradise."

"You have a stunning home," Tavar admitted. The merchant's eyes lit up at the words.

"That's an Alfaran accent I'm hearin' is it not? You brothers don't come here too often. Still a bit of animosity if truth be told," he shrugged. "But not from my side. Each brother needs to be judged on himself. God alone can guide us, no matter where you from."

"I'm not Alfaran, though I did grow up there."

"Hmmm… My baba grew up there, tough times. Much better being here in paradise."

Tavar agreed and handed over two bronze coins, accepted three bananas with a smile.

"Enjoy your time on my island, brother. You can relax on the Arrow Islands. Sun is always shining and people are always smiling. All the love." Tavar took the man's hands and accepted the hug before following Alice and Marcus down the dusty pathway between the stalls.

"Always making friends," Alice smirked as Tavar caught up and handed her the banana. Marcus took his gift and sniffed it. Must have smelled fine as he started peeling it before long. Tavar peeled his own and bit into the top. It was much sweeter than the bananas he was used to. Definitely worth the bronze coins.

"They are a friendly people," he said, taking another bite. Most nations would be on edge, keen to take revenge on Alfara for what had been done to their people. But they seemed to have brushed it off and took solace in ignoring their neighbour, choosing to love their own home than hate that of their old foe.

"I've travelled far and wide on this continent. This island is far and away my favourite place. Surrounded by water, soaked in sunshine and welcomed by shining white teeth everywhere you go. If I ever were to settle down..." Alice's voice trailed off as the thought passed her mind. Tavar wondered how often she had thought about it over the years. Giving up her life of piracy to settle down on the island.

"Maybe once we're done with Alfara..." Tavar let the idea hang there. There was no point forcing the issue. Alice had had enough time to think about it on her own without him forcing it upon her.

They strolled for a while longer, taking in the relaxed atmosphere and accepting the smiles and greetings from the locals. A holy man stood at a crossroads dressed all in white, a small cap shading his dark, bald head. "God is watching my brothers and sisters. At all times he is watching. Act with the knowledge that his eyes are upon you and you will rejoice. Our people have walked through the fires of hell and now is the time for us to rise and live as a united people. The waters of these islands can suffocate any fires placed before us now. Believe and be saved!"

Behind him, a choir of men, women and children were swaying together, singing in the old tongue of the Arrow Islands. Though Tavar couldn't understand the words, he felt himself caught in the flow and rhythm. It was impossible not to clap along or click your fingers.

"It's just a little further," Alice said, wiping sweat from her face and blowing her cheeks out.

A small, coral stone building greeted them amongst a canopy of green trees. A few people lay out on the benches out the front, chatting and laughing together. Tavar followed Alice into the building and took his headdress off, holding it low as a sign of respect.

Rows of beds ran down the length of the building. Patients sat or lay on their beds, a few of them had visitors next to them, cheering them up. Some just lay there, staring at nothing as the doctors ran around, checking on them.

Alice ignored them all, determined steps pulling her towards a woman dressed in a light blue dress stitched with a red circle and cross to signal her profession as a doctor. The doctor turned around as Alice tapped her on the shoulder.

Tavar rushed to catch up, ignoring the sweat pouring through his clothes.

"Well, isn't this a pleasant surprise!"

Tavar beamed at the woman, throwing his arms around her and basking in her musical laughter. "How have you been, Cassie?"

"Most of the injuries are self-inflicted. Too much alcohol and walking through dark jungle don't mix too well," Cassie chuckled to herself. "We get a few fights, mostly fools with too much pride to back down. The Island Watch aren't troubled too often though. Masani is the Watch Captain, she's a lazy bitch but she clamps down on any problems that arise. These people don't want trouble. They've had enough of that." Her eyes kept drifting to Alice, as though she was itching to have her alone.

"Are you happy here?" Tavar asked her, thanking the barman as he brought over their drinks. His eyes lingered on the barman's sparkling silver and sapphire jewellery that dangled from each ear either side of his bald head. He smiled at Tavar with painted red lips before walking away, his bright orange dress swaying in the breeze that flowed through the open tavern. The people really were free to live as they chose. Only Marcus seemed to stare overly long at the different style.

"Yeah. I have a purpose. I'm helping people. Only one thing missing…"

"We spoke about that," Alice snapped, her mood souring instantly.

Just in time, a young boy, of barely ten years, crashed through the trees and leapt into Cassie's open arms with a wide smile on his face. "Aunt Cassie!"

"Ade!" Cassie said, pinching the boy's cheek and shaking her head. "You weren't meant to be back here so soon. Where is your mother?" She looked over the boy's shoulder and frowned. Tavar followed the look and stood from his seat. A dishevelled woman stood on the simple stone pathway, breathing heavily, a scimitar in her hand. He was glad to see that the weapon was unbloodied.

"They're back…" Lilian said, face drawn and still as though she had seen a ghost.

Halfor and Medda came crashing down the wooden steps that led to the upper floor of the tavern. The Naviqing had his warhammer in hand and a resolute look on his face.

"Ships on the horizon," he spat. "Waving the flag of Alfara."

Medda twisted the spear in her hand. "Payback for the Islanders who helped us escape."

It made sense. "How many?" Tavar asked, already hearing the whispers call through him from the blade hanging at his hip.

"Three. Reckon they'll have around a hundred fighters. Not enough for a full-on attack but enough to teach a lesson."

"We don't have soldiers. We have farmers, builders, and merchants. We're not a military nation. People will be slaughtered!" Cassie argued, holding hands over Ade's ears so as not to frighten the boy.

Bells rang out across the island and urgent shouts and screams followed as the people of the Arrow Islands prepared for the invaders.

"We will give them more than a bloody nose. The people here still have weapons. They'll defend this paradise with their dying breaths," Lilian said through gritted teeth. As if on cue, the barman stepped out amongst them, a huge machete in hand and a grim look on his face.

"No need for our dying breaths, sister. The trouble with paradise is people get green with envy. We know how to defend our island, even if we wish we didn't have to." He winked at them and gave his weapon a few swings through the air. "You'll see."

The beach had been transformed by the time Tavar and his allies returned. The smiles had long gone from the faces of the locals, replaced with grim resignation. Men and women held a mixture of military weapons and homemade carved spears and bow and arrows. Whatever they could find. Timber from trees had been cut into spikes and planted into the sandy beach pointing towards the invaders.

"How have they prepared in such a short amount of time?" Halfor wondered out loud, staring around at the makeshift army of three hundred.

"We've had years to think about what happened to us before. There's not many of us but we've always known they'll be back," the barman answered. "And we knew that we wouldn't stand aside and let such atrocities happen again."

"Brave and just," Halfor nodded, impressed. "You should be proud of your people."

"Always have been."

"My name is Halfor, warrior of Naviqand."

"Ekon."

"It shall be good to stand with you Ekon."

"And you, Naviqing."

Many of the islanders had retreated further into the heart of the island in the hope of hiding the children and vulnerable from the worst of the fighting. Those left stood in the shade of the trees, watching and waiting.

"New Meat!" A familiar, booming voice sounded from the trees.

Tavar turned and greeted the large figure with a smile, tapping his chest. "Zaif. It's good to see you." A smaller male walked in the warrior's footsteps. Leaner and younger but with the same mischievous eyes and wide jaw.

"Looks like we'll be fighting side by side once again." The warrior bumped a fist with Halfor and saluted Medda, sharing smiles even amongst the nervous atmosphere of the battlefield. "We'll send these Alfaran bastards packing. Dump them back into the sea and let the

Gods of the Ocean deal with them. Won't we, son?"

"Yeah, Baba," the younger once answered, eyes not leaving Tavar. He looked barely sixteen years but he held the scimitar with confidence and his muscles were toned and mature.

"This is my son, Xane," Zaif explained. "Today we draw blood together for the first time. The gods will be pleased. You become a man."

"I'm already a man," the boy argued, frowning as his father laughed and ran a playful hand across his shaved head.

"So you keep saying!"

The boy continued to stare at Tavar until he felt compelled to say something.

"Can I help you with something?"

"You have their skin," Xane replied bluntly. "Same as the people who invaded."

"Can't deny that."

"So why are you standing against them?"

Tavar bit his lip, thinking about how to explain it. It must be strange for the boy to see someone who looked like the people who had caused so much harm to his companions stand against them and expect to be trusted.

"They may look like me. But I make my own decisions. I fight for the people I care for and people who need my help. No matter what colour skin someone has, or where they are from, they must be judged by their actions alone."

Zaif lowered his head next to his son and kept his eyes on Tavar. "This is the one who killed the Immortal. We can trust him."

Xane's eyes lit up at that and he offered a small bow, something which draw snorts of laughter from Halfor, Alice, and Medda.

"There's no need for that…" Tavar muttered, feeling his cheeks heating up.

"They're almost here," Alice said, eyes turning to the ships as they neared the coast. "Don't engage until they're past the line in the sand. They cross that, and we unleash hell."

"Unleashing hell in a place like heaven," Tavar smirked. "Gotta be something poetic about that."

"Where's Marcus?" Alice asked, cursing as she looked around for the man. "Qassim!" she turned on the frightened Alfaran. "I told you to keep an eye on him. Bastard is probably drinking that bar dry."

"Sorry, boss," Qassim said, looking ashamed. "He must have slipped away. I could go and get him?"

"Too late now. Weapons ready."

The Alfaran warriors marched down the docks in two separate units. Spearheading each unit was a soldier holding a long pole, waving the flag of Alfara in front of the crimson uniformed men and women who marched together onto the beach, only stopping as their boots left the wooden slats of the docks and met the sand.

A single soldier stepped out from the unit to Tavar's right, silver helmet obscuring most of his face. He planted his spear in the sand and took the helmet off, holding it in the crook of his right arm and using his free left hand to wipe the sweat from his face. The beard was greying and his black hair was thinning slightly more than Tavar remembered but his face was almost unchanged other than that.

"It's good to see you, old friend," he called out to Tavar. "Last I heard, you had fled to the Okadan Empire. It would have been best if you had stayed there."

"And you *Commander* Adnan," Tavar called back, noticing the blue sash that ran across the soldier's tunic. "It would be best for everyone involved if you got back on that ship and sailed for home."

"If only I could. I have orders. And soldiers follow orders."

"Even if they don't agree with them?"

"Especially then. It is not my role to question my betters. I have been tasked with coming here to arrest those who aided in your escape. They will join the other foolish prisoners who helped you in Kessarine where they will be questioned and judged."

"Hung on the wall, more likely."

Adnan shrugged as if such a matter was inconsequential to him. "If the Gods decide."

"If Uhlad decides," Tavar spat back bitterly.

"Yes." Adnan's face tightened. "If *King* Uhlad decides. There doesn't need to be bloodshed today. I wasn't ordered to bring you back. It could slip my mind, if those who helped you come quietly."

"Not happening. Once this blade is drawn, there's blood, Adnan." Tavar unsheathed the blade and held it high to roars from the Arrow Islanders. Halfor licked his lips and nudged himself ahead of the others, eager to quench his warhammer's thirst for blood.

Adnan sighed and placed the helmet back on his head and picked his spear from out of the sand. "So be it, old friend. You saved my life once. This saddens me more than you can imagine."

A horn blasted loud and clear. Then they attacked.

CHAPTER THIRTY-ONE: BLOOD ON THE SAND

Tavar screamed for the islanders not to lose their heads but some still rushed ahead, letting the nerves and excitement of the battle get the better of them. He cursed under his breath as the swarm of Alfaran soldiers professionally eliminated those strays, picking them off with ease. They couldn't afford to lose too many, otherwise it would be a slaughter. He glanced at Alice, acutely aware of the difficulties of their situation. She sighed and swore.

"Fuck it," she muttered and slammed her dagger arm against the shield held in her hand.

Halfor and Zaif rushed first, darting away like arrows that had been pulled too far. The rest followed, not wanting to be left alone at the back. Gaps opened in the immaculate frontline of the Alfaran soldiers and Tavar took full advantage. His kyushira sliced through the thin armour like cutting fruit. He ignored the blood splattered across his face and spun to block an attack before twisting his blade, stabbing his enemy in the gut and releasing it with ease, spinning his body back around and finishing off the first soldier with a clean slice across his neck. The joy of the blade washed over him as it tasted blood for the first time, quenching its thirst and dripping with red as he turned towards his next victim.

The islanders were fighting valiantly, throwing themselves furiously into the battle and taking down as many soldiers as they could. Halfor and Zaif were clearing paths through the enemy lines, swinging their weapons with relentless fury and roaring battle cries whilst drenched in blood mostly not their own. Alice blocked a strike aimed at Xane and pierced the back of the attacker with her dagger before pushing the boy out of the way of another attack.

"Zaif! Come and get your fucking kid!" she cried to the bloodthirsty warrior.

Distracted, Tavar twisted and raised his weapon too late as a sword sliced towards him. The blade clanged against steel and allowed Tavar the chance to poke his blade into his attacker's chest. He looked to his right, grateful for the interception.

"We're almost even now," Qassim said with a laugh. "I still owe you one, though." He bounded across the sand, throwing himself in amongst the chaos of the battle.

Deafening blood pounded in Tavar's ears and he scrambled back into the disorder and violence. He ducked a thrust spear heading his way smashed the hilt of his blade into the attacker's face. He winced as Medda stepped in, moving with the grace of a dancer and the fury of a demon. Her spear spiked up through the man's chin with enough force to pierce his skull and send his helmet spinning away. She kicked at the soldier and pulled her weapon away with a disgusting squelch, not even bothering to catch Tavar's eye as she darted across the sands.

Halfor and Zaif continued their path of destruction, fighting with the relish of beasts smelling blood. Alfaran soldiers dropped back, retreating to stay out of the way of the two blood-soaked warriors.

Alice screeched with pain as a spear ripped past

her face, catching her cheek and sending her black hat flying onto the sand. She pushed forward fuelled by fear and anger, knocking the spear aside and jabbing forward with her dagger and sword, forcing her opposite onto his back foot. He slipped as his boot drifted into the sand and she took full advantage, leaping forward and cutting through his armour with a great cry, straight through his chest.

The fear and confusion on the Alfaran soldiers' faces proved that they hadn't been expecting such a battle on the calm Arrow Islands. They had come to collect the guilty and nothing more. Instead they were fighting for their lives and being forced back onto the wooden docks. A few broke ranks, dropping their weapons and rushing towards their ship.

Across the chaos of soldiers and steel, Tavar's eyes found Adnan just as the soldier pulled his blade free from a fallen islander. Through a great tangle of spears, shields and swords, a parting opened upon, as though the gods themselves had decided what must be done. Adnan gazed up through the gap and frowned. Tavar felt a familiar sinking feeling in the pit of his stomach and walked forward as Adnan echoed his movement. An Alfaran flag lay in the sand, half of it had been stomped beneath the sand in the madness of the fighting so Tavar stepped over it with ease. Adnan looked down at the flag and then back up at him.

"It's a crime to desecrate the flag of Alfara," he said to Tavar wistfully, holding his sword loosely at his side as the battle raged on around him.

"You can add that to my list, if it makes you feel better," Tavar replied as a woman in a ripped dress rushed at Adnan, machete in hand. The soldier diverted the blow and brought his knee up, allowing her momentum to take her to the ground. He slashed across the woman's fallen body nonchalantly and continued his march to Tavar.

"I might let you off with that one. It pains me to do this. You saved me once. I wish that I could have returned the favour."

"You still can," Tavar pleaded. "Take your men and return to Alfara. I will be there in half a moon. You have my word. There has been enough bloodshed."

Adnan's face dropped, looking genuinely saddened by the words. "If only I could accept such a proposition. My men will only retreat upon my death," he spat on the sand and glanced back at some of those who had fled to the ship. "Apart from those cowards. They will be dealt with."

"I don't want to fight you."

"Nor I, you. But this is the path God has chosen, cruel though it may be. Die well, Tavar Farwan." Adnan tapped his chest and smiled weakly as the gesture was reciprocated.

Tavar dodged the first two attacks, dropping a shoulder and falling back out the way of the sword as it whipped across his chest. Adnan was already on him again, using his experience to keep the upper footing and keep Tavar stepping back in the sand. The quick strikes flashed dangerously close but the kyushira rose to meet each one with speed that even frightened Tavar. He grinned at the look of incredulity on Adnan's face.

"A fine blade," the soldier said through heavy breaths.

"The last Al-Taabi," Tavar answered, enjoying the widening of his opponent's eyes.

This time, he attacked first.

The kyushira danced through the air nimbly. Three attacks were blocked: high, high, low as he sensed the blade guiding him to its preferred destination. He pushed his weapon forward, forcing his face to within inches of Adnan's. They glared at each other, straining with the effort as the kyushira pressed Adnan's weapon against his own cheek, drawing a slither of blood. A stamp on his foot snapped Tavar from his focus, and the hilt of a blade smashed into his nose. He ignored the crunch and black spots floating in front of him and whipped his sword up, glancing an attack to the side as he stumbled back.

An unfamiliar figure jumped in between the two of them, sword guiding its way towards Adnan. The experienced soldier diverted the attack and with unnerving speed, slipped his blade through the defence and straight through the figure's stomach. Tavar shook his head and breathed, watching as the figure fell to its knees, Adnan's sword still stuck in his belly. Tavar seized the opportunity and flashed forward, slicing down on Adnan's hands, severing his body from them as they continued their grip on the hilt of the blade.

Adnan's eyes widened in horror as he stared at the blood pumping out from the stumps where his hands had once been. His mouth moved but no sound would come. But it was another who screamed through the fighting.

Zaif smashed through the soldiers, clearing them out of his way with great hits of his huge shoulders. He stopped as he reached Tavar, eyes focused on the kneeling figure. He dropped next to him, holding his face in his hands.

"Xane. My son…" Tears ran silently down the warrior's blood-stained face as he stared into the open eyes of his only son.

"Baba..." his son said, looking down with confusion at the sword still piercing him. Then his eyes flickered and finally closed. Tavar thought how much he looked like a child now and not the young man he had met earlier.

Zaif caught his son's body as it fell back. He guided his son gently onto the sand, his chest rising and falling with increasing speed. He kissed him softly on the forehead and stood, sword in hand. Turning on a defenceless Adnan with a cold fury, he placed one hand on the Alfaran's head and slowly pushed his sword through the man's right eye, ignoring the screams of anguish and agony. He didn't stop until the blade popped out the other end of the soldier's skull, taking with it the blood and pieces of brain it collected on the way.

Frightened soldiers dropped their weapons and fled to their ships losing their will to fight after watching the torture of their commander. The islanders didn't chase. They were too exhausted, happy to finally rest and stop the bloodshed.

Tavar looked around at the many bodies lying scattered on the beach: the damage of the short skirmish, and he wondered what it would be like when they attack Alfara. How many more people will die before Uhlad's tyranny was at an end? Barely thirty men and women still stood, bloody and battered but still alive. Zaif knelt beside his son's motionless body, running a slow hand over his head and leaning down to breathe in his smell.

"Zaif," Tavar said, walking over to him and placing a gentle hand on his shoulder. "He fought well. I'm so sorry."

"This is my fault," Zaif replied, his voice barely

audible, even with the shocked silence of the beach. "It was too soon, and he was not ready."

"It was a battle. Even the most experienced of men fall in battle." Tavar pointed his bloody sword at Adnan's corpse. "Look at him. Your son fought with heart and that's all we can ask for." It wasn't enough and Tavar knew it. Just words he had once heard to calm the grief of loved ones. Battles were random and there was no certainty that anyone would make it out alive. A mix of skill and luck, and things weighed heavily in favour of those with the latter. That was the way of war.

"Yeah." Zaif sniffed and wiped the wetness from his face. "He fought with heart. He made me proud. Prouder than I have ever been. Prouder than I ever made him…"

Tavar made to walk away, searching for his friends among the shocked warriors stumbling back to their family and loved ones. Halfor was checking a wound on Medda's shoulder that looked like it would need cleaning up before they departed. Zaif looked up and caught his eye. "You're going to Alfara, aren't you?"

Tavar nodded. It would all end where it had started, for good or ill. "We're raising an army across the Undying Sands."

"I'm coming with you. They'll pay for doing this." Zaif stroked his son's peaceful face. "It's what he would have wanted."

Tavar was too tired and drained to think about that. Was it really what he would have wanted? He thought that the fallen would do anything to end the fighting and bloodshed, they were the ones who had suffered the worst of it after all. The last thing they would want would be more death. But Tavar wasn't a father, and he could not deny the thirst for vengeance burning behind Zaif's eyes like the fires of the hells themselves.

Without a sound, the people of the Arrow Islands came out of hiding and marched to the beach, backs straight and chest out. They hid their pain and instead chose to be proud of what they had achieved. They had fought back and defended their island. Those alive and well began to take care of the bodies, covering them in shawls to give them dignity in death. The injured were helped to their feet or carried away into the trees, most likely heading for the hospital where they could be checked over properly. The number of dead would undoubtedly rise before darkness came.

"We lost a lot of good people today," Cassie said, clutching Tavar's hand walking in front of him to block his path. "You can put that away now."

He looked down at his still dripping kyushira. The blade's thirst had been quenched, for now. He blinked a few times before releasing Cassie's hand and sheathed the blade. "I'm sorry we brought this to your island, to your home."

"No apology necessary. It's not the first time foreigners have fought on our land and it won't be the last. You were just an excuse for them. They'll find another before long. That's their way."

Cassie skipped across the sand as she saw Alice heading towards them, her face splattered with blood. Some of her own and some not.

"You look a mess," Cassie said, hugging her tightly before inspecting the cut across her cheek.

"And you look as beautiful as always," Alice answered, stroking a thumb across Cassie's dark skin and staring into her eyes. "Come with us.

"What?" Cassie asked, confused.

"One more fight. Stand up against Alfara and then that's it. We can make a home here. No more fighting."

"You're serious, aren't you?"

Alice nodded. "I'm tired, Cass. No promises that I'll make it out alive but no matter how it ends, that's it. No more blood. No more death. Just you and me, together as it should have always been."

Cassie planted her lips against Alice, falling into her embrace and ignoring the blood and sweat. "One more fight."

"One more fight."

"You have a plan?"

Alice smiled and looked over her shoulder at Tavar. Cassie followed her eyes.

Tavar rolled his tongue around the inside of his mouth and rubbed his hands together. "I'll tell you on the way."

CHAPTER THIRTY-TWO: GHOSTS OF THE PAST

Wind whipped a cloud of sand around them, dense enough to block their vision. Traversing the Undying Sands with clear sight was difficult at the best of times but with this added obstruction, Tavar wondered how in the hells Medda was able to find her way as she took point, trudging across the dunes with frightening determination.

All four of them wore scarves on their faces to protect from the dancing sand but it still managed to get into their eyes. Tavar peered through the pain, glad that he could still make out the figures of Halfor and Alice as they kept pace with Medda. She had insisted that only the four of them travel to her homeland. The Blood Nation was not used to guests and more than four would be considered an aggressive act. Tavar had reluctantly agreed, eventually caving in and telling Tajira and Qassim to take the others to the villages on the edge of Alfara. If they were going to get any help in Alfara, it would be from those who suffered on the edge of the nation, forgotten by the nobility of Kessarine.

At the very least, those innocent people needed to be warned that an army may be marching through their land soon. Too often it was the innocent who fared the worst in times of war.

Crossing the sands brought back memories of Tavar's last journey in these lands. Every step he took reminded him of riding next to Adam, laughing with

Adam and Bushy and catching Carver's eye. So much had happened since he last wandered through the desert. So much had been lost. He wondered if there was a point where he could have changed things. A point where if he had taken another option, lives would have been saved. Adam would have still been here. Carver wouldn't have betrayed him.

Wasted energy, Kenji used to call it. Fretting over the past to the detriment of the future is a fool's past time. Learn from the past to walk the right path in the future but do not worry for what has gone, only for what may be. He would have given almost anything to have the blind man's words of wisdom right now. But Tavar was still breathing, and he still had friends. Some were stuck in Alfara, needing his help and he wasn't going to distract himself with the past if it meant losing them. He tightened the strap on his pack and leaned into the wind, urging himself forward.

Tavar ignored the gritty dryness of his mouth, unsure how long he would need to make his water last him. His cracked lips were sore and dry and his legs were beginning to ache with the constant change of incline over the dunes. He remembered why he hated the desert. Just an endless dry landscape of sand and not much else.

Medda grimly dragged them onwards. The orange sun dipped below the horizon just as the wind died down, casting a pink glow over the sky. Now he remembered why he also loved the desert. Such sights could warm even the coldest of hearts.

"We should set a camp here," Medda informed them, taking off her bag and throwing it on the sand. "There's enough cover with the dunes so that we can start a fire. I'll hunt for some food." She accepted the bow and arrow Alice handed her and trudged away.

Halfor made to follow.

"No," she said to the big man. "Stay here, keep warm. I won't be long."

Halfor frowned but nodded, understanding. She gave him a soft smile and he kissed the top of her head before she ran off across the starlit desert. A half-moon watched her journey as Tavar dropped his bag next to Medda's and fell beside it.

"She'll be okay," he said.

Halfor grunted and growled under his breath, unused to not being useful. He was a warrior of action. Sitting around and waiting wasn't in his blood.

"Hope we're not too far away," Alice said, holding her waterskin up and tilting the remains into her mouth. "I don't fancy dying of dehydration out here."

"Here, have some of mine." Tavar offered his own which she begrudgingly accepted. "Medda will make sure we're okay. These are her lands."

He pulled the wood from out of a bag and began to pile the small logs together as Halfor grabbed the stones and started making a boundary for the fire. They were lucky that the wind had died down. After a few tries, they had a roaring fire to keep them warm in the cool night of the desert.

Tavar lay back and stared at the stars. A few birds glided with ease, blocking out some of the light as they made their own journey across the unforgiving land. His eyes grew heavy as he leaned back against his spare clothes, his body craving rest after the harsh march. Halfor's low snores brought a smile to his face and he heard a small chuckle from across the fire.

"Nowhere near as bad as Adam, is he?" Alice

said, making Tavar sit up. She was stabbing at the sand with the dagger at the end of her arm, unable to rest.

"If he was here, enemies would have been able to hear us all the way in Yorkland," Tavar agreed, enjoying the sad smile curling at Alice's lips.

"Do you still think of Vandir?"

"Every single day. There's always some little thing that reminds me of him. Halfor might do something stupid and I'll think that I need to tell Vandir as he would love it, then I remember he's not there and my throat closes up and it's like losing him again."

"Yeah. I hear Adam's stupid little quips whenever someone says something that annoys me and it makes me laugh when I really shouldn't," Alice agreed, sniffing and laughing at the same time. "He always knew how to make me laugh. I'd give my other hand to have him back."

"It hurts to think that Vandir gave his life to help me escape. I feel like it's a debt I can never pay back. He's gone and there's nothing I can do about it," Tavar admitted, telling her what had been gnawing at him ever since he had escaped Kessarine.

"He was your big brother," Alice explained. "That's what big brothers do. There's no debt to be paid. You just have to continue living. That's all you can do."

Tavar lost himself in the dance of the flames, following the rhythmic flickering and swallowing the growing lump in his throat. "We're doing the right thing, aren't we? Going back to Alfara, fighting?"

"Honestly?" Alice blew out her cheeks and leaned closer to the flames. "I have no fucking idea. Cassie used to say that fighting should only be a very last resort. After all we've been through, I feel like this is what we need to do. Marek and Hashem helped you out, you wouldn't be able to live with yourself if you didn't do the same."

"Yeah..."

"Since Adam died, it's felt like something is missing. Like a part of me is just gone forever. Maybe helping others out will fill that gap. If nothing else, it's what Adam and Vandir would have done. They threw themselves into flames and fights without thinking of themselves. If we want to pay them back, we need to do this." Alice's voice grew more determined as she spoke, convincing herself of what must be done.

"One last fight," Tavar said.

"One last fight."

"A fight with whom?"

Tavar snapped up at the unfamiliar voice, his hand reaching for the kyushira at his side.

"No need for that..." the voice said. Tavar looked up to see that they were surrounded by ten warriors, all with arrows nocked and aiming at them.

Halfor had sat up and was staring angrily at the closest one, as though daring them to shoot him. Alice had managed to stand and was pointing her dagger at a fearsome looking warrior almost as tall as Halfor. All ten of them had the same reddish-brown skin as Medda. Dark, alert eyes stared out from faces painted with red lines smeared in various symbols. Some of them wore scarlet headbands that held back their long-flowing jet-black hair from their faces. Both the men and women wore beige trousers that flared out at the bottom but not much else. Some of the women wore brown tunics decorated with a collection of feathers that was cut off just beneath their breasts, though a couple unashamedly kept the top half of their body free from clothes.

One of the warriors stepped into the light of the fire, giving Tavar a better look at him. Around his eyes was a black paint that spiked down in pairs from each eye and dropped to his thick, closed lips. His headband was black with golden zig zags running across it. The way he walked instantly let Tavar know that this man was in control.

"What are you doing in our lands?" He spoke the common tongue well with barely a trace of an accent. He sounded almost exactly like Medda, but deeper and more menacing.

"We seek help," Tavar answered, thinking it best to keep his responses short and concise.

"The Blood Nation do not help those who never helped us. Give me a reason to kill you quickly. Or we will have fun and ensure a slow and entertaining death…" His fellow warriors sniggered at their leader's words, pulling their arrows tighter against the bowstrings.

"Because they are with me." Medda stepped into the light, spear aimed at the leader.

A collective gasp sounded from the circle as they all stared at her. Two plucked birds hung loosely at her left hip. Even in that moment, Tavar's stomach growled with hunger.

The leader hid his shock and lowered his eyebrows, allowing the hint of a smile to reach his face. "It's been a long time," he said, scanning Medda and stepping forward, ignoring the deadly spear aimed at his chest. He allowed it to press against him before he stopped and smirked at the deadly weapon pressing against his skin. Medda didn't move an inch. "How are you, sister?"

"It's good to see you, brother."

CHAPTER THIRTY-THREE: BLOOD PACT

The sand dunes gave way to red rock and small green shrubs that had been capable of adapting to survive in the extraordinary heat. Dried up rivers had carved a meandering path through the landscape, creating great canyons and ravines. There was enough green for animals to live close by: wild dogs eyed the group eagerly but kept their distance, birds of prey flew overhead, waiting for the expectant scraps of food that they thought would come their way.

The blood warriors stayed silent for most of the journey, offering Tavar and the others water and food without a word, which they accepted gratefully. They guided them through across the rocky land and away from the sands, weapons always at hand, a continued threat but nothing made Tavar feel that he was in any danger.

Medda marched ahead, conversing with her brother in their native tongue, arguing at times as her arms flailed wildly whilst her brother scowled at her. Halfor watched the whole scene play out with a grim scowl of his own. The big man was soaked in sweat and struggling without the large amount of food his huge frame was used to. Alice found things easier. Two of the warriors had taken a liking to her, inspecting her metal hand with interest and holding their red-brown skin against her pale but slightly pinking skin. They laughed at the comparison and smiled at her but not in mockery. Being with Medda had relaxed most of the group, even if they weren't too fond of speaking to them.

A rocky archway curved overhead from each cliff on either side of them as they strolled down the natural pathway. Tavar held his hand over his eyes as he strained to look up as dark figures crept out of hidden caves behind the rock. They stalked across the archway, eyes intent on the group and large, white bows in hand. More blood warriors. Guards watching over their land for intruders.

"Friends of yours?" Tavar shouted to Medda. She turned back and followed the incline of his head.

"Different tribe but we are all one people. They won't attack if you don't give them a reason to," she answered. "We're close."

Further through the canyon, the stone either side changed from the natural effects of an ancient river to decorations of people. This rock had been carved by hand, displaying perfectly crafted columns and house designs that surrounded cave entrances that led into the rock. Curious men, women and children peeped out of these caves, observing and pointing as the group passed. Excited mutterings and waves broke out as more left their enclosures. Some children ran ahead, eager to spread the news that visitors had arrived.

The carvings grew more elaborate as they progressed; great statues of warriors holding spears and shields loomed high overhead and looked down upon them, judging them. Tavar studied the variety of animals that had been created in the red rock, immaculate constructions of eagles, falcons, wolves and snakes. They must have taken lifetimes to complete with such perfection. Some stood an intimidatingly five hundred paces high or more, he guessed. How they had managed such amazing work out here, he could only imagine.

As they reached a peak in the canyon, Tavar

gasped. He looked down the valley and scanned the city opened out in front of him. At the edge of the horizon, a river lazily meandered out towards the glistening sea. The red rock lessened, turning to greenery around which there were a myriad of tents and houses of wattle and stone. Thousands of houses were dotted in the valley, all lined towards a large pyramid structure in the middle made of red stone that rose from four corners leading up to a single point on which stood a large pole with a carved symbol of a wolf baring its teeth. Smoke drifted up from some of the houses and dissipated amongst the thin white clouds failing to block the searing heat of the sun. Tavar felt beads of sweat at the base of his beard begin to pool and drip down his neck. Shade, food and a cool bath would be worth the world to him right now.

"Welcome to the city of Nhizoni," Medda's brother said, walking backwards so that he could face them all. He opened his arms up and smiled, displaying rows of white teeth. "Home of the Blood Nation."

Tavar marvelled at the size of the tent he found himself in. The room was larger than that of Uhlad's back in the palace in Alfara. A circular hole had been dug in the corner of the tent and filled with water poured over hot stones. A simpler bath than he was used to but welcome, nonetheless. Halfor had already lowered himself into the water, his piercing blue eyes staring at the animal skins hanging from the rope that ran from one side of the room all the way to the other.

Tavar joined him, dropping his head beneath the water and rising out again, pushing his long hair back away from his face. It had grown past his shoulders now. Soon he would be challenging he Naviqing himself for the longest hair in the group.

"I need a shave and a cut," he said to the solemn warrior.

"Nah, suits you," Halfor complimented him. "There's a tale from my tribe of a warrior who grew stronger as the length of his hair increased. It is the sign of health and strength for a Naviqing."

"It is the sign of laziness and filth in most of Alfara," Tavar retorted. "No idea what my people would have thought. My father always kept his short. Mother said it was practical."

Tavar cupped his hands and splashed more water against his face, attempting to rid himself of the sand and grit that covered his face. It would take more than one bath to get rid of the uncomfortable feeling of dirt and filth he had claimed crossing the Undying Sands.

"Where's Alice?"

"Medda took her somewhere to clean. Men and women aren't allowed to clean together apparently. We can join her for a meal tonight, though." Tavar sat back against the rim of the bath and frowned at the sad look on his friend's face. "What's troubling you, Halfor?"

"I've known her for years. She'd never wanted to speak about her homeland and I was fine with that, we all have a past that we don't want to remember. But you saw the way they looked at her. She's no civilian. She and her brother were looked at with respect by the others. I just wish she had trusted with me enough to talk to me."

"She'll have her reasons," Tavar said, attempting to cheer him up. "We don't know the whole story."

"We don't know any of the story!" Halfor moaned, splashing a fist against the water and cursing. "If she was so embarrassed or even scared of coming back here, then surely we should know why, at least before we came here and walked right into the jaws of the city."

"Too late for that, now," Tavar admitted. "We need to trust her."

Halfor growled and dropped beneath the water. When he broke the surface, he breathed out and roared. "I feel better," he said with a grin. "Reckon they have any drink around here?"

"I'd be upset if they didn't," Tavar said, glad that it was so easy for his friend to avoid black clouds that passed over him.

"Then let's get some clothes on and grab Alice. Time to make some new friends."

They waited outside a small red stone house as children ran by, heads twisted towards them no matter where they were. The children giggled and screamed as they neared Halfor and he roared through a big smile, prompting squeals of delight from the kids as they stumbled away. They had tried to enter the building, only to be shooed away by a group of older, stout women shielding Alice. The women barked at them through frowns in their own harsh but melodic language. Tavar didn't understand a word they were saying but he got their meaning. The pushing and screeching definitely got their message across.

"Hope you haven't been waiting too long," Alice said as she sauntered out of the building. A patterned beige dress fell low from her right shoulder and down to just above her knees. Her left shoulder was exposed to the sunlight and a necklace of coloured shells and bone hung low down to her collarbone. For once, she had decided against a hat and wore her hair to the side, letting it flow down to just above her hip. She looked stunning. "Don't fucking laugh," she warned the two of them, spotting the shocked expressions on their faces.

"You look amazing," Tavar said, holding back a laugh as he saw her cheeks blush. "Seriously. It suits you."

"Fuck you."

"He's right," Halfor agreed, calming her down. "This is no joke. You would turn heads if you were to walk into any city on this continent."

She arched an eyebrow but let whatever snarky comment she had prepared go. "You seen Medda?"

"Nah. Still with the chief. We thought we'd have a look around the city while we can. It's not every day you get welcomed into a secret nation." Tavar looked down the pathway and smiled at the three warriors glaring at them, spears in hand and stormy looks on their faces. "Though welcomed might not have been the best choice of words. Seems like a few of the locals aren't too keen on us being here."

"They've not had outsiders in a long time, if ever. We're the shiny new playthings to them," Alice said, waving at the children still running back and forth and squealing anytime Halfor looked at them. "To others, we're a threat that must be watched at all times. Can't blame them, really. The only time they've had any interaction with outsiders is when they're killing each other. I wouldn't trust us either."

They strolled between the tents and stone houses, ambling over to the river. A few of the children followed them, at a distance, still grinning sheepishly whenever the

Naviqing turned a sparkling eye their way.

"You're good with the kids," Alice commented. "Thinking about settling down here once the battle is over?"

"The world is too big and I have too much life to live before Halfor the Mighty thinks about such things!" Halfor bellowed, his big frame shaking with good humour. "There are still places I must see and foes to defeat. What about you? Your skin tells me that your blood will call you north before long."

"Grandparents were a mix of Albion, Yorkland and Naviqand. I'll head north one day," she answered as she faced up to the sky and closed her eyes. "Too much of a sun-worshipper to go anytime soon. The ice and snow don't appeal much to me."

"The ice and snow reveal who you really are!" Halfor argued, sweat beading on the tips of the hairs of his beard. "If you think the Undying Sands were unforgiving, you should spend time crossing the White Wastelands. Facing the snow bears and running with the wolves. It's a whole new world."

The river was wide and calm. Women swam and cleansed themselves in the water as buffalo drank on the opposite side, at ease with the laughter and frolicking. Animal skins had been lain out across the grassy patches of land near the river and men and women sat eating whilst their children ran carefree around them.

"They seem happy here," Tavar said. "Reckon we'll be able to convince them to fight?" Putting himself in their boots, he didn't know if he'd be convinced. The warm smiles and jovial attitudes of the people proved how comfortable and relaxed these people were here across the canyons. Pulling them away to fight for his cause would be difficult.

"They have their reasons. Generations of hatred can't be washed away with distance and smiles," Alice argued, finding a patch on the ground suitable to sit on. "Alfara has a funny way of attacking those who find comfort. These people know that they are on borrowed time out here. They can't isolate themselves from the world forever."

Tavar and Halfor joined her on the ground. A woman watched them from the banks of the river, frowning. Tavar noted her talking hurriedly to her friends before picking something from the ground and running towards them.

"For you," the woman said, thrusting a large animal skin their way and pointing at the grassy ground.

"It's fine," Tavar said, shaking his head but smiling wide. "Thank you."

The woman scowled and thrust more urgently until Tavar reluctantly took it in his own hands. "Please," she said. "Take." She gave an awkward bow and smiled as Tavar tapped his chest and nodded to her.

"Thank you," he said again before she ran off back to her giggling friends by the river. He threw the skin down and they each sat upon it.

"Our friends are following us," Halfor said, rolling saliva around his mouth and growling low at the back of his throat. The three warriors from the street had followed them to the river and were standing a short distance away, eyes fixed upon them behind the dark paint on their faces.

Tavar stood with a sigh, deciding to put the warriors at ease. He strolled over easily, hoping that a warm smile would show them that he meant no harm.

They tensed as he approached, twisting calloused fingers round the dark wood of their spears. He pressed his hand to his chest and spoke. "My name is Tavar. My friends and I are here seeking help. There is no need for worry or anger. No need for violence. We are not a threat to your people." They looked at him as though he had just told them his plans were to fuck their mothers and beat their sisters. He scratched his head and failed to keep the smile on his own face. "Is there anything we can do to put you at ease? We mean no harm," he insisted.

The man in the middle, taller than Tavar but shorter than Halfor, passed his spear to one of his two friends and stepped closer to Tavar until their chests were nearly touching.

Tavar looked up at him square in his dark eyes, not moving an inch. He knew when to stand his ground and when to back down. He'd faced up to people like this in the arena dungeons and he wasn't going to back away now. The blood warrior had black paint horizontally running across his eyes and all the way to his ears. His head was shaved but for a thin strip in the middle that had been coloured red as blood, just like the paint that looked like crimson tears running from his eyes and down his cheeks. He looked a bit older than Tavar but his skin had been tested and damaged by exposure to the heat of the desert sun.

"You should leave," he said to Tavar, breath smelling like an animal had crawled into his mouth and died before anyone could save it. That, more than anything made Tavar want to put more distance between them but he held strong, ignoring the stench and the look of hatred in the man's dark eyes. "Our people have had enough of your kind entering our home without permission." He lowered his forehead to Tavar's and pushed him back a step. "Too long have you treated my people with disdain and contempt. Leave."

"My people are a travelling people. Alfara has done as much damage to me as they have to you," Tavar answered. "If not more…"

The warrior held his hand out and his ally threw him the spear which he caught without a look. Tavar leapt back and drew his sword without thinking. The blade sliced through the wood of the spear, taking the steel point from it as though he had been slicing fruit.

"Stop!" All eyes turned to a blood warrior pacing towards them, fury and frustration covering his dark features and wearing a familiar black headband with golden zigzags. Medda's brother.

The foul breathed warrior instantly dropped what was now just a stick and lowered his gaze to the floor as his comrade strode his way. Tavar made to sheathe his blade but felt a force fighting against him, whispers demanding blood. Sweat dripped from his head as he fought to encase the deadly kyushira as he remembered Keito's warning. The blade needed to be bloodied.

"Apologies Sachem Red Mist." The warrior's cheeks reddened as Medda's brother approached.

"Drawing a weapon on guests is not allowed in this city, Neolan," Red Mist reminded him, his eyes darting to the still drawn blade in Tavar's hand.

"It needs to be bloodied," he explained to the Blood Sachem.

Without missing a beat, Red Mist, grabbed a hold of Neolan's hand and pressed it against the blade, pressing hard and ignoring the man's wince as it cut easily into his palm. He released him and inspected the wound as the blood seeped over his hand, darkening in the lines in his palm and dripping onto the ground. Tavar checked the blade and nodded at the stain of blood before finally sheathing the weapon, satisfied.

Neolan wiped his hand against his bare chest, smearing the blood over his dark skin before standing tall to face his leader.

"As Sachem, it is my role to make sure the people of Blood Nation abide by the Chief's rules. Continued abuse of the laws of our people lead to one destination, Neolan. What do you think that is?"

"Exile, dear Sachem."

"Exile," Red Mist agreed. "Now think on that as you take a walk. And take the branch with you," he added, looking with disgust at the broken spear.

Neolan nodded and motioned for his two friends to follow him as he skulked away from the riverside. Red Mist sighed and knelt, picking up the iron arrowhead that Tavar had cut from the spear.

"My role would be much easier if you didn't get into any altercations in this city during your stay."

"Believe me, a fight wasn't what was intended." Tavar raised his palms to protest his innocence. "However, I will always defend myself." He glanced over his shoulder at the sound of laughter as Halfor and Alice strolled over to them. "Thanks for the back up," he said sarcastically.

"You had it covered," Halfor smirked. "It'll take more than an angry man with a stick to kill you."

"Hmm…" Tavar grumbled, before letting his smile break through.

"My sister has spoken with our Chief. They both wish for the three of you to join us in the Temple of

Spirits. They will discuss your request in front of the elders of our nation."

The Temple of Spirits was unlike anything Tavar had seen in his life. The great stone pyramid in the centre of the city had one opening at its base that led into a welcoming room. Men and women wearing nothing but colourful paint on their bodies and large, wooden masks with painted animals of all kinds upon them greeted them as they entered. In their hands, they swung an iron ball dangling from a long chain that wrapped around their wrist. From the ball emanated a sweet-smelling scent that followed a smoke drifting the ball's path and rising up and out of the pyramid through small holes in the structure's ceiling. The scent hung in the air around them as they walked on through the room, vision blurred slightly by the leftover smoke.

Halfor coughed, drawing a wry grin from Red Mist. "The scent prevents any bad spirits from entering the temple and desecrating our most holy of places. This is the most sacred place in the whole of the Blood Nation, designed so that we can speak to our ancestors when guidance is needed. This is the heart of our people."

The next room was larger but there was no smoke or naked tribespeople to distract them. The room was bare but for a circle of wooden carvings taller than Halfor that stood in the middle of the room. Each carving depicted what looked like warriors from the tribe. They held different weapons in their hands: bows, spears, swords and one even held a roped blade similar to the one Tavar had fought against in the arena. On top of each of the warrior's heads were different wooden animals: bears, eagles, hares, and buffalo. As he passed them, he marvelled at the precision of the carvings and the way their eyes seemed to follow him, no matter where he stood.

"The twelve Great Ancestors of our nation. Chiefs who fought valiantly for the tribes who then became part of the Blood Nation. It is to these spirits who the Elders confer with when guidance is needed. These men and women are respected above all amongst our people," Red Mist explained.

Seemed like the air in the room was thicker than others. Tavar's breathing slowed as he walked past the carvings, his lungs working harder for the air they craved. Maybe it was the spirits surrounding them, he thought, hiding his amusement from the warrior.

"Have you ever spoken to these… spirits?" Alice asked, eyeing the wooden statues with distrust.

"Only the Elders speak to them. I've listened to other spirits, though it is a difficult process."

"My people claim to speak to spirits, though it is often only after they had drunk the equivalent of a lake of ale…" Halfor threw in with a chuckle, not noticing the offended look on their guide's face.

Red Mist stopped as he reached a closed wooden door at the end of the room, the first they had encountered in the Temple. He gave the three of them a stern look as they caught up. "In the next room are the Elders and our Chief. I will warn you that they are not overly fond of outsiders. Treat the room and them with respect or you will be asked to leave."

He opened the door with care and stepped aside, allowing them to enter ahead of him.

The room differed from the others in that silken sheets dyed a variety of colours had been tied around the walls and pulled in to create a circular space in the centre of the room. The ceiling was much higher than the others. Tavar looked up and could barely see a hint of light at the top, peeking through one of the holes that allowed the smoke out from sweet smelling scent boxes that lay around the edge of the circle.

Four old women and two men sat at the edges of the circle, each next to one of the scent boxes. Their eyelids drooped low and heavy as they swayed back and forth and side to side as though in a trance. Grey hair and wrinkled skin informed Tavar that they were living out the last stages of their lives and they didn't seem to care too much for clothes; only wearing small patches of animal skin to hide their private areas. Two of the women wore small triangular coverings that draped over their shoulders and covered much of their torso though the other two seemed perfectly comfortable with displaying everything else. Their comfort shocked Tavar, so used to the Alfaran way of dignity and respect through covering one's skin. The Blood Nation had a different way of showing respect, he guessed. They had allowed him to carry a deadly weapon into their holiest of rooms so he certainly wasn't going to complain that they weren't covering their bodies in front of him.

In the centre of the room sat a woman younger than the Elders. Her dark eyes were alert and searching as she scanned Tavar before moving onto the others. She sat with her legs crossed, dyed red hair falling past her knees and a beautiful face painted with two thin lines of black that curved up from the edges of her lips, making it seem as though she was always smiling. She wore a great jacket that covered her shoulders and kept her torso from view. The jacket was from animal hide, by Tavar's guess, though it had been painted and dyed to show small images of what looked like a battle, with warriors throwing spears and others who held raised shields and wore silver helms. Next to her sat Medda. She didn't smile as their eyes met, if anything, her face dropped as the three of them stood before her, silently. Tavar's eyes darted from the woman in the centre to Medda and he felt his jaw slacken. The likeness was uncanny.

"My daughter tells me that you are trusted and hardened warriors," the woman said, playing with a long, thin pipe in her hand. Her voice was deeper than he expected and there was a weariness to it that wavered around the commanding aura of her words. This was a woman who was used to being in charge. "You request help with defeating our sworn enemies in Alfara yet offered nothing in return. What do you have to say?"

He felt Alice and Halfor's eyes burn into him from either side as they silently chose him as their speaker. He made a note to thank them for it later as he cleared his throat and ignored the watching eyes of the Elders as they continued to sway in amongst the haze and smoke.

"Alfara held us as prisoners for many years, treating us as something they owned and playing with our lives for the amusement of the people. We escaped but they have friends of ours and are threatening to kill them. We need help to take over the city and end the tyranny of King Uhlad," he said, finding himself walking in the space between himself and the chief as he pleaded with her for assistance. "A long time ago, I defended myself against a warrior of the Blood Nation. He died with honour and a smile on his face after warning me that his people would rise against Alfara. I'm asking you to help us achieve that, to bring truth to his final words."

The chief watched him carefully, holding her head up to get a better look at him as he spoke. "Generations ago, a ruthless King of Alfara burned down our towns, killed our men and took the women and children as slaves," she spoke with a cold detachment, as if she had spoken the words so many times that they no longer had a hold over her. "Bloodlines died and were lost forever, families torn apart and never allowed the comfort of a final word. Bodies were desecrated in ways that stopped the dead from taking the long walk to the Old Lady of our people, the one who will welcome us all with open arms when it is time. We have rebuilt our people, we have reclaimed land once lost to us, and we have restrained from vengeance in the belief that the lives of our people are more important than the deaths of our enemies. Now you come her and ask me to inform them that it is time, that we should fight and risk our lives to help you. Is that what you desire?"

"I…" He stopped and sighed, pushing his hair back and taking a moment to think before he answered the Chief. *Errors made in haste cannot be taken back with such speed.* That's what Kenji had once told him. "I just want to save the innocent people who helped me. I want to save my friends. I lost my parents. I lost my brother. I lost two of my best friends. I'm sick of losing those around me to the plague that is Alfara. For once, I want to save them, instead of watching them die."

The Chief rubbed at the paint on the edge of her lips, not even blinking as she judged his sincerity. "My daughter's words displayed how close you have all become. Protecting friends and loved ones is understandable. The Elders have decided that we will speak to our people. The Blood Nation does not decide for everyone. They must make their own decision regarding this matter." Tavar grinned as Halfor punched the air in victory and Alice allowed herself a smirk. "We shall speak to the Spirits and seek their support in the battle to come. My daughter has already agreed the price to be paid for our allowing you to enter our secretive city and assist you."

Tavar frowned. "What payment has been agreed?" he asked, a flicker of annoyance rising at the idea of being left out of such a crucial discussion. He looked at Medda and the annoyance left him at her slumped and defeated frame.

The Chief's smile widened, and her eyes flashed at the question, shooting to her daughter as she answered. "She has agreed to return after the battle and marry a tribesman of *my* choosing. Then she will take my place as Chief as I finally join the Elders."

Halfor's shoulders dropped and the blood drained from his face at the news. He stared at Medda but she kept her head bowed, unable to look him in the eye. The energy between them did not go unnoticed by the Chief whose smile only further increased. She sat there like a victorious chess master. She had moved her pieces into the positions she desired, now all she needed to do was watch as the events played themselves out to the very end.

Tavar frowned as all the fight drained from Halfor's form and he too dropped his head, staring at the floor in the hope that it would swallow him and take him away from such a feeling of loss. They had come here to gather an army. On that matter, they could see this as a win. But as they walked out of the Temple of Spirits and into the cool night air, Tavar had to wonder if they had lost something greater.

CHAPTER THIRTY-FOUR: ALL JUST SHADES OF GREY

"The Alfaran has been showing some of the villagers what to do should they get caught up in it," Tajira said, looking out from the balcony across the farmland. "They like him. Still keep a fair few paces away whenever I go down there but..." he shrugged.

"Do you blame them?" Tavar asked, genuinely curious for the answer.

"If anyone of them can press a hand to their chest and tell me that they've lived a guilt-free life then I'll jump from this balcony onto the nearest spear and end my existence. We have all done wrong in the time given to us."

Tavar opened his mouth but held back his tongue, struggling to find the right words for his counter argument. "You are covered in scars displaying all of the people you murdered in cold blood for an organisation called the Court of Shadows. Might be a bit different to little Tasneem once calling her mother a bitch."

Tajira turned his head and pushed his face close enough to Tavar for him to see the tiny pricks of hair growing on his cheeks following his last shave. For a moment, he wondered whether he should draw his kyushira, then the warrior's face cracked into a wide smile and he leant back, laughing up at the clouds above him. Tavar couldn't work out which unnerved him more, the stare or the laugh. Either way, he was happy to have kept his blade sheathed.

"I guess you're right," Tajira said, wiping away a tear as another chuckle broke free and faded into the night. "Suppose I am more of a bastard than they are."

They stood together, watching the rows of villagers twisting spears and copying Qassim's thrusts and turns. They were brave, standing up against the might of their king and his army. Most had run, seeking shelter in the towns and villages that would be farther from the fighting, heeding the warning that Marcus and Qassim had passed throughout the land. A wise decision, in Tavar's mind. They didn't want people caught up in the fighting who didn't want to be there. The loss of innocents was against everything they were fighting for.

"Why are you still here, Tajira?" he asked the shadow warrior. "You could have left after speaking to Keito. Yet, here you are, preparing to fight in a huge battle against an enemy who outnumber us and are better prepared."

"The Court has told me when to eat, when to fight, when to shit, when to breathe for my whole life. They sent me across the ocean to a land I'd never been to and they left me to rot in a cell with the scum of a foreign land to satisfy someone I was never able to meet. I think it's time to make my own decisions, the Court has left me alone so I must make decisions on my own. Fighting alongside warriors I respect seems like a good enough plan for the moment. It doesn't matter if I fight for Alfara or against them. People in every land are a mix of good and bad. No one is ever truly good or evil. They are a blend of their choices and actions and in the end, they all die the same way."

"Well," Tavar cautiously patted him on the

shoulder. "I'm happier with you on my side than against me. You're welcome with us for as long as it makes you happy. Anything you do will be your own decision. We won't make them for you."

Perhaps he was imagining it, but Tavar thought he saw a flicker of thanks in the killer's eyes. He left Tajira to his thoughts and headed down the steps leading out into the open farmland. A stray dog jumped back from him and trotted off into the growing darkness, looking back every now and again to see where Tavar had got to. He knelt and whistled, calling the dog back. After a moment of hesitation, the scruffy grey animal inched closer. Tavar pulled a scrap of pork out of his pocket. The dog sniffed it suspiciously before greedily taking it from Tavar's hand and munching on it whilst allowing a few strokes on his head and enjoying scratches beneath his chin.

He stood and ambled over to the tavern. Halfor would be in there, no doubt drowning his sorrows in the hope that another drink would help him forget his pining for Medda. The journey from Nhizoni had been tough. Chief Tamaya had provided horses for them to cross the desert and speed them on their way with the promise of an army to follow. Medda was to stay and help to convince as many of the warriors to join in the battle as possible. Halfor had said a tense goodbye to her and then barely spoken on the whole way across the Undying Sands. Alice had suggested that Tavar speak to him but in all honesty, he didn't know what to say to cheer up the Naviqing warrior. He'd entered the village and stormed straight to the tavern, emptying a barrel of ale before Tavar had even had the chance to settle the horses and catch up with Qassim and Lilian.

Medda had always been the one with the magic

touch, the one person capable of snapping him from his dark moods whenever they struck, which thankfully was rare. Without her, Tavar didn't know what to do to drag the warrior away from the storm cloud attached to him.

Outside of the tavern, a washed and clean soldier leant next to the frame of the door leading in. His beard had been clipped short and trim, still showing dashes of grey by his chin. Hair that had once been wild and unkempt was now cut short in the military style that reminded Tavar of a much younger man. Alert eyes warmed as Tavar walked towards him. The soldier placed the end of a long pipe between his lips and sucked in before letting out a long, sweet, scented cloud of smoke. Much better than the smell of stale alcohol and piss that Tavar had expected.

"Is there a curse on my brain or is this Commander Marcus I see before me?" Tavar winked at the soldier and shook his head with amazement at the transformation of the experienced man.

"Don't be stupid," Marcus scoffed. "We both know you don't have a brain. And I'm no commander."

"New robes?" Tavar observed, eyeing the forest-green tunic and black trousers.

"Lilian had them made for me," Marcus answered, peering down at the immaculate clothes and patting a hand on his stomach. "Even manged to mostly conceal the pregnant male look that I've acquired in the past few years. Impressive."

"You look well." Tavar stared at the ex-Alfaran soldier, dropping the humorous attitude and letting the man hear the honesty ring in his statement. It had been a long time since Tavar had seen Marcus look anything but a man on his way out of life, stumbling drunkenly on a path of self-destruction.

"We're fighting for a better Alfara. It's what Sett and I always wanted. Lilian reminded me of that." He took another blow of the pipe and pushed open the tavern door. "Though, it now appears we have another who has taken my place. And this one won't be as easy to drag out against his will…"

Tavar entered and found himself immediately drawn to a standoff between two men. One stood peering up at the other who was almost twice his size. He nervously rubbed his knuckles as he politely requested that the other man left the tavern.

"Leave! You want me to leave?" the larger man roared, scaring the men and women huddled on the other side of the room. "I am going into battle for the Alfaran people. I'm not from here. My people are in the far north of this continent. But I'm staying here and fighting for people who can't? And what will I get out of it?" He spread his arms out, spraying ale from the jug in his right hand and almost hitting the poor man brave enough to have requested that he leave. "Nothing…" Halfor leant towards the man so that their faces were almost touching. "She's marrying someone else and once all this is done, I'll crawl back to the hole I came from and be right back where I started. Halfor the Mighty, indeed," he said, slurring his speech. "More like Halfor the Foolish."

"I think it's best if you step outside, friend," Tavar insisted. "The fresh air will do you good."

Halfor turned and his eyes rolled into the back of his head as he stumbled. Tavar rushed forward and caught the big man, struggling to keep him on his feet. Marcus joined him, taking an arm and pulling it over his shoulder.

"Come on, Halfor. Let's grab some food and

enjoy the fresh air." Tavar thanked the barman and smiled an apology at the frightened patrons in the corner of the room as he pulled Halfor past them and out into the moonlight. Qassim had ended his evening's training and in the centre of the field, a large bonfire was burning. The smell of roasted meat and wafted through the air and perked Halfor up.

"She should be here," he muttered. "To drink and feast. She should be here," he repeated.

"I know," was all that Tavar could think of saying. Halfor pushed the two of them away and stood on his own, hands on his hips and breathing heavily. His pale skin was flushed and his long nose had turned purple with the amount of drink he had consumed. "She'll be here soon."

"But she won't, will she? Not *here*! Not like she should be," Halfor argued, pressed a hand against Tavar's shoulder before flinching away and growling to the sky. He picked a rock up from the ground and flung it into the distance with another roar. It sailed past the single acacia tree on the hill and was lost to the dark of the night. "She's not coming back."

"Halfor…" Tavar called as the Naviqing strode off after the rock.

"I need to be alone, Tavar."

He made to follow his friend but an arm cut across his path.

"Leave him," Marcus commanded. "Trust me. He needs to help himself out before you can help him. He knows where you are. Don't force it."

"He needs a friend, Marcus."

"I agree. And he has one. More than one, in fact.

But people aren't that simple and easy. Sometimes you just want to get pissed and storm off without anyone bothering you about it. Nothing wrong with that. He'll come back. Believe me, I should know, better than any."

Tavar pursed his lips and sighed, giving in.

Marcus had been correct in saying that Halfor needed time on his own. The Naviqing stayed away from everyone for three days, hunting alone, eating alone and heading into the village only to collect a barrel of ale before heading back out into the open fields. Tavar spent his free time meeting more of the villagers, chatting to them and getting to know them as well as he could. They had taken to bowing to him and whispering *Immortal Killer* or *Izad Slayer* whenever they greeted him. He'd tried asking them to stop but Lilian had told him to let it slide. They would fight and die for someone with his legend. To them, he wasn't just an ordinary man, he was something more. A symbol. Something worth dying for, as they knew that he would die for them.

Sleep evaded him as the old nightmares returned. Any rest he managed to get was short and brief and broken by screams and a cold sweat. The first few nights had been especially difficult, not exactly helped with his room placed next to Alice and Cassie's. Before he had taken to camping out in the field under the stars, his nights were full such passionate moans and groans that at one point he wondered if they were being attacked by banshees. Still, it was worth losing a bit of sleep to see their beaming smiles as they walked hand in hand around the growing camp of soldiers.

Slow drips of men and women continued to join the camp. People from the Arrow Islands, Yorkland and even Vanizia, the water city to the west. People all over had heard the message and were looking to settle old scores with the ancient city of Kessarine.

A week passed before Halfor finally found him again. Tavar was lying close to the acacia tree, looking out over the open land and mulling over the strategy for the battle. Until the Blood Nation arrived, the numbers wouldn't be clear and so he had begun to develop different strategies with Marcus and Alice, hoping to figure out solutions to various problems that they expected could arise.

"Sleeping?" Halfor bent over him and looked at him with bloodshot eyes.

"Nah. Take a seat."

The big man sat beside him with a groan. He let silence take over for a while. Tavar didn't mind. It was comforting just to have his friend back next to him. Without Halfor and Medda, the past few days had felt like he was missing a limb. Alice had scoffed and shook her head at the phrasing when he had mentioned it to her.

"I'm sorry for how I have behaved since leaving the Blood Nation," Halfor eventually said, picking at a small flower standing between his tree trunk-like bent legs. "I am ashamed for my outburst and will apologise to the villagers tomorrow."

"There's really no need," Tavar insisted. "It was a bit of a show for them. No one was hurt. How are you, anyway?"

The Naviqing sighed and looked up at the moon before twisting his body to face Tavar. "Since leaving Naviqand, all I've had is blood and battles. I loved it.

Then she came along." Halfor licked his lips as the moonlight caught his sparkling blue eyes. "Fiery, beautiful, strong, powerful, and a breath of fresh air. I never thought I'd meet anyone like her. And I don't think I'll meet anyone else like her. In the dungeons, we comforted each other but knew that any moment might be our last together. It was an intense and passionate bond that we shared. Once we had escaped. Things evolved. We could choose who we wanted to be with and we still chose each other. There was hope for a future and still we stayed together. Then we head to her city and everything changed again…"

"You know how much she cares about you. Medda loves you."

"Yes. And that's why it pains me so much. I would prefer it if she was running away from me because she wasn't happy and wanted something more. But this doesn't make her happy. And I would burn a thousand cities to the ground if it meant making her happy."

"Speaking to her might be the better option," Tavar proposed. "Less burning. Just a suggestion."

"When will I have time? As soon as they arrive, we will go to battle. Then she's heading back home to lead her people. I'm out of time."

"Find time. *Make* time. Convince her to stay. What do you have to lose?" He held onto the thread of hope that sparked in Halfor's face and pulled. "I know not everything is as simple as black and white, but some things are. She loves you and you love her. Everything else can go to the fucking hells."

Halfor nodded and laughed, looking back to his old self. "I've missed our talks, little one." He pulled Tavar in for a hug and laughed again, a booming laugh that shook the ground beneath them.

"Wait, Halfor…" Tavar pushed the Naviqing away as the laughter stopped. But the shaking continued.

Scrambling to his feet, Tavar looked out to the distance and caught the flickering of lights on the horizon. "An army, heading this way…"

"Blood Nation?" Halfor asked hopefully, following Tavar's gaze.

"From that direction? There's only one army," Tavar said, his stomach turning at the realisation. "Alfara is coming."

CHAPTER THIRTY-FIVE: AS THE WAVE BREAKS

Villagers scattered around, hastily pulling on their crude cuirasses and helms, clutching swords and spears, and prepared the arrows; placing them beside the fires being lit as Qassim and Marcus rode a straight line on horses across the hilltop. The high ground gave them the advantage but the overwhelming numbers would allow Alfara to send wave after wave of men to suffocate them. They had proven in the past that soldiers were an expendable commodity. There would always be more.

Horns blew from all sides of the village and panicked, ashen faces flashed to Tavar for guidance as he strode by, searching for his commanders.

"Immortal Killer, what shall we do?" one particularly pale villager asked him. Must have been barely eighteen years.

"Listen to your commanders and your unit leaders. The Blood Nation will arrive to support us. We need to hold them off until then. We have the high ground, do not fear." It was the best he could do. Four-hundred ill-equipped men and women against the might of two-thousand trained soldiers. At best, they would all die a quick death.

"Alice!" Tavar called. Alice spun at the sound of her name. Cassie quickly helped her with the clasps on her waist band before the Pirate Queen hurried over to him. "Take those with spears and place them at the front. Qassim and Marcus have what cavalry we've been able to muster on the flanks, so you and Halfor will hold the front line, just in case Alfara feel brave enough to risk a frontal assault. I doubt they will at first, but we need to be prepared."

"No problem. Tajira and Zaif have already made for the top of the hill with their unit," she answered, biting her lip. "You sure we shouldn't be running in the opposite direction?"

"They'll come. We just need to hold them off for long enough. If we run, they'll slaughter us and I'm not dying with a spear in my back."

Alice nodded resolute and determined. "Let's make them pay."

"Be careful, Tavar," Cassie added, pushing onto the tips of her toes to plant a kiss on his cheek. "Now is not the time to die on us."

"You too. Stay safe and look after each other."

Alice winked at Cassie and kissed her on the lips quickly. "You got it. Not letting this one out of my sight."

Tavar stalked through the mass of villagers scrambling up the hill to their positions. He stopped an especially panicked man who had fallen in his haste to reach the hill.

"Calm," he said to the frightened man. He looked a year or two younger than Tavar, a mere boy in some cultures. "You're of no use to anyone on the ground. The hill will still be there if you walk." He took the man's helm from the floor and helped to line it correctly on top of his head, ensuring that the nose guard would protect him properly. "This could be the difference between life and death." The man just nodded as his chest heaved up and down beneath his crude cuirass. "I'll be right there with you, at the front. Stay strong, okay?"

Another nod and the villager ran away. Tavar watched his path for a while, making sure there wasn't another fall. Satisfied that he was the last of the villagers making their way up the hill, he turned and followed.

Reaching the top of the hill, he saw with relief that the meagre number of fighters had been moved into their respective units. They parted to allow him through to the front of the line, pressing a hand against him as he made it past them. He smiled hopefully to them, trying his best to offer confidence in a situation where there was little at hand. They smiled back with hope filled eyes, staring as he trudged forward through the lines. Confident that there was nothing else for him to do, he searched for a familiar face.

"They look up to you, you know," Alice smirked as he reached her. She was holding a spear low in her left hand, her right fitted with a long dagger that gleamed in the moonlight. "You should say something. It'll give them a push to fight to the end. The gods know they need something. Wouldn't blame them if they turned and fled with that sight before them." She pointed the tip of her dagger towards the oncoming army. "Balls of fucking iron, this lot."

Tavar glanced down the line and felt a surge of pride at the brave faces staring back at him. He turned and looked down at the oncoming army, marching like one giant beast ready to wipe them from the face of the world.

Balls of fucking iron indeed.

He stepped out in front of them and, taking a

deep breath, he turned and looked back at them, trying to find the right words.

"Some of you have stood with me in battle before. Others have heard of battles I've fought in. I'm not going to sweeten my words: battles feel like the hells have risen and taken dominion over the world. You will face an enemy that wants to kill you, an enemy that will show no mercy. But I'm asking you to face that malice, that hatred. I'm asking you to stand beside me today and fight with everything you have. Fight for the people Alfara has taken from us before their time. Fight for the brothers and sisters that stand with you. Fight for yourself!" A few of the rookie soldiers cheered and pumped their fists, encouraging others.

"We fight for you!"

"We fight for Hartovan!"

"We fight for the Arrow Islands!"

Tavar nodded grimly, appreciating each call. "For too long Alfara has been a nation that has used their size and might to push around their neighbours. Today, we stand together, people of different nations, races, and creeds. We stand together and show them that their actions will no longer be tolerated. We show them that five hundred men and women can bloody the nose of a giant.

"People will sing songs of this day for generations to come, a warning to any country who wishes to prey on those smaller than them." Tavar paused and drew his kyushira, knowing that when it was next sheathed, it would be soaked in blood. Every set of eyes flashed to the majestic sword and waited for his final words. Halfor caught his eye and grinned, his eyes twinkling with tears as he raised his great Warhammer into the air.

"Let's give them a song for the ages! Five hundred stand together to show the world what can be done with hope and strength. When dawn breaks, it will light up a new world. We'll make sure as few of those bastards live to see it!" Everyone before him raised their weapons and roared as he finished, relieved to have said his words. His heart hammered against his chest as he twisted and faced the enemy. His ears rang with the cries as Alice moved closer to him.

"Nicely done, kid."

"Let's try and make sure they're not my final words, yeah?"

She had tears glistening in her eyes. "You got it. For Vandir and Adam."

Marcus rode across the front of the line, riling up the soldiers with his own sword high in the air. Slowing down as he reached Tavar and Alice, he bent down so that they could hear him.

"A word of warning. Do not rush ahead. Wait for them to come," Marcus advised, patting his steed on the neck as he sat back up in the saddle.

"I know, the high ground, right?" Tavar asked, slightly confused.

Marcus winked back at him before urging his horse away. "Not just that. Qassim and I have a little surprise! Prepare for the worst and hope for the best, that's what I was always taught!"

"What do you think that's about?" Alice asked, a bemused look on her face as Marcus rode away.

"No idea," Tavar answered, pulling on his beard as he looked back at the advancing Alfaran army. "Guess we'll find out soon enough."

It didn't take long for Tavar to find out about Marcus and Qassim's little surprise. Alfara dispensed with the pleasantries of battle. There were no pre-battle talks between leaders like on the Arrow Islands. They had come to purge and destroy. Words would only delay what they saw as the inevitable.

They rushed towards the unmoving five hundred, labouring up the hill, cavalry first. Three of the four units waited at the bottom of the hill, watching as the first wave ripped towards what Tavar hoped would be an unbreakable wall of hope and strength. He gripped his kyushira and stepped a few paces forward, ensuring that he would be first in line as the wave broke against them. Lead by example. Most commanders and generals enjoyed waiting at the back and watching the battle play out but Tavar didn't have that luxury. He had to show his people that he was willing to draw blood and die for them if needed. Anything else would allow doubts to set in.

Alice called for the first barrage of arrows to be unleashed as the cavalry were halfway up the hill. Dipped into the various beacons that had been lit and lined up beside them, the arrows lit up the night sky like shooting stars, descending upon the first wave to screams and yells of anguish as some met their mark whilst others bounced against shields or were extinguished with dull thuds as they buried themselves into the ground.

"Loose at will!" Alice cried as the enemy neared.

Halfor lifted his weapon in the air, ready to make his own command. "Shield wall, forward!"

A row of soldiers snapped their shields forward

and set them against each other to create one giant barricade for the advancing army. Tavar saw looks of determination and grim faces outnumber the scared and worried glances that he had expected.

"This is it, brothers and sisters! Stand strong! Stand together!" he cried, staring out at the cavalry.

Then the first wave broke. But it broke before reaching the wall.

Horses fell into the ground, throwing their riders from the saddles whilst some fell beneath their steeds, crushed and unable to move. Across the line, Tavar found Marcus raise his own sword and urge his mount forward on the left flank whilst Qassim mirrored his actions on the right.

From out of nowhere, Tajira stepped out of the shadows. "Now!" he yelled as the shield wall broke in six separate places and in their space came six barrels of hay rolling down the hill towards the stricken and fallen enemy. Flaming arrows rained down on the fallen whilst some were shot perfectly into the rolling barrels, lighting them up as they raced on their way into the advancing army. Frightened and confused, some of the Alfarans broke ranks and fled, only to be chased down by the five hundred's cavalry, Marcus and Qassim leading the way with gleaming swords.

Too far away to hear him, Tavar silently urged them back, not wanting them to draw in the second wave too soon. As if on cue, the two experience warriors turned and led their units back, cleaning up any of the enemies who had been scattered in the chaos. Some were aflame, running around the battlefield and screaming as their flesh burned away.

"Clever bastard…" Alice muttered, impressed

with her old commander's tactics. "Looks like the old dog still has a few tricks left to play."

"They'll be more cautious on the next attack. We need to be careful," Tavar warned, pushing down the growing hope in his chest and trying to think logically about what the next attack would contain. The flaming hay barrels had lit tunnels of flame that Marcus had set up prior to the barrel. When Alfara attacked next, they would need to risk funnelling their attackers down thin channels between the flames as they trudged up the hill or be forced to take their time and swing around the army, giving Tavar and his allies the advantage. "It's a good start, but that's all it is. They still have the numbers."

"But we have the belief," Alice said, glancing at the cheering soldiers behind her. "You can crack a smile, you know?"

Tavar winked at her and allowed the corner of his mouth to curl. "Maybe later. They're regrouping."

He twisted the blade anxiously in his hand as he watched the soldiers at the bottom of the hill move like ants busying themselves and regrouping. They broke into six separate lines, avoiding the flames as they marched towards him.

"Fuck your caution," Alice said with a dark chuckle. "They have the numbers and you know what that means."

"They don't care how many die…" Tavar answered with disgust.

The Alfaran soldiers did their best to avoid the heat of the flames, marching forward with shields held high and spears poking through a curved indent at the top of the shields. Tavar stepped forward, eager for them to come and aware that they would find it difficult to surround him. Halfor had surmised the same thing. He looked across at the Naviqing and grinned as he watched him give the warhammer a few gentle swings in the wind.

"Ready, brother?" Halfor shouted, catching his eye, the thrill of battle taking over.

"Always!"

Alice, Tajira, Zaif, and Cassie spotted what they were doing and marched to the edge of the flames. They would be the first line of defence. The wave would break against them. Tavar grimly inclined his head to them all, proud to stand alongside his friends as the Alfaran soldiers upped the pace.

A poor decision.

"Errors made in haste cannot be taken back at such speed," Tavar muttered to himself and allowed a moment to smile at the memory of his old friend. "This is for you Kenji."

He couldn't even hear his own battle cry as he rushed past the flames, swiping his sword across the midriff of his first attacker and dropping low to dodge the incoming spear. Without glancing back, he snapped the blade up and felt it slice through flesh and bone, already focusing on his next victim. He raised his knee and kicked the shield from his enemy's grip and slapped the spear to the side with a swat of his kyushira. One thrust later and the blade popped out of the back of the soldier's neck, dripping with crimson blood and shining in the light of the flames either side of him.

He could sense the blade dragging him onwards, begging him to rush to the mass of wide-eyed soldiers running between the flames to meet their death.

He ignored the pull of the blade and stood his ground, just as an arrow whistled past his head close enough for him to feel the rush of air. Distracted, he snapped his blade up but only managed to divert the spear towards the edge of his helm. He rocked back as the helm flew from his head and he staggered, arms flailing to keep his balance.

Another attacker leapt forward with a roar and waved his sword wildly in Tavar's direction. He raised his kyushira blindly, still recovering his balance and attempting to get his head back in the fight as the sounds of battle turned into a steady ringing in his ears. He diverted the thrust but left himself open for the hilt of the blade to loop over his guard and catch him right on his cheekbone. He finally fell, dazed and staring up at his would-be killer. Scrambling back, his free hand caught on a rock and drew more blood. Just his luck.

The Alfaran soldier leered at him gleefully, amazed with his luck, eyes solely on his fallen victim and the promise of glory for defeating so infamous a foe. His eyes widened first in victory, then in shock. His arms slumped and the sword fell from his grip. He peered down and fumbled uselessly with the small hilt of a dagger sticking out from his chest. The poor bastard looked up at Tavar in confusion, as though asking him for answers before dropping to the floor, eyes staring up at the moon.

"Can't have you dying out here in the middle of fucking nowhere can we?" Tajira growled, pulling his dagger free from the corpse and placing it back into the leather belt around his waist.

Tavar cleared his head and stood gingerly. "They're realising their folly. No point running the channels up the hill. Trying to take the flank instead."

Tavar flinched as he carefully pressed a hand against his cheek and felt the swelling already starting.

Ignoring the pain, he glanced across the battlefield. The channels of flames were empty other than the piles of bodies of unfortunate soldiers on both sides. Even over his thudding heart and broken breaths, he could hear Halfor's battle cries boom into the night.

Still alive. Still fighting.

Behind him, the five hundred had turned to face the enemy attempting to flank them. He climbed the hill and looked down at the heart of the battle. Qassim and Marcus's units were still fighting valiantly but in vain. The remaining few of the cavalry were now turning back as the Alfaran army pulled together and engaged their second and third units.

"They want this over as quickly as possible," he said more to himself than anyone else. Tajira just grunted in return, watching the chaos as the men urged their horses to back up the hill.

Tavar peered through the darkness and caught sight of Qassim slashing wildly as Marcus called for him to retreat. He looked past the soldier to see row upon row of Alfaran archers step forward as one and ready their arrows. "Shit," he muttered, realising what was happening. He ran through his own soldiers, screaming at them as he pushed them out of his way. "Shield wall! Now!" Men and women jerked into action at his words, fixing their shields together to create one guard for the entire unit. Tavar didn't have time for anything else. He raced past them, bending low to pick up a fallen soldier's shield as he ran towards Qassim who was lagging behind the retreating remainder of the cavalry. Finding himself caught between the two armies with only Qassim near, he heard wails in the night, his name being screamed into the void of the battle. It was too late to turn back now.

Qassim's horse panicked and fell, toppling the

soldier onto the floor. Tavar thanked the gods that it didn't crush him but he kept running as Qassim staggered to his feet, without his weapon.

The bows twanged, followed by an unnerving silence as the arrows arced through the air.

Tavar stopped and gazed up at the ominous black cloud of arrows above them, thick enough to block out the light of the stars. Cursing, he knelt and held the stolen shield above his head, helplessly looking across at Qassim.

The Alfaran noble tried to run but his left knee twisted awkwardly and he dropped with a cry. He caught Tavar's eyes and nodded solemnly, accepting what was to come. Two arrows penetrated his armour: piercing his shoulder and back. With the first volley over, Tavar ran towards his injured friend. He slid across the floor and covered Qassim, placing him on his side and peering at his wounds.

"Bad, isn't it?" Qassim coughed as Tavar placed his shield next to them and looked him in the eyes with grim resignation. "You've saved me enough, my friend. Finish what we started. There's hope in Alfara, embers of something better. You just need to ignite it again. It's not all bad. Nothing is."

"I'll do my best, I promise."

"That's all anyone can do. Breast pocket," Qassim said, his eyes flickering down. Tavar's bloody fingers fumbled with the soldier's jacket and pulled out a piece of folded parchment. "It's for my sister. If you ever get a chance to see her."

"I'll give it to her, I promise."

"You're a good man, Tavar Farwan. Better than most. Don't forget that." Qassim groaned and reached for the shield beside them. He pulled it over Tavar's head and waited with a grin. "We're even now…"

Tavar's brows lowered in confusion. Then he heard the whistling of arrows in the air and felt the shield push against his back and head as the second volley of arrows slammed with a thud against it.

"We're even," he agreed as the shield fell from Qassim's grip and his chest ceased moving. Dark eyes stared up without seeing. Tavar pressed his own forehead against Qassim's and muttered a small prayer for the Alfaran, tapping his chest twice with a gloved hand. "Rest well, my friend."

The sound of thousands of boots hitting the ground at once pulled Tavar away from his loss. There was no time for grief.

He looked up and sighed as the Alfarans marched forward, every soldier pressing on together, leaving none behind. Wearily, he pushed himself to his feet and held his bloody kyushira to the side. An thirsting energy emanated from the weapon, the excitement it felt as the soldiers marched towards him. He glanced over his shoulder and gave a wry smile as Halfor and rushed towards him, both covered in the red of battle. Alice's shield hung low, her left shoulder looking slightly out of place from the battle. Halfor was bleeding from an open wound on his forearm but he still managed that winning grin of his that Tavar loved so much.

"If we're gonna go out," the Naviqing said, "then we might as well go out together."

"Seems like the right thing to do," Alice agreed.

"See you both in the hall," Tavar smirked. "I've decided my favourite heaven is Halfor's. Enough drink and feasting to last an eternity."

"You've made a wise decision," Halfor said. "You'll both be greeted with open arms and the largest jug of ale you can imagine."

"It's been an honour, gentlemen." Alice dropped the shield and drew a curved dagger. "Let's go out in style."

They roared together and smiled at the wave of sound crashing towards them from the remaining warriors behind them. The Alfarans had broken into a run now, the whites of their eyes clear in Tavar's vision.

"Give them hell," he commanded to his forces. The ground shook as though the world itself was breaking and Tavar roared once more into the night, ready to draw blood in his final moments as the wave of red threatened to crash upon them and drown them all.

A rush of movement whipped past him at the last moment as he saw the fear in his enemies' eyes. Horses leapt past him from behind and smashed into the wave, spears and swords slicing through the rows of soldiers and forcing them to scatter and retreat.

"Blood Nation?" Alice asked incredulously over the sound of screams and cries of battle.

Tavar cheered as he spotted the painted warriors mounted on the horses, thousands of experienced fighters pouring down the hill to wipe away the Alfaran soldiers. One of the newcomers stood with ease on top of his horse as it raced down the hill, shooting his arrows with an unnerving accuracy before leaping from the animal and drawing a double-bladed sword before slicing through the shocked and confused soldiers around him with glee.

"You just going to stand there?" Tavar spun at the sound of the familiar voice. "Sorry, I'm late." Medda winked and urged her horse onwards towards the retreating wave of soldiers.

He blew out his cheeks and couldn't help but chuckle at the open mouths of Halfor and Alice as the blood warriors tore through the retreating army. "Looks like we're not done yet..." The blade flashed in his hand and he pushed forward with a cry, feeling a surge of renewed energy race through his body as those behind him joined in his cry and followed, a second wind forcing them forwards.

They had escaped the jaws of death and now was the time for vengeance.

CHAPTER THIRTY-SIX: THE BURDEN OF LEADING

The warriors of Blood Nation showed no mercy. They slaughtered the retreating army to a man, unwilling to take prisoners, much to Tavar's disgust. But he wasn't in a position to argue against it. They saved his life and the lives of one hundred men and women ready to make a last stand. He was in their debt and he knew it. They revelled in decorating their faces and bodies in the blood of their enemies, covering their hands in the flowing blood where possible and smearing it over themselves with cackles that sent chills down Tavar's spine.

"They've waited a long time for this," Medda explained uneasily. "It's like releasing a starved wolf amongst sheep. They will devour all without a single thought for mercy. It is their way. It always has been, as long as I've been alive anyway. I'm not even sure if there is a word for mercy in our language…"

"Our bodies would be cold and resting in a pile waiting to be burned," Tavar said to her with a shrug. "We're in no place to complain. We're breathing and that must be enough. Let's hope Lilian's message got through to the civilians in Kessarine. I don't want innocents dying because these warriors don't have a word for mercy."

"I'll speak to my brother. They'll be more likely to listen to him."

"Thanks. You spoke to Halfor yet?" The last

Tavar had seen of the big warrior, he had been pacing around the battlefield at the crack of dawn, offering quick deaths to friend and foe alike who were taking a longer journey to the heavens than was preferable. Such suffering didn't help anyone. Some of the blood warriors had snickered at the Naviqing as they watched, unable to understand the compassion in his actions. He had merely growled before continuing his merciful work.

Medda scratched the shaved part of her head and looked away from Tavar. "Not yet. I don't know what to say. Or how to explain things to him."

"Just tell him how you feel."

"It's not that easy," she moaned. "Though I wish it was…"

Tavar sucked in a breath and blew out long and slow, surveying the battlefield in the light of dawn. "He's hurting. And you might not have much time left. Regret is a horrible thing, Medda. It eats away at you like a dog gnawing a bone. After a while, it'll consume you. I should know, I'm full of the bastards."

"I'll speak to him. Just need a bit more time."

Tavar squeezed her shoulder and walked away, wanting to give her the space she desired to make her own decision. His words weren't needed any more. He had done what he could and now it was up to the two of them to work things out. They were adults. And they acted like it, most of the time anyway.

"General." A weary, battered man offered a confused salute as he stopped in front of Tavar. His black skin was bruised and cut in numerous places and there was swelling above his left eye which was bloodshot to the point where Tavar could hardly see any white. They had spoken briefly a couple of days before. A farmer who was held in high esteem by the other villagers for running off bandits the previous year. A man of strength.

"Ali. It's good to see that you are safe," Tavar said, glad that he could remember the man's name. He had met all of the villagers before the battle, wanting to show that he was one of them and that they weren't just fighting alongside an uncaring figurehead like so many soldiers had to. "What can I do for you?"

Ali played nervously with the bronze bracelet enclosed round his wrist, twisting and pulling it as he hesitated to speak. "Those of us who… who survived… we've been thinking…"

"You want to go to your families," Tavar said with a sad, knowing smile. He had presumed as much. They had seen warfare and it had done what it did to so many before them. Scared them shitless.

Ali's good eye widened at his words. "Well, yeah. We'll go with you all the way if you want, Tavar. But we're shattered and there's so few of us. You have these new warriors now and if I'm honest, they scare us about as much as the Alfarans did, probably more!"

"They scare me a bit too," Tavar said to shared laughter. He held out his hand and Ali shook it happily. "You all fought so well. You should be proud as you head back to your families. Rest and enjoy the time you have together. I would never command anyone to follow me into battle. We can handle it from here."

Ali tapped his chest and his grin threatened to reach his ears. "May the gods bless you Tavar Farwan. You're a good man. Folk been saying you could be descended from Izads. I don't blame 'em. Got a fire about you that I've not seen in most people. Good luck." He turned and trudged away to share the news with his fellow villagers who sat together, nervously glancing at the passing blood warriors.

"Descended from Izads?" Marcus scoffed, his body jerking with the action as he limped his way towards Tavar, wincing every time he placed any weight on his right leg. "Must have had too much Okadan whiskey."

"You okay?" Tavar asked, his eyes flashing to the leg. Marcus had cut the bottom of his trouser leg off at the knee. His ankle had swollen and had already turned a worrying shade of purple. "You shouldn't be walking around on that."

"There's a lot of things I shouldn't do. And yet, I always seem to be doing them," Marcus joked, unable to force the humour into his expression. "I'll be fine. Get through the whole battle with a few scratches and then fall awkwardly jumping from my horse. Humour of the gods, I suppose. Bastards." He spat on the floor and cursed. "I've wrapped Qassim's body up. Thought we could all be there, when… you know." His eyes fell to the ground, his meaning clear. "Thought you might want to say a few words. He really liked you, in the end. He wanted to go back for you straight away after Hartovan. Kept saying how he owed you for saving his life. Never shut up about it, to be honest. He was a good kid, after all. Typical noble bitch at first, but he grew on me. Really seemed to enjoy the chaos of our new lives and I can't say that about many."

Tavar tapped his fingers against his chest, feeling for the parchment in his breast pocket. He'd make sure it found its way to Qassim's sister. As long as he was breathing, he'd do that for his fallen ally. "He was a right bastard when we were younger. He was a changed man outside of Alfara. Actually saw him smile. Totally different to that scowl he used to always wear. He'll be missed." He sniffed and remembered the warm smile Qassim had given him at the end. The warrior had died a noble death: fighting for others and protecting his friends.

"We've all changed since we left Kessarine. People talk of how we shape our surroundings but sometimes I think that it is the surroundings that shape us."

"That gut is definitely shaped by the taverns you've been surrounded by of late," Tavar smirked, poking a finger into Marcus's protruding belly. He took the jibe in good humour, forcing the belly out further and laughing.

"I've been working on this for years!" he cried, rubbing his gut protectively. "My pride and joy."

"I'll grab the others. Alice and Cassie will want to be there. Halfor too. He liked him in what little time they had together."

"Qassim mentioned travelling to Naviqand once this was all done," Marcus said, frowning at the realisation that he would no longer get to achieve that goal. "He loved to travel. Always wanted to find a spot on a hill and overlook the land around him. I thought we'd bury him under the acacia tree. Good view from there."

"Good idea," Tavar agreed. "Once we're done, it will be time to leave. We have a long march ahead of us. Rest that foot."

Marcus spun slowly, flinching as his foot hit the ground. He raised a hand without looking back. "You got it, General."

The march was slow and steady. Such numbers made it difficult to move with pace across the rocky land. The blood warriors spoke to each other in their native tongue, rarely switching to common when Tavar or one of the others asked them questions. Medda rode on ahead, leading her people alongside her brother as they leant towards one another, lost in constant discourse throughout the journey. She had joined them for the Qassim's funeral at least, taking time from her duties as the future chief to hear Tavar and Alice's words over the fallen soldier's body. Then they piled the earth onto his lifeless, wrapped up body and found a large enough stone to inscribe his name and a short message:

Here lies Qassim ir Alisson. A noble warrior who died saving others. May he find his way to the heavens.

Alice had been the one to decide on the inscription. Tavar liked it: short, simple and it spoke the truth. They had bid a fond farewell to the villagers returning to their families before turning for Alfara and another battle. It was a bittersweet feeling. They needed as many fighters as possible but Tavar was glad that they were safe and alive.

"Won't be long now," Zaif said, pulling Tavar from his daydreaming. The big warrior had sunk into himself since the battle on the beach. The few times he had spoken with Tavar, he had been withdrawn and used few words. If Tavar briefly mentioned Xane then the warrior's eyes would tear up and he'd create a sudden and random excuse to leave. Tavar thought it best to steer things away from thoughts of his son now. Give the man the space to grieve in his own way.

"Should be there by nightfall," Tavar answered.

"Good, good..." Zaif muttered, his narrowed brows and unfocused eyes clearly at odds with his words.

"Sooner we're there, sooner it's over."

"Yeah. Thought about what might happen after the battle?"

"No clue. I wanted to fight alongside my boy, watch him grow as a man on the road. Now, things ain't clear. All muddy, like. The world's a big place and I don't know where I belong. Spent too long in those damn dungeons away from him. Wasted years. I'll make Alfara pay for taking that from me. Then I'll see where the dice lands."

"What did you do before the dungeons?" Tavar said, wondering why he had never the question before.

"Mercenary for hire." Zaif smiled and licked his lips. "Got a good price too, in most places. Had a warm bed and a cooked meal in any village I ended up in. Bit of thieving here and there, some piracy. Anything for a bit of coin and some food. Simple times. Now we're waging war against the power of the northern drylands. Life can be funny at times."

"I find myself laughing more and more," Tavar admitted. "I find it's easier than the alternative."

"You think we'll win?" Zaif asked, knocking Tavar off guard with the blunt question. "This battle with Alfara. It'll be hard. Damn hard. That skirmish on the beach and the battle on the hill were won because of the enemy made errors and were reckless in their arrogance. That won't happen in Kessarine. They'll be ready and behind the wall. A siege is good for no one, and I doubt this lot will be up for waiting long," he said, nodding towards a few of the blood warriors passing by on their horses.

"They've not fought a battle like this for a long time," Tavar explained. "They won't have enough food prepared to last a siege and the wall isn't strong enough all around the boundary. They've wasted units in the last two battles, and they'll be scared. But it will be difficult. Kenji used to say armies are like any beast, take the head off and the body dies. If we can take out their leader and get to the king, the city will fall. That has to be our aim."

"What then? What's stage two of the great plan?"

"Honestly? I have no fucking idea." They laughed together at the stupidity of it all. "I'm still crossing my fingers about stage one. Don't think I can give any of my energy to stage two."

"Well, if it all falls apart, at least we will all die together with the fresh air around us. Free warriors with weapons in our hands and songs on our lips. That's the way I've always wanted to go. What about you?"

"Old and in a warm bed. Surrounded by as many of my friends as possible and a few empty bottles of wine scattered about, preferably," Tavar said to Zaif's amusement considering the loud snort he gave. "We haven't done all this just to return to Alfara and die. Even if we have nothing else, we have hope."

"Yeah," Zaif agreed. "We have hope."

"I thought it would be… bigger," Red Mist said, looking utterly dejected as he frowned across the open lands at the giant wall surrounding the city of Kessarine.

"You thought it would be *bigger*?" Halfor asked, incredulously, glancing at Tavar in amazement before looking back at the disappointed warrior.

"I've heard nothing but tales of this city since I was a small boy. The imagination of a young boy is a powerful thing, prone to exaggeration. I'm disappointed."

"The wall has stood for generations," Marcus explained, feeling an urge to defend his home city, even if they were about to attempt to overthrow its king. "It has stood as a warning to its people and others that Alfara is not to be messed with and Kessarine is the heart of that kingdom."

Red Mist shrugged. "It's not a problem for me. We'll tear it down and build a new one. Much bigger and more intimidating than this one."

Tavar scratched his head, trying to imagine what could be more threatening than the monstrosity surrounding Kessarine. "Let's focus on the task at hand before we start moving in and choosing what colour paint we want to decorate the city with."

"Let me guess, red?" Halfor asked Red Mist, unable to hide his contempt. Medda just looked away, pretending to be distracted by a large crow flying around them.

Red Mist leant towards Halfor, staring up at the tall warrior, not intimidated in the least by the Naviqing. "Blue, actually. It relaxes me. Like the ocean," he said, grinning wide and defiantly. Halfor growled and stomped away towards the tents that the warriors had begun to erect.

"I have a feeling the pale man isn't happy with me for some reason," Red Mist said to the rest of them, brushing his hands together and licking his dry lips. "Was it something I said?"

"Don't worry about him, pre-battle nerves," Tavar explained, glancing past Red to watch Halfor stomp towards the tents. Medda jumped in the Naviqing's way and dragged him back into her tent. Finally!

"Understandable," Red said, nodding and staring at the city before him, completely oblivious to Halfor and Medda's impromptu meeting. "I heard that there are still Naviqing slaves in the city of Kessarine. They serve their masters by cleaning their clothes, bringing their food and even bathing them when fingers are clicked. I would be ashamed and nervous if I were him. My people were never taken as slaves. We fight to the death." He beat on his chest like some kind of proud beast, inching his chin up far too high for it to look impressive. Tavar thought he looked more like a child trying to impress a bemused peer.

"Well, you'll have your chance to prove that," Marcus said, stroking the stubble on his recently shaved chin. "They won't be taking slaves though. It will be death or the wall for all of us."

"And what are the women like in the city?" Red crept close to Marcus and slowly pushed his face closer to the Alfaran. A bit too close for Marcus, considering the way he edged back from the warrior. "I've heard tales that there are women of all kinds in the brothels. Brown, black, white. Tall, short, fat, and skinny. The spoils of war gets my blood rushing," he said, his eyes flashing as he released a lecherous moan from the back of his throat and stuck his tongue out, laughing at them both. "We will have some fun, my new friends. The night will bless us with blood and the morning will shine down on a new kingdom." Red slapped his hand roughly against Marcus and winked at Tavar before sauntering off to his men.

"He's not exactly growing on me," Marcus declared. "How that idiot is related to Medda, I've no idea."

"I'll explain it after the battle," Tavar smirked, "If we make it that far."

"When is Lilian leaving?"

"She's already left," he answered, wondering where in that colossal, chaotic city she would be right now. "Didn't want to drag it out. Crept in with the last of the merchants allowed before they closed the gates. She knows what she's doing."

"Never failed before," Marcus agreed, still casting a nervous eye over Kessarine and silently praying that she was safe. "And she won't now. If there's a woman that can convince men to join her, then it's that one."

Tavar smiled and made to head back to their camp. There wouldn't be time to rest, they were too close to nightfall and the nerves of battle had already begun their slowly attack his mind and body. That's when he heard it. The creak and ring of the metal chains as the bridge lowered, revealing the jaws of the city.

He turned, narrowed brows and alert eyes facing the bridge as it ground to a halt, resting against the rocky ground and shooting a plume of dust into the air, blocking his view of the city.

The mood of the camp changed as the warriors rushed for weapons and untied the horses to the cries of the unit leaders. Tavar spotted a dishevelled looking Halfor leap from tent he had been in, hair a wild mess and soaked in sweat. His legendary hammer was to hand as he marched over to Tavar. Medda crept out after, eyes darting either side as she patted down her tunic and pushed her hair up on its end. She checked her belt and pulled the spear from her back to hand as she stormed across the camp, bellowing orders to her fellow warriors.

"What are they doing?" the Naviqing asked, sniffing and wiping the wetness from his beard. His eyes jumped everywhere but at the smirk on Tavar's face.

Tavar pushed his bottom lip out and shrugged. He thought the next time that gate would be open would be after they stormed the city. Kessarine had been locked up for the night in his mind.

He brushed a finger across the hilt of his blade, rubbing the weapon to relax himself as the dust settled. Silhouettes of a small unit of soldiers passed through the dust. Draped in infamous gold of the Immortals, ten of the soldiers marched together, surrounding a thin, spindly man dressed in more understated garments, though no less impressive. The man's grey robes fell to just above his silver sandals on his feet and he wore a look on his old, weary face of one who was perturbed slightly by the large army camped outside his home. An insignificant pest that needed to be dealt with and nothing more. Like Halfor when he would grow frustrated and slam his hand down on the annoying flies that would circle him after the heat of battles whilst he enjoyed a victory drink.

"You know him?" Halfor asked, frowning at the man and his retinue of gold. "Must be important to have those warriors with him."

"Important?" Marcus scoffed, holding a hand out to point at the weary man before turning to Halfor and Tavar with a look of incredulity. "This is a mockery. Uhlad is laughing at us right now."

"His name is Ahmed," Tavar answered calmly, rubbing at the itchy heat on his neck beneath his beard. "He is the king's head servant."

"A slave," Marcus corrected. "And nothing more. We should rain arrows on them all and begin the attack."

Tavar raised a palm, warning Marcus to relax. "No. I want to hear what he has to say. Ahmed has been nothing but brutally honest with me when we have spoken. It would be remiss of me to have him killed like this. Let's hear what he has to say. Then we can attack..."

As they drew closer, Tavar spotted one further figure at the back covered in brown robes and wearing a bag over their head as they stumbled after the Immortals. "Tell Medda and Red to keep the soldiers on guard." Marcus nodded and rushed off to relay the command as Tavar faced Halfor. He unbuckled his belt and held it out to the Naviqing. "Take this and look after it for me. You'll know what to do." He handed the belt over with the kyushira resting in its elegant scabbard.

Halfor took the item in his huge hands, unable to keep the sadness from his eyes. "Not everyone is as trusting as you, brother. Walking into a pit of vipers without a weapon is folly."

Tavar chuckled as he strolled off towards Ahmed who had stopped and was waiting with the Immortals and the prisoner. "Who said I was without weapons?" he called back to Halfor. The big warrior grinned and shook his head as Tavar turned.

He tried to ignore the thousands of eyes burning into his back as he strolled to the waiting company. Swallowing his nerves, he hummed softly to himself, an old tune his mother had once sung to calm him whenever he had been frightened. He knew that anyone of the Immortals could kill him within a second if they wanted to. The daggers hidden in his trousers and latched onto the back of his boots wouldn't be able to help him much if they attacked but still, they at least made him feel slightly better.

"Tavar Farwan..." Ahmed drew out the syllables before clicking his tongue against the roof of his mouth and bowing. He tapped his chest with a skinny hand and smirked. "The gods have blessed you indeed since last we spoke."

"What do you want Ahmed?" Tavar said, aware that ten sets of eyes were staring out at him between golden scarves and headdresses. Just one click of Ahmed's fingers and he would be dead. "I have a city to overthrow."

Ahmed sighed and, using a finger and thumb, picked at a speck of dust on his fitted grey robe. He rubbed his hands together and looked back at Tavar. "Topple Kessarine. The city that made you who you are, whether you like it or not. Such petulance is unbecoming of a man of your stature."

"The city ruled by the king who enslaved me and took my entire family away from me," Tavar bit back through gritted teeth. "What do you want? Or should I ask, what does *Uhlad* want?"

"He wants what any king wants. He wants peace," Ahmed said, peering at Tavar as though he was a fool who needed an explanation about why one shouldn't drink their own piss. "Kessarine is not a city that wishes to see blood. Especially not with those…" he peered over at the camp behind Tavar where thousands of warriors were watching and waiting, weapons in hand and ready for war. 'S*avages*!" His nostrils flared at the word before he glanced back to Tavar, his eyes alert and eager. "Uhlad is burdened with the great weight of leadership and you know what leadership in Kessarine means. Four of the most powerful men and women tug on the strings of Uhlad like chaotic puppet masters playing their little game. He never wanted to be your enemy, Tavar. You must believe me."

"He didn't do enough to help his people. If he wanted a better Alfara, then he should have fought the

Judges."

"If only it was that simple. Sever one head from the body and another grows in its place. The eternal leadership of Alfara." Ahmed sighed and his genuine dismay unnerved Tavar. "I digress. I bring a gift, a sign of peace, so that you may do as I ask of you." Ahmed clicked his fingers and the dark figure at the back of the group were brought forward by two of the Immortals. The golden warriors pulled the bag away to show an old friend, beaten and bruised.

One of Hashem's eyes was closed shut and a worrying shade of purple. The other eye flashed at Tavar and he managed a grin that displayed his broken smile. At least three teeth were missing, leaving bloody gums behind.

"What have you done to him? Tavar asked as the Immortal shoved Hashem into his arms. "Go to the others." Hashem nodded, unable to speak as he stumbled to the camp where Marcus was already rushing to collect him.

"I'll tell you what we didn't do," Ahmed said, stepping forward to Tavar and away from the Immortals. "We didn't put him on the wall. We didn't kill his father, or his mother. We showed restraint."

"How generous of you," Tavar mocked, scrunching his face up in distaste.

"I needed him alive so that I could speak to you…" Ahmed pressed closer, voice dropping to a whisper. "There is someone who wishes that you join us in the city. Someone who needs to speak with you urgently. If you enter the city, I can promise you safety and we will release all of the prisoners that we caught following your little escape from the arena."

Tavar stuck his tongue into the side of his cheek, thinking on the request. The release of prisoners would be a huge coup for him. The safety of those who fought for him was vital to him.

"If you still wish to attack the city once you have had your discussion with a mutual friend," Ahmed continued, "then so be it."

"Who is it?" Tavar asked. "Who wants to speak with me?"

Ahmed flashed a wicked smile. "The Queen of Alfara herself. Carver ir Edemer."

CHAPTER THIRTY-SEVEN: OUT OF THE SHADOWS

Hands tied, Tavar entered the city to the fury of the locals. Rotten fruit and vegetables were pelted his way along with a few bottles of what smelled like piss. It was only when one of the Immortals drew a sharp blade that the crowds lining the streets calmed enough to only hurl insults his way.

His soul was damned for all of eternity. His mother had laid with goats. The fires of all hells would consume him from here to the end of days.

He'd heard it all before. Dished some of it out too, in all honesty. People he recognised screwed up their faces and joined in with the hatred. To them, he was a deserter and a criminal; the man who had brought a savage army to their doorsteps and killed soldiers on the beach of the Arrow Islands and in their own backyard. He understood but that didn't ease his pain at all.

"Glad to be back?" Ahmed asked with a wry smile.

"Couldn't keep me away," Tavar responded, flinching as a rotund, bald shopkeeper pulled back and launched a mighty ball of saliva onto his cheek. "Disgusting…"

The streets seemed smaller than he remembered. Hordes of men, women and children crammed in between the rows of stalls and houses and left little room for the Immortals to march towards the golden dome in the centre of the city. At one point, a particularly irate merchant stormed through the other angry folk and managed to get within five paces of them. Tavar's hands instinctively reached for his kyushira. His heart sank as he recalled handing the blade over to Halfor. Still, better to be with the Naviqing than in his enemy's grasp. The merchant pushed against one of the golden guards and found himself lying on his back in the dusty street, face looking up at the night sky as his head slammed against the ground. More roars and curses spat through the air as a concerned stall owner rushed to the man and held his bleeding head up.

"That was your fault!"

"Traitor!"

"Take him to the wall!"

The cries died down as the group met with lines of soldiers, ready for battle with their spears facing out towards the baying crowd. The grounds around the palace were deserted but for the few guards marching the perimeter and looking out for any signs of trouble on the brink of battle.

"Take him to the queen," Ahmed commanded the guards. "I have business to attend to." Looking at Tavar, he offered what could have passed as a smile if he had managed to control his narrowed eyebrows. As it was, the servant ended up looking confused. "Don't try anything funny. The Immortals know that should you try anything... *reckless.* Then they are to kill you without a thought."

"Got it. Nothing reckless," Tavar replied, holding back a smirk as Ahmed released a small groan before spinning away in the direction of the palace.

The guards led him round to the side of the

palace along the coloured brick path and between excessive and gauche nude busts draped in colourful flowers of all varieties.

A ceiling of lavender, daffodils and chrysanthemums twisted overhead to shade them on their walk in the sun until the path opened up into a wide myriad of rectangular patches of perfectly cut grass and stone benches. The gentle splash of water from the various fountains caught his ear and he looked to his left and laughed at the marble statue of a muscular hero fighting a leviathan with his bare hands. The water sprouted out from the monster's mouth and crashed into the circular basin beneath. A wooden bench covered in further flowers Tavar didn't recognise stood next to the fountain. The woman sitting on the fountain looked as beautiful as when Tavar had fallen in love with her. There was more sorrow in her dark eyes and she wore her hair up, tying it tightly into a bun whilst allowing a few wavy strands to fall loose. She waved the guards away who bowed and retreated to the shadows of the garden, leaving just the two of them.

"I would bow," Tavar said. "But my knees are aching from the march."

"Then sit," Carver commanded, moving up on the bench to allow him more room. He took the seat and stared out in awe at the mass of colour and vibrancy in the garden. "Beautiful, isn't it? We live in one of the hottest kingdoms in the world and yet even here, there is beauty and growth to be found."

"Life always seems more beautiful when you're staring out at it at a distance from your golden tower," Tavar snapped. "You have your own gardens, probably your own servants. You are a queen."

"I am. I did what I had to do, for my family,"

Carver bit back, an icy edge to her voice. "You see the world as black and white. You think people either do good things or bad things, but it's not like that! If I'd have ran away with you that night in Hartovan, my mother would have been all alone, the remaining member of a family of traitors in a kingdom with a penchant for torturing its people on a giant fucking wall!" Tavar felt his annoyance with her draining as she ranted at him.

"I couldn't leave her alone. I had to give Uhlad something. *You* were that something. You helped others desert. You let Marcus get away. He was due to be killed when he returned but you let him slip through Uhlad's fingers. With you, I had my bargaining chip. My mother was allowed to stay in her house in the country and I could continue using my father's name."

"And then you decided to marry him. *Uhlad.*" Tavar felt revulsion at the bottom of his gut as he thought about it. To him, Carver was still that young woman he had fallen in love with in the tent in Hartovan. "You wanted more. To be a queen. To have power. You always were greedy for more." His neck twisted with the impact of the slap across his burning cheek. He rubbed at it gently before turning to face her, suddenly embarrassed as she glared at him; fury and sorrow waging battle on her face.

"It was the only way," she hissed through gritted teeth. "It's difficult to explain…"

"Try me."

She sighed and flicked an errant piece of hair from her face, the way she always used to. "Uhlad has some power. The people believe him to be an Izad descendant, so he always has that. But he's not greedy. He's comfortable in this kingdom. But there's someone else guiding Alfara, pushing her towards war and conquest."

"The Judges..." Tavar frowned and sighed. He ran his tongue across his teeth, thinking about what Uhlad had told him about them.

"Uhlad has only ever loved two things in his life. Sett, and Alfara. He doesn't want to see his kingdom fall, though the people above him are doing their very best to get rid of him."

"What about the prince?" Tavar choked out, hating the thought. "What about *your son*?"

Carver shifted uneasily on the bench and averted her eyes from Tavar's gaze. "Uhlad helped me when I needed help. He has looked after me and given me a good life. So I gave him a son. A son who he has adored and cared for from the day I found out I was pregnant. In the last year, the king has been acting paranoid. Every time we have spoken, he has warned me that people in the shadows are out to get him, to steal his throne. He warned me that they would come for my son next. I couldn't allow that, and neither could Uhlad. That's why I smuggled him out of the city when Lilian arrived."

"What?" Tavar shot up from the bench as Carver cleared her throat loudly and flashed her eyes to the shadows.

"Sit down!" she hissed at him. He sat sheepishly, unable to calm his beating heart.

"Where is Lilian now?"

"She made it out of the northern gate. Marcus and a small band loyal to me will be opening the gates any moment now and your army will have their chance."

"And what about Uhlad?"

"He is with a group of Immortals searching for

the Judges. They will end this sickness in the chaos of battle before seeking peace with your army. He will do anything to protect Alfara," Carver said with a sad smile.

"And what about his son?" Tavar asked, wincing with the dull pain in his chest. "How does Uhlad feel about him leaving the city with Lilian?"

"That's another thing I wanted to speak to about…" Carver said, blowing hard from her cheeks and swallowing a lump in her throat, making the silver necklace rise and fall with the motion. "Prince Amir isn't Uhlad's son. Uhlad has never lain as much as a finger on me. Amir is your son, Tavar. *Our* son."

Tavar's legs shook and buckled beneath him. He fell to his knees, breathing fast and struggling to focus as a ringing sound rose in his ears, blocking out Carver's words as she dropped next to him, her face wrinkled with worry. He closed his eyes and rocked back and forth, feeling the heat rise in his body as his forehead dripped with sweat. The ringing abated just in time for him to hear cries in the distance.

"They've done it…" Carver muttered, a calming hand still on Tavar's shoulder. "The gate is open. We need to go." She stood and dragged Tavar to his feet, slapping him harshly across his face. "Now isn't the time for those stupid questions running around your head. You need to get out of Kessarine. Your son needs you."

My son. The thought ripped Tavar back into the moment just as Carver drew an ornate, purple-hilted dagger and sliced open the bonds around his hands.

"I can get you past the Immortals but you're on your own then. Find your friends, make sure they are safe, and meet me out the back of the palace. The gate will be open," she commanded.

"What about you?"

"I need my sword. Here, take this," she winked and Tavar felt his heart skip a beat at the sight as he caught her dagger. "Time to kill some Judges."

CHAPTER THIRTY-EIGHT: BRAVERY

He stuck to the shadows of the palace walls before rushing to the shelter offered by the stone buildings lining the King's Street.

In the chaos of battle, stealth would be his ally. The sound of hundreds of boots bounding against the stone roads filled the city as soldiers marched towards the commotion. As he left the royal district, he was met with the panic of citizens weaving in between the marching units of soldiers. Some were rushing with weapons of their own to join in the heat of the battle whilst others grabbed loved ones and headed towards barricaded homes, banging on the wooden doors and screaming for help.

Tavar raised the hood on his cloak and pulled it tight across his face. In the dark of night, he hoped that he wouldn't be recognised. His survival most likely depended on it.

Following the clang of metal smashing together and the cries of pain and anguish, he found himself on the edge of Market Street. He looked to his right and spotted a familiar shop. The Apothecary. Flashes of memory of days spent laughing and joking with the owners flooded his mind. Adam smiling at the herbs Tavar had brought him made his stomach lurch. He swatted it away and focused. He couldn't be distracted. That wasn't what Adam would have wanted right now. He needed a vantage point.

Glancing around and checking to ensure he wasn't being watched, he jumped into the alleyway beside the apothecary and grinned as his eyes fell on the rope ladder hanging from the side of the building. He pulled on the rope and was glad to find that it held tight. He began to climb before he heard a scream above him and looked up to see a frightened woman holding a knife against the rope, her hands trembling.

"Give me one good reason why I shouldn't cut this rope, you thief!" the woman cried at him. He almost fell from the ladder laughing as he realised who he was staring at.

"Because you were always so kind to me and Adam. Your whole family were," Tavar replied with sincerity. "How's your father?" he asked, still hanging halfway up the side of the building, nervously glancing at the drop beneath him. It wouldn't kill him, but he liked his ankles unbroken and in working order.

Yasmin's quick, green eyes flashed under her black headdress as she took a closer look at him. "Tavar?" she asked herself, pulling a hand to her mouth in surprise. "By the gods, it is you!" She backed away from the rope as Tavar grunted and scrambled up onto the roof of her shop. "What in the hells are you doing?"

She crouched low, pressing her body against his in a welcomed hug. "I thought you would be in the dungeons by now. I saw you entering the city."

"I bet you were the one who threw that rotten tomato," Tavar grinned at her.

"You were a good boy and were always kind to my family. That isn't something I would forget easily."

"How is your family?"

"Dad passed away three years ago. Heart stopped

whilst he was asleep. Hit Tasneem hard. She's moved out near the Moon Coast and sells her own wine. She writes when she can. Met a nice guy," Yasmin shrugged and smiled. "How are *you*? I heard what happened in the arena. I'm sorry about your brother."

Tavar brushed off her concern with a wave of the hand. "I'm okay. I need to find my friends amongst this... *chaos*," he said, motioning to the battle. He peered over the edge of the wall surrounding the flat, stone roof of the apothecary. Blood warriors poured through every gap and crashed against row upon row of hardy Alfaran soldiers.

"Good luck," Yasmin snorted. "Unless they are holding one of those flags, you won't be able to spot them from here."

"You're right, I need to head down there, into the battle."

"You're mad! You'll get yourself killed!"

"Maybe. Let's hope not, though," Tavar winked and placed his arms on the woman's shoulders. "You still have the basement beneath the shop? With all of the herbs and liquids?" She nodded back, frowning. "Head down there and don't come out unless you hear a friendly voice. It won't be safe for you anywhere else." He pulled out the dagger Carver had handed him and passed into Yasmin's shaking hands. "Take this with you, just in case. Now, go."

The apothecary kissed him on the forehead before he wheeled away, running across the rooftops and towards the sounds of battle, trying to formulate a plan in his head. He was in between two armies with no weapon and no sense of where his allies were. Off the top of his head, he couldn't think of many more dangerous situations that he had been in. Things couldn't get much worse. Or at least that's what he hoped.

He paused as he reached a gap between buildings, peering down. A pile of litter and gods knew what else was packed against the side of the building. His best bet for landing safely.

With a quick prayer he leapt down and landed against the pile of stinking scraps of discarded food and broken plates. Wincing, he stood and peered down at the small cut on his hip where the edge of a broken bone had dug into his skin on landing. If that was the worst of his wounds tonight, then he would consider it a good time.

Brushing himself off, he ran to the edge of the street. The Alfaran army was being pressed back further onto the centre of the city, towards the palace but they were making the blood warriors fight for every step forward. Tavar saw through the torchlight in the doorways around him that the fight had even spilled into some of the houses. Seeing a door smashed to pieces and lying on the ground outside one of the limestone houses, he dashed towards the doorway in the hope of taking a soldier unaware and stealing a weapon capable of defending himself better in the battle raging on throughout Kessarine.

He stormed past the wooden falcon hanging on top of the doorway with a roar only to be met with silence. Confused, he frowned at the shadows of the empty home. It was a simple room that he found himself in. A carved aurochs hung on the wall and three crude wooden chairs had fallen onto the sapphire rug covering most of the stone floor. One of the chairs had snapped a leg, most likely due to being propped up against the now destroyed door lying outside. The wooden, rectangular shutters were closed, so that the only source of light streaming into the room was from the open doorway. He tilted his head as the sound of muffled sobs reached him from further in the house. He crept forward and pressed his back against the wall before chancing a look into the next room.

A single bed pressed up on the blood covered wall. On the floor beside it sat a blood-soaked warrior trying his best to stifle his crying as he held the lifeless body of a young boy in his arms. Next to him were three blood warriors, all covered in wounds. The killing weapon, a long, wide sword covered in red lay discarded in the corner of the room.

The warrior looked up, tears streaming down his wet face. "I tried to stop them. He's just a kid. I tried to stop them." *Zaif.*

Tavar gently walked to the big shoulder and crouched beside him. The warrior's large arms closed tighter around the dead boy, shielding him from Tavar. "Zaif. You did your best. You fought well. These things happen in battle."

"But why?" the man roared suddenly, rocking Tavar back with the outburst. "Why do we carry on, we who deserve death. We've taken lives without remorse and yet it is the young who leave for the heavens before us. It isn't fair," he sobbed, sniffing as snot dripped down in the stubble above his lips.

"I should have saved him. It should have been me who died. I should have saved him." Zaif pressed his face into the boy's hair and broke into uncontrollable shaking cries. Tavar realised that this wasn't about the dead Alfaran anymore.

"He was a good kid, Zaif. He loved you and you should be proud. I saw the way he looked at you before the battle. He died a soldier's death. There was nothing more you could have done."

"They cut through the family in here. The kid's parents are in the other room. They were defenceless. Sick bastards are these blood warriors," he said, inclining his head to the fallen soldiers beside him. "I don't want to go back out there, Tavar," Zaif said, shaking his head and wiping the sleeve of his tunic across his face, taking with it most of the liquid that had pooled upon him. "Every time I see the flash of a blade, I see him, lying there, waiting for me to come and save him. But it's too late. It's always too late."

Tavar held Zaif's hand and looked him in his wet, bloodshot eyes. "There's a woman a few doors down. In an apothecary. She's hiding in her basement. Go there and call for her, tell her that you were sent by Tavar Farwan. If she doesn't believe you, tell her that she used to always laugh at how pink Adam would get. Wait with her, away from the battle. If soldiers come for you, then protect her like you tried with this boy. For me, please?" Tavar asked. Zaif sniffed again and nodded.

"I can do that. Protect her. I can do that." He picked the boy up and placed him on the bed, gently resting his head against his pillow.

Tavar searched the dead soldiers and found a decent sword. Thicker than he was used to but it would have to do. "I'll find you after the battle, Zaif. Be strong."

The blade pushed through flesh and bone easily enough. He pulled it from the chest of the nearest soldier and moved on, dodging the horse belting past him and flinching at the howls of the bloodthirsty warriors as they swept through the scattered lines of the Alfarans.

The battle was close enough now to the palace for the archers high on the wall to fire down on the invading army. Tavar ignored that and pushed towards the gate, searching desperately for any sign of his friends. A tap on his shoulder snapped him from his thoughts and he swung his blade wildly at his opponent. The blade missed, digging against the head of a warhammer Tavar could never fail to recognise.

"That is one of the worst greetings I think I've ever received," Halfor said with mocking disgust. "Next time, I'll just leave you alone." The Naviqing laughed and unbuckled the scabbard at his waist. "I believe this is yours," he said, handing over the stunning blade.

"Have I ever told you that I love you?" Tavar said, jumping up and kissing the sweaty warrior on the cheek. He stank of blood and the musk of working men but Tavar didn't care.

"Often. More than once I've thought that you had intentions of running away with me," Halfor joked. "Let's get the battle out of the way before we get down to any funny business though."

The warrior glanced out of the corner of his eye at the incoming horse heading his way. He rolled to the side and swung the hammer up and cleared the shocked and screaming Alfaran from his mount. The horse didn't miss a beat as it kept on running through the stream of fighting soldiers.

Tavar drew his sword with a moan and licked his lips as he felt the surge of joy emanating from the magical Al-Taabi blade. He stepped closer to the fallen soldier and with a flick of the wrist, the kyushira sliced through the man's neck, pouring blood across the stone street.

"Where are the others?" he asked, spinning the

blade in his hand and grinning at the reunion.

"Somewhere in the chaos," Halfor replied rather unhelpfully. "Medda led the warriors in with her brother. Tajira stalked into the shadows after muttering something to himself. Didn't seem too keen in rushing headfirst into the fight."

"How strange of him…" Tavar said with a smile.

"How strange indeed," Halfor smirked. "And so unlike him."

"We need to push forward to the palace. We can end this battle with the death of the Judges. They are the true power in this kingdom. Once they are dead, the blood can stop."

"Lead the way, brother."

Buoyed by the sight of the gleaming kyushira and the mountain of a Naviqing warrior charging into the melee, tired blood warriors roared, energised with new life as they swept towards now frightened and panicked Alfarans who had only moments ago been roaring their own battle cries.

It was in that moment that Tavar felt bravery was a strange thing. In the blink of an eye, a soldier can go from feeling capable of taking on the world to worrying that his world was about to end abruptly. It all depended on how the stones fell, bravery.

The blood warriors had marched for days with minimal rest and were teetering on the edge of annihilation, peering over the bloody cliff leading to death and wondering what was next. Now they were charging forward with abandon, spears and swords flashing towards the enemies backing off closer to the palace.

Blood poured onto the streets. Flesh tore open. Metal clashed and rang out a song of death across Kessarine.

Tavar dodged a spear-thrust and ducked under the next attack, tracing a killing cut along the soldier unfortunate enough to face him as Halfor cracked his hammer against a man's skull, destroying what was meant to be a protective helm and cracking the man's head wide open like an egg. And still the invaders poured forward. Like a predator stalking wounded prey, they smelled blood and the end of the conflict.

Tavar cut through his next attacker with ease, dodging the weary strike and sliding his sharpened blade across the soldier's throat. A sword dropped to the floor as the soldier clutched uselessly at the open wound as it released a river of blood down his leather armour and he fell to the ground looking aghast at Tavar's gall for killing him in such a way. Funny how soldiers never seem to feel that their death would arrive. It would always come at another point. Another battle. Another war. Another fight. Death was always an unwelcome guest in battle and hardly ever greeted with a smile. That was the way of things, he supposed.

He heard Halfor grunt, gritting his teeth as a spear glanced off his shoulder, barely an inch from piercing his huge frame. A mass of sweat and blood-soaked hair tangled about his face as he screamed and slammed a fist into the soldier who had had the nerve to land even a glancing blow against him. His neck snapped back with the impact but Halfor didn't stop there. He launched his large body forward and brought a mighty knee straight up beneath the man's chin and the soldier's body tightened and fell to the ground like the felling of a great oak.

For good measure, the Naviqing raised his hammer and dropped in against the lifeless man's face with a crunch. Tavar flinched as he unwittingly found himself glancing at the mess of what was left above the soldier's neck. Alfarans close to the scene bolted, racing back to the cheering of blood warriors who for once paused, unwillingly to chase them across the city.

"Hold!" a voice commanded the warriors. "Let them flee. We hold the city!" Red smirked as though he alone had pushed them back from the streets. He looked around him at the cheering warriors and motioned up with his hands, wanting them to raise the level of noise to intimidate their enemy.

One soldier stayed where the others had fled. His helm had been knocked off some time ago by the look of the grazes and cuts on his head. His dark hair had been cut short though he had let the back hang slightly lower towards his shoulders. A thick moustache sat above his lips though part was missing where a white scar ran from his cheek down to the base of his chin.

"You always had a fondness of pink friends," Harun said with a nervous smile, his panicked eyes darting to Halfor. The Naviqing lowered his hammer and pushed his chest out in warning to the Alfaran. "I saw you fight in the arena. You won me a small fortune."

Tavar stepped forward as the blood warriors paced around the solitary soldier, creating a square around the two of them. "You should leave, Harun. Kessarine is to fall," he pleaded with his old ally. He didn't want to fight Harun; they had been on the same side and struggled together. If it could be avoided, then swords need not be drawn.

"Then I shall fall with it," Harun answered, eyes brimming with tears. "This army gave me more than I ever deserved. I can't just turn my back during its hour of need, as easy as that would be."

"Bushy still around?" Tavar asked, remembering the close bond between the two young soldiers he had shared a room with alongside Adam.

Harun's eyes dropped and his voice shook in reply. "Died a couple of years ago. Found him in our room after we got back from a skirmish near the Moon Coast. He was more sensitive than he let on, Bushy. Watching those you stood beside die with a swipe of a sword or an arrow in the back takes its toll after a while. He chose his own path to the heavens. I suppose I'll meet him soon," he raised his bloody sword and smiled sadly. "The end is here for me but I'll face death head on at least. I'm glad it's you, if that's worth anything."

Tavar grimly stepped forward and held his blade straight up, looking past it to the weary soldier. "I'm sorry it's me…"

An arrow flashed past Tavar's head, whistling by his ear and digging itself straight through Harun's throat. The Alfaran grabbed helplessly at the missile as Tavar ran forward, catching his old friend before he fell to the floor. Harun gazed up in sad bemusement, eyes locked on Tavar's as his body toiled to take his final breaths.

He watched as Harun's chest slowed and eventually came to a final stop. A cold fury swept over him as he looked up from the fallen warrior and searched for the culprit.

Red nonchalantly slung his bow over his shoulder as his warriors parted, alarmed by the furious stare beaming from Tavar's face. Medda's brother smirked as he looked over at Tavar and shrugged, brushing his fingers against his chest. "I aimed for his eye. Guess I should improve my aim for next time."

Like a warrior possessed, Tavar sprang up and flashed towards the fool, kyushira leading the way. Cold, bloodied steel glimmered against Red's throat as Tavar's other hand clutched the back of his neck, keeping him in place. To the warrior's credit, he didn't squirm or panic like most would have. With a controlled calm, his painted eyes slowly glanced either side of Tavar, falling on the rows of warriors all aiming their arrows, spears and, swords in his direction. Halfor growled, rubbing his hand along the large hammer and eyeing up the surrounding warriors, attempting to identify a way out of their predicament. Tavar just kept his cold gaze on Red.

"He deserved an honourable death in the square," Tavar spat, saliva flicking onto Red's face. "He deserved to die by my hand!"

"He was an enemy in the midst of battle," Red argued without passion to Tavar's further fury. He felt the kyushira begging for the man's blood but he stayed his hand, for the moment. "This is a war, Tavar Farwan. Old alliances and friendships mean nothing to me. I will kill every last fucking one of them, innocent and guilty, good and bad, if it means that I can take Kessarine and piss on it as it falls to its knees."

"There are ways of taking a city."

"Yes!" Red laughed, eyes flashing at the comment as he pushed his neck closer against the blade. "And this is *our* way. You came to us begging for our assistance. The blood is as much on your hands as ours. Don't you dare try and wriggle your way out of the grasp of truth. You may have read your books about warriors with honour but I'll tell you what happened to those men and women. They're like him. Dead. This is a real battle, Tavar, and I mean to win, by *any means necessary*. Kill me if you wish, but my army will destroy you, your friends and everyone in this forsaken city if you do. They will tear the city down stone by stone and rebuild it in my image. Or you can release me like a good soldier and we can finish this."

His breathing rushed from his nose like a bull as he thought over Red's words. As much as it pained him, the bastard was right. One slice of Tavar's blade and this would have all been for nought. He knew what he was doing when he sought help. The blood was on his hands. He eased the blade from Red's throat and let go of the man's collar. "If you do anything like that ever again, I'll cut you into so many pieces, not even the gods will be able to put you back together again."

"Ah, empty threats," Red said, spitting on the floor and looking Tavar squarely in the eyes. "I've had more of those than I've taken shits. If I do something like that, come and find me. We'll settle things my way. No fucking *square*." He clicked his fingers and the weapons were lowered, though most of the eyes stayed on Tavar and Halfor as Red marched towards the palace.

Tavar turned and saw Medda standing there, watching it all unfold. Her brother charged past her, taking the men and women with him, leaving only Tavar, Halfor and Medda left in their dust.

"Don't know if anyone has ever told you this before," Tavar said, biting his lip until he could taste his own blood. His hands quivered with rage until he tightened his grip on the enchanted blade. "But your brother can be a fucking cunt at times."

She smiled wearily. "You should have seen him as a kid..." She pushed her hair up and sighed. "The Alfarans retreated to guard the palace. One last push and we can break through. You coming?"

"I need to get in there before any of your kin," Tavar said. "There is a gate round the back. Can you keep them distracted?"

She smirked, similar to her brother's expression but with a warmth that Tavar knew directed her every choice. "I think the big man and I can think of something…"

Halfor grinned wide and kissed his hammer, unaware of the blood being transferred from his weapon onto his lips. "A distraction made for the ages. Let's see how brave these soldiers of Alfara can really be."

Striding over to the Naviqing, she leant up and kissed him passionately on his bloodied lips. Halfor took her in his arms as they both turned to Tavar. He swallowed and nodded, breathing out slowly as he looked at two of his greatest friends, hoping to the heavens that he would see them again.

"Remember Kenji's advice," Medda said to him, winking. "Kill the bastards, and don't fucking die."

"Great words to live by," Tavar chuckled at the memory of his fallen friend. "Find the others, keep them safe if I don't…"

"We'll keep them safe until you get back," Halfor said with an exaggerated nod and wink. "You will get back. If there is one thing that I am sure about in this life, Tavar Farwan, it is that the gods have blessed you, Immortal Killer. We shall stand together again in this life. Believe it."

CHAPTER THIRTY-NINE: CUTTING THE STRINGS

Scrambling up the wall, Tavar prayed that the vines would be strong enough to take his weight. His hands turned red raw with the effort as he clung on to the natural green ropes and pulled himself higher. With a mighty heave, he held his breath, groaning with the strain as he pulled himself over the wall and dropped to the grassy patch beneath, breathing heavily and rolling to break his fall. The plants and fountains sheltered him from watchful eyes but he raised his hood up nonetheless, taking no chances.

He crept through the gardens, keeping as low as possible and ignoring the strain on his weary knees. Braziers burned on both sides of a white stone archway as Tavar ducked through, racing towards where he knew the bolted gate leading into the palace kitchens would be. Pausing, he peered between two palm trees, spotting the open gate. Two Alfaran soldiers dressed in the crimson red of their unit lay on the floor, blood pooling around their bodies.

He darted forward, stopping only to glance at the bodies and frowning as he saw multiple wounds on both of them. They weren't given a chance. Their weapons were still clasped to their belts and their robes had been slashed in numerous places across the chest and stomach. *Surely Carver wouldn't have been so ruthless and unnecessarily violent?* She would do what had to be done but whoever killed these soldiers had enjoyed the attack;

had delighted in the violence.

He pressed forward with renewed urgency as he pushed into the palace kitchens. As soon as he entered, he knew something bad had taken place.

Blood painted the stone walls and splattered against the pots, pans and bottles shelved and placed upon benches and tables. The bodies of palace staff pointed the way of the killer for Tavar. Defenceless, they had fallen with ease but again, both men and women had been torn apart by what he guessed were multiple strikes of a swift sword. Wounds could be found all over the bodies. Legs, backs, chests, faces, and guts. They had been carved up by a warrior with skill and little remorse for what they were doing.

Tavar stopped just short of the next open door. He peered around the doorway and into a larger kitchen; a small fire on which sat a large, empty, circular pan was burning in the centre of the room. Bottles of wine had been smashed to pieces, the dark, red liquid pouring across the floor and blending with the blood of more men and women caught in the wrong place at the wrong time. An Alfaran soldier lay next to his curved sword. He had died with his weapon in hand at least. Perhaps the screams of the staff had alerted the soldier to the kitchens where he had been struck down by the unknown invader.

Tavar took a closer look at the soldier and grimaced. The blood had darkened and congealed. He had been killed a while ago, certainly not in the time since the Blood warriors had stormed into the city. Disturbed, Tavar continued cautiously through the kitchens and out into a large room with tall paintings of leaders dressed in their finery and a long, wooden table standing on a golden rug. The boundaries of the room were lined with vases and statues from around the world. Opulent snobbery at its finest. Nobles and royalty were often quick to speak of their own greatness and the inferiority of other countries, but they still coveted items and decorations from other lands. The hypocrisy of the elite.

Six bodies weaved a path through the dining room. Tavar didn't stop to check the wounds. There was no time. Carver was somewhere here and so was this crazed killer.

The entrance room was wide open and welcoming to the king's guests most of the year. Tavar walked out from the shadows of the curved stairs and heaved, holding back the vomit threatening to escape his gut. The marble floor had been decorated in the blood of the ten soldiers contorted into a specific line, their bodies and the blood leading up one of the staircases and soaking into the golden carpet. Two of the soldiers wore the gold of the Immortals but they had been taken down just like the others. Leaning against the wooden banister, Tavar regained control of his breathing, trying to look away from the horrific scene before him, instead focusing his eyes upwards at the chandelier hanging from the ceiling, sparkling in the torchlight of the flames hugging the walls around him.

He stepped over the bodies that had been dragged up the steps, holding his breath to escape the acrid smell of death that permeated his surroundings. The double doors at the top of the stairs were open, leading into the reception room for King Uhlad. Tavar walked on the tips of his toes, opening the door further with his forearm as he drew his sword with care, pointed it forwards to warn those who may wish him harm.

The reception room was a grand room designed for the sole purpose to intimidate guests and emissaries from other lands before they were taken into the throne room. The high ceiling gave Tavar the feeling of being small and insignificant as he stepped past the large, ornate, wooden doors. Paintings three times his size displayed stern and grim kings and queens from Alfaran history who glared down at any who entered the room. Black marble busts of tormented heroes decorated the edges of the room, one had fallen from its plinth and smashed into a dozen black, jagged lumps on the sapphire carpet beside a rectangular set of cushions and backboards designed for comfort in the daunting room.

Uhlad had to provide at least some level of comfort for his guests.

Gold and green curtains covered the floor to ceiling windows on the one side of the room next to which sat an oaken roll top desk stained with blood. Tavar rushed over and pressed a finger against the blood. *Still wet.*

"She said you would come…" Tavar spun, sword leading the way as the words reached him from the far side of the room.

He jumped over the cushions and peered down at the singular body in the room. King Uhlad lay with his back against the wall, chest rising and falling as a purple gloved hand rested against the bleeding wound on his neck. Tavar scanned the ruler of Alfara and winced at a much larger wound that had opened the king's gut, allowing parts of his insides to escape from the deadly exit. The king wasn't long for the world, of that, he was certain.

"Uhlad…" Tavar muttered, kneeling beside the king and checking the fatal wounds.

"Not too pretty, are they?" Uhlad coughed slightly with the attempt at humour.

"I can ease your pain," Tavar said, motioning with his kyushira.

Uhlad shook his head and grimaced. "Not necessary." He turned his deep, dark eyes on Tavar and lifted a weak hand, grasping at Tavar's blood-stained tunic. "I never meant for any of this, you must believe me. I did what they asked of me out of fear. I didn't know about this. I didn't know about *him*." He broke into a coughing fit, only further pushing out his guts and quickening his meeting with death. "You must leave. There is nothing but darkness in there for you. Darkness and death. Leave now and find your son. He is a good boy and he will need you. I did what I could to keep him from being a part of any of this. You must leave *now*!"

The king's eyes bulged as he strained to catch his breath, choking, and jerking with the motion. His head dropped and rested against his chest as his hand loosened on Tavar.

Tavar said the words and tapped a hand to his chest before standing to his feet, weapon gripped tightly in his fist. His son was waiting for him outside of Kessarine. Only the gods knew what was waiting for him in the throne room. Uhlad had told him darkness and death. But in the end, isn't that what was waiting for everyone? Not even the swiftest of soldiers can escape that final meeting. He didn't believe in the gods but in that moment, he closed his eyes and prayed to the heavens, prayed that his son would be safe. That his son would live a good life, away from all this blood. That he would have a different life to that of his father.

Then he opened the door.

Red and gold carpeted the walls and six pillars stood tall, leading the eyes towards the two levels of steps that led up to a large rectangular golden seat laden with cushions and a softly smoking pipe which stood to the side in a silver dish. Orange embers glowed in the dish beside a smug looking man with eyes only for Tavar, mean, piercing eyes that flashed with a petrifying mix of malice and wisdom.

"Like how I've decorated the place?" the man asked, spinning his thin, skeletal hand up and guiding Tavar's eyes to the ceiling.

He almost choked in disgust as he spotted the softly swinging bodies above him. They were naked but for the masks they always wore. Masks that had been tainted and tarnished with their own blood into a sickening smiling face with red lips that ran all the way to their ears. A mass of small cuts criss-crossed over their skin, none deep enough to have caused death. They had died suffocating from the tightened ropes still pulling at their throats.

"The Judges…" Tavar whispered, his voice carrying across the cavernous room.

"The Judges," the man on the golden throne agreed. He was dressed as though in mourning. All black. A long, tight robe fell to his knees. A short, tight collar wrapped around the light brown skin of his neck. "Four men and women who have been acting out my orders and wishes for years, a welcome buffer should any issues ever arise. Now, they have no purpose, so I thought I would let them swing."

Tavar stared at the man with loathing and shame, feeling the heat building in his cheeks as he realised his folly. "Ahmed," he said through gritted teeth as a soft throbbing pain built up behind his eyes. "It was you in control all along."

The servant stood and bowed with a flourish of

his hands to the side. "A fabulous display of acting and skill, one might say. I must admit, I am rather proud that I managed to convince so many people that I was a mere servant. Years of training and working my way up to becoming an Acolyte of Shadow and then I had to tear all of that down and play a servant to an emotional king with a lust for men and a will to bring progress to Alfara. The Court of Shadows has watched and waited for too long. We thrive in chaos and you helped me to create it, Tavar Farwan. Obviously, you were pushed slightly by those under my control…"

From out of the shadows, Tajira stepped into the torchlight, blood covering his face and his dark tunic ripped across his torso, displaying a thin wound that sliced across his body.

Tavar shook his head, not willing to believe it.

"Tajira has been my man all along. A brother of shadow who has watched as you created a war between the Blood Nation and Alfara. With both nations weak, this continent is ripe for the picking. Soon, my people will stroll in and do as they wish."

"But… you saved my life!" Tavar screamed at the blood drenched warrior, refusing to believe what his eyes were telling him.

Tajira just shrugged back at him, unmoved. "Saved a few people. Killed a load more."

"He was the one who saw your use," Ahmed continued. "Forging Uhlad's message and cutting the heads from those men I sent with him was all part of the plan. His plan. He's good with those kinds of details. He was the one who made up your mind to come back here. And he knew you needed help. Having that savage bitch from the Blood Nation with you only made it all that much easier. The strings are so easy to pull when the puppets play their part willingly."

"Where's Carver?" Tavar asked, raising his sword and keeping his eyes on Tajira as the warrior paced towards him.

"The whore you lay with?" Ahmed smirked. "I do like a happy reunion." The Acolyte pointed a lazy hand past Tavar who slowly turned, fighting the logic that warned him not to.

Her body had been forced against the wall with four separate daggers, each piercing her hands and feet, holding her up so that her stomach was at Tavar's head height. His tears fell silently as he peered up at her drooping head, as still as a statue. A single wound was all he could see other than those caused by the daggers. One cut across her throat. He stared only at her face, ignoring the damage, and focusing on her soft, closed eyes and long lashes that he knew so well. Focusing only on her face, he could almost convince himself that she was merely sleeping, her dark, wavy hair falling to one side like he had always loved it to. He remembered the way she would smirk and twist her head, flicking the hair from her face as she licked her lips at him.

Burning with rage, he screamed and twisted, swiping his bloodthirsty blade at Tajira who snapped his twin, curved swords up from his waist and defended the attack. Tavar didn't stop. He flicked his wrist under the warrior's guard, opening up the defence and slipping the blade forward with a speed that shocked himself.

Tajira's eyes widened with the unexpected ferocity of the attack and he leant back, his head just dodging a deadly blow. As though in another world, Tavar could hear Ahmed's pleasure as he clapped and chuckled with the fighting display before him. He swore to end this swiftly. He would not be one to amuse that bastard any more than he had.

Remembering the shadow warrior's fight in the arena, Tavar paused, allowing the warrior to lead the attack, just as Kenji had once done. Spinning on the balls of his feet, Tavar dodged one of the swords and snapped the other skywards before unleashing his own strike diagonally down, slicing through the warrior's leg above the knee, cutting flesh and bone.

Tajira didn't scream. His body dropped onto the carpet beneath him and he sat staring at the bleeding stump where his leg had once been.

Tavar wasted no time. He stepped over the warrior just as he opened his mouth to speak. He could have been pleading for mercy. He could have been begging Tavar to remember some of the warm conversations they had shared. He could have been telling him to go fuck himself. A sword through the traitor's mouth ended any chance of Tavar finding out.

"Bravo!" Ahmed clapped, grabbing at a bowl of dates to his side and plucking one out to throw into his mouth as Tavar stomped forward, a grim frown etched on his face. "A fight for the ages, no doubt. Though, I must say, you seem to forget what all this has been for, Farwan. I am an Acolyte of Shadow. The Court of Shadows will arrive, they will send more. I am a mere blade in their vast armoury. Losing me will mean nothing to them. The Blood Nation will fuck this city up more than it already has been and the continent will soon fall. You'll see. They will send more and they will come for you, for your son, too."

Tavar didn't waste another breath on the smirking fool.

There was no anger on his face. No sadness. Just a void of emotion as the kyushira whipped through the air and took his head off in one go. The dates fell from the bowl, replaced by the head, a peaceful expression on Ahmed's face as the blood poured into the bowl.

Tavar walked back down the steps and straight to Carver. He pulled the daggers free from the wall and caught her body, resting her gently on his own, her head falling over his shoulder in a final embrace. He carried her out past the fallen king and onto the balcony overlooking Kessarine.

The curtains were pulled open, allowing him an uninterrupted view of the city and the land of Alfara and beyond just as the sun was beginning her descent on the horizon. He looked down at the mass of fallen bodies down in the city, at the cheering warriors of the victorious Blood Nation and he sighed. He wanted this to be the end. The end of the blood. The end of the fighting.

As the tears fell down his cheeks, he stroked Carver's hair and wondered if this was just the beginning.

CHAPTER FORTY: USED TO IT

The sun fell behind the hills as Tavar lent back against the acacia tree and sighed at the memories. Even after all these years, the pain still tore at his heart as he remembered her smell and the way she felt in his arms as he peered down at the chaos of Kessarine. Too many people had died that day. Too many innocents. He supposed people could say that about any battle. He was just an old fool looking back on his regrets and wishing things had been different. Perhaps that was the purpose of life though. You don't learn from your mistakes; you just tell others in the hope that they don't repeat them.

"That battle is spoken of in hushed whispers across the whole continent," Jassim said, eyes wide as he leaned towards Tavar. He had listened well. Mouth shut and ears open. He'd done better than Tavar could have hoped for. Maybe there was hope for the next generation. "Though the way I hear it, you killed Uhlad in a fit of rage."

"Uhlad died at the hands of Ahmed. The only person that the bastard actually killed himself, if my memory serves me well. Tajira did the rest. The Dog of Shadow, some people called him, at least in the songs I heard over the years. The sight of those bodies doesn't leave you soon enough, I can tell you that."

Jassim absently picked at the grass and gazed up at the setting sun. "How did Medda's brother come to rule that kingdom? From what you've said, surely Medda would have been in line to rule."

"She chose love over duty," Tavar answered with a weary smile, warmed by the memory of his two friends together after all they had been through. "Her mother didn't like it, of course, nor her brother. They vowed that if she crossed paths with any member of the nation again, that her life would be forfeit. She wasn't too bothered about it. She'd lived most of her life out from their shadow and she was never one for servitude. A life on the road with Halfor appealed far more to her." He pushed his shoulders back and grimaced at the cracks that followed.

"I've told you my tale, as best as I can. Now I think it is time for you to tell your truth. You have the look of Alfara on you but your accent is off." Tavar tapped the emerald blade at his hip and dropped any pretence of warmth from his face. The time for honesty was at hand. He had delayed for long enough. "If I even think you are lying to me, then I take your head and stick it on a spike to warn any other fucker who thinks to come into my land with lies and threats of violence. Speak quickly."

The colour drained from Jassim's face as his eyes darted from Tavar's to the blade threatening death. He wriggled up on the grass, palms facing Tavar, begging for forgiveness as his lips frantically moved, straining for the right words but offering nothing at first. He stood slowly and backed away as Tavar just sat still, eyes burning towards him.

"You've got it all wrong," Jassim pleaded, still backing away. "I need your help."

"Funny way of asking for it. Lies and blood. Could have just asked."

"I couldn't. I had to know it was you, before they

came," Jassim moaned, eyes wide and panicked.

"*They…*" Tavar repeated, finally standing and strolling to the defenceless and wounded man. "Who are they?"

"I married a gorgeous, kind woman who means the world to me," Jassim stammered, swallowing his nerves. "Three moons ago, her family angered dark warriors from across the sea. Men dressed in black who fought with a ferocity I had never seen before. My family told me to find you, the Legend of Alfara. The Nightmare of Kessarine.

"I met my love when travelling in Okada, eager to escape the hell of Alfara. Your legend was backed up by an old blind man who lived in the next village along. I know that you are the only one who knows what they are capable of, Tavar Godslayer. You are the only one who can help me find my wife and save her from whatever horrors they had planned. Please, you have to believe me."

Tavar glared into the man's eyes. He was telling the truth. That much was certain. "The Court of Shadows…" he sighed and cursed, pushing his long hair back and mulling Jassim's words over in his head.

"Kill me if you want to," Jassim said, his shoulders dropping as he winced and grasped at the healing wound, still obviously causing him severe pain. "But find her. Save her, please. To many, you are a hero. Keito said you were the only one. He made that blade for you. The final Al-Taabi."

"*Keito.* I paid that debt many years ago," Tavar barked, pointing a finger venomously at him. "I dragged his niece, Mako, away from slavers on the Bone Isles. I owe him nothing more." He spat the words but inside he knew it was just bravado, he cared for the old man as though he was family, but he wasn't going to let this fool be privy to that information. "And here you are, drawing your blade in my home and telling me it is my duty to go after the deadliest order in the known world. They rule the dark continent and their grip over here is tighter than you could ever understand. They would have followed you here. You'll be dead within days and I'll be needing to bleed my kyushira sooner than I would have liked. You're a fool."

Jassim made to step forward, brows curled up as he opened his mouth to answer, only to find a long, thin blade preventing his throat from any kind of further movement. Tavar grinned at the look of complete shock on the poor fool's face.

"He's got more than a few days left, I reckon." A woman's face popped up over Jassim's shoulder, her lips close to his ears as she hissed at him. "Killed two of the bastards back at the farm. Woke up poor Amir during his afternoon nap. Good job we decided to visit this moon or the poor kid would have been waking up with a dagger in his gut." Another woman stepped out from the night beside Jassim. Her skin was dark as the night where her ally's was as pale as the moon.

"What shall we do with him?" the darker woman asked, tracing a finger along Jassim's jawbone and tutting at him. "Cute kid. Would be a waste to kill him. But I can do it."

"Easy, Cassie," Tavar growled. "He's under my protection. For now." He raised his eyebrows at Jassim, making sure that he knew he wasn't in the clear just yet. "It's okay Alice, you can drop it."

The pale woman shrugged and lowered the blade attached to her elbow before strolling over to Tavar and kissing his cheek softly. "There could be more coming. Stand and fight? Or run?"

Tavar frowned at Jassim, watching the man swallow the lump in his throat. "Looks like we're moving out. Fancy sending a message to some old friends?"

"Been a while since we headed to Naviqand," Alice grinned at her wife, flashing her eyes eagerly. "I think we can manage the trip."

"You won't regret it, Tavar," Jassim implored, growing increasingly animated at the thought that maybe he might make it through the day without ending up as a corpse. "I promise."

"Save your breath, kid. You'll need it for the journey the five of us are going on."

Jassim frowned, eyes darting around as he silently counted and came up one short. "*Five?*"

Tavar nodded down the hill as a young man trudged up, carrying a large bag and dressed all in grey. His dark hair fell effortlessly to his shoulders and his beard was trimmed close to his jawline in the fashion of the northlands. The man smiled widely at the meeting on the hill and dropped the bag, still smiling as two bloody heads rolled out between Tavar and Jassim.

"Had some visitors earlier today," the young man said, voice ringing with pride as though he was happy with such a meeting. "I'm assuming by their clothing and the weird fucking weapons they had that this is it, right? The Court of Shadows is finally here."

Tavar scratched at his beard and sighed. "Looks that way. You're keeping an eye on this one," he said, motioning to Jassim with a hand. The newcomer pushed out his bottom lip and sniffed as he eyed up the wounded man. "He'll be fine in a few days, just make sure that he doesn't die. And that he doesn't kill any of us," Tavar warned, marching off towards his house, followed by the two women as Alice draped an arm around Cassie's shoulder.

"My name is Jassim." The newcomer took his hand and smiled at him.

"Amir, you passed by my farm with another guy the other night, before the storm. Where is he?"

"Tavar killed him," Jassim shrugged. "It's no loss. It was almost worth it to see the way that man controls the kyushira."

"Yeah," Amir grinned and chuckled softly, kicking at one of the heads by his feet. "Dad can be like that sometimes. You'll get used to it."

THE END

Aaron S. Jones

Acknowledgements

There are a million people I should thank for creating this book and you all know who you are.

It was written during the beginning of the coronavirus pandemic in a time when everything felt like shit and I had nothing better to do with time as I was working less and I had just handed *Flames of Rebellion* in for the editing phase. I had written the first three chapters of *Paths of Chaos* but felt like I needed a break from that world.

Inspired from my time in the Middle East and deep within my third read of *The Name of the Wind* and a late-night screening of *Unforgiven,* I wanted to write a book about an older warrior looking back on his life and all its glory and regret. The guilt, the joy, the despair. All of it. I didn't want a medieval setting and I didn't want it to seem like a carbon copy of anything else that I had read. I felt confident enough as a writer to explore themes and ideas that I hadn't manage to touch on with *Flames*.

I am so proud of this novel. I love the characters. I love the world. I love the themes and I love how I was led on this journey as much as most readers will have been.

The world has moved on in the 18 months or so since I first started writing about the weary warrior being attacked in his home during a storm. I hope we never forget how difficult that time was. How difficult it was to be cut off from loved ones. How difficult it was to lose loved ones. I hope in some way that this novel will always be a reminder of that. There will always be memories of blood and shadow, but we can learn from such times and band together with the people we have, to live a better life and ensure that we appreciate every moment we have together. Isn't that what life is really about?

Printed in Great Britain
by Amazon